The train bombing in Italy was the beginning. Relentlessly the hunter stalked his quarry from Europe to the trackless wastes of Africa, across the Atlantic to an affluent Florida stronghold and back again. But each time the hunter thought he had finally run his prey to ground, he realized he had found only the changing face of evil. The hunt had become a game—and the game was deadly.

Until the hunter came full circle.

DON PENDLETON's

MACK BOLAN

A GOLD EAGLE BOOK FROM

WORLDWIDE

TORONTO • NEW YORK • LONDON • PARIS
AMSTERDAM • STOCKHOLM • HAMBURG
ATHENS • MILAN • TOKYO • SYDNEY

First edition October 1986

ISBN 0-373-61406-3

Special thanks and acknowledgment to
Peter Leslie for his contributions to this work.

Printed in Canada

"I'll be the judge, I'll be the jury," said cunning old Fury; "I'll try the whole cause, and condemn you to death."

—Lewis Carroll

It is not for me to judge; I am the Executioner. But sometimes, in the dark places of the world, a situation arises where judgment and execution are no more than two faces of the same coin. At such times I do not pause to ask questions. I act.

—Mack Bolan

To the memory of Swedish Prime Minister Olof Palme,
who was assassinated in Stockholm, February, 1986.

Chapter One

The first shot from the Winchester repeater gouged chips of stone from the cornice only moments after the big stranger appeared through a trapdoor leading to the roof. Pigeons flapped angrily into the dawn sky as the sharp crack of the rifle echoed across the deserted piazza.

The stranger was dressed in close-fitting black, and there was a 9 mm Beretta 93-R automatic holstered in a shoulder rig beneath his left arm. He ducked behind one of the white marble statues that dominated the cornice.

The sniper fired again. Aristotle, second in the line of ten sculpted figures, and with a hand raised to compel attention, lost an index finger. Hidden by the folds of the Greek sage's robe, the stranger checked his face for blood where marble chips had stung his cheek. He unleathered the silenced autoloader now, and scanned the buildings on the far side of the square.

The third shot ricocheted off the tiles of the shallow roof. And gave the gunner away. Diagonally across the piazza an ancient archway, flanked by two pyramid towers, led to the winding streets of the old town. It was from the top of one of these towers, above Perugia's massive ramparts, that the gunman was shooting.

The man in black took in his surroundings. He was three stories above the street, perched on the roof of a rectangular Renaissance palace. He realized that he could ill afford to let the rifleman pin him down. The stranger hoped the sniper would not get lucky with his fourth shot. But mere wishing, the black-clad man knew, would not help him if he stayed where he was any longer. The sky was lightening. And time was running out.

The terrorist he had chased up onto the roof had vanished—either escaping while the stranger was tied down by the unseen rifleman or working his way around the central stack to rake him with gunfire.

From the roof to the tower, he estimated, was about 250 yards—which put the sharpshooter way out of range of the 93-R autoloader. Between him and the trapdoor stretched twenty-five feet of empty asphalt, sitting-duck territory for a guy with a high-powered rifle firing at less than half its effective range.

There was a possible escape route immediately behind him, where the cornice turned at right angles to cover the building's main facade, and again there was open ground to be crossed—no more than eight or nine feet, but still a death trap if the marksman was as good as his weapon.

The stranger knew that the Winchester carried its 200-grain slugs in a tubular magazine that could empty at a rate of fifteen rounds per minute. He decided to offer himself as a tempting target until the remainder of that magazine was exhausted, then cross the danger space while the killer reloaded.

The man in black exploded into motion and began to sprint, ducking, weaving, varying his pace and his attitude until he reached the eighth statue. He hid behind it for a moment and then, as if deciding that he couldn't make the far side, turned and dodged back. He plunged to the asphalt below the figure of Aristotle as the fifteenth bullet struck the cornice and screeched off into space. His gamble had paid off.

Now, hastily but surely, he crawled back to the corner of the building.

For an instant—the moment of maximum danger—he knelt upright on the coping, a perfect target in silhouette. Then, grasping the stonework, he lowered himself into the void beyond.

The first round from the new magazine cracked out as his head sank below the coping and he saw the last marble figure with its hand lifted in valedictory salute. The slug hit so close to his own hand that he felt the wind of its passage, and a sliver of stone gashed his thumb.

He hung at the full stretch of his arms, supported by four fingers of each hand. He looked over his shoulder. Sixty feet below, a small Fiat sedan nosed around the corner of the palazzo, passed the wide steps leading to the entrance and headed for the arch. Otherwise the square was still empty.

The stranger altered his position, inching away from the corner hand over hand. Two hundred-odd pounds of solid muscle dragged at his locked fingers and crucified the tendons of his shoulders. His breath hissed through clenched teeth.

The muscle was itself locked into a husky frame measuring slightly more than six feet. This, plus the length of his arms, enabled him—he had gambled on this, too—to touch the apex of a protruding triangular window frame in the palazzo's upper story.

He dragged in a lungful of air, lowered his heels gingerly to the sloping stonework and released his grip on the coping above.

He was standing facing the seventeenth century wall with his weight evenly supported on both legs. Now came the difficult part. One side of the frame or the other, he had to make the base of the triangle. If he attempted to do so while upright he would surely slip and fall. But if he bent or crouched, to get a hand down to the level of his feet, he would risk pushing himself a sufficient distance from the wall for his center of gravity to lie outside the edge of the frame; with nothing to hold on to, he would drop backward into space.

With infinite care, flattening himself against the facade as much as he could, he swiveled one leg, splayed out the knee and slowly began to bend it.

At the same time he tilted sideways from the waist with an outstretched hand arcing down toward the slanting stone. Muscles all over his body were on fire by the time his fingers touched the stone and he could transfer his weight to that hand. Now he folded the knee beneath him and slid until he was lying full length along the opposite slope. He released his breath in a long sigh of relief.

The exhalation translated itself from chest to hip and his weight shifted. A fragment of weathered sandstone crumbled away from the edge of the frame. His body toppled outward and he fell.

Only a desperate two-fisted grab saved him from a death plunge to the street. The full weight of his body jerking suddenly as his outstretched arms jolted him so savagely that his teeth rattled in his head. He gasped, once more extended with only the strength of his fingers between him and oblivion. And this time there was no stonework beneath his feet.

With hands now bleeding and raw, he lowered himself down the last few feet of the slope until his toes touched the top of a column. Finally, he rested.

And at that moment he heard movement above him...looked up...and saw the terrorist he was hunting lean over the coping with a 9 mm Uzi machine pistol in his hand.

The stranger fisted the Beretta from its shoulder rig once more and triggered a 3-shot burst in a single fluid movement before his enemy could fire.

The face above him—swarthy skin, hook nose, black mustache—vanished in a cloud of blood, brains and bone fragments. The Uzi fell into the street. The terrorist's body slumped over the coping with arms trailing, slid slowly beyond it and then dropped to the cobbled sidewalk of the Corso Garibaldi.

By the time the thump of the impact reached him, the man in black was sliding down the Corinthian pillar to a wide sill outside the double windows.

He knocked out one of the square glass panes with the butt of his Beretta, reached in to unfasten the latch and stepped into the room beyond. It looked like a schoolroom, with maps on the wall, a dais, a chalkboard and a semicircle of tiered desks.

From a pouch clipped to the belt at his waist, the stranger took a wadded nylon packet, which shook out to become an ultralightweight, unlined windbreaker. Thrusting his arms into the sleeves, he zippered the front to hide the reholstered automatic, left the room and took the wide mosaic stairway down to the entrance hall.

The sextuple doors already stood open. On the steps outside, a man in dark blue uniform lounged, smoking a cigarette. "You're early, sir," he remarked in surprise. "Classes don't start until eight, you know."

"Classes?" The stranger also looked surprised.

And then it dawned on him. Gold lettering cut into the marble architrave above the pillared doorway spelled out the words:

Università per Stranièri.

University for foreigners...or strangers.

Of course, the big man in black thought. This was Perugia, capital of the province of Umbria, and the Palazzo Gallenga was famed worldwide as a center for students of all nations taking postgraduate courses on Italian history, culture and language.

That figured: it was the abduction of a student that had brought him here in the first place. And it was the protection of the ancient Greek educators lined up along the cornice above that had saved his life!

"I guess I already learned my lesson for today," he told the uniformed janitor. "And who knows, maybe I taught one too...."

He walked on down the flight of steps. Boys and girls with bikes or mopeds and on foot were now converging on the piazza. He turned along the side of the building away from the arch, skirted a chattering crowd gathered around the body on the sidewalk and strode unhurriedly down the grade to the parking lot where he had left his rented car.

Chapter Two

It started with a train wreck more than two hundred miles to the north.

The first headlines reported forty-one dead, but the chief of carabinieri—Italian police—directing the salvage operations told the tall American with ice-blue eyes that the final count could be much higher. One of the buckled sleeping cars at the front of the train had been reserved for a party of foreign students on their way from Perugia to Vienna. "A block booking," the commendatore—police chief—said. "We have no idea how many boarded the train."

"Surely you know how many sleeping berths there were in the car?"

"Naturally. Still, it would certainly have been overcrowded. Lying in the corridor, resting on backpacks, even sleeping two to a bunk." A Latin shrug. "You know the young people today, *signore*."

"So I guess there'll be no record of the number of persons passing the barrier at Bologna with tickets for this train. Or of those who joined it farther south, at Perugia."

"That is correct, *signore*."

Light fog rolling up from the Lombardy plain had shrouded the valley when the disaster occurred. The first explosion was small, and although the locomotive shuddered at the concussion, the engineer assumed it was a signal torpedo placed between the rails to warn him that visibility ahead was too poor for him to read the signals.

After viewing the wreck, the officer told the foreigner, the police figured that a second charge, much larger and expertly placed, detonated between the rear of the engine and the baggage car that preceded the passenger coaches.

The train was traveling at more than one hundred mph when the blasts were triggered. The locomotive and seven of the sixteen cars were blown off the rails. The baggage car disintegrated, and the first three of the wrecked sleepers folded into less than a quarter of their original length.

"You see what I mean," the policeman said. He gestured toward the blackened and still smoking debris littering the tracks. A wrecker on the southbound line was winching up a mass of twisted steel from the remains of the first sleeper, but there was still a chaos of metal, cloth and splintered wood beneath. Men from one of the salvage crews were operating cutting torches around the impacted panels of a compartment overlaid by the second mangled sleeper.

The tall American watched two attendants in white coats carry something heavy wrapped in a sheet toward the rows of plastic body bags laid out along the riverbank. Moisture seeping through from the contents darkened the heavy curve of the sheet at the lowest part of the load.

"You guys are sure it was a terrorist attack?" the American asked.

A decisive nod of the head. "Very certain. There is a hole big enough to hide a bus underneath all that. Besides, the bastards responsible have already phoned headquarters to boast about it." The officer glanced at the capsized locomotive. Diesel fumes from its ruptured fuel tanks tainted the mountain air, which was already sour with the stench of death and burning. "And why here of all places...?"

He stared helplessly around him. Early-autumn sunshine had driven away the mist in the six hours since the Rome-Vienna streamliner had been dynamited. The valley, twisting through the eastern foothills of the Dolomites, ran between Venzone and Carnia, below the long grade that rose past Malborghetto to the Austrian frontier. The town of Udine lay twenty miles downstream.

The place was more than two thousand feet above sea level, but thin skeletons of vines still clung to the stony terraces beside the tracks. On the far side of the Tagliamento River, the gray slate roofs of a village showed among the trees at the edge of a chestnut forest.

"Who did you say is claiming responsibility for this attack?" the American inquired.

"You have a particular interest? You are not, I think, a newspaperman, Signore...?"

"Bolan. Mack Bolan."

The policeman frowned. Mack *Bolan*? Surely... But yes! This was the category B foreigner on the latest printout from the Interpol computer: six feet three inches, two hundred pounds, dark hair, blue eyes and craggy, determined features; hold for questioning at the request of CIA, NSA, MI6, DSGE, Mossad,

Garda and whomever. There could be no mistake: this was the man they called the Executioner!

Another shrug. The American was not wanted for anything in Italy. The officer had received no specific orders; what with this damned terrorist bomb, he had quite enough on his plate already without running into any more—possibly international—complications.

"I am looking for a girl named Suzanne Bozuffi, the daughter of a friend of mine. She was with the student group," Bolan said.

"Bozuffi? An Italian girl?"

"American. But her grandfather was born in Siena."

"My home town! I am a Tuscan myself," the officer exclaimed. "Signore Bolan, what can I do to help you?"

"Tell me where I can check out the names of the dead. And of course the survivors." Bolan had hitched a ride to the disaster site on the wildcat tanker puffing the wrecker crane up from Udine. He had no idea how the local authorities were handling the administrative side of the disaster.

"The injured have been flown to Udine by helicopter," the policeman told him. "Some of the rescued continued their journey by bus. Others returned to the plain. Some may still be in the village." He nodded across the river. A TV camera crew, curious onlookers, peasants from the village and a handful of reporters were being held back on the far bank by a line of carabinieri. "You will find the details at the town hall."

"And those still under the wreckage?"

The police chief spread his hands. "Just those first three cars now. Certainly there will be more casualties there. But alive? I fear it is unlikely, *signore*."

He shouted something to the wrecking crew. For a moment the roar of blowtorches, the rasp of saws and tapping of hammers ceased. The normal sounds of the valley were audible once more. The salvage boss standing on top of a section of coachwork that looked as if it had been squeezed in a giant fist shook his head. There were no more cries to be heard beneath the wreckage. The crews resumed the search for the dead.

"You have of course the description of this Suzanne?" the *commendatore* asked.

"Uh-huh," Bolan replied. "She has red hair, shoulder length. She was traveling with a white leather suitcase. Most of her companions carried the usual student gear: bedrolls, rucksacks, that kind of thing."

"It is as well to know," the Italian said. He glanced at the lines of body bags. "Matters of identification can be very...delicate. It is perhaps a good thing the girl's father could not come himself. But one thing I can tell you: nobody of that description is among the dead so far recovered."

"Okay," Bolan said. "I'll talk to the people at the town hall and come back later. Maybe she took a walk along the train."

"It is unlikely. The explosion was at four o'clock in the morning."

Bolan thanked the police chief, then turned his back on the wreckage. That section of the river was shallow; he had no difficulty wading across. It was going to be a hot day. At the head of the valley, the mountains stood bare and brown against the blue sky.

The town hall, set back between plane trees at one side of a dusty square, was in chaos. Several dozen of the shocked survivors were still being cared for in a schoolroom hastily converted into a makeshift medical center. Anxious teenage villagers carrying sheets of paper scribbled with names and addresses ran between the mayor's office and an antique telephone switchboard.

But there was no redhead with shoulder-length hair in the schoolroom. And no record of any passenger named Bozuffi being transported to the hospital in Udine, or boarding the bus that ferried the braver to the next railroad station up the line. Nor was there a white leather suitcase among the collection of baggage and effects stacked beneath the plane trees. Bolan went back to join the *commendatore*.

By dusk that evening twenty-three more bodies had been located. Many were facially unrecognizable but none of them had red hair.

Seven had been so badly burned in the fire after the explosions that there was no trace of hair left on their incinerated bodies, but other factors were inconsistent with Suzy's description.

Bolan hired a cab in the village and returned to Udine.

Beyond the arched cloisters of the hospital, low-power electric lamps lit the crowded wards. Whispering nuns and interns in white coats moved among the injured, attempting to quiet the babble of voices in the out-patients department where the walking wounded awaited attention.

Some of the casualties in Out-patients were still in shock, but Bolan found one girl—a blond nineteen-year-old Californian with a ponytail—who had suffered no more than a broken arm. "I guess I was lucky," she told him, flourishing the plaster cast protruding from the ripped denim sleeve of her jacket. "I walked down the train to the john. I was booked in the second sleeper and there were some Dutch guys sprawled all over the aisles. They were going to..." She faltered for a moment, shook her head, blinked and then continued. "Suzy Bozuffi? Sure, I knew her. We stayed at the same pensione in Perugia. I mean we're not bosom pals or anything. Suzy's, you know, kind of ritzy. The leather suitcase, expensive clothes and all that. But she's okay."

"Did you see her on the train?" Bolan asked.

"On the train?" The girl wrinkled her nose as she concentrated. "Come to think of it, I don't believe I did. But she must have been there. We checked out of the pensione together, along with a group of kids from... Hey, why all the questions about Suzy? Is she missing?"

"You tell me," Bolan said.

He was about to give up when a distraught young man was brought in who had been found wandering on the mountainside hours after the wreck. He had been in charge of the Vienna group, and he had miraculously been thrown clear while most of his charges had died.

"My God!" he cried. "Their parents... What am I going to say? How can I possibly justify—"

"Take it easy," Bolan said gently. "Nobody's blaming you. Did you make the block booking for the sleeper?"

"Yes, of course. But I never imagined—"

"Suzanne Bozuffi. Was she on that train?"

The guy knuckled his eyes. His hands were trembling. "Now you mention it...no, she wasn't. She missed the train. I was worried about it but there was nothing I could do. There were all the others to think of, you see. I had to—"

"So she left the pensione with the others but she never got on the train, right?" Bolan interrupted for the third time.

The young man pulled himself together with an effort. "But, yes, that's correct. Thank heaven for her it is."

Bolan checked in to the Albergo della Posta and called Suzanne Bozuffi's father in Turin.

Michael Bozuffi was an industrialist. He built ships, light aircraft and electronic equipment. He was part-owner of a chemical factory in northern Italy and mining concessions that extended from South America to West Africa.

Mack Bolan was an outlaw, a dedicated warrior in the battle of right against wrong. He fought the hydra-headed menace of international terrorism wherever he found it, with whatever means he considered best, and for his pains he was himself on the hit list of most of the world's major intelligence and security networks.

Two men, two lives, two stories. But they had one point in common; there was one place where they converged.

They had shared a foxhole during the Tet offensive in Vietnam.

Courage in the face of continuous danger breeds respect, and the two veterans, so different in upbringing and approach, had remained friends ever since the three days of hell they had endured together.

Right now Bozuffi was hospitalized, recovering from a minor hip operation. Since Bolan was passing through Turin and had stopped to say hello to Bozuffi, he had agreed to check out the fate of the industrialist's only daughter as soon as they heard the news of the train wreck over the radio. But now he felt the investigation was at a dead end.

"She probably took off with a boyfriend, or simply missed the train," Bolan reassured the anxious father. "I'm sure you'll hear from her."

"Suzy doesn't have boyfriends. In any case she would have told me. We're very close," Bozuffi said. "Mack, I don't like it. Something smells. I want to find out where my daughter is." He was silent for a moment, then said, "Could I ask you a big favor?"

"Name it," he said.

"Would you backtrack for me, go to Perugia and see if you can find out what happened from that end?"

"Don't worry, Mike, I'll see what I can do," Bolan replied.

THE FOLLOWING MORNING Bolan asked the clerk at the reception desk to help him find a rental car.

Another American was checking out of the hotel at the same time—a tall, thin character about forty years old, wearing a tweed sport jacket that looked as if it had been made for a heavier man. A cigarette drooped from the corner of his mouth.

After Bolan had left, the thin man spun around the register and scanned the entries for the previous day. Scrawled illegibly on the page he saw "M. Blanski." He called back the clerk and asked to use the telex in the hotel's leisure room.

At the keyboard he tapped out a message to the Paris bureau of the Chicago *Globe*:

PSE SEND SOONEST UDINE POST OFFICE BIOG DETAILS MACK BOLAN AKA THE EXECUTIONER REPEAT EXECUTIONER STOP CONCENTRATE RECENT CAMPAIGNS ANTITERRORISTS STOP METTNER STOP

Jason Mettner II was the *Globe*'s roving ace foreign correspondent. His nose for news had taken him from Nicaragua to Nanking, from Cape Town to Kabul, from the carpeted quiet of the EEC headquarters in Brussels to the rent-a-mob slums of Khaddafi's Libya. Mettner II had followed in the footsteps of his father, a crime reporter for the same newspaper in the rough-and-tumble days of prohibition and the gang wars.

Mettner had heard of Bolan and had seen artist's renderings of him. And despite the Blanski name on the register, the features were unmistakable. The guy interested him, partly because he had showed here at the scene of one of those dime-a-dozen terrorist attacks from which the whole of Europe was suffering, and not least because many of the Executioner's victories had been won against the Mafia descendants of those hoods whose shady exploits Mettner's father had recorded.

But before he followed up Bolan's unexpected presence in this corner of Italy, the newspaperman had work of his own to do. He tore the copy of his previous message from the machine, lit another cigarette and tapped again, squinting to keep the smoke spiraling up from the cigarette out of his eyes.

METTNER ADD TRAIN WRECK STORY STOP RESPONSIBILITY FOR BLAST CLAIMED BY AFL REPEAT AFL (ACTION FOR LIBERTY) SMALL ULTRARIGHT-WING ITALOTERRORIST CELL ALREADY CREDITED ELEVEN MURDERS MODERATE LEFT-WING POLITICOS STOP WELL INFORMED CIRCLES SUGGEST BLAST STAGED THAT NEIGHBORHOOD AS REVENGE GESTURE STOP PIETRO RINALDI FASCIST FATHER OF AFL CHIEF MASSIMO EXECUTED THERE BY PARTISANS AT END WORLD WAR II STOP CHECK DETAILS GLOBE MORGUE STOP MESSAGE ENDS

Before he left the hotel, Mettner thrust a fistful of lire notes across the reception desk and told the clerk, "Look, there'll be more for you if you can find out from your friend at the rental agency exactly where and when Signore Blanski checks in his car. I'll call you tonight and again tomorrow to find out, okay?"

MACK BOLAN STOOD OUTSIDE the Pensione Estrellita in a narrow alley that wound down to the Via Bartolo in back of Perugia's fourteenth-century gothic cathedral. The stout, motherly Neapolitan woman who looked after the pensione remembered the students leaving. Why wouldn't she? They had been with her three months and it was only the day before yesterday.

"There were two special buses waiting to take them down to the railroad station," she said. "For the connection to Rome. But what a terrible thing, that bomb! So many dead...so young... How could anybody...?" She dabbed her eyes with a corner of the flowered apron she wore over her black dress.

"You actually saw them board the buses?" Bolan asked.

She shook her head. "They were around the corner, by the fountain in front of the cathedral."

"But you are sure Suzanne Bozuffi was with them?"

"Certainly. I waved goodbye as she turned the corner, just before I returned to clear up the mess they left."

"Did she have any...special men friends? Perhaps somebody older, more sophisticated? I believe she was a little more...mature...than the others."

"Men friends? Not that one." The head was shaken more vigorously. "Except when her father came. A real gentleman; he spoke very good Italian. But otherwise—no, not even among the students. If she went out at all, it was with a crowd. But usually she was studying in her room."

"Did she ever come back late? I mean, after the others returned?"

"Suzanne?" The fat lips blew out in a Latin expression of total ridicule.

Bolan walked down to the piazza in front of the cathedral. Sitting around the three-tiered fountain, and on the cathedral steps old men dressed in black gazed soberly at nothing. All of them had been there the day before. And the day before that. Unless one of them died, they would be there again tomorrow. Most of them remembered the students' buses leaving.

"Did you notice a girl, a foreigner, with red hair and carrying a white leather suitcase?" Bolan inquired.

"The red-haired one? Oh, I knew her all right," one of the old-timers replied. He chuckled. "I had looked at her very often. A student. Remarkable."

"Yes, yes," quavered another. "Beautiful clothes—and always a smile."

"But did you see her get on the bus with the others?"

A short silence. And then one man said slowly, "It is curious that you should ask that. I remember now. She was heading for the bus, a little after the others, hurrying. But I think she was taken ill."

"Ill?"

"A fainting fit. If it had not been for her friends..."

"What friends? The other students?"

"No, no," offered a man who so far had not spoken. "They were already on the buses. Her friends with the car, the ones who took her away."

"She went away in a car?"

"But yes," the first man said. "She was passing these three young fellows when she staggered...if they had not caught her she would certainly have fallen. And then of course they took the suitcase and helped her into the car—"

"Did you see what kind of car?"

"Of course. It was a Fiat. A gray Fiat."

"Nonsense!" someone else shouted. "It was a silver color. A Peugeot, I think."

Bolan left them to it. He started toward the pensione. It seemed clear now that his friend's daughter had been kidnapped. Three men, a waiting car, probably an aerosol spray or one of those KGB-style umbrellas with a needle tip to thrust into the unwary calf. And the Executioner was betting that there would soon be a ransom demand.

It was a disheartening story to take back to Bozuffi. But Bolan had done all he could. Despite certain disquieting overtones, he felt that such tragedies, all too common in Italy today, were best left to the official police.

That was the Executioner's reaction until the plotters made the mistake of attempting to thwart his investigation. The irony was that as far as he was concerned it was over, but they did not know that. Three separate and increasingly vicious attempts on his life in the following twelve hours not only convinced him that the affair must be more serious than he had realized; they also angered him to the extent that he determined to stay with the investigation personally until it was resolved.

The proof that this was something more than a simple abduction came before he even reached the pensione again. Pigeons swooping down from the cathedral roof skimmed the alley, and Bolan, mentally rehearsing what he was going to say to the girl's father, instinctively ducked his head as one flashed close by.

The stream of bullets from a silenced automatic splatted against the brickwork beyond his shoulder, staining the air with red dust. If it hadn't been for the pigeon, they would have taken the top of his head off.

Bolan's reactions were honed by years of combat in the hellgrounds of the world. He hit the cobblestones, snatching his Beretta from inside his jacket as he went down. Flat on his stomach, he swung around with the autoloader at the ready.

But the assassins were on a mission that was strictly hit and run: two figures on a Lambretta scooter at the end of the alley, anonymous in visored crash helmets. The engine screamed and they swerved out of sight before Bolan could fire.

He scrambled to his feet, decided against a second visit to the Estrellita—the Neapolitan lady was unlikely to have noticed three strangers in a gray or silver car—and checked in to a hotel in the Corso Vannucci.

He called Bozuffi. The industrialist agreed to contact the police and report his daughter as missing, probably kidnapped. Bolan promised to return to Turin the following day. Despite the attempt to put him out of the way and kill any investigation of the girl's disappearance, he still intended to offer his friend no more than moral support.

That was before the second attack.

It happened during the night. Bolan was wearing the skin-tight combat blacksuit, complete with shoulder harness, that had become his personal trademark in the guerrilla wars that ravaged the world. Always a light sleeper, with a catlike ability to wake instantly with all systems go, he was off the bed and crouched in a corner by the old-fashioned closet before the stealthily opened door was wide enough to let in the first intruder.

The light in the passageway had been switched off, and the guy was no more than a darker blur against the faint radiance of a late-rising moon that filtered through a distant window.

Bolan waited until the second man glided in, then rose silently to his feet. He saw the dim light glint against steel as they circled to stand on either side of the empty bed.

An explosion of movement. The two assassins fell to the bed, stabbing viciously downward where Bolan should have been. But the Executioner was behind them. He launched himself into the air and landed astride the back of the man nearest the door, whose shape was more clearly defined. He hooked a forearm beneath the hood's chin and reached at the same time for the second man's head, slamming the two skulls together.

There were cries of pain and alarm, and the three of them collapsed face downward across the rumpled covers.

The killers were taken by surprise, but they were tough and they were experienced. A blade sliced through the blacksuit sleeve and traced fire along Bolan's biceps before he could pull over the man who he had in a headlock and use him as a shield.

As they writhed and squirmed, striving for an advantage, the second man struck again. His arm rose and then savagely fell. But the blade homed on flesh the instant Bolan succeeded in rolling onto his back and dragging his half-choked assailant on top of him.

The killer uttered a strangled groan. His body arched and then went limp. Bolan hurled the body aside and heaved himself out from under to meet the knifeman's renewed assault.

Moonlight on the bloodied blade saved Bolan again. His hand shot out to seize the knife hand before the blade scythed in. The two men knelt face-to-face, their breath hoarse in the night, wrestling for possession of the weapon. Bedsprings creaked. The blademan jerked backward, attempting to pull Bolan on top of him; Bolan blocked the move and twisted to the left. The thug released Bolan's arm and clawed at his face. Bolan skimmed the heel of a callused palm against his adversary's throat.

Another spasm of exertion and the couple, still locked in combat, toppled from the bed and crashed heavily to the floor. A pottery lamp was dragged from the the night table and shattered. Maintaining his viselike grip on the assassin's wrist, Bolan achieved the nerve hold he had been seeking and the knife skated away beneath the bed.

With manic force, the guy thrust Bolan away and sprang to his feet. He leaped for the open door and pounded down the passage that led to the stairs. Bolan raced after him.

The sounds of the struggle had already awakened other guests. Doors opened, lights were switched on, querulous voices complained.

Bolan ran past them all. On the stairway a cool breeze blew from open doors beyond the entrance lobby. He dashed into the dark street. The moon was below the rooftops now but he could make out the figure of the killer, dodging between parked cars on the far side of the road. Bolan sprinted after him.

The guy ran across the piazza in front of the cathedral, traversed a long colonnade and stumbled out into the Via Rocchi. Halfway down the slope toward an Etruscan arch, Bolan caught up with him and dropped him from behind with a flying tackle.

Grappling fiercely, they rolled across the cobbled street, elbows, knees, fists and butting heads in the harsh yellow illumination of a streelight.

Bolan had not figured on a backup. He had assumed the two hotel intruders were the hit specialists who had escaped him on the scooter. But there had been a third man with the kidnap team in the car.

Now the Executioner's danger sense registered the bellow of the tiny high-compression motor as the scooter weaved in and out of the colonnade arches and into the Via Rocchi.

The guy he was fighting would have to wait. Bolan shoved him aside, firing a quick kick to the side of the head, and scrambled upright. He darted for a recessed doorway at the corner of an alley as the Lambretta sped toward him. The rider carried a rifle—it was a Winchester, Bolan saw—slung across his back and there was a blued steel automatic pistol in the left hand resting on the handlebars.

Bolan unleathered his silenced Beretta. When the scooter was just within range, he loosed off two 3-round bursts. The shots were muffled burps in the narrow street.

Battered sideways by the impact of the 9 mm skullbusters, its tire ripped to ribbons, the Lambretta's front wheel folded under. The machine cartwheeled, catapulting the rider forward to crash against a cast-iron hitching post cemented into the sidewalk.

The first attacker was on his feet and running. Bolan left the Lambretta pilot stunned on the cobbles and gave chase.

The hit man raced through the archway and across the square beyond.

Somewhere above them, a window was thrown up. An angry voice called inarticulate obscenities at the predawn sky. Bolan paid it no mind. Something he had seen on the far side of the arch had triggered an alarm inside his head.

In the light from the street lamp, he had caught sight of a three-letter monogram tattooed on his assailant's wrist. The letters A, F and L.

Action for Liberty.

The neofascist guerrilla group claiming responsibility for the train wreck in the Tagliamento valley.

So although she had not been on the train, it seemed as if Suzanne Bozuffi had been abducted by the same terrorist group who sabotaged it.

As the girl's father had suggested, something smelled.

And if the kidnapping was a terrorist deal, Bolan was in for the duration. Damn straight.

For the suppression of international terrorism, the fight to allow ordinary, decent men and women to live the lives they chose outside the shadow of fear, that was the number-one priority in Mack Bolan's book. Right now it was the only entry; he was dedicated to that fight.

The bomb in the supermarket, the hijacked airplane, machine-gunned restaurants, departure lounges and places of worship—these were the escalating threats that weighed more heavily on civilized society every year, every month, every week now.

And for the animals who planned and carried out such crimes against humanity, the Executioner offered no quarter.

Bolan had long ago decided that the governments of the world were too soft on such carrion.

Yeah, a hell of a sight too soft. The Soviets were soft on all terrorists because it suited them to have the West destabilized. The governments of the West were soft on Arab terrorists because they were scared of losing their oil; they were soft on terrorist acts committed by the Irish, the Israelis or the Germans because they were scared of losing votes. Why they were soft on Turkish and Armenian and Cypriot terrorists, Bolan didn't know.

Whatever, the scum of humanity who coldbloodedly gunned down women and children, who callously "executed" hostages, could rely on money, a safe passage to a "friendly" country or a prison sentence that was only nominal—until the next hijack made their release a condition of the hostages' safety.

Unless they happened to run up against the Executioner.

Mack Bolan did what governments and international organizations were too timid—or too corrupt—to do.

He hit back.

Hard.

It was no use obeying the rules when you were fighting people who denied the existence of rules.

Bolan did not need to know if the killer he was chasing had been a deprived child with an unhappy home life; he did not need a psychiatrist to analyze the guy's political beliefs: the Executioner had his own method of making the bastard talk. After that he would most likely kill the scum. It depended on the answers.

The man raced past the university for foreigners, looked over his shoulder and then—seeing that Bolan was closing in—dived through an open doorway in a wall behind the building.

Bolan followed him across a yard and in through another open door to a furnace room. The killer was already on the stairs beyond. Bolan took them three at a time, arrived in a marble and mosaic entrance hall, saw there was no elevator and continued on up a wider stairway that led to the upper floors.

His quarry's footsteps clattered on, two flights above him. A door slammed. Bolan arrived on the top floor.

He was in a deserted hallway. Glass-paneled doors blocking off empty lecture theaters. A single wooden door with a notice advising it was an emergency exit to the roof.

Bolan tried the handle. The door was locked.

He fisted the Beretta again and shot off the lock. Beyond the door a narrow wooden stairway spiraled upward. At the top of the stairs was a trapdoor. He shoved it open and emerged onto the roof behind the row of statues. There was no sign of his quarry.

And by this time the third killer, the rider of the Lambretta, had regained consciousness and taken his rifle to the top of the tower that flanked the Etruscan arch....

Chapter Three

After the gunfight at the university building, Bolan drove slowly out of town, northward toward Città di Castello and Arezzo along the Corso Garibaldi, through the old fortified gateway and then across the plain below.

Perugia had been founded on a rocky highland with flatlands all around; it stood now as an ancient enclave rising above a sprawl of modern railroad yards, warehouses and factories.

From a vantage point such as the tower above the Etruscan arch, a watcher could follow a car clear through the suburban housing that ringed those yards and see which road he took across the plain. Especially if the watcher had field glasses or a telescopic sight.

Bolan drove slowly because he wanted the rifleman on that tower to see which road he took. He wanted to be followed.

He chose the Arezzo road because it was relatively straight, with no main intersections for many miles, an easy road for a tail anxious to pick him up. The rented Fiat was a bright red, easy to spot between the poplars lining the route.

As far as the hotel was concerned, the management was welcome to keep the few things he had left in his room: their loss was nothing to the headache he would have explaining to the local police the presence of a dead man on his blood-soaked bed.

The tail picked him up before he had driven five miles. The car was neither silver nor gray: it was a putty-colored Volkswagen station wagon. There was just the one guy behind the wheel, Bolan saw with relief.

But there could be no doubt this was the killer. The VW stormed into view in Bolan's rearview mirror, trailing a cloud of dust above the sunny roadway...and then slowed at once and maintained its distance when the driver identified the red Fiat.

He wasn't bad. He never closed up too much, Bolan saw, and where possible he left at least one other vehicle between him and his quarry. But there was very little traffic; he would have needed a city street to prove whether he was really expert. In any case it didn't matter a damn: so long as the Executioner didn't let on that he knew he was being followed, the plan might work.

Bolan stopped in Città di Castello's central square and got out of the car. The VW wagon drove sedately past and pulled into a space one hundred yards down the street. The driver appeared to be making some minor adjustment beneath the hood—something that kept the engine of the VW running.

Bolan entered a grocery store and bought a couple of bread rolls, cheese, a carton of milk and a bunch of grapes. He returned to the Fiat and continued his journey. The driver of the VW, evidently satisfied with his tinkering, climbed back behind the wheel and followed at a discreet distance.

Two miles farther on, Bolan turned right onto a minor road and drove through a stretch of undulating country surrounded by wooded hills. He soon found what he was looking for: a long, straight grade that slanted down to a bridge over a stream and then rose up the far side of the valley. At the top of the hill trees grew on either side of the road, and there was a grassy space beside the bridge where a car could pull off and park by the waterside.

Bolan coasted the Fiat to a halt and got out. He sat on the grass with the food around him, the picture of a driver with a long way to go stopping to take in a breath of fresh air and eat a wayside breakfast.

He was gambling, but he had calculated the odds very carefully. The success of his plan depended on three things: that the tail was unaware Bolan knew he was being followed, that there was only one place beneath the trees at the top of the hill where a car could be conveniently parked off the roadway, and that it was once again a hot day.

From the corner of his eye, the Executioner saw the VW slow down, then bump across the grass shoulder to stop in the shade of overhanging branches. The driver got out and opened the tailgate. He would, Bolan knew, be taking out the Winchester repeater. A moment later, light flashed briefly from the lenses of a pair of field glasses. The killer was checking that Bolan was alone and defenseless.

Resting his elbows on the station wagon's hood, the rifleman took a preliminary sighting through his sniperscope. The distance was about four hundred yards.

Since the killer's sightline traversed the road surface, the mirage effect of the haze produced by the half-melted pavement should make Bolan's image in the Winchester's sight appear higher than it actually was, as if he floated a foot above the ground.

It was a hell of a risk, because the guy was a good shot.

Bolan accepted the risk. But the hairs prickled on the nape of his neck as he glanced sideways up the hill while he ate and drank.

Every muscle in his body was wound tight, the arms ready to thrust, the legs, tucked beneath him, prepared to straighten. He sensed rather than saw the rifleman taking final aim. At that moment the valley was deserted; road and fields extended empty in all directions. But farm laborers, a tractor, another car could appear at any time. The efficient murderer must act decisively and fast.

Bolan saw the twinkle of fire at the Winchester's muzzle and launched himself forward and down. He had been waiting like a sprinter for the starter's gun, but even with the illusory effect of the heat haze he would have been hit if he had not anticipated the shot. The bullet parted the hairs of his head as he crashed facedown among the remnants of his meal, scattering bread, fruit and milk over the grass. It seemed a long time afterward that he heard the crack of the rifle.

Bolan lay motionless. Everything now depended on the killer's faith in his own skill. If he thought it prudent to loose off a second shot, the Executioner was a dead man. But Bolan was betting on the belief that he would play safe, not wishing to attract attention with a second shot.

Bolan released his breath in a long sigh when he saw that the gamble had paid off. The killer was striding quickly down the hill toward him. There would be a pistol in his pocket, but he had left the Winchester in his car. Bolan assumed the pose of the newly dead—no problem, since he had seen enough corpses—one leg doubled beneath him, his head at a strained angle, an elbow bent awkwardly. But beneath the bend of the elbow the muzzle of his Beretta, held against his chest, pointed menacingly up the grade.

When the terrorist was ten yards away he looked cautiously right and left and then drew an automatic from his pocket. It was the same one he had carried on the Lambretta. Squinting through half-closed eyes, Bolan figured it for a SIG-Sauer Model P-226—a tough gun to argue with at short range.

As the man raised the pistol Bolan fired without altering his position. He wanted the guy out of action but alive.

From beneath the crook of Bolan's elbow, the Beretta choked out one...two...three...triple bursts that smashed across the terrorist's knees and thighs like iron whips.

He fell screaming, clawing at his bloody legs, collapsing like a puppet whose strings had been cut. The pistol dropped into the long grass.

The Executioner was on his feet. He leaped in and grabbed the killer by the lapels, hauling him upright. The guy was still yelling, mouth gaping, face a mask of agony.

Bolan kicked the gun out of reach. "All right," he growled, savagely shaking the injured man. "Suzanne Bozuffi—where is she?"

The killer's lips snarled back from his teeth. "Drop dead," he gasped. "Never heard...of...the bitch."

Bolan drew back a fist and smashed it into the swarthy face. The head snapped back. Blood streamed from the hood's broken nose.

"Where is she?"

"Go fuck yourself."

Bolan seized the hood's collar and dragged him toward the river—the useless legs jerking and twitching, the guy yelling again as shards of splintered bone grated together.

Bolan dumped him facedown on the bank. He pulled the guy's head and shoulders forward until they projected over the stream, and then he leaned down and dunked the terrorist's head in the water.

The yells turned to gurgles. Pink-tinted bubbles broke surface and skeins of scarlet from the broken nose swept away on the current. Above the hips the body writhed and threshed.

Bolan grabbed a fistful of hair. He yanked the head back until the face was clear of the water. "Suzanne Bozuffi?" he rasped.

The hood coughed, spluttered, spit blood and water.

"Okay, okay," he choked. "I'll talk, but I don't know where the hell she is."

"You worked the snatch, right?"

The hood sicked up water, spit again, nodded. His breath rattled in his throat.

Bolan dragged him away from the edge and propped him in a sitting position against the stonework of the bridge. "Okay," he said grimly. "Now talk."

"Damn all to say." Hate-filled eyes stared venomously out from beneath the sodden thatch of hair.

"Me and Ugo and Marcello—we were told to snatch the girl. We did. End of story."

"Not quite," Bolan said. "How did you snatch her?"

"You know damn well how. You've been snooping around long enough. We gave her the stuff, shoved her in the heap and away."

"You gave her what stuff?"

"Shit, the antimugger spray. The aerosol. You know. Stuff that puts them out for a coupla minutes. After that it was the hypo."

"So where is she now?"

"I already told you...." The gory face contorted with pain, and a long shudder shook the hood's body. "Jesus, my *legs*! Look, mister, for pity's sake, I'm losing a lot of blood."

"Me, too," Bolan said. "My heart bleeds...for you. Where is she now?"

The killer screamed as Bolan rose menacingly over him with a raised fist. "I don't know. Don't hit me.... Honest, I swear, I don't know where they took her."

"Where did *you* take her?"

"We took her to Cortona. To the strip. The way we were told."

"The strip?"

"There's a flying club there, a private field. We delivered her to a plane where some other guys took care of her, some black guys."

"*Black* guys? And they were flying her out? Where was that plane going?"

Painfully, the terrorist shook his head. His breath snorted through the blood in his nose. "Search me.

We had to board our own crate. We took off before they did."

"And where did you and the other two go?"

"To Udine, for the train."

"So the three of you bombed the train?"

"And three other brothers from the cell. A rush job."

Bolan frowned. "What was the hurry?"

The thug groaned and eased his shoulders against the stonework. Bolan repeated the question.

"It had to be that train, didn't it? I mean she was supposed to be on it. And we had to cover up the snatch, for God's sake. It wasn't an ordinary ransom routine."

A terrible suspicion was forming in Bolan's mind.

"It takes time to fix those things," the hardman went on. His voice became stronger, tinged with pride. "It was delicate work. It had to be just right. She had to blow between the locomotive and the baggage car, to make the biggest mess possible of those first three sleepers, see. Turned out a real neat job, especially after we fired them. And I'm telling you, that needs real skill when they're traveling at high speed. I mean, to be that accurate."

He turned his head aside to spit blood. "With luck they'd have written the kid off as if she'd been there. Except—" he glared at the Executioner "—you had to poke your goddamn nose in, you son of a bitch."

Bolan suppressed a surge of rage before he spoke. "Are you saying that the only reason you wrecked that train, killing more than sixty people, was to cover up the kidnapping of the Bozuffi girl?"

The terrorist stared at him incredulously. After all, who could make up a story like that?

"Okay," Bolan seethed, still trying to restrain his temper. "I have another question. Why did you choose that particular valley. Even vermin like you, I guess, have *some* reasons for their actions."

"You follow orders, that's all."

"Why that valley?"

"It seems there was a good cover story, something to take their attention away from the girl. Something to do with Massimo's old man."

"Massimo who? Is that the punk who gives the orders?"

The thug clamped his mouth shut. "I ain't saying any more."

Bolan hit him again. He had no pity. The man was a murderer many times over. "Massimo who?"

"I shouldn'ta said that. They'll kill me."

"They won't need to."

Suddenly the man's body was convulsed with sobs. Tears streamed from his eyes. "They'll kill me, they'll kill me," he repeated. "Look, mister, you gotta get me to a doctor. An ambulance."

"Think about all those people you killed, the kids burned alive. And the women who'll stay crippled for life."

"Fuck them. They belong to the old order, don't they? They gotta make way for the new. They gotta die sometime so we can clean up this shithouse world."

Bolan sighed. Like most bullies, the terrorist was a coward; like all fanatics he was narrow, insensitive and stupid as well as cruel.

"You gotta get me to a doctor," he pleaded again.

Bolan looked at the crimsoned grass around the guy's dead legs, at the earth that was already turning brown as the blood pumping from ruptured vessels sank in. "You wouldn't last long enough," he said. "By the time a doctor got here you'd be dead. I'll make it easy for you... and quick."

He placed the muzzle of the Beretta against the terrorist's temple and squeezed the trigger.

Chapter Four

Cortona was a small town perched on a hillside between Perugia and Siena. It boasted a dark and somber cathedral, a diminutive museum and a view on fine days of the Trasimeno lake.

The airfield lay on the plain below—a clubhouse, a single hangar and a stretch of grass where a small Cessna, a Beechcraft, a Piper Cherokee and a couple of Cubs were tethered against the breeze sweeping in from the east. A World War II pursuit monoplane, captured from the French in 1940, was mounted on a plinth in the center of the graveled area in front of the clubhouse.

By the time Bolan arrived it was after midday and the parking lot was deserted.

A man in a white jacket was polishing glasses behind the bar in the empty lounge. He had a shock of black hair and heavy, dark eyebrows above a puckish face. "Ninety percent local stuff—joyrides, flying instruction, parachute jumping and gliding at the weekends, that kind of thing," he said in answer to Bolan's question.

"Apart from club members or people with their own planes, I guess there aren't too many intercity flights or foreign traffic, right?"

"You said it. We have a couple of regulars with estates down here who fly their own planes to Milan or Geneva. You know, business types. But on the whole, like you say, it's the homegrown talent."

"So you'd remember anything recent on the international scale?"

"Try me," the barman said.

"Three days ago. A ship with a black crew. Probably foreign registration. Something local flying up to Udine at the same time."

"Sure I remember. The foreigner was a Fokker. Not the F-27, something smaller, but big stuff for us. Normally they won't put them down on grass fields. This one was registered someplace in North Africa."

"And the crew?"

The barman shrugged; the black eyebrows rose. "They were okay. No uniforms. Didn't drink. Didn't say much. Once the ambulance arrived they took off again."

"Ambulance?"

"With the sick chick. Some tropical disease, they said. They were taking her to some special clinic. Too bad, she was pretty too, red hair, all the curves. You know."

"Was she conscious? Did she say anything?"

"They were way out on the apron, I was here. She was on a stretcher, looked as if she was asleep, or unconscious."

"And the three guys who brought her?"

"They were going to Udine. There was a chopper waiting for them. Civil version of a Bell Cobra. Unless I fucked up on the registration letters it was a rented job from Milan."

"What about the ambulance?"

"There was a fourth guy. He drove it away."

"Just one more thing. On a small private field like this, any pilot doing anything more than joyriding has to file a flight plan. Am I correct?"

"Sure, he does. No sweat if it's A to A. But if it's a case of A to B, he has to file. International regulations."

"Okay. So this Fokker would have filed a flight plan with your guys here and the area control, right?"

The barman nodded.

"I have to contact the sick girl urgently. Family business," Bolan said. "But I don't know where this clinic is. And I doubt the air traffic controllers at Florence would part with the information to a stranger. You figure I could persuade anyone here to divulge that Fokker's flight plan?"

"For that," the barman said, "you would have to be real nice to our flight controller."

Bolan looked out the wide glass windows at the deserted field. It was still sunny, but the wind had freshened, bending the cypresses on the far side of the perimeter track. "How long do I have to wait before the guy shows?" he asked.

The barman took off his white jacket and hung it on a peg. He walked around the end of the bar counter with an outstretched hand. "Meet the flight controller," he said.

Bolan grinned. He peeled bills from a roll and laid them on the polished mahogany counter. "When the barman returns," he said, "buy him a drink on me."

The black brows rose and fell again. The bills vanished and white teeth appeared in a fleeting smile. "I don't even have to check out the ledger,'' the man said. ''We get so few international flights in and out of here, I keep a computer behind my eyes.'' He scribbled a line on a notepad, tore off the page and handed it to the Executioner. ''This here's the plane's registration. The pilot filed a flight plan taking him due south, with a refueling stopover at Catania, in Sicily. He gave his destination as Tripoli.''

''I KNOW YOU WON'T ACCEPT MONEY,'' Michael Bozuffi said, ''but anything you need in the way of travel expenses, transport, weapons, contacts—well, just name it. I have a certain amount of influence and I'm not a poor man. It's all at your disposal if you can just locate Suzy.''

''I may need that help,'' Bolan said. ''I don't like the way this is shaping up. I don't understand why this terrorist group should make such a big deal out of snatching your daughter. Especially since there's been no ransom demand.''

''She's got to be found and she's got to be safe. I know you'll do all you can, Mack. I rely on you.''

''Where terrorists are concerned,'' Bolan said, ''you can count on me.''

He drove back to Udine and asked to see the police chief he had met at the site of the train wreck.

''Massimo?'' the *commendatore* repeated. ''And the man who quoted the name was a member of this AFL nonsense?''

''He was. Like one of his friends who... disappeared, he had this monogram tattooed on his wrist.''

"Then it must be Rinaldi," the officer said. "Massimo Rinaldi. Said to be head of this terrorist group, but nobody can prove anything. Besides, he has protection. His father was a big wheel under Mussolini. Killed by the partisans at the end of the war."

"And Junior continues to preach the extreme right?"

The police chief heaved his shoulders in a Latin shrug. "But carefully, my friend. Very carefully. The night the train was wrecked, for instance, Massimo was at La Scala in Milan, the guest of a respectable politician. At the time your supposed kidnapping took place he was provided with an equally unimpeachable alibi: hosting a luncheon for fifty members of France's Front National, who had come to Italy to air their anti-Semitism and their Hitlerian views on immigration."

"Nice guy," Bolan said. "I think I'd like to visit him. He might find it difficult to get protection from me."

"It is supposed to be a secret—once more the protection, you see—but I can give you an address." The *commendatore* wrote on a sheet of paper, which he handed to Bolan. "It is, of course, my duty to warn you that we cannot tolerate any kind of punitive activity that is outside the law."

"Of course."

"But apart from that, if there is any way I can help..."

"You could have your bloodhounds check out a couple of registrations for me," Bolan allowed. He passed over the details he had gleaned at the Cortona airfield. "The Fokker's from North Africa. I believe the Bell's a rented ship from some company in Milan, but I'd like to know who hired it three days ago."

A telex machine began chattering beyond the filing cabinets ranged along one wall of the *commendatore*'s first-floor office. "I shall do what I can," he promised.

He rose to his feet, tore off the paper when the telex machine ejected it through the plastic slit in the lid and began to read the message. The phone on his desk rang. He picked up the receiver and held it against his ear. Bolan scanned the paper with Massimo Rinaldi's address on it. Unexpectedly, it was a small seaside town between Alassio and Imperia, on the Ligurian Riviera.

The police chief laid the handset carefully back on its rest. He glanced a second time at the message in his hand.

"Signore Bolan," he said uncomfortably, "I am truly sorry, but I have my duty to do. It is a task that is personally unpalatable to me, but this time I have received specific orders...."

Bolan looked up, frowning. "Meaning?"

"It concerns a man found dead last night in a hotel room in Perugia. The room had been booked by someone who answers your description. A second man was found dead on the sidewalk outside the university early today. He had, it seems, fallen from the roof. Again, a person fitting your description was observed to leave the building shortly afterward."

Bolan said nothing. The policeman cleared his throat. "I am instructed that the local police require that you be held for questioning. There is also a third death—all of them, curiously, members of this AFL commando—about which they feel you may be able to help. A man found by the roadside near Città di Castello. You must forgive me, *signore*, but my orders are to place you under arrest."

The Executioner rose to his feet. "I understand," he said. "You have your duty to do; you must obey your orders. But first, tell me—how much would it cost to replace that window if it was broken? And the shutters beyond if they should become damaged?"

The policeman stared at him. "I... really do not know. Something perhaps in the neighborhood of 950,000 lire. It would depend, of course, on the damage."

"Great." Bolan peeled bills from a wad he took from his pocket. He laid them on the desk. "Let's hope this covers it," he said. "If not, you must let me know somehow... and in the meantime my apologies for a hasty departure."

Shielding his face with crossed arms, he launched himself at the window and burst through into the night in a shower of broken glass and splintered wood.

Chapter Five

Laigueglia is an Italian fishing village not far from the French border, with a twelfth-century watchtower, a single short jetty and an extraordinary twin-towered church that presides over the catch from the lower slopes of hills rising from the Mediterranean shore.

Not the place, on an early-fall afternoon at the end of the tourist season, where a man expects to be struck between the shoulder blades by a 14.6 mm slug from an elephant gun.

The ocean was smooth that day. Half a mile offshore, water and sky merged in a uniform oyster-gray. The sun was hidden. Moisture beaded the white wrought-iron tables on the deserted café terrace and brightened the paint of fishing boats drawn up on the damp sand.

Even indoors, where Mack Bolan sat nursing a beer, the humid air caused the walls to glisten and misted the panels of the espresso coffee machine. Apart from a couple of students necking in back, the café was empty. The proprietor, elbows resting on the countertop, was reading a newspaper.

With the sleeve of his jacket, Bolan wiped a clear space in the center of the steamy window. He saw fishermen in shorts and vests crouched over a net that was stretched along the dock. A small speedboat nosed in toward the jetty. In a few minutes the contact he was waiting for would arrive.

The man was four minutes early. A chunky guy wearing a windbreaker and sunglasses, he braked a knobby-tired Honda trail bike to a halt and leaned the machine against one of the empty terrace tables.

After a quick glance around he walked into the café and sat down at Bolan's table. Renzo Gandolfi was a part-time burglar, small-time fence and smuggler and full-time scavenger of information, which he was prepared to sell.

It was two days since the Executioner had burst out of the carabinieri office in Udine. According to the newspapers, authorities were on the lookout for him at docks, airports and railroad stations. But he had an idea that the police chief, while fulfilling his duty to the letter, had nevertheless omitted to mention to his superiors that the person they wanted was likely to pay a visit to a man in Laigueglia—a man whose address he had himself provided. Certainly Bolan had received no suspicious looks either here or in San Remo, where he had passed by the musty antique store that Gandolfi operated as a front.

"You have the intel?" Bolan asked.

The Italian nodded. "You were right about the chopper, it belongs to Italavia at Milan. It was hired on the day you mention for a straight three-point run—Milan to Cortona to Udine, and then back to Milan. The pilot was a company man. He received his orders, picked up the clients, delivered them and then went home."

"And the name of the client renting the helicopter?"

"Renato Colibri. If it's the same Colibri, he works as a chauffeur and bodyguard for Rinaldi."

"It'll be the same one," Bolan assured him. "Did you find out about the North African Fokker?"

"It's registered in Libya. Based in Tripoli. But in fact it belongs to Anya Ononu, part of his private fleet."

Bolan whistled. "Ononu? The dictator of that West African—"

"Montenegria, that's right. I guess he must be in with Khaddafi."

"That's great," Bolan said sarcastically. "A crazy black fascist shacked up with a mad Arab Communist! And talking of fascists, what do you have on this Massimo Rinaldi? I checked out the property, uphill on the far side of the tracks, but I waited to get the lowdown from you on his security organization before I took it any further."

"Renato Colibri looks after that," Gandolfi said. "Apart from the dogs and his three thugs, there's the wire—"

The snitch never completed the sentence. Gandolfi reared up suddenly from his chair, knocked over the table and hurtled headfirst into the wall on the far side. He slid to the floor with blood frothing from a grotesque hole beneath the collar of his windbreaker. At the same time Bolan registered the crack of a distant shot. Glass from the shattered window cascaded to the tiles.

Bolan was out on the terrace by the time the proprietor reached the dead man. The sound of a fiercely accelerating engine cut through the babble of voices from tourists and fishermen, who stood horrified among the nets and lobster pots. Beyond the jetty, riding high on its creaming bow wave, the speedboat streaked out to sea.

A fat guy with a beard had dropped a basketful of sea bass. "Un-b-b-believable," he stammered. "Standing at the end of the jetty, cool as you p-p-please! He had a rifle with a telescopic sight."

"He must have sighted through the clear patch where I wiped the glass," Bolan said.

Back in the café the proprietor had blood on his hands. "What kind of a gun is that?" he asked dazedly. "To send a man crashing over a table?"

"Big-game stuff," Bolan told him. "A safari gun, probably a Mannlicher."

Bolan didn't need anyone to tell him who was responsible. Clearly the word had gotten around that he was hot on the trail. Three members of the AFL cell were already dead, the cops were looking for a certain Mack Bolan, otherwise known as the Executioner—and the guy had the nerve to show up in the very town where Action for Liberty's boss had his headquarters!

So it wasn't all that surprising that an organization with so little regard for human life should eliminate anyone likely to help out.

Okay, Bolan thought grimly, elimination was a game where more than one could play. Renzo Gandolfi might have been small fry, a dispensable piece on the board, but he would be avenged.

Yeah, as soon as the Executioner collected the necessary intel and the so-well-protected Signore Rinaldi could be confronted in his lair.

Bolan figured it would be wise to lose himself. If the terrorists were this well informed, if they were prepared to waste anyone who tried to help him, he himself would be a marked man, the prime target on their hit list.

They had gunned down Gandolfi first, he guessed, because he happened to be the clearer target and they dared not wait around for a second shot, and as a warning to others not to cooperate with Bolan. Or maybe because they wanted the Executioner alive—and they figured on jumping him if he attempted to break into the Rinaldi property.

Either way, he had to go underground...in case the guy with the elephant gun came after him again or a second killer was unleashed on him. That meant before the cops arrived and started to ask questions.

Bolan walked out of the café. If anyone thought of stopping him, a look at the expression on his face was enough to deter them.

As soon as he left, the two students in back slipped out through the kitchen of the café. A quarter of a mile away, they went into a bar on the Via Roma. The girl headed for a booth with a pay phone. She dialed a number and waited. Then, "Your man was a little late," she said. "Gandolfi had already begun to talk...but I don't think he had time to say much. The big guy split."

By now it was dusk. Bolan was three blocks away. A salt breeze blowing off the sea carried a hint of drizzle along with the fish odors, and the promenade was deserted. He could hear nothing but the crashing of waves and a desultory rhythm picked out by a guitarist in the empty depths of a disco bar with a red neon sign that flashed Hell's Kitchen.

Bolan turned down a lane so narrow that arched buttresses had been built high above to keep the houses apart.

It was here, from a flight of stone steps half-hidden behind a solitary palm, that the man with the Mannlicher fired his second shot that day.

And for the second time, an involuntary movement saved Bolan's life. He was passing a gun shop stacked with sports and fishing equipment, and an unusually designed suede shoulder rig caught his eye. He momentarily checked his pace to glance at the window display.

In the instant he slowed down, during the tenth of a second that his head turned, the killer squeezed his trigger.

The report from the huge-caliber rifle was deafening. The bullet, aimed fractionally ahead of Bolan on the assumption that the pace would not vary, fanned his ear and smashed through the plate-glass window of the gun shop.

Bolan dived to the cobblestones, and crawled for cover behind a concrete trough planted with geraniums, before the echoes of the shot died away—the unleathered Beretta already in his right hand. High on the wall above him, the gunsmith's burglar alarm shrilled.

Bolan lifted his head and peered through the aromatic leaves, wondering if the gunman would fire again.

He saw movement, a play of shadows below the ancient walls. He heard running footsteps, the creak of hinges, a wooden door slamming. Evidently the rifleman had decided against another shot right away. Shutters had been opened, windows thrown up, a chorus of voices demanded to know what the hell was going on. The alarm continued to ring.

Bolan jumped to his feet and sprinted for the steps. Beyond the doorway a small lobby, poorly lit, separated a curving flight of stairs from a corridor. A few yards along, a flimsy door was still swinging. Bolan charged through the door.

In the confined space the second shot, fired from a corner at the far end of the corridor, sounded even louder than the first. The muzzle-flash revealed peeling walls, a boarded-up window, broken floor tiles. Plaster flew from the wall beside Bolan's head as the heavy slug channeled an exit route through layers of stucco. The killer vanished before the Executioner could shoot.

He continued the chase, pounding along another dark passage, down more stairs and then out of the warren of old houses into a piazza where an immense brass ship's anchor lay cemented to a memorial plinth. Hunter and hunted dashed across the Via Dante Alighieri and passed Hell's Kitchen. Through an arch at the far end of the lane, fishing boats were visible on the sand by the jetty. But the gunman turned left and raced along an alley that led to the main highway. He was holding the unwieldy rifle slanted across his chest.

He continued straight over the roadway and through a tunnel that burrowed beneath the railroad embankment. At the top of a twisting grade on the far side there was a parking lot in front of a modern schoolhouse. The 320-series BMW that Bolan had rented in San Remo was there.

So was the killer's car. The Executioner was halfway up the grade when an engine roared to life and a Mercedes sedan rocketed past, tires screeching as it slewed around the corner in front of the tunnel. Bolan jerked open the driver's door of the BMW and slipped behind the wheel.

He had to make a quick decision whether to chase the hit man or head straight for Massimo Rinaldi's property. He opted for the former because the Executioner preferred action to the waiting game; and partly because he hoped to catch up with the killer, force him off the road and choke out of him some of the details Gandolfi had been about to reveal.

By the time Bolan wrenched the BMW out of the tunnel and into the main drag, the taillights of the Mercedes were disappearing around a curve four hundred yards away where the road followed the shore again at the far end of town. He floored the pedal and the German car howled in pursuit.

Laigueglia was a desert. It was the dead end of the season: most of the hotels were closed; green shutters blinded the severe rectangular facades of the waterfront houses. A scooter, ridden by a youth dressed like a speedway ace, and a small Fiat backing up out of a cul-de-sac were the only vehicles in sight. Bolan swerved around them both, trying to close the distance between himself and the fleeing Mercedes.

The Mercedes streaked up a long grade that led around a headland, past dormitory developments that sprawled over the hillside on the outskirts. The contorted strata of a cliff face showed up as the killer switched on his headlamps. Rounding the point after him, Bolan saw the lights of Laigueglia slide sideways in his driving mirror and then vanish. The two cars roared westward along the coast road.

Andora was a featureless downhill straight lined by apartment blocks bordering a marina. Traffic lights flashed green and amber at the far end of the street. The Mercedes raced through, leaving Bolan still two hundred yards short of the intersection when the signal changed from amber to red.

He gritted his teeth, shifted down, kept his foot on the gas. Horns blared, brakes squealed, angry shouts whipped away behind him as he shot between two cars, narrowly missed a bus and briefly clipped the curb. Gunning the engine, he heard the shrill of a police whistle fade.

Some miles before Diano Marina, the coast road swooped and twisted below high cliffs towering over the ocean. Traffic was heavier here. The lights of cars and trucks, strung out along the dark, curving littoral, disappeared, swung back into view, vanished again and then reappeared with dazzling brilliance around a shoulder of the mountain.

Yard by yard, making the most of the BMW's superior cornering power, Bolan was gaining on the Mercedes. He could hear the big car's tires screeching in protest on every bend. The hum of his own exhaust ricocheted off the rock face to his right.

He had closed up to within eighty or ninety yards when the killer pulled out to pass a slow-moving pickup. Through the sedan's wide rear window, Bolan could see the driver silhouetted against the glare of oncoming headlights. He was steering with one hand, holding a portable microphone in the other.

Bolan assumed he was calling up reinforcements. The Executioner began to keep a wary eye open for rockfalls, hidden marksmen, any kind of ambush. At the same time he glanced continually at the rearview mirror, on the lookout for vehicles coming up fast from behind.

There was a temporary lull in the traffic and Bolan saw a sign flash by, indicating that he was approaching a double S-bend at the head of a creek indenting the coastline.

The Executioner hurled the BMW around the first curve at close to seventy mph. The brake lights of the Mercedes blazed as it slowed for the second.

Suddenly a huge dump truck nosed out from behind a rock outcrop to block the roadway.

There was only one thing for Bolan to do. Straight ahead, no brakes in the world would save him from a collision that would certainly be fatal. On the right, the cliff face ran close to the truck. His one chance was to try and squeeze the BMW through between the truck's front fender and a low parapet bordering the road where it circled the steep slope at the head of the creek.

Holding the gas pedal to the floor, he flicked the wheel to the left.

The truck was still moving. To avoid it, Bolan was forced to run the BMW's offside wheels over rough ground between the roadway and the parapet.

A cloud of dust mushroomed into the air. Stones rattled against the bodywork; the engine screamed as spinning tires scrabbled in the loose surface. There was a jarring crash when the oil pan scraped solid rock. Then he was through and lurching back onto the macadam.

It was there that the ambushers played their trump. A second vehicle—a jeep hidden from view by the dump truck—accelerated obliquely across the road and nudged the fender of Bolan's rental with the iron bar protecting its own front wheels.

The BMW was barely under the Executioner's control.

The impact jerked the wheel from his hands. A front tire blew. The car slammed against the parapet, reared up into the air and then cartwheeled over the edge and plunged toward the sea.

The slope was almost vertical, steep and stony, with clumps of furze and brushwood among the rock outcrops. The car smashed onto its side halfway down, rolled over twice, bounced off a granite boss and dropped the final fifty feet upside down to hit the surface of the water with a noise like a grenade exploding.

It sank at once.

Before it hit the slope, Bolan had enough time to unsnap his safety belt, thrust himself away from the steering column and hunch down beneath the dashboard on the passenger side.

He was aware of space and darkness and the rush of air before the final impact...then blackness, a pounding behind his eyes and the cold, dead clutch of the ocean.

The car undulated down through forty feet of saltwater and settled on sand.

Chapter Six

Jason Mettner II folded his lean frame into an armchair by the window of his room on the second floor of Laigueglia's Albergo Splendido. He lit a cigarette. It was dark outside; the drizzle had been blown away by an offshore breeze, but the roofs of the old houses across the tiny piazza still shone with moisture in the misty lamplight.

Mettner picked up a tape recorder no bigger than a pack of Chesterfields and thumbed the button that set the miniature spools turning.

The message would be flown by courier the following morning. Personal to Allard Fielding, Mettner's editor in Chicago.

"I'm making this a verbal memo, Al," Mettner said, "because you know how many eyes scan a cable or a telex before it makes your desk, and I want to keep this strictly between the two of us.

"I'm holed up in this dinky fishing village in a hotel room not much bigger than a telephone booth, and I'm wondering what the hell I'm doing here—not because there's no story but because there are too damned many! You sent me here to do research for a feature on the increase of terrorism in Europe, remember? So I'm checking out this Udine train wreck when an American industrialist's daughter gets snatched. Nobody knows who by. No ransom note received by distraught daddy. But—wait for this!—the girl was supposed to have been with a group of students written off in the sabotaged train. Yeah. You're dead right. There has to be a connection."

Mettner tipped ash from his cigarette into the saucer beneath an empty coffee cup, swallowed a slug of bourbon from a leather-covered hip flask and replaced the cigarette in the corner of his mouth. He continued his report.

"Meanwhile, at my hotel in Udine, I find this Mack Bolan character. He wasn't registered under his own name, but I figured it out. You'll have a file on him in the morgue, but to save time and trouble I'll give you the rundown I got from the Paris bureau. It seems he was a Nam vet, a guy whose skill as a sniper and penetration specialist won him the title of the Executioner. And it seems he was known at the same time as Sergeant Mercy on account of his compassion for Viet civilians.

"According to the cuttings, it was compassion of a different kind that brought him back stateside. He received emergency leave to bury three members of his family in Pittsfield, Massachusetts. Stories vary on the details. The most likely has old man Bolan in debt to Mafia loan sharks, kid sister hustling to raise the dough to pay them off and then Dad finding out and liquidating the girl, his wife and finally himself in a fit of rage and grief and humiliation. There was a kid brother, too, but he seems to have only been wounded.

"What's for sure is that the tragedy was the springboard for Mack Bolan's one-man war against the Mob."

As he spoke, smoke from the wagging cigarette at the corner of Mettner's mouth spiraled up into his eye. He picked the butt off his lower lip and dropped it into the coffee dregs. With a grimace of distaste, he gulped another mouthful of bourbon, lit another cigarette and resumed his message.

"With most of the Mafia families wiped out, Bolan was supposed to have croaked in an auto fire. But one of the *Post*'s investigative specials a couple of years back turned up a cosmetic surgeon who claimed to have given a guy answering Bolan's description a new face. The piece asked us to believe that the face was owned by a certain Colonel John Phoenix, U.S. Army, Retired. The good colonel was said to have masterminded a worldwide antiterrorist campaign with tacit White House approval. But there was some kind of frame, supposedly organized by the KGB, which had taken some hard knocks during the operation. And suddenly, no colonel! Equally suddenly—surprise, surprise!—back onstage trots Mack Bolan. Except now, he's an outlaw. No more White House sanction. But still, apparently, on the warpath. You see, the woman in his life was killed by an attack on Bolan's command center somewhere in Virginia.

"Let me tell you, Al, this is one colorful character. He's big, around six-three, and muscle all the way. Big, too, by way of personality. He has these eyes that dare you to lie—and scorch through you when you're telling the truth, to find out why! He's a husky dude, attractive as hell, I'd think, in a macho way. Yet there's no lady in his life, although it's been some time since he lost his woman."

The newspaperman fished a small notebook out of his pocket, rested it on his knee and riffled through the pages.

"I'd like to read you a few lines," he said, "from a profile published a year ago in a London adventure weekly. Quote. Bolan believes that the savages, the evil legions of animal man, should not be allowed to inherit the earth; he considers their defeat his vocation; he is prepared to sacrifice love, a home life, a normal career, to fight those legions. He wants to halt their advance so that the gentle civilizers will no longer live in fear.

"Learning his deadly skills in the jungles of Vietnam, this modern crusader, who knows that each victory only brings him closer to the next threat, has transferred those skills to the urban jungles of the West in a cause to which he consecrates every ounce of his soldier's resolution. Unquote."

Mettner crushed out his second cigarette, closed the notebook, tossed it onto the bed and tipped the flask to his lips once more.

"Okay, so I've got Bolan, I've got the girl, and I've got the terrorists. You figure those for three separate stories? No way. Something tells me these three leads are all part of one big story.

"Now, don't blow your top, Al, but I'm asking you to let me stick with this Bolan dude. Because that's where I figure the action will be. It may take me some time, and you'll miss out on that terrorist piece, but believe me, if it comes off you're going to have a front-page lead with a six-column heading that'll knock every other daily off the newsstands."

Mettner grinned. His battles with Fielding over where to go and what to write were legendary around the world's press clubs. He lit a third cigarette and blew a long plume of smoke at the ceiling.

"That's why I'm here," he said. "I followed Bolan from Turin, where he saw the missing girl's father. And he's not here a half hour before some two-bit crook from San Remo gets his head blown off in a waterfront café! Add to that the fact that Bolan's wanted by the Italian police for questioning in connection with three other killings. And then guess who the victims were. That's right. Terrorists. Members of the gang who sabotaged the train. You see what I mean?

"No kidding, Al, it's all happening. Because some maniac with a hunting gun shoots up the display window of a sporting goods store. And a few minutes later I'm backing my rented Fiat up along the main drag and what should I see but a Merc sedan hotfooting it out of town driven by some guy with a rifle leaning against the passenger seat. Seconds later I'm rocked on my springs by a BMW going like a bat out of hell.

"A goddamn chase. And guess who's behind the wheel of the BMW? Right, again. M. Bolan, Esquire.

"So listen, Al, whatever you say, I'm hanging in here until I get the lowdown on what goes on. I have to find out what's with this guy, okay?"

Mettner lifted the flask, shook it, scowled and lobbed it empty into the wastebasket. His cigarette had gone out. He picked up a box of matches. That was empty, too. He swore. "I'll be in touch," he growled into the recorder.

Chapter Seven

Panic was not a word that Mack Bolan cared to accept in his personal vocabulary. If he had permitted himself to panic, he would have drowned in the sunken BMW within two minutes, wasting his energy and exhausting the oxygen that remained in his bloodstream by battering vainly at the inverted wreck.

But he knew there must be a pocket of air trapped—as he was himself trapped—inside the car. He knew, too, that the imprisonment of the air was only temporary; the pressure of the water was forcing it to escape; he could hear it, hissing past the instrument panel, bubbling out the holes where the pedals projected into the cockpit.

Unless he could use that air while it lasted, his own imprisonment would be final.

A fleeting, ironic thought crossed Bolan's mind. He had survived Nam, and all the hell miles in his War Everlasting, only to die, trapped in a submerged car beneath the Mediterranean. No way was he going to go out like that. He had to replenish his lungs and make his escape before the cockpit was totally flooded. He'd try the doors. They were designed to open, after all, he should be able to inch one open wide enough to let his body through.

He dragged himself out from under the dash and pushed himself to the surface of the water inside the car. With the top of his head against the floor, it was lapping against his chin.

He took a deep breath and submerged. Then he stretched his frame fully across the width of the car and pulled on the door latch. With his feet fully braced against the other door, he found that his knees were still flexed because he was taller than the space across the inside of the car. He started pushing, his temples throbbing, the blood thundering in his chest. But the crumpled steel would not budge.

He came up for another gulp of air, and found that the water level had risen so much there was very little space between the surface and the seat. Besides, the center console and gear lever pushing into his midriff made the whole exercise even more difficult.

He was running out of oxygen. Calling on all reserves of strength, Bolan tried it again.

Movement, and he pushed even harder, determined not to lose it all in what he considered would be an ignominious death. When he died, he wanted to be standing upright, facing the enemy.

Finally he had the aperture large enough to squeeze through.

With the last reserves of his energy, Bolan pushed himself under and out, still shoving upward with both hands.

A huge bubble of air, released from the suddenly opened door, burst out and sucked him with it. Lungs now bursting, too, he shot to the surface.

The dark wind was chill on his face. He lay on the sea, gratefully breathing in the cold.

Around the creek, he saw stationary headlights. A few flashlight beams probed the slope, moving down toward the water. There could be guns in their owners' free hands.

Bolan floated until his racing pulse had quieted. Then he dived beneath the surface and swam underwater with long, powerful strokes toward a jetty on the far side of the creek where a dozen pleasure boats were tied up, bobbing gently on the somber swell.

The water was warm in the shallows. He rested his arms on a weed-slimed wooden crosspiece beneath the planking of the deck. It was immediately clear to him what he must do now.

Salvage crews would be unable to locate the wreck of the BMW before daylight. By the time it had been winched up out of the water, it would probably be midday.

According to his waterproof digital it was not yet eight o'clock. That meant he had sixteen hours or more before anyone knew there was no drowned body trapped in the sunken vehicle. And even then nobody could be certain that he was not dead: submarine currents could sweep corpses out to sea; the drowned sank for some days before they surfaced.

There was no better time, while he must be presumed dead, to call on Massimo Rinaldi.

Yeah, attack was the best method of defense, the element of surprise accounted for three-fourths of the successful battle, and like that.

Bolan had no idea how far he was from Laigueglia. He wondered if he could make it in time without transport...and, more important, without running into any of the AFL hit teams sent to ambush him.

From beneath the jetty he looked around him.

Sure he could. The killer with the elephant gun had been sent into battle by sea; Bolan would counterattack the same way.

He waded to a ladder and climbed to the wooden deck of the jetty.

Surveying the craft moored there, he saw at once that most of them were too cumbersome, too ostentatious for his purpose. In fact the choice narrowed down to two boats—a small sailing dinghy and a dory with a twenty-five-horsepower outboard tilted over its stern.

The sailboat would be less obtrusive to get under way, but the breeze was still blowing off the sea. He would have to beat against it part of the way—and once the moon rose the craft's silhouette would be much more noticeable against the reflected light on the water.

If he used the outboard, on the other hand, there was the risk of discovery when he started the motor. Several large villas overlooked the creek and the noise could alert a suspicious owner.

He lifted the tarp and saw that there was a pair of oars in the vessel. He decided to take the dory. It would allow him more time at the other end and the course would be more direct.

Provided there was enough gas in the tank.

He rocked the small boat experimentally. It sounded as if there was.

In the shelter of a boat house at the inner end of the jetty Bolan dismantled his Beretta and stripped off his outer clothes. There was no more drizzle and the wind was warm. By the time everything was dried to his satisfaction it was past ten o'clock. The onlookers and their cars no longer choked the road at the head of the creek. Even the flashing blue light on the roof of the police car had vanished.

He dressed, slipped the 93-R into its shoulder rig and stepped down into the dory. With the tarp folded and left on the dock, he took up the oars and rowed silently across the dark water. Only when the boat was rocking on the swell, clear of the headland on the eastern side of the creek, did he lower the outboard, switch on the fuel supply and jerk the starter cord.

The engine fired at the third attempt. It sounded every bit as loud as Bolan had expected, but no lights appeared among the villas overlooking the creek; no angry voices shouted. He settled down with one arm resting on the tiller and headed for the distant promontory that masked the lights of Laigueglia.

Once around the point, he cut the engine and allowed the dory to drift ashore with the tide. He beached the craft between two clusters of rocks beyond the promenade. It was way past midnight: the roadway—long streamers of yellow radiance reflected on the damp pavement beneath the streetlights—was deserted. Bolan hurried across and headed for the dirt road that led up into the hills toward Rinaldi's domain.

The property ranged over a series of terraces below a small wood. It was surrounded by a high stone wall topped with half a dozen strands of barbed wire. The wooden gates were ten feet high. Beyond them, four towers rose above the tops of ornamental trees that surrounded the house. From the upper windows the ocean would be visible, between two shoulders of the mountain.

Bolan knew the place would be well guarded. But the only intel he had gleaned from Renzo Gandolfi before he was shot concerned guard dogs, the bodyguard Colibri and three other hoods, and something unfinished about "the wire."

A rubber-encased pencil flashlight clipped to the inside of Bolan's jacket had survived the wreck of the BMW. He used it now, slanting the thin beam toward the top of the wall.

He could see nothing special about the barbed wire.

Ten yards before the gateway, a tall chestnut tree grew on the far side of the dirt road. Bolan hauled himself up among the branches and lodged himself in a fork above the level of the wall. He played the flashlight's beam on the wall.

Now he could see a primitive but very effective alarm system. Below the inward-leaning wire barrier, a second strand had been strung with small bells too heavy to be actuated by the wind but sensitive enough to register the slightest touch. It would be impossible to cut the wire, blanket the barbs or cross the wall in any way without setting at least one of them jingling. And among the fruit trees planted on the far side of the wall, small microphones hung every few yards.

Any attempt to enter the property that way would thus immediately be signaled, together with its exact location, to some central listening post inside.

Bolan guessed there would probably be electronic sensors planted among the trees as well, although how these would operate if there were dogs patrolling he could not guess.

He was still evaluating his discovery, trying to work out a way to beat the alarm system, when he heard the sound of an automobile laboring up the grade behind him.

It was the killer's Mercedes that he had chased along the coast road. The sedan was followed by the dump truck that caused the accident.

The Mercedes halted with its front fenders inches away from the gates. Bolan couldn't see how many men were in it; he reckoned three. Add the driver of the truck and that made Gandolfi's info accurate.

The driver signaled with light taps on the horn—three short and two long. The gates swung slowly open. Electronically controlled, Bolan noted, for no sentry was visible.

Headlight beams showed up a flagstone courtyard, a double flight of stairs curving up to a balustraded terrace, a stable block at right angles to the main building.

The Mercedes moved forward. Gears grated as the driver of the dump truck shifted into first and prepared to follow.

The truck was immediately below the tree fork where Bolan was perched. The high cab blocked the view of anyone looking out the rear window of the sedan. Bolan made a sudden decision: the hell with it, he would go into the Rinaldi stronghold with the hired help.

The steep-sided rear section of the truck was empty. Hanging from a branch at the full stretch of his arms, Bolan was just able to touch the steel tailgate with his feet. He transferred his weight, balanced precariously for a moment on the edge and then lowered himself inside as the truck lumbered forward.

The two vehicles passed a gate house. By the stone steps the sedan stopped and Bolan could hear the occupants climbing out. Somebody laughed. A door slammed. The truck continued around the corner of the house and parked beneath a eucalyptus tree beside one of the turrets. The driver switched off the engine and jumped down from the cab.

Bolan leaped onto the man's shoulders and dropped him.

A forearm across the throat and a savage blow behind the ear with the butt of the Beretta took care of the guy before he could do more than utter a choked-off yelp of alarm.

Bolan stared up at the dim bulk of the house. In fact, however well guarded the property was on the outside, it was surprisingly easy to break in once you were past the gates.

The terrace ran around three sides of the building. Bolan pulled himself up and scrambled onto the balustrade. From the top of one of the stone urns set at intervals along it, he could reach the lower branches of the eucalyptus. After that there was another climb of fifteen feet, a stack pipe within easy reach and finally an unsecured skylight in the conical turret roof.

Bolan moved stealthily down a winding staircase and found himself in a long hallway flanked by bronze busts on plinths. From the floor came the murmur of voices.

He crept down a second, wider flight of stairs and found himself in an unlit corridor terminated by double doors beneath which a strip of yellow showed.

Crouched with an eye to the keyhole, he could see a man who was obviously Rinaldi leaning back in a wingback chair.

Rinaldi looked to be about fifty years old, with crimped silver hair and tanned features etched with a network of lines. He was wearing dark trousers and a short crimson silk smoking jacket.

Shifting his position slightly, Bolan saw the one-shot wonder with the elephant gun, the back view of another burly hood and a tall, muscular dude he assumed must be Renato Colibri.

This was one mean character, with small eyes, a slit of a mouth and crew cut blond hair.

"You're dead sure this person went down with the car?" Rinaldi was asking. "No chance he could have hopped out on the way down?"

"No frigging way," Colibri said. His voice was as disagreeable as his looks. "We searched the whole goddamn slope and there wasn't a sign. Nobody could have left that heap before it hit the water."

"And afterward?"

"It just disappeared. He'll be trapped beneath it."

"Very well," Rinaldi said. He looked as if there was a bad smell just below his nose. "Now about next week's hit in Modena..." He paused, glanced at the thin gold digital watch on his wrist. "Where the hell's Eduardo? I want you all in on this."

"He's parking the dumper," the elephant gun man said.

"He sure takes his time. Giancarlo, go find the lazy creep and tell him to take his finger out."

The burly man rose from his chair and opened the door of the room. He strode down the passage toward the stairs. The door swung shut behind him.

Bolan was waiting in the darkness of a half landing. The hardman walked into a rock-solid fist that sank into his solar plexus with all of the Executioner's two hundred sinewy pounds behind it. The breath whooshing from his tortured lungs was blocked in his throat by the edge of a hand, plank hard, that smashed the cartilage of his Adam's apple. He toppled forward into a night that held no tomorrows.

Bolan caught him before he hit the floor, snaring a gun from the holster beneath his jacket. Unfortunately the guy was heavier than Bolan thought. He was thrown off balance, forced to let go. The hood's body thumped down the remainder of the staircase with a noise like a roll of thunder.

On the upper floor, a door was flung open. Voices called angry questions. Bolan took the stairs three at a time, lay facedown along the last flight with his elbows resting on the floor of the hallway above.

Unwilling to trust the rounds in the Beretta after the weapon's saltwater immersion, he was holding the gun he had taken from the hood. It was an M-39 automatic, a well-balanced 9 mm Smith & Wesson creation that lay snugly in the Executioner's big hand.

Elephant gun stood in the doorway with a similar pistol. In the light streaming from the room he suddenly saw Bolan's head and shoulders low down at the head of the stairs. He spit out an exclamation and raised the gun.

Bolan fired first. Two shots that momentarily deafened him in the confines of the hallway. The rounds slammed the hood backward, and he hit the wall and slid to the floor with a fist-size hole separating the splintered remains of his fifth and sixth ribs.

Bolan was already running for the door.

Surprise had been total. He was flattened against the jamb, the M-39 trained in the direction of the two men left in the room, while Colibri was still halfway to his feet with a hand between the lapels of his jacket.

"Drop it!" Bolan snapped. "Take it out slow and easy...then drop it on the table."

Colibri hesitated, face snarling, knees still flexed.

"Play the odds, asshole. Guess how many rounds left in here," the Executioner warned. He raised the autoloader. "Move!"

Reluctantly the bodyguard unleathered a long-barreled Walther PPK and laid it on the table.

"Now unfasten the jacket," Bolan said. As he had expected, there was a broad-bladed throwing knife tucked into the hood's waistband. Bolan gestured threateningly and it joined the gun on the table.

Massimo Rinaldi had not moved. He leaned back, apparently relaxed, in the wingback chair. "Under the car, at the bottom of the creek, I think you said?" he remarked conversationally.

"Anybody can make a mistake," Colibri growled.

"Only once in your case," said Bolan. And then, to Rinaldi, "All right, you, stand up."

The neofascist boss sighed and rose slowly to his feet.

"Open up that pretty negligee."

"I am not in the habit of carrying weapons," Rinaldi said coldly.

"Open it up."

In a pantomime of injured dignity, Rinaldi loosened the crimson silk belt at his waist, opened the smoking jacket, raised his hands.

No knife, no gun, no shoulder rig. Bolan was not surprised. This kind of creep would always be clean; he left the dirty work to the hired help. "Okay, hands on the top of your head, both of you," he ordered. "And stand up straight."

"I suppose it is pointless to ask the meaning of this puerile charade?" Rinaldi said. "I think, however, that you will live to regret it. If, that is, you live at all."

"You think so?" Bolan said. "I don't think so. In case you were wondering, all three of your heavies are now out of commission. The big-game hunter, as you know, on the floor behind me, Giancarlo at the foot of the stairs and Eduardo sleeping peacefully by his truck."

"So what, punk? You think that's all the soldiers we have on call?" Colibri grated.

"I *know*, for sure," Bolan lied, "that's all I have to worry about right now. Okay, so now we get down to business, right?"

"Yes," Rinaldi said, "perhaps you would enlighten us. Maybe we could be favored with an explanation? What right do you have, in a country not your own, to indulge yourself in this orgy of killing? Why must you meddle in affairs that do not concern you, Mr...?"

"The name is Bolan. As you damn well know."

"Yeah," Colibri sneered. "The guy who calls himself the Executioner. The one who thinks he's Superman."

Bolan let that one go.

"I suppose, like everyone else, you can be bought?" Rinaldi said.

"Just try me."

"Very well. What is your price in this particular situation? How much would I need to buy you off?"

"Money wouldn't help you. I want the answer to two questions, that's all."

Rinaldi raised his eyebrows. "And supposing we were able to supply the answers you require, what could we expect in return?"

"I'd kill you quick and easy, instead of drawing it out."

Rinaldi turned to his bodyguard. "I assume the fellow's joking?"

"I was never more serious," Bolan said. "Now, enough talk. Where have you sent Suzanne Bozuffi—and why? Those are the two questions."

"Bozuffi? I don't believe I've had the pleasure," Rinaldi said.

"Go fuck yourself, big shot," said Colibri.

Bolan thought quickly. A question-and-answer routine here was going to get him nowhere fast. Rinaldi was an unknown quantity, but with a punk like the bodyguard it had to be the big stick. Bolan had to show who was top dog from the start. Colibri's gutter-bred toughness would only bow before something tougher still. "You heard what I said," he rapped. "I want an answer."

"And you heard what *I* said, asshole. I don't aim to waste breath repeating it."

Bolan raised the barrel of the Smith & Wesson and shot the bodyguard through the palm of his left hand.

The nickel-jacketed, 9 mm hollowpoint smashed its way through flesh and bone and cartilage, slamming Colibri's arm back against the chair he had left. Blood spurted from the hole and flowed down his wrist. His yell of pain and fury was lost in the ringing echoes of the report.

"Ready to talk?" Bolan asked.

Colibri was doubled up with his knees pressed together, nursing his shattered hand in the shelter of his crotch. "Drop...dead, you...bastard," he groaned.

"For the last time, where and why?"

The Italian straightened up. Bolan had been right about the knife at his waistband. He hadn't bargained for the second one, strapped to the left forearm beneath the bloody sleeve. Colibri had secretly been working it loose; now he flicked the deadly blade straight at the Executioner's chest.

Taken by surprise, Bolan barely had time to shift sideways as he saw the bloodstained steel glint in the light. The knife ripped the shoulder of his jacket, searing the base of his neck as it passed. At the same time Colibri leaped forward and knocked the gun from his hand.

Bolan lost his cool. It was the second time in less than a week that he had been gashed by the knife-wielding thugs of this damned terrorist group. It was time to even the score.

Colibri was diving for the M-39. He crashed to the floor with a cry of agony as Bolan leaped on his back.

The Executioner dragged him upright by the lapels of his jacket. The bodyguard reeled dazedly as a hard fist slammed into his face again and again.

"Now tell me, where is that girl, and why?"

Colibri went limp in his grasp. Bolan let him drop and kicked him on the jaw. He placed his heel on the maimed hand. "Why was she snatched?" he snarled.

"All right, all right," Colibri cried, seeing the foot resting lightly on his hand. "It was just a job. Ask the boss."

Bolan turned toward Rinaldi, who had remained rooted to the floor, staring in horrified astonishment at the savaging of his second in command. "Just... a job?" Bolan repeated softly. "More than sixty dead, God knows how many injured, and this girl abducted?"

He picked up the gun, stepped over the squirming Colibri and jammed the muzzle against Rinaldi's belly. "Tell me," he said.

The terrorist leader swallowed. "You must understand, we are a political organization," he said. "At the moment, because of the corruption sapping the energy of this country, we are forced to lead a clandestine, undercover existence. Until we are... accepted... we have to raise finance where and when we can."

"Cut the bullshit," Bolan said. "You mean if there's dirty work to be done—an Israeli to be murdered on behalf of the PLO, or an interfering newshawk silenced to please the KGB—you're only too glad to help? Is that what you're saying?"

"I wouldn't put it exactly like that—"

"But that's the way it is, right? Okay—who paid you to snatch the Bozuffi girl and organize a train wreck to cover up? Where was she taken after the plane landed in Tripoli?"

"The affair of the train worked in with our own plans. The destabilization of a society rotten with—"

"Spare me the crap, I said," Bolan cut in. "So it suited your breed of 'politics' to stage a terrorist attack. For the last time, who's paying you?"

There was sweat on Rinaldi's brow. "Part of the deal—perhaps the most important—is secrecy, discretion," he said nervously. "We are paid to keep our mouths shut as well as to act. Any kind of betrayal... well, the client would be most unhappy."

"And he might come gunning for you if he found out? Well, that's an occupational hazard in your line of business," Bolan said, curling his lip in contempt. "When you're up to your neck in filth, you have to put up with the smell. So who's the client?" He jammed the muzzle of the automatic harder between the edges of the red robe.

Rinaldi shivered. "Ononu himself."

"The bloodthirsty dictator? Okay, where and why?"

"They were transferring her to another plane in Tripoli and then flying on to Montenegria. To Ononu's palace in the interior. That's all I know, I don't know why."

Bolan dragged the gun muzzle up the whole length of the terrorist leader's body, pressing hard, until the snout lodged beneath his chin.

"I don't know," Rinaldi yelped. "I swear. It was part of a package deal.... There were two other girls, delivered earlier. I don't think any of them were for a ransom. He sent no demands."

"Who were these other two? When were they kidnapped?"

Rinaldi's glance flickered sideways. The expression of fear on his face faded. Before he could reply, Bolan whirled.

Colibri had wormed his way toward a coffee table, reached up his good hand and grabbed a hand mike. Now he pressed the button and shouted, "Gate house! There's an intruder here! Get him—"

Bolan shot him in the back of the head, cutting the sentence short. Brain tissue sprayed over the carpet; blood flowed from the hood's gaping mouth.

Rinaldi took advantage of the diversion and swooped on the Walther PPK that still lay on the table. Bolan shot it out of his hand, fired again and caught Rinaldi in the right shoulder.

The room hazed with gunsmoke. Rinaldi gave a high pitched scream and staggered back against the wall, clapping his left hand to the wound. The red silk, liquified, appeared to pump out through his clenched fingers.

Bolan bolted toward the door and dashed down the hallway outside. Above the stairs at the far end, there was an open window.

He climbed through, found himself on a shallow roof, ran to the edge and dropped fifteen feet to the terrace. The dump truck was below the balustrade. From the front of the house he heard footsteps and shouts, from upstairs Rinaldi frenziedly calling.

Bolan vaulted the balustrade and pulled himself up into the cab of the truck. He turned on the headlights, twisted the ignition key and the still-warm engine rumbled to life. Slamming the lever into first, he gunned the huge diesel and sent the truck roaring around the corner toward the flagged yard and the electronically operated gates.

The gates were closed. In the headlight beams he saw men on the terrace, men in front of the gate house, two men with shotguns in the center of the yard.

Bolan drove straight at them. Flame blasted from both barrels of the guns, peppering the truck's hood and fenders with a hail of shot. There were pistols, too, firing from the terrace. The cab's rear window exploded inward, showering the Executioner with granules of toughened glass; the windshield starred.

Taking one hand from the wheel, he emptied the M-39's magazine at the guys in front of the gate house, sending them scurrying for cover. Then he was on the shotgun pair. One leaped aside, the other was run down, his body tossed aside like a broken doll when the steel grill protecting the truck's radiator smashed into his chest.

Bolan held the pedal flat on the floor, aiming the dumpster at the junction between the two great wooden doors. There was a jarring crash as the grill burst them apart, then the truck was through in a storm of splintered planking and twisted metal framework. A fusillade of small-arms fire followed. The truck veered wildly toward the side of the road as a front tire blew and wrenched the wheel from Bolan's hands.

He wrestled the truck back onto the trail, but it was slewing right and left, almost out of control... and then, from a gate he had not noticed before at the far end of the property, a heavy sedan nosed out and halted dead across the roadway, completely blocking his escape.

Bolan spun the wheel and ran the dump truck in among the undergrowth that fringed the wood at the side of the track.

It crashed through a screen of bushes, uprooted several saplings and tore down the lower branches of trees. Finally it came to rest with the grill against the trunk of a huge acacia. Bolan leaped out and ran past the steaming radiator, farther into the darkness of the wood. Beyond the improvised roadblock, the trail looped around in a wide curve. Bolan figured that if he could strike through in the right direction, then he could hit it again farther downhill.

But the thugs from the gate house were not far behind. And three men from the sedan, guessing Bolan's intentions, were running through the wood lower down, hoping to cut him off. He could see a trio of flashlight beams bobbing between the trees.

From behind and off to one side, shots rang out. Bullets thwacked through the branches, twigs snapped and leaves fluttered down around the fleeing warrior.

Bolan was sprinting flat out. He was always in fine shape, muscles and reflexes honed to combat standard. Once he was back on the road he was confident he could outdistance any pursuit. But here in the forest—difficult target though he was—with the undergrowth plucking at his feet and unseen branches thrashing his face as he forced his way through, it was not so easy.

The flashlight-carrying gunners from the sedan were less than one hundred yards away on his right when he saw a lighter patch between the dark mass of trunks ahead of him. He sprinted the remaining distance, jumped down a bank, twisted an ankle as he landed and almost fell.

He was standing at the side of the road.

Parked under the trees a few yards away was a small car. The engine was running quietly.

Bolan hesitated. Through the rear window he could see the glow of a cigarette above the steering wheel. The soldier wondered if this was yet another stalling action staged by the AFL terrorists.

He did not have to wait for an answer.

Suddenly the passenger door swung open and a voice drawled, "Jump in quick, Mr. Bolan. I believe you could use a ride into town."

It was the American newspaperman, Jason Mettner.

Chapter Eight

"Thanks," Bolan said, "but how did you happen to be there, at that time, waiting by the road in the middle of the night?"

Mettner grinned through the layers of cigarette smoke weaving beneath the low-power lamp above his bed. Despite its name, the Albergo Splendido boasted no night porter, and he had been able to smuggle the Executioner in with a passkey he had cajoled earlier from the receptionist.

"Partly luck and partly news sense," he said. "I was in town because I followed you from Turin. I was following you because my news sense told me there was a story in you. Then I happened to see you chasing that rifleman in the Mercedes. That was luck. The rest was legwork. I had to come back here to record a message—my Fiat could never have kept up with you two, anyway. But when I was through with that I drove out along the coast road. it was only a hunch, but pretty soon I was halted by a traffic holdup that stretched half a mile, and I was told a car had run out of road and dropped into the ocean.

"'No hope for the driver,' they said, and the wreck couldn't be salvaged until tomorrow morning. I stuck around just the same. And right enough, after everyone had split, someone rowed this motorboat out beyond the point before the engine started. So, I thought to myself, someone who wishes to remain unobserved! Naturally I observe. I tracked the boat all the way back here—and then, from way down the main drag, I saw you come ashore and start up the dirt road leading to the Rinaldi place.

"I figured you had to be heading there. It's an open secret that Rinaldi's behind this Action for Liberty crap. And since they claimed credit for the train wreck, and the three guys you are supposed to have knocked off worked for the same group, it seemed reasonable that the chick whose dad you saw in Turin was snatched by the same team. Am I right?"

"No comment," Bolan said.

"Anyway," Mettner said, "for my money that ties you in with the train, the snatch and the terrorists. So I stick around some more, and after a while this Mercedes and a big truck pass me on the way to the house. Not long after that I hear shots. There was shooting up there, wasn't there?"

"I believe I did hear something that could have been gunfire," Bolan said blandly. "Poachers in the woods, I guess. You know the Italians."

"Is Rinaldi still alive?"

"He was the last time I saw him."

"You won't tell me what happened up there?"

"I think," Bolan said, "you can be pretty sure that Action for Liberty will be keeping kind of a low profile for quite some time."

"Great. But can't you give me some of the details? Somehow I don't think they're going to set up a welcoming committee for reporters and photographers—and you're the guy, after all, with the inside story."

"The details? Maybe," Bolan said. "Later. In return for a piece of legwork you can do for me."

"It's a deal," Mettner agreed. "What do you want to find out?"

The Executioner hesitated. It was against his principles to involve a third party in the middle of a mission. But the intel he needed could be important—and if it was, time could be vital. "Two other girls were kidnapped," he said, "probably by the same team who took Suzanne Bozuffi."

"Rinaldi's henchmen?"

Bolan ignored the question and continued, "I don't know exactly when—not too long ago, I guess. They may have been taken to the same hideout as the Bozuffi girl. The only other thing I know is that neither has been the subject of any ransom demand. I was...interrupted before I could find out more."

"And you want to know...?"

"I want to know who the girls were, who their fathers are, where they were snatched and how. Could you run a check on that through your office files?"

"No sweat," Mettner said. "I can do better. I can get someone in the Paris bureau to write a program that will not only come up with the information you want: it will also comb the crime-sheet data banks for any similarities between the two cases and the Bozuffi abduction. How does that grab you?"

"I like it," Bolan said.

"And if I do this for you, I get a first-person piece on tonight's scenario? Plus the waterfront killing yesterday afternoon and your escape from the sea?"

Bolan shook his head. "No first-person material. I'll background you on the events here in the village.

No comment on the escape. And, on strict condition that my name be kept out of any story you write, I'll fill you in on the Rinaldi deal. Take it or leave it."

"This is too good to be true," Mettner said.

"There is one other favor you could do for me."

"Name it."

"I reckon it'd be an idea if my face wasn't in evidence around here tomorrow. I've done what I came to do and there's no reason for me to stay. In particular I want to avoid any brush with the local law, because... well, for obvious reasons."

"Testimony on the waterfront shooting—and then they'd find out you were on the wanted list." Mettner nodded understandingly. "You want me to help you get out of here, is that it?"

"Uh-huh."

"Let's go now," Mettner said. "I'll bring the car around to the rear entrance and we can take off right away. The bill's paid; I always settle up each day when I'm on an assignment. That way I'm free to leave any time I want, without any hassle."

"Better still."

"Where do you want to go?"

"Turin," Bolan said. "It'll be easier for you to contact Paris there. And I have to get back to Bozuffi and make certain financial arrangements, put in a request for special equipment. The way things look, I'll be heading for Africa pretty soon."

JASON METTNER CONJURED UP Bolan's intel before midday.

Nineteen-year-old Joy Helder, whose father was a midwest plastics king, had been missing for three weeks. She had been returning from a vacation in Greece aboard a TWA plane hijacked over the Mediterranean and flown to Beirut. One hundred eighty-nine passengers had been taken off and held hostage in the Shiite quarter of the war-torn city. When terms had been negotiated and the hijackers paid off, the passengers had been returned safe and sound.

All except one.

Seven days later Rachel, the twenty-one-year-old daughter of Conrad Meyerbeer, owner of America's most profitable hotel chain, had failed to return from a water-skiing expedition in Montego Bay, Jamaica.

Her playboy escort had been found drowned—in the cockpit of his powerboat, along with the girl's undamaged skis.

Nothing had been heard of either girl since.

The *Globe* Paris computer had found no similarities between the methods of abduction; such abstracts as callousness and ruthless behavior could not be expressed in binary mathematics. Apart from shared interests in tennis, horse riding and water sports, no correspondence between the girls' life-styles was traceable.

It was in the business interests of their fathers that Bolan found the link he was seeking.

Each of the three tycoons possessed a large holding in Montemines Corporation: between them they controlled more than eighty percent of the stock. Each had a seat on the board of directors, and each was a major shareholder in a subsidiary concern trading under the name of Negrimin International. There was a fourth director on the Montemines board but he held very little stock.

The Montemines Corporation had been formed four years before to exploit a huge mineral concession in the mountainous northern part of Montenegria.

Negrimin was the marketing organization that processed and distributed the tin, copper, zinc and other industrial materials extracted from the ores.

"Each of those kids is being held by that bastard Ononu, that's for sure," Bolan said to Antonio Bozuffi. "So I'm going to take you up on your offer. I'll need arms, ammunition, transport and a certain amount of specialized equipment. But I'm going on in and free those girls if it's the last thing I do."

It was while they were discussing the logistics of Bolan's rescue operation that they heard the news, on a television set at the foot of the industrialist's hospital bed.

Palomar, seventeen-year-old daughter of Lucino Varzi, millionaire Italo-American at present living on the isle of Ischia, had been abducted at gunpoint from the family box during a performance of *La Bohème* at La Scala in Milan.

Varzi was the fourth director on the Montemines Board.

Chapter Nine

Like the true dictator that he was, Emperor Anya Ononu ruled Montenegria, a West African nation of just under five million people, with an iron fist. The country itself, Bolan had learned from his friend Bozuffi, was a wedge-shaped enclave with an area of fifty-one thousand square miles, sandwiched between Liberia and the Ivory Coast.

The country was rich in minerals, which included copper, zinc and tin.

The Doulas river split Montenegria almost in two. Twenty miles upriver, Lake Gadrany drowned a winding valley at the foot of a ridge that formed the central backbone of the country.

And it was just below the crest of this ridge that Mack Bolan now braked his Land Rover.

Behind him, cliffs towering on either side of the pass blotted out the stars. Below, the dark landscape fell away toward a paler, sinuous blur that marked the position of the lake.

Bolan adjusted night-vision goggles over his eyes and scanned the rocky trail that wound steeply down to the flatlands lying at the base of the mountain range.

With luck he could coast maybe two miles without the engine running. After that the recon would have to be on foot: no way could he risk alerting watchers below that a foreigner was making a night entry into Montenegria by this route.

Bolan's objective was Anya Ononu's summer palace, which was built on an islet at the head of the lake, accessible only via a suspension bridge with a gate house and armed guards at both ends. It was here, he believed, that the kidnapped girls were being held prisoner.

Here, too, that most of the elite palace guard, drawn from Montenegria's most warlike tribe, were quartered. "You want to watch your step with those boys, Mack," Antonio Bozuffi had told the Executioner. "Anything you saw in Vietnam's kid stuff compared with them. Impalement, castration, crucifixion, having your guts pulled out and fed to the palace guard dogs—those are the least of your worries if they don't like the shape of your nose."

Between the ridge and the lake, the lunar landscape revealed by the NVD lenses passed from barren mountain slopes, through scrub-covered foothills to an upland savannah dotted with thatch-roofed villages surrounded by squares of cultivation. It was here, in the country's more temperate climate, that the self-styled emperor preferred to spend most of his time.

The warrior eased off the hand brake and allowed the Land Rover to roll. The track was rugged, alternating loose granite chippings with shelves of bedrock.

During the previous three days Bolan had seen worse.

He was determined to have his own specialized transport in Montenegria; at the same time there had to be no record of his arrival. In a heavily policed dictatorship this presented problems. Bozuffi, who knew the place well, solved them in a single stroke.

The Tunis-Monrovia Rally was about to take place. This tough transcontinental event required contestants piloting anything from a 250cc motorbike to a race-bred Porsche or a three-ton truck to dash across the southwestern fringe of the Sahara, cross a mountain range in southern Mali and complete their torturous journey through the tropical rain forest of Liberia.

The latter part of the route passed within a few miles of Montenegria's northern frontier.

In the wild and trackless wastes of that stretch of Africa it was easy enough—and believable enough if he happened to be caught—for a driver to lose his way and stray across that border. Bolan's Land Rover had accordingly been entered in the rally.

The crossing had taxed neither his courage nor his skill. There were few frontier posts, and travelers were more likely to be refugees wanting out than visitors wanting in.

There was an additional advantage, for Bolan, to this route. Since the Tunis-Monrovia attracted the world's top rallymen, there was international interest in the event and big-deal media coverage. Customs and immigration formalities in the countries traversed were therefore minimal.

That suited the Executioner just fine. Like all the other vehicles, his Land Rover carried extra tires, jerricans of fuel, provisions and spare parts. Unlike them it concealed beneath its floorboards a quantity of specialized equipment and weaponry supplied by Bozuffi at Bolan's request.

Once safely in Montenegria, he had stripped off rally license plates, destroyed check forms and paperwork and substituted local plates. Bolan himself was provided with papers identifying him as a consultant mining engineer employed by the Montemines Corporation with duties that required him to commute between the mines in the north and the dockside installations owned by the company at Port-Doulas. The Land Rover was certified as one of a fleet owned by Negrimin International.

The cover would be useful later, when he was overtly moving around the country. It gave him no reason to be where he was now, east of the palace and the lake. But that wasn't a problem he was going to waste any time on: with only the unreal vision provided by his goggles, it was all he could do to hold the Land Rover on the stony track, alternating between the brake pedal and clutch, and his hands moving from gear lever to steering wheel on each hair-raising corner.

Soon the odor of overheated brake linings wafted into the cab. The squeal of overtaxed disks was audible over the scrabbling of tires on the loose surface. The breakneck descent continued through a dozen hairpin curves, up a slight rise, slowing now as the trail slanted upward, then accelerating again until perhaps one mile and a half had been covered. Here the route flattened out. The Land Rover gradually lost speed, approaching another grade that preceded the final plunge to the valley floor.

Bolan bucked and swayed in the driver's seat, trying to urge the utility up to the crest and gain another few hundred yards on the far side. But the vehicle's inertia and the rolling resistance of tires and running gear to the rough surface of the track remorselessly braked his advance. The crest was still seventy yards away when the Land Rover lost momentum entirely and began to roll back down the slope.

Bolan turned the wheel and steered it off the trail between two outcrops of rock. He climbed out, lifted the floorboards and prepared himself for a scouting expedition on foot.

First the skintight combat blacksuit, then black cosmetic to mask the pale glimmer of his face. From the neatly packed arsenal in the special hidden compartment he withdrew and unwrapped Big Thunder—his stainless steel AutoMag—a pulverizing flesh-shredder with wildcat .44 cartridges. He shrugged into military-style webbing, holstered the gun low on his right hip, drew on thin black gloves and picked up a pair of heavy-duty 105 NVD binoculars. He started to walk.

He had perhaps another mile of rocky hillside to negotiate. After that the land flattened into a series of mild undulations that gradually descended to the lake. The trail twisted between orchards and patches of corn and groundnuts, past plantations of coffee and avocado pears. The savannah beyond was lush, with long grass punctuated by clumps of acacia and the occasional thorn tree.

Twice Bolan had to make a wide detour through fields head-high with sunflowers to avoid a village. But although dogs started a frenzied barking in one, nobody challenged him and he made the twelve miles to the lake in just over two hours.

Crouched on a huge granite outcrop projecting over the still water, he unslung the field glasses from around his neck and scanned the far shore, looking for the bridge and the islet on which the palace was built. As soon as he had the place in focus, he knew that any single-handed attempt to rescue the four kidnapped girls was foredoomed to failure. All the outer walls of the extraordinary building plunged straight into the water; the bridge, at a slight angle to the shore, led straight to the rectangular entrance court. And each of the two guard houses, he had been told, was staffed with a thirty-six man permanent garrison, twelve of whom, armed with Uzi submachine guns, were on alert at any time during the day or night.

Even if he was able to get in there, Bolan realized, he wouldn't have a chance in hell of getting out with a quartet of helpless, possibly sick or drugged females.

He would have to rely on his backup plan, which he favored less because it involved third parties. But he had no choice. The only solution was an armed assault on the palace. And for this he had to recruit professionals opposed to the dictator.

There was only one place he could get them.

Twenty-four hours later he was studying it through the same binoculars from a distance of two miles.

Ononu's jail for political prisoners was on the coast. Ten miles east of Port-Doulas, the strip of dunes separating the equatorial forest from the shore rose into a low bluff. And this in turn was overlaid by a shelf of rock rising to a cliff on whose highest point the prison was perched.

The dictator's enemies were usually butchered by the palace guard and their remains hacked up and added to the pig food processed in a factory at Assano. It was said that the heads were preserved in a custom-built refrigerator in his private suite at the palace.

But for a group of army officers who had narrowly failed to overthrow him in a military coup some weeks before, Ononu was reserving a special fate, involving a show trial and public executions. It was these men—there were eleven of them, now in a high-security wing of the jail—whose help Bolan hoped to enlist.

Logistically and operationally, there were three separate problems involved.

First, the Executioner knew he had to contact the dissident officers and confirm that they would be prepared to go along with him. For this, he had to somehow smuggle himself into the jail... and out again.

Secondly, he would have to organize a jailbreak to free these men and their supporters.

Finally, using their specialized knowledge, a successful attack on the palace had to be planned and carried out.

It could be, Bolan thought, refocusing the binoculars, that phase one would prove the toughest.

The prison's central core was an ancient coastal fortress built by Arab slave traders in the seventeenth century. Within this rectangle of massive sandstone cubes quarried from the horizontal strata of the cliff, four concrete cell blocks had been constructed in the form of an X. Outside it a wall with four watchtowers enclosed a compound that included cook houses, a laundry, storerooms, an administration block and sleeping quarters for the guards.

Since the land inside the compound sloped toward the cliff, Bolan could see over the wall and estimate the possibilities.

It was not an encouraging sight.

The walls of the old Arab fortress—pierced in one place only by tall iron-studded gates—rose to a height of twenty feet or more and looked impregnable to anything less than a marine commando with boarding nets.

The outer compound, too, had only a single entrance: behind a wall at the end of a curving approach track guarded by a gate house with a sandbagged machine gun emplacement outside it.

The ledge behind the battlements was patrolled regularly, and in any case there was a hundred-yard strip, bare of any vegetation, surrounding the compound wall on three sides.

The fourth side rose sheer from the cliff.

Since any clandestine entry or exit there looked impossible, that was exactly where the Executioner decided to try. He reasoned that the guards patrolling that sector would be less alert.

For the rest of that night Bolan charted, timed and noted the frequency of patrols, the changing of guards, the activity of the men in the watchtowers.

It was clear that however tough it would be getting inside the prison, making it out again would be even more difficult. He'd be in the same position as a prisoner trying to escape; and the whole place was designed to prevent just that.

There was a single advantage. Ononu's jail was run by the military. And Bolan knew from experience that efficient military administration depended upon precision. Personnel movements were regimented; Bolan had discovered already that the activities of the guards were as well regulated as a clock mechanism. The life of the prisoners would be equally well-drilled. They would take their exercise at the same time every day, in the same way, in the same place. The movements of the men watching over them would be equally predictable.

Bolan spent the daylight hours in Negrimin's dockside offices, reinforcing his cover as a mining engineer, digesting intel on the prison and the captive officers as far as Bozuffi's local superintendent was able to hand it out.

He was stopped three times by military police on his way into Port-Doulas, but the papers and visas supplied by his old Vietnam buddy were evidently in order, because each time the sour-faced cops waved him on after only a perfunctory examination. Just as well they didn't search the Land Rover, Bolan thought.

He opened the secret compartment beneath the floor soon after midnight.

This time he took out the blacksuit, climbing boots, NVD goggles, army webbing and three weapons: Big Thunder in fast-draw leather on his hip, the silenced Beretta, holstered beneath his left arm and a commando knife strapped to one ankle. Three stun grenades were clipped to one side of his belt, and a coil of nylon rope with a grappling hook looped to the other. He carried no spare ammunition: unless something went very wrong this was to be a soft probe.

The Land Rover was backed up among trees on the fringe of the rain forest in back of the coastal strip.

Bolan walked across the dunes to the bluff at one side of the sandstone cliff.

The rock face was vertical but not smooth. The horizontal beds were stacked like the pages of an uncut book, each leaf a thin slab of sandstone. It was therefore not difficult to make the climb, toes wedged in between two layers, fingers grasping a third higher up.

It was not even too much of a problem when the cliff soared up to meet the prison wall. What brought the operation its special danger was the fact that sandstone is easily pulverized: the weathered face could crumble any time it was subjected to weight or pressure.

That and the sound of waves breaking against the foot of the cliff fifty, sixty, seventy feet below.

Bolan had several near escapes—once a narrow section broke away and he was left with his feet dangling in the void—but nothing as spine-chilling as his escape from the killers at the foreigners' university in Perugia. Finally he arrived beneath the outer wall of the jail and dragged himself up the last few feet until he was immediately below the stonework. He uncoiled the rope from his waist.

The difficulty now was to find a strong enough single handhold that would allow him to lean outward and swing the rope with his other arm.

He made it at the fourth attempt. The three-pronged hook, tossed high up toward the moonless sky, dropped down to clamp securely into one of the firing slits in the battlement.

He tugged hard to check that the rope was firmly fixed, then he started to climb upward hand over hand. The rope was halfway between the two southern watchtowers. The tropical night was dark and steamy. He had exactly two and one-quarter minutes before the next patrol passed this sector of the perimeter wall.

Bolan made the battlements, glanced swiftly right and left, then dropped the rope on the far side and lowered himself into the compound.

He raced across a narrow stretch of ground separating the wall from a storage building. Beyond this there was a cook house with a covered passageway leading through the sandstone rampart of the central redoubt to the cell blocks.

Bolan hesitated, trying to decide if he should force an entry here and then use the corridor. He decided against it. The kitchen personnel would be long gone, but he had no clear picture of the wardens' movements; there would be too much risk of running into the enemy once he was inside the jail.

He looked at the luminous digits on the face of his watch. Two and three-quarter minutes before the compound patrol passed on the far side of the storage building. Nine minutes after that the soldiers on the battlement parapet would pass in the other direction. One half hour before the guards on the watchtowers were changed.

Bolan knew he had to make contact with the leader of the dissidents and be ready to leave the prison while that was happening. He uncoiled the rope again and swung the hook up to the top of the sandstone rampart.

The rough sedimentary blocks were easier to climb than the stonework of the outer wall. Bolan was already on the ground outside the eastern cell block when he heard the footsteps of the first patrol.

Each cell block was two stories high, but the soldier had been told that the lower floors, which housed the high-security, solitary-confinement prisoners, were four-fifths below ground. The barred windows, high up in the wall of each tiny cell, were level outside with the beaten earth surface of the exercise yards.

In this eastern yard, if his information was correct, the window he wanted was seventh from the left. Dark as the night shadows within the walls, the warrior crept along at the foot of the concrete facade.

At the seventh window he dropped to his hands and knees and then lay with his face against the close mesh of inch-thick iron grillwork. A fetid odor drifted up through the glassless aperture. He had heard that prisoners in this block were denied the most basic sanitary arrangements.

"Colonel Azzid?" Bolan whispered.

There was no reply. Somewhere in one of the other blocks, a voice cried something unintelligible. A shouted command, repeated, brought silence broken only by the distant crash of waves against the cliff below the jail.

"Colonel Azzid!"

There was movement in the blackness behind the bars. A creak of wood, a slithering noise. Then a sleepy murmur, barely audible.

"Wha'—? Who's there?"

"Azzid! This is a friend. Can you hear me?" Bolan dared not make his whisper any louder.

A sudden rustling, a slap of bare feet on stone. Finally, higher up near the window, came the same voice, but stronger now. "I hear you. Who are you? What do you want?"

"Colonel, I'll make this fast," Bolan replied, enunciating each whispered word as clearly as he could. "I'm going to crack the summer palace. Ononu's holding people there that I want out. I need soldiers and I need backup. If I bust open this jail tomorrow and free you and your friends, will you help me?"

"Possibly." The voice was tinged with suspicion. "What would be in it for us?"

"You get a second bite at the apple you lost."

"What?"

"To depose Ononu. The failed coup. You get a second chance. Are there still soldiers in the garrison you could count on, or have they all been liquidated?"

"There are still some. Maybe thirty, forty. If we could get to them."

"Enough. Would they command armor?"

"How's that?"

"Armor," Bolan repeated urgently. "Look, time's short. Could they lay their hands on tanks, APCs, mortars?"

"Affirmative."

"Okay. I'd make sure you got to them all right. Are you with me then?"

"What's in it for you?"

"I told you. I want these hostages free. End of story."

"That's all? You don't want any part . . . that is, we can deal with Ononu any way we want? You're not concerned with the future running of the country?"

"Not one little bit. So will you help?"

There was a deep-voiced chuckle from within the cell. "What can we lose?" Colonel Hassani Azzid said. "We already know the sentences; there's only the trial to come."

"Okay. Now what time are you exercised?"

"Me personally? Fifteen hours fifteen."

"What do you mean personally?"

"While the other prisoners take their hour, we get five minutes each. But never two of us out at the same time. They like to keep just enough life in us to make the torture amusing."

"Hell. That complicates things." Bolan stole a glance at his watch. "In less than fourteen minutes, I have to split. You'll have to waste a guard when the time comes, grab his keys, and free as many of your ten buddies as you can before I blow the outer wall."

Again the chuckle. "With my bare hands?"

"I can't do too much tonight," Bolan said, "but I can help some." He unzippered a section of the web belt that housed a small pocket. From this he removed two small sausage-shaped packets of C-4 plastic explosive, detonators, firing caps. He unclipped the stun grenades from the belt. Finally he reached up the commando knife from his ankle. "Take these," he whispered, passing the items one by one through the grillwork. "If you're never together in the exercise yard, is there any way you can contact your friends, to alert them?"

"Only the guys on either side of this cell. We have a signal routine."

"That'll have to do. If they can pass the message on, great. Now listen carefully, Colonel, here's what I'd like you to do...."

Bolan talked rapidly and concisely for eleven minutes. Then, telling the captive officer goodbye, he rose to his feet and stole back to the wall sector where he had left the climbing rope hanging.

He was on top of the rampart, paying out the rope on the other side, when he realized he had made a miscalculation that could be fatal. In his determination to wise up Azzid on every possible contingency in the planned jailbreak, he had delayed a fraction too long outside the seventh cell.

The watchtower guard details had already changed over.

The moment of inattention on which the Executioner had counted, perhaps a brief exchange as the reliefs arrived—that short but vital period was past. The soldiers who had been up in those towers were already filing down from the battlements, on their way to sleeping quarters on the far side of the compound.

Bolan slid down the rope. He stood beside the cook house passageway. Six feet three inches of hellground black, he was invisible in the angle of the wall. But it wasn't enough to remain unseen: he had to get out.

If he waited for the relieved detail to muster in their quarters, he risked being spotted by the compound patrol or the men up on the parapet when he made his bid to scale the outer wall.

If he tried to make it before they turned the corner of the central block and drew level with him, on the other hand, there was a chance he wouldn't be fast enough . . . they would hear him move . . . he would be seen by the battlement patrol. . . gunned down from the towers while he was helpless, halfway up the wall.

The hell with it. Bolan hated inaction. He'd make it *now*, before the detail came his way. He flip-jerked the rope to free the grappling hook.

The hook didn't move.

He tried again. And a third time.

One of the prongs was caught fast in a crevice between two of the sandstone blocks. Try as he would, he was unable to free the rope.

Bolan started to run. Silently he sped around the ancient fortress ahead of the advancing detail. But some slight sound as the rope slapped against the wall had alerted a soldier in one of the towers.

There was a warning shout. Dazzlingly bright, a searchlight on the tower scythed apart the darkness and exposed the sandstone rampart in its cold brilliance.

And the rope dangling from the top of the wall.

There were more shouts. A whistle blew. Somewhere above, a deep toned alarm bell began to jangle.

The returning detail broke into a run. On the far side of the prison the two patrols about-faced and hurried toward the tower that had sounded the alarm.

Bolan unleathered both guns as he ran. He kept close in to the rampart, passed the laundry and an armory, then dodged around the admin block.

Lights were springing up there and in other buildings around the compound. A second searchlight blazed to life. So far they hadn't picked up the fleeing warrior; they were still concentrating on the area near the cook house where the rope was visible.

But the Executioner would be sandwiched between the compound patrol and the returning detail at any moment. He had made almost an entire circuit of the central redoubt. Panting, he leaped for the flight of stone stairs leading up to the battlements.

He was almost below the first watchtower, in the darkness below the searchlight beam.

But it was not quite dark enough. He heard a triumphant cry from one of the approaching soldiers at the far end of the parapet. Flame pierced the night, and heavy slugs chipped fragments from the stonework as the stutter of an SMG echoed between the prison walls.

Bolan flung himself flat. Big Thunder roared. Fifty yards along the wall there was a scream of agony. A body pitched over and clattered down into the compound.

Now the men of the detail had arrived at the foot of the stone stairway.

They carried only handguns on watch in the towers, the guards were armed with swivel-mounted machine guns.

Eight soldiers toting heavy-caliber revolvers—those odds were a bit high even for the Executioner.

Left-handed, with the Beretta, he pumped out three lethal, almost soundless rounds. A trio of black soldiers, incautiously deployed too near the pool of radiance cast by the searchlight, slumped to the ground. One rolled into brilliance, twitched, raising a small cloud of dust, and then lay still as the earth around him darkened.

Bolan rolled over on the stone ledge—slugs were splatting against the wall on either side—and fired two more thunderous shots from the AutoMag. He followed up with a 3-round burst from the silenced Beretta.

All hell was breaking loose. The guys on the parapet were now firing from behind the collapsed bodies of dead comrades. The alarm bell continued to jangle. Officers shouted orders from the far side of the compound. The second searchlight was swinging slowly around to pinpoint the warrior in its merciless glare.

He was in dead ground for the machine gun in the watchtower immediately above him, but he would be a sitting duck for the crew in the second tower once they had him in their sights.

The soft probe had gone hard. Very hard.

Scrambling to his feet, he triggered the remaining rounds from his two deathbringers and leaped for the outer wall of the battlements.

For an instant he stood in one of the firing slits, a night dark shape poised hawklike over the cliff.

With no choice but straight down.

Chapter Ten

Mack Bolan knew the risks. He knew, too, that there was no other way out. In the hellgrounds where his life was spent, a false step, a moment of inattention, an instant of extra concentration on the part of an enemy could bridge the gap between life and death. The tightrope across that gap was a path the Executioner trod every moment of his waking life.

And there was no safety net below the rope.

Nor, for the guy balanced up there, was there time for reflection, for indecision.

With these thoughts in mind, the warrior launched himself off the wall.

He felt a rush of cold air that was both endless and immediate. With both guns holstered and arms outstretched before him, he plummeted sixty feet toward the cold, black water of the ocean.

He judged his approach perfectly.

Fingertips broke the surface between two swells as he plunged into thirty feet of saltwater with scarcely a splash.

It seemed an eternity before he rose gasping into the healing air. He could feel his heart thudding against his ribs; his blood tingled through every limb; seawater pressed cold against his skin.

But he had suffered no damage.

Bolan lay on his back and allowed the tide to carry him ashore east of the jail, facing the dunes. In the distance, over the swash of water, he could hear the faint trill of the prison alarm.

For the moment he was safe. He'd let the military figure out how a prisoner escaped but nobody was missing when they called the muster. Let them worry how that nonexistent escapee came to be equipped with a climbing rope and two guns that fired real bullets.

The Executioner hoped they would be so worried that the investigation inside would take their minds off normal security *outside* the jail. Because he had to approach the perimeter wall once more, unseen, before daylight.

For the second time in one week he waded ashore out of the sea on potentially hostile territory. But this time it was with an even firmer determination to see this particular mission through to the bitter end.

Yeah, okay, it was because of the women. And, yeah, he had personal reasons, compelling personal reasons, to feel bitter about the human savages who preyed on women.

Maybe the Executioner was a killing machine. Maybe. But Mack Bolan, Sergeant Mercy—the names stood for a man of high ideals.

The scumbags of the Mafia were responsible for the prostitution and ultimately for the death of his beloved kid sister, Cindy. Scumbags of a different color had killed April Rose, the love of his life, in a KGB-engineered raid on his antiterrorist headquarters when he was working secretly for Uncle Sam.

They came in all colors, the savages of the underworld. And color had nothing to do with evil, Bolan knew. Not all white men were bad; not all black men were good. At this moment his target was a black African—a bloodthirsty tyrant whose inhuman excesses had not been paralleled since Idi Amin had been chased out of Uganda to seek refuge with the crazy Marxist fanatic, Khaddafi, in Libya.

Releasing the women from this dictator's evil clutches, Bolan felt, would in some small way cancel a part of the debt.

And help avenge the deaths of those ladies he had loved.

Except that, if he had his way, there would be no free ticket to Libya for Emperor Ononu.

With the help of Colonel Azzid and the men who remained faithful to him, Bolan hoped to erase the name of Ononu from the list of the ungodly who held high office in the world.

But before Azzid could help, certain preparations had to be made, precautions taken, a number of arrangements set in motion, without which two men, one inside and one outside, could not hope to free up to a dozen prisoners from a high-security jail.

Bolan's immediate imperative was to secretly storm the outer walls of the prison and place delayed-action charges that would act as decoys when the time came for the break.

He could not rely on a single massive charge to breach the wall. He had no idea about the structure and consistency of the stonework, and he sure as hell could not make a close examination. The plan he had worked out with Azzid, moreover, was based on a series of small shocks rather than one big one.

The disadvantages lay in the timing. Bolan was using the old urban guerrilla technique involving wristwatches with the minute hands removed. Wired to a small battery with one terminal attached to the hour hand and the other to a pin piercing the watch face, the circuit was completed and the charge detonated when the hand touched the pin. All the saboteur had to do to set the device was back off the watch hand the number of hours corresponding to the planned delay.

Theoretically, the maximum time lag possible was thus eleven hours and fifty-nine minutes, when the hand would be set fractionally ahead of the pin with an entire circuit of the dial to complete before the two were in contact. In practice, since it was difficult to place an hour hand as precisely as a minute hand, the delay was usually restricted to eleven hours and fifty minutes.

Bolan's problem was that the break could not be organized before 1515 hours the following day, when Azzid was due for his five-minute exercise period. This meant that he dared not set the timers until 0325 hours.

It was not yet two o'clock. He hoped the investigation inside the jail would be rigorous enough to keep the guards' attention for another ninety minutes.

Back beside the Land Rover, Bolan checked through the specialized equipment he would have to use the next day, and then selected two packets of C-4 each weighing one pound. These, he reckoned, would create enough damage to persuade the prison authorities that something serious was on the way in the area of the explosions.

He pushed detonators into the puttylike plastique, wired up batteries and watches, inserted the pins and moved the hands counterclockwise until they almost touched the metal shanks.

At twenty after three he was standing at the edge of the forest on the western side of the prison. One hundred yards away across a pale blur of sand, the outer wall was silhouetted against a faint glare from the lights inside the compound. Bolan wound the two watches, checked that they were ticking and wrapped each timed charge in a strip of sacking. Slowly, he started to walk across the sandy strip.

He was relying on the hope that the watchtower guards, as well as the battlement patrol, would be more than usually alert for any more signs of a break from within the prison...and that much less aware of movement beyond the walls. Normal duties in any case oriented their attention inward rather than outward.

Nearing the dark bulk of the building, Bolan could hear raised voices still, both angry and sullen, from the interior. He knelt at the foot of the wall and scooped a shallow hole for the first charge, covering it with sand once he was satisfied it was hard against the foundations.

Thirty yards nearer the cliff, he started a cautious manual exploration of the stonework at the height of his own shoulders. There were plenty of crevices, but most of them were too narrow for his purpose. Eventually his hands touched some thistlelike growth sprouting between two of the weathered blocks, and with a little digging he was able to dislodge the roots and pull the plant free. The opening revealed was four inches wide and deep enough to swallow his hand as far as the wrist.

A thin trickle of earth, tiny pebbles and fragments of stone pattered to the sand. Bolan froze.

The noise sounded alarmingly loud to him, but it provoked no outcry from the battlements high above. After a full minute of anguish, he expelled his breath in a long sigh of relief.

Working with infinite care, he molded the package of plastique into the aperture, tamping it firmly into position and then checking that the wires were still attached.

He laid his ear to the wall. The watch was ticking.

Finally he picked up the plant and replaced it, packing sand around the roots until it would remain in place without his steadying hand. Unless there was a violent downpour during the next few hours it should stay there as long as he needed it. He looked up, above the dark mass of the wall. Stars shone brilliantly in a cloudless night sky.

Satisfied, Bolan turned and made his way back across the strip to the forest—silent as a shadow on his avenging path.

AT TEN O'CLOCK the following morning, once more playing the role of consultant mining engineer, he was in the Montemines office on the Quai Muhammad Khaddafi in Port-Doulas.

The superintendent who represented Bozuffi and the other directors was a tall, spare man with close-cropped white hair and heavy horn-rimmed glasses. His name was McTavish.

"Ononu's army," he was explaining to the Executioner, "lines up just one division of ten thousand men. But with the equipment they have, that's quite a force."

"Modern equipment?" Bolan queried.

"You can say that again!" McTavish replied. "They have a squadron of A-4 Leopard tanks, for starters."

Bolan whistled. He knew that the A-4s sported 105 mm turret guns and ten-cylinder engines.

"Right. And the Leopards are backed up with the same number of Roland missiles on trailers, plus half a dozen M-109 self-propelled howitzers. I mean like heavy stuff."

"Air support?"

"Limited," McTavish said. "Two AH-1G choppers armed with Rockwell hellfire missiles. There are four Soviet-built Hinds as well, but those are strictly ferries. They carry no armament."

"That's quite a package," Bolan admitted. "But what about the guys who operate them? How do they rate?"

"In combat? Who knows? But I can tell you they're certainly on the ball when it comes to mopping up tribesmen armed with muskets."

"Apart from the Hinds, that's all GI or NATO equipment, isn't it?"

McTavish nodded. "Bought through France—with money contributed by Khaddafi, the Syrians and possibly Moscow," he said dryly. "I know for a fact that the Hinds were a birthday present to the dear Emperor from the Politburo."

"Bosom buddies. But I bet they're all looking over their shoulders," Bolan said. "Did you manage to contact the officer I called you about?"

"He'll be sitting at the counter of the Palm Bar on the rooftop terrace of the Lido at eleven. He won't be in uniform. Look for white tennis shorts and a blue-and-white-striped sweatshirt."

"Thanks," Bolan said. "Unfortunately I can't tell you what it's all about. But Mr. Bozuffi figured it would be better if you forgot this whole thing."

McTavish nodded once more. "I guess he's right at that."

"Before I see this guy," Bolan said, "tell me about Ononu. What makes him tick? Does he have some kind of chip or is he just naturally mean?"

"He's an asshole," McTavish said. "An uncouth, sadistic, insensitive asshole."

"I take it you don't like him," Bolan said, smiling.

"Who could? He hates our guts."

"Why? Surely the two companies are making him rich. Isn't he on a percentage, like the Arabs?"

"He thinks the percentage is too low. He reckons the figure should be one hundred rather than fifteen."

"He wants it all? Is he planning a takeover, some kind of nationalization?"

"Nothing he'd like better, but there are certain considerations, other commercial and political interests, certain pressures, let us say, that tell him no. He wants to renegotiate."

"At what figure?"

"He says he'll accept nothing less than fifty-fifty."

"And your directors disagree, right?"

"Why the hell should they agree?" McTavish was indignant. "Shit, he'd never even know the bloody lodes were there if it wasn't for us. We prospected and discovered the goddamn minerals. We put up the cash to sink the bores, organize the surveys, exploit the mines. It's our money that pays for the extraction of ore, for processing and selling the product!"

"What's his line on that?"

"He's mad because he claims he was tricked into signing the original concession treaty. But there's nothing for him to bellyache about: he was guaranteed a fixed sum for ten years even if we discovered the lodes were unworkable. He had nothing to lose and everything to gain. As it is, he still risks nothing and rakes in plenty. He's just a greedy bastard and that's the truth of it."

Bolan pursed his lips. Things were beginning to make sense. If you wanted to renegotiate a deal with four guys and they refused because they held all the cards...hell, it would sure strengthen *your* hand if you happened to have a reputation as a monster and you held their daughters hostage!

Which was why, maybe, one of the guys was so damned anxious to have a certain antiterrorist warrior named Mack Bolan take up the case....

Bolan left McTavish and went to the Lido.

The day was heavy with damp heat. The sun glared brassily from a burnished sky. Around the Olympic-size pool, topless black girls wearing Western-style wigs oiled themselves on striped mattresses. From the rooftop terrace the Executioner looked out over a wide esplanade to the lines of surf rolling in from a leaden ocean.

Shiny automobiles cruised the seafront and there were brightly colored umbrellas shading the tables of the beach cafés. If it weren't for the scrawny chickens pecking the dirt roads that led to the shantytowns on the city outskirts, an observer could have rated Port-Doulas as the symbol of a flourishing society.

Lieutenant Edmond Ogano, in blue and white as advertised, was nursing a whiskey sour at the bar. Bolan slid onto a stool beside him and ordered the same.

Ogano was a tall, lithe man with ebony-colored skin and a bushy mustache. Bolan liked him immediately.

"Colonel Azzid regards you as a friend," he said, once the identification routines had been completed.

The African sighed. "Maybe not friendly enough," he said. "If he'd had more support, he might not be in jail."

"If your friendship had been too obvious," Bolan replied, "you'd be in jail with him. As it is, you can help get him out."

"I guess that's right," Ogano said. "Naturally I'll do anything I can. What do you have in mind?"

"Azzid tells me your party can count on perhaps thirty or forty men. Is that right?"

"In principle, yes. But getting them together, in the same place, at the same time, might be difficult. They don't all belong to the same unit."

"Okay. How many could you rely on one hundred percent—I don't mean rely on their loyalty but on their availability."

"Perhaps twenty. It would depend on the day and the time."

"Tomorrow afternoon. Are any of your guys connected with the Leopard tank squadron?"

Ogano shook his head. "Not one. They're all infantrymen. From the Yanga tribe, like me. Nothing but the more menial tasks, the gun-fodder role, for them. No higher than captain for me." The lieutenant sounded bitter. "Ononu takes very good care that nobody but the Oriwady gets within a mile of the tanks and artillery and missiles. He dare not."

"Too bad," Bolan said. "And the choppers?"

"Choppers?"

"The helicopters. Are the pilots Oriwady, too?"

"The men who fly the missile gunships certainly are. I could count on a couple of the Hind fellows, of course, but they don't have—"

"I know. The civil version. Unarmed. Still, they could be useful. Do your guys have access to APCs—armored personnel carriers?"

Ogano brushed the ends of his mustache outward with a forefinger. "We could lay our hands on maybe four mechanized infantry combat vehicles. They're good value—American XM-723s, only in service since 1980."

"So we make it with four MICVs and a couple of civilian choppers. It's better than a foot patrol. Now here's the big question: are you, personally, in a position to order those MICVs out of base camp—and maybe raise the choppers too—without any awkward questions being asked? Is there any chance of them being within reasonable distance of the prison around three in the afternoon without some kind of alarm being raised?"

The young officer thought for a moment. "I guess so," he said finally. "There's a cleanup campaign in progress—against the use of ganja and the hard stuff in the shantytowns. We act on information received. Like fast, to catch the pushers with the stuff on them. It's an infantry job—and if the tipoff comes from here or Kondani, well, we'd pass the jail on our way into town from the base camp at Oulad."

Bolan clapped him on the shoulder. "We're in business!"

FIFTEEN HOURS TEN. The heat of the sun, fiercer each minute, had metamorphosed an atmosphere already heavy with humidity into a haze that blanketed the forest trees and blotted out the ocean horizon. At the edge of the forest, half-hidden behind a screen of tropical undergrowth, Bolan's Land Rover faced the dirt road that skirted the dunes and passed the prison.

The Executioner sat in the outside passenger seat. Cradled on his left shoulder and projecting from the open side of the utility was the stubby barrel of an RPG-7V rocket grenade launcher, most unwieldy of the weapons carried in the secret compartment below the floor.

Bolan's big hands were wrapped around the RPG-7's two pistol grips. His right forefinger remained poised, ready to curl around the forward trigger, his eye pressed to the rubber shield in back of the optical sight. The skirt of the bulbous five-pound grenade was already in place over the launch tube's muzzle.

The warrior's forehead furrowed in concentration. Was it the distant grinding of gears, the threshing of tracks driven by 280-horsepower diesel engines that he heard?

Fifteen fifteen. There was a sudden puff of brown smoke above the prison's western wall. Two seconds later the thunderclap of an explosion.

Before the cracking detonation died away, there was a vivid flash and another eruption of smoke billowed over the wall. Fragments of masonry spewed out from the center of the blast. The shock wave of sound rolled across the strip of sand.

Bolan nodded in satisfaction. Through the RPG-7's optics he saw the shapes of men passing the firing slits in the battlements. They were running toward the sector where the delayed-action charges exploded. Sounds of confused shouting came to him from the western end of the compound.

Bolan shifted his position, centering the sight's cross hairs on the parapet at the eastern extremity of the jail's outer wall. He could definitely hear the approach of tracked vehicles now.

But he waited, fingertips tingling, every muscle in his body tense.

Fifteen seventeen.

Brown smoke drifted over the battlements. Two more detonations, muffled this time, reached him from within the prison. They were followed by a volley of revolver shots and the deeper stammer of a submachine gun—abruptly cut short by two thudding bangs, quite different in quality from the explosive charges.

The Executioner imagined the scene being played out in the high-security wing: Azzid knifing the guard due to escort him to the exercise yard, freeing his companions and using the plastique to blow his way out of the block and into the passageway that led to the cook house, then using two of the stun grenades to put any guards blocking his escape out of action.

Holding his breath, Bolan squeezed the launcher's trigger.

A roar of flame belched out from the rear of the tube, exiting on the far side of the Land Rover's cab. The grenade leaped from the launcher at a speed of more than one hundred yards per second; four stabilizer fins unfolded, then the rocket motor cut in to increase the speed to three hundred yards per second. The fiery warhead streaked over the road and the sandy strip to burst with a shattering crash and a gush of orange flame just below the parapet.

Fifteen twenty. Bolan reached down to the floor of the Land Rover and picked up a second rocket grenade. He fitted it over the tube. Through the sight he could see a breach in the battlement perhaps seven or eight feet across and four deep. Rock dust and fumes from the explosion hung over the gap.

Four hundred yards away along the dirt road, four MICVs, each carrying half a dozen armed men in uniform, materialized beneath a miniature sandstorm raised by their tracks. The machine gunners in the watchtowers hesitated, unsure if the carriers were enemies or reinforcements.

Bolan fired the second grenade. This time he aimed a few feet below the breach. Solid blocks of stone tumbled to the sand. Smoke tinged with flame boiled out and up as the blast enlarged the gap in the wall.

Beyond the western end of the jail, Bolan watched as the MICVs left the dirt road and rumbled across the sand toward the battlements. From the open turrets, 7.62 mm PKT machine guns spit flame.

Some of the watchtower guards fired at the armored vehicles, some shot down into the compound. The concussion of the last stun grenade...a rattle of small-arms fire. By now, Bolan reasoned, Azzid and his companions would have seized weapons from the fallen wardens and be blasting their way toward the breach.

The Executioner aimed his third grenade some way below the hole in the wall. When the dust cleared he saw that although the explosion had not pierced the rampart, it had pulverized the stonework enough for the section above to collapse. The jagged, wedge-shaped opening in the wall now reached halfway from the parapet to the ground.

A pall of smoke hovered above the prison. Bolan had agreed with Azzid that the escapers would make it through the gap immediately after the third HEAT missile exploded. Still, he decided to cover them now with a fourth from his total stock of half a dozen. The gunners on the watchtower nearest the break sprayed death in the direction of the breach. The warrior angled the barrel of the bazookalike launcher upward.

The rush of flame. The screech of the rocket engine.

A direct hit. Platform, railing, gun mounting and roof disintegrated in a holocaust of flame. The girdered pylon supporting the platform buckled and tilted, showering blazing debris into the compound. Red-hot metal trailing spirals of smoke jetted skyward, and a threshing shape licked by tongues of fire dropped screaming to the sand outside the wall.

Fifteen twenty-seven.

Bolan slid behind the wheel, started the engine and drove the Land Rover out, across the road and toward the prison. The tracked MICVs were churning around in front of the breached wall, hosing lead at the remaining watchtowers.

Emaciated figures in drab prison uniform, some of them with SMGs, some without, appeared in the gap, jumping down ten feet to run in the direction of the rescuers. The Executioner counted seven.

But there was a hail of fire raining down from the battlements now. Two men fell. A third staggered, almost pitched full-length, but was picked up and dragged to the nearest carrier by two companions.

Bolan could see Lieutenant Ogano in the turret of the leading MICV, gesticulating urgently.

Finally all the escaped prisoners had been hauled aboard except one tall, sinewy man with cropped gray hair and a seamed face. The Executioner assumed correctly that this was Colonel Azzid; he was down on one knee, coolly covering his men with short bursts from an Uzi. Bolan gunned the Land Rover's engine and swooped across in a shower of sand to pick him up.

Azzid's denim prison uniform was dark with sweat. He tossed the SMG into the back and sank gasping into the passenger seat. Ogano's MICVs were already back on the dirt road heading east.

"Problems?" Bolan asked, wrenching the utility onto the trail and accelerating after them.

"As expected," the colonel said, panting. "No more, no less. Without this it could have been difficult." He produced the commando knife. The blade was dark with congealed blood.

"I used it to write off two wardens," Azzid continued. "So once I had freed the first of my fellow officers, we were able to use both sets of keys and liberate the rest twice as fast."

"You got them all out?" Bolan asked.

"The ten of us concerned in the failed coup, yes. By the time the first of the plastique charges you had given me blew the cell-block doors, we were ready to rush through and blast open the way to the kitchens with the second. But the guards in the exercise yard were quick off the mark: we lost two men killed and one wounded and recaptured." Azzid shook his head. "Poor bastard, I wouldn't like to be in his shoes."

"Plus two more dead and another wounded between the wall and the carriers," Bolan added. "So effectively there's just yourself and three other officers, and of course Lieutenant Ogano, to lead the men?"

"Correct. How many men has Ogano organized?"

"Twenty-four including himself, I think. With another three who should be crewing one of the Hind helicopters."

"Only one?"

"Ogano wasn't sure he could rely on the second. In any case only one would be used in a genuine antidrug cleanup operation. So we figured it safer to avoid suspicion and base the plan on a single aircraft."

"Very well." Colonel Azzid turned to look out the Land Rover's rear window. So far no pursuit vehicles had emerged from the jail. "What exactly is the plan?" he asked.

Bolan told him. He had worked it out with Lieutenant Ogano.

The first priority was to get across the idea that this was simply an escape, an attempt to flee the dictator's wrath, and not in any way the preliminary to a second coup. Accordingly, the convoy was to head east and north through the forest as if making for Halakaz and the Ivory Coast.

But even on forest trails, four MICVs and a Land Rover were not likely to elude the vigilance of an enemy deploying four or five helicopters, two of them armed with missiles. So it had been decided to junk the wheeled transport and hide the vehicles beneath the trees once a direction—and by implication the flight to a neighboring country—had been established.

The Hind that was theoretically on Ogano's imaginary cleanup mission would then pick up the entire company.

Lake Gadrany and the summer palace were 162 miles away in a straight line. By road the distance was more than two hundred miles. The Executioner had decided, in view of this, to make the escape and the assault on Ononu's fortress a single operation. The quicker they were able to strike, the less chance there was that the dictator would realize they had no intention of crossing the frontier into the Ivory Coast—and the less time he would have to react and call up reinforcements loyal to him.

But because the ungainly civil version of the Soviet helicopter was too easy a target for ground-to-air missiles and rockets fired from other aircraft, the small attacking force was to be divided before they reached the killzone.

One of the escaped officers and three handpicked men were to be set down on the rooftop helipad of the Radio Montenegria tower in Bomiko-Kassi.

The four men would be given orders to penetrate and take over the station's continuity control room, silence the armed guards, then force the broadcasting personnel to continue normal transmission until they received word from Azzid that Ononu had been overthrown. There would then be radio silence until the colonel himself went on the air from the dictator's own studio in the summer palace and announced the takeover.

The most important part of the mission was the speed and precision with which it had to be carried out: the four men had to seize control of the radio station before anyone could raise an alarm.

From the capital, the chopper would then fly northeast to the lake and set down Ogano, two more of the escaped officers and eighteen infantrymen with their weapons and certain elements of Bolan's arsenal from the Land Rover. Disembarkation would be behind a belt of woods half a mile from the lakeshore.

Finally, Bolan, Azzid and the two remaining soldiers were to take a chance on the time it took for base control to figure out that the chopper was involved in the jailbreak and not with any antidrug swoop. They would stay aloft and make an airborne attack on the palace while Ogano's task force neutralized the gate house garrisons at either end of the bridge linking the islet with the shore.

"It's a crazy plan," Bolan said, "but it's got to work. With the main radio station in your hands, plus the linked studio at the palace, do you think you could swing the rest of the army your way?''

The colonel nodded. ''If General Shagari is at the palace—and he's Ononu's right-hand man so he usually is—then there should be no problem,'' he said.

''But even with Shagari in your hands, too, won't the rest of the Oriwady officers at Oulad prove something of a headache?''

''Once your hostages are out of the way,'' Azzid said grimly, ''I have no doubt we can...persuade Ononu and the general to issue certain orders that will make our task easier.''

He turned again in his seat and looked back down the forest trail. There was no sign of pursuit. ''In any case,'' he said for the second time, ''what have we got to lose?''

Chapter Eleven

Emperor Anya Ononu was a large and powerful man. He was not particularly tall, but he was very wide, deep chested, long armed and packed with hard muscle. He weighed 210 pounds.

At noon on the day Colonel Azzid escaped from jail, Ononu's face was devoid of its habitual sullen expression: the corners of his mouth turned up in an anticipatory smile and his small eyes, yellow flecked with red around a black iris, shone with eagerness.

Each day at 1400 hours, ever since the industrialists' daughters had been delivered to him, he selected one to be ceremonially—and publicly—raped. While four soldiers held the young woman spread-eagled on a marble table in the summer palace's huge mirrored reception hall, Ononu would strip naked and violate her in front of an audience composed of servants, off-duty military and any sycophantic members of his entourage who happened to be around.

Most of them made it a point to be around—no one wanted to rouse Ononu's temper, which was mercurial at best. He liked to show off his physique and his virility. It flattered his ego to hear the spectators gasp as he plunged into the unwilling flesh. But most of his satisfaction was mental; he could, if he wished, take his pleasure anywhere in Montenegria, at any time. It was the humiliation, the repeated subjugation of these haughty females—and with it the vicarious supremacy over their fathers—that slaked his thirst for revenge, for domination of the hated foreigners who had pillaged his land and cheated him out of his rightful share of the profits to be gained from its exploitation.

It helped, too, from the propaganda point of view, to keep his subjects persuaded that his power was unchallenged: the subjugation was a convenient—and agreeable—symbol of the emergence of black Africa and the final suppression of colonialist rule.

Today, the emperor decided, he would take the Bozuffi girl again. He had personally tortured each of the kidnapped young women when they arrived, but she had been the toughest to break.

Today he would make sure he broke her spirit, her will. There was great satisfaction to be gained when such a victim finally lost all self-control.

Each beating and each rape had been filmed. It would be both amusing and flattering to his ego to run the movies later in front of other leaders who lusted for Western humiliation. The soundtracks of the films had been transferred to tape. There was almost enough material now. Suitably edited, copies of each girl's tape would be sent to her father—with the ultimatum that unless new terms for the mining concession were satisfactorily negotiated at once, arrangements would be made for the recording of further tapes.

Ononu's carnal pleasures were not restricted to the domination of women. The "interrogations" of his enemies, which again he liked to oversee personally, were a constant source of joy.

The rumor that he kept their heads in a refrigerator amused him. And he was careful to ensure that the rumor was never denied; subversives and upstarts from inferior tribes were less likely to challenge a ruler with that kind of reputation.

The truth was in fact no less bizarre.

Ononu was of that vile breed of men turned on by suffering. He liked to watch his enemies drown. There was a room in the subbasement of the summer palace that could be flooded from the lake, right up to the ceiling level. The room had one glass wall, with floodlights and a viewing cubicle on the far side.

Better still, in the cellar he used for his torture sessions there was a row of hooks from which seven-foot-deep sacks in transparent heavy-duty plastic could be suspended. The victims were immured in these sacks with their arms bound, and the sacks were then filled with water. In this way, Ononu could watch the frantic jerkings of the water-filled bags and the contorted faces of the drowning men.

If he was feeling generous, the emperor would invite his intimates to these sessions and take bets on which victim stayed alive the longest.

Last-to-survive wagers were also made on two more favorite techniques of "execution." In one, two men were roped tightly together face-to-face and placed in a bath containing just enough water to submerge one of them. Ononu found the resulting struggles diverting, especially if the victims were friends.

The second system involved a rope passed over a beam. There was a noose at either end of the rope, and each noose was fastened around the neck of a handcuffed man. The length of the rope was then modified so that when one man could just touch the floor with his toes, the other would be suspended and choking. Provided the two men were of equal weight, the seesaw battle for life could be prolonged for quite a while.

Finally there was a clever technique of torture that Ononu had learned from the descendants of the Thugs in India. A naked man or woman was held upright and a razor incision made from navel to pubis. It was surprising how little this would bleed.

A sharp, well-directed blow with the heel of the hand on the victim's diaphragm would then cause an involuntary abdominal spasm that convulsed the intestines so that they burst outward and spilled through the opening.

The high point was the victim's reaction: to see if he gave himself up for dead, or tried to wrench open the slit in his own belly and stuff his guts back in.

There were still enough prisoners in the palace dungeons, most of them survivors of the recent coup, to satisfy Ononu's desire to enjoy all of these arcane pleasures. For the moment, however, the red-haired Bozuffi girl topped the list.

Ononu left his luxurious private suite and went to check with his second in command. The emperor wore a pale cotton suit with a high-buttoning neck in the style preferred by Chairman Mao, with five gold stars on each shoulder strap. The contrast when he stripped would show off his virile animal body to perfection.

General Shagari was waiting in the Long Room—an ornate salon furnished with gilded console tables and antique chairs imported from Paris. There was a seventeenth-century spinet with an ivory-colored case in one corner, but the effect was rather spoiled by the wooden figures displayed in floridly decorated niches along the room's western wall.

These, many of them crudely phallic, represented the juju gods of war and fertility as imagined by a succession of indifferent Oriwady tribal artists whose cultural tradition went back no more than fifty years.

The general was wearing a silver-gray uniform with large gold epaulets and seven rows of medal ribbons. A Browning automatic with mother-of-pearl butt plates nestled in a white suede holster clipped to his belt. He was a squat man, shorter and wider than Ononu, with similar eyes and tribal marks on his cheeks.

Ononu rubbed his hands together. "Is everything ready?" he asked.

Shagari bowed. "As you ordered it, Majesty."

"The table, the lights, the film crew briefed on close-ups? The four men holding the girl instructed to keep out of the way of the camera?"

"Yes, sir."

"Good. And the audience?"

"Seventeen off-duty men and three officers from the palace guard, the deputy duty officer, the palace comptroller and his wife, the three dancers from Freetown and, of course, all the servants."

"Excellent. The bitch has been fed?"

Shagari nodded. It was an idiosyncrasy of the emperor that captives in the palace should invariably be well fed and in good shape.

Ononu disagreed with the Oriental concept that emphasized the inferiority of prisoners by reducing them to the state of animals. Surely it was much more satisfying to reduce a smart, healthy man in a well-pressed uniform to a blubbering wreck than it was to terrorize some filthy, unshaven wretch who would cringe if a dog barked?

It was a clearer lesson, too, in the matter of one's own supremacy, the domination of a worthier adversary.

The same thing was true of the women.

In the emperor's mind he was all-powerful. Anya Ononu considered himself the inspiration of warriors, forger of dynasties, destroyer of the unworthy—even the scented darlings of the Western world lay prone before his masculinity!

If any of the spectators ordered to attend these ritual violations had reservations because the scented darlings were being held down by four men, they were careful not to voice them.

"Have her prepared," Ononu ordered.

The general bowed again and left the room.

In the reception hall floodlights glared. A murmur of anticipation ran through the assembled spectators as the camera crew moved in on the marble table. Suzanne Bozuffi was led in through a side entrance. She wore a knee-length dress in flowered silk, gun-metal tights and white high-heeled shoes. Her long red hair was brushed and glossy.

The young woman was handcuffed and the steel bracelets were attached to a chain held by the Oriwady corporal in charge of the three other jailers. Her head was held high and she was doing her best to look disdainful, though from time to time her body shook with an uncontrollable shudder.

The corporal unlocked the cuffs and two of the jailers grabbed Suzanne's arms. She made no resistance when the NCO and the fourth man unzippered the dress, unhooked and removed her brassiere and stripped the tights down to her ankles.

She stood naked before them, her body discolored with bruises, her back still crisscrossed with the marks of a whipping. General Shagari clicked his fingers and the four men lifted the girl, placed her face upward on the big table, stretched her arms above her head and spread her legs. Tears trickled from beneath her closed eyelids but she made no sound.

Ononu strutted into the hall.

From behind the spectators a young man in the uniform of a major ran up to the marble table.

"Majesty!" he said, panting. "A message... Forgive me, but a most important message..."

The emperor turned and scowled. "You dare to interrupt?" he shouted. "You know perfectly well this is forbidden. The duty officer is capable—"

"But, sir—" the young officer's eyes were staring "—there has been an attack on the prison! Colonel Azzid and his men have escaped!"

"*What!* What infamy is this?" Ononu's face was suffused with rage. "You *dare* to bring me news...." Backhanded, he slashed the major across the face with such force that the young man crashed to the floor and slid six feet along the polished boards.

"Majesty, it is true," the officer babbled. "I swear it. We have received a telex from the governor. A detachment of traitors from the base at Oulad with foreign support... They are heading east for the border, but so far they have gotten away...."

"Those Yanga dogs!" Ononu stormed. His rage was terrible to see. "Must I continually be surrounded by imbeciles? Is there nobody fit to trust with the simplest task? I can see I shall have to handle this myself. Shagari—warn the garrison at Halakaz. I want these men brought back alive. All of them. Heads will fall if any escape."

He glared around at the silent crowd. "The rest of you—wait here until I give you permission to leave. I shall attend to this white trash as soon as I have been to the radio room and issued my orders." With a glance at the trembling girl on the table, he strode from the hall.

Chapter Twelve

Sitting at a bamboo table near the window of his room on the top floor of the Hotel Imperial in Kondani, Jason Mettner stared at his miniature tape recorder. The newspaperman rubbed his eyes, trying to collect his thoughts before speaking into the machine.

Mettner was tired, but excited. He had been two nights without sleep following a lead that brought him to this backwater town in the armpit of Africa.

This guy McTavish *had* returned Mettner's call with news of a jailbreak apparently organized by Mack Bolan. Mettner himself *had* arrived exhausted after an off-the-cuff decision to follow through the kidnapping of the four industrialists' daughters. He hesitated, staring out the window. Between the broad leaves of a banana tree he could see the muddy yellow waters of the Doulas estuary. On the far side of the river, self-propelled cranes transferred ore from a line of railroad hopper cars to the hold of a freighter—one of several berthed alongside the Port-Doulas dockside quays.

What the hell. The research for the terrorist piece for the Sunday supplement could wait. Right now it was better to stay close to the news, whatever his editor, Allard Fielding said. Mettner picked up the miniature voice recorder and pressed the button.

"Al," he said, "this is your wandering ace correspondent. Forget the terrorist feature. Okay, okay—I know it's the second week running. But it looks like all hell could break loose here and I figure it's better that I stay where the action is rather than waste cigarettes composing a scholarly thesis in a hotel room. If there's a military takeover here, I shall be the only Westerner able to give you a firsthand account. You could even have a scoop, guy!"

The newspaperman stubbed out his cigarette and lit another.

"Where is here?" he continued. "Kondani, Montenegria, no less. Third most important town in the 715th country in black Africa to achieve independence. Treasury full, courtesy of Moscow and Tripoli; one anti-American vote in the U.N. General Assembly up for rent.

"Al, let me fill you in. Four tycoons' daughters snatched, each presently in the hands of the big shot. Each the apple of Daddy's eye. Each father connected with the local mining concession. Add the fact—for which I owe this guy McTavish—that the emperor considers he was done in by said daddies, now wants to grab a larger slice of the royalties, and what do you come up with? The hottest blackmail story this year.

"But this, baby, is not all. The ever-present Mr. Bolan is present. This time he contacts buddies of the ruler's jailed enemies, rubs his magic lamp and presto, the enemies are out of jail!

"I was too late for the party. By the time I got there, there was nothing left but smoke. No comment, of course. A minor accident with an explosive charge while hollowing out the rock for the prisoners' new swimming pool. But I heard the gunfire and I saw the holes in the wall.

"They're said to be heading for the border. Not for my money: ducking out from under ain't the Bolan way. Me, I'm heading for the boss's safehouse in the interior. Don't be surprised to find a cabled Flash on your desk. You could even dust off those old headlines about the Red Monarch Ousted by Military Junta. But remember, this time the soldier boys are the good guys."

Mettner killed his second cigarette, stretched, yawned and favored the darkening sky with a crooked smile. "Watch this space!" he told the recorder.

Chapter Thirteen

Mack Bolan climbed down from the sky. The sky was now gray, darkening in the southwest, with low clouds tumbling inland from the ocean. The steamy heat of the early afternoon had been dissipated by the wind; soon, as the dusk thickened, there was going to be a fierce tropical rainstorm.

Bolan's rope ladder hung from the open hatchway of the Hind. The bulbous chopper, with its swept-back stub wings and the twin air intakes above the bullet-proof-Plexiglas canopy, was hovering over the southern wing of Anya Ononu's summer palace.

Halfway along the steep roof an octagonal tower was built out from the facade. The tower was open-sided and housed a wide spiral staircase bordered on the outside with stone balustrades.

Surmounting the tower was a smaller octagonal structure and it was on the flat roof of this that Bolan and his companions intended to land.

The continually curving staircase would give them maximum protection from any shooting within the palace. At the same time they could exit from any of the five floors where the battle was fiercest.

Before he stepped off the ladder and signaled Azzid and the soldiers to follow him, the Executioner had to make sure that the opening stage of the assault was going as planned.

There was no way of telling whether the ruse suggesting that the escaped prisoners were trying to make it to the Ivory Coast had fooled the bloodthirsty dictator. Even if it had, he would be jumpy as hell, knowing his opponents were free; he would certainly be protected by a nucleus of his own toughest fellow tribesmen.

And those guys were certainly going to be trigger-happy, even if they hadn't heard the chopper was involved in the jailbreak, even if nobody wondered why it was hovering over the islet, even if Bolan and his ladder hadn't been observed.

But they had been observed.

Beyond the slated roofs, Bolan saw a sentry outside the gate house at the landward end of the bridge, legs astride, head tilting back, finger pointing skyward.

The man turned his head to shout a warning to the guards inside the gate house.

At that moment a single shot cracked out from behind a line of bushes on the far side of the lakeshore road. The sentry dropped. He lay on his face with his arms outflung.

Bolan wondered if the guard had had time to get his message across. The sentries—maybe the people inside the palace—would know there was a chopper overhead. But was anyone else wise to the fact that someone was about to land on the roof?

Whether or not Ogano's marksman had dropped the sentry in time swiftly became an academic question.

Small-arms fire erupted all along the leafy margin of the road. Lying in a trench behind the bushes, the attackers hosed lead from Kalashnikov AK-74 automatic rifles at the two guardhouses.

Three soldiers had run out to check what had happened to the sentry. Two of them fell; the third dodged back inside the doorway. Then a withering stream of return fire from perhaps a dozen Uzi submachine guns opened up through slits in the walls of both buildings.

Bolan stepped off the rope ladder onto the flat roof of the octagonal structure above the tower, signaling to the others to follow him with a sweep of his arm. Azzid and the two soldiers slid down to join him. The helicopter, with its three-man crew and the wounded officer aboard, soared up and flew away toward the wood.

It was to land there, out of sight of the palace, and await a radio call from Azzid, who would need transport to the base camp once the assault was over.

In the huge rectangular entrance courtyard, out of sight over the rooftops, Bolan could hear shouting and the stamp of feet. Gunfire continued from the two gate houses and along the far side of the lakeshore road.

One of the attackers, dashing between two bushes, was slow off the mark; sandwiched in a lethal stream from both ends of the bridge, he crashed through low branches onto the road, rolled over twice and then lay still. Tentacles of blood spread out from beneath his body, reaching for the grassy margin.

Bolan was waiting. From his shoulder he unhitched a compact and deadly Ingram MAC-11 SMG fitted with a suppressor, checked that the AutoMag and his silenced Beretta were smoothly leathered and turned to Azzid and the soldiers. "Any moment now," he gritted. "But I think we should make the top of the stairway first."

The colonel nodded. One by one they dropped, light-footed, from the roof of the octagon to the flat parapet on top of the tower. One of the eight openings gave access to the stone stairway.

The Executioner hesitated again. Then he heard the sound he was waiting for. The sporadic gunfire from below, which could bring the assault force nothing while the defenders were protected in their stone shelters, was punctuated by a heavier, thudding report.

A streak of flame pierced the bushes.

Towing a fiery tail, one of the two rocket grenades Bolan had reserved leaped for the lakeshore gate house. The HEAT warhead thundered into the wall just below the roof and exploded with a shattering roar. Blocks of masonry were sent spinning high into the air and one side of the building collapsed, sending tiles showering to the ground in a cloud of plaster dust.

The launcher tube spewed flame again, and the last of the RPG-7 bombs scored on the inner gate house. The explosion smashed a hole in the wall and sent gunners reeling out through the smoke. Ogano's men shot them down.

"Okay, this is it!" Bolan yelled. Thumbing the fast-fire Ingram onto full auto he pounded down the stairs. Azzid and the two soldiers, each carrying an AK-74, followed close behind.

At the first turning of the spiral, Bolan looked out above the slanting stone balustrade...and checked his stride.

The clatter of rotors had increased in volume, all but drowning the gunfire below.

Through the open side of the tower, Bolan saw that the attackers were, as planned, taking advantage of the chaos caused by the grenade explosions to emerge from behind the bushes and rush the bridge. Firing from the hip as they came, Ogano's men fanned out to saturate the first gate house.

But above them, sideslipping down from the angry sky, whirled one of Ononu's AH-1G helicopters with Hellfire missiles nestling in launch tubes above its skids.

Colonel Azzid uttered a shocked exclamation. Bolan's mouth opened but he said nothing; there was nothing they could do. The unarmed Hind, an ungainly sitting duck, had not yet sunk from sight behind the trees.

From beneath the smaller helicopter's cabin, a missile detached itself in a deceptively leisurely fashion, trailing fire. Then, accelerating in successive stages until it was no more than a brush stroke of flame against the dark canvas of the landscape, it homed on the Hind's hot jets, burst into an orange fireball and blew off the helicopter's five-bladed rotor.

Blazing, the Hind dropped like a stone. An instant later black smoke marbled with crimson boiled up from behind the trees.

Clearly they had underestimated Ononu's intelligence organization. As soon as the Hind appeared, the dictator had known it to be connected with the escape and had called up his air support.

The AH-1G banked, angling its remaining Rockwell Hellfire projectile at the troops attacking the bridge. But two of the MICV crews had dismantled the 40 mm cannons from their turrets before they left the vehicles in the forest. Set up now behind the bushes, the two guns opened up at a range of less than five hundred feet as the chopper drifted nearer.

Over the roar of the cannon, the attackers on the tower stairway heard the HE and incendiary shells smacking into the underside of the gunship's fuselage. Flame engulfed the aircraft. The tail section and the rear rotor dropped off. The AH-1G reared up like a startled horse and slid backward into the lake. The remaining missile exploded as the chopper hit the water. Another fireball seared the sky, raining blazing fragments across the steaming surface.

The rebel troops had taken the first gate house. Weaving left and right, they were sprinting across the bridge. Three of them were left immobile among the ruins of the demolished building along with eight or nine of the defenders. One of Ononu's soldiers, wounded in the belly, was vomiting among the fallen tiles. Another took to his heels and fled along the lakeshore road. A third had toppled from the bridge and floated faceup on the surface of scarlet-colored water.

Bolan and his companions passed the fifth floor and then the fourth. They saw no one. They were on the third when the Executioner realized that many of the ornately decorated apartments in the palace were in fact unused.

He saw stenciled crates stacked among acres of dusty gilt furniture; refrigerators, dishwashers and other electrical household appliances still sheathed in polyurethane reflected in vast eighteenth-century looking glasses. An alcove hung with green silk curtains and expensive tapestry housed a wooden box from Omnipol, the nationalized Czech arms manufacturer. Standing open on a marble occasional table, the box was packed with Skorpion machine pistols in oiled plastic wrappings.

The warrior and his band were halfway around the next staircase spiral when, with shocking loudness, automatic fire opened up on them from the floor below.

The rounds pulverized the stonework. One of the soldiers cried out as he was flung backward on the steps. He cursed, clapping a bloodied hand to the shoulder of his combat jacket.

Azzid, Bolan and the other soldier dropped below the balustrade. Bolan inched forward and down, circling the staircase's central core. Eleven stairs farther on, he could see through the balusters into a long hall floored with mosaic tile. Pillars faced with mirror glass supported the arched ceiling and a small lobby separated the room from the stairway.

It was from behind an alcove wall dividing this lobby that the gunman had fired. Bolan motioned to Azzid, higher up the stairs, to fire a couple of rounds from his AK-74. The soldier with him followed suit. As soon as the two burps of automatic fire died away, the guy reappeared to take a rapid snap shot at them.

Bolan caressed the MAC-11's trigger and the gun choked out two asthmatic rounds with no more noise than an apologetic butler's cough. The .45 ACP slugs carried away the top of the gunman's head, leaving a halo, rapidly tarnished, of blood and brain fragments. He fell full-length and his Uzi skittered away across the floor.

There was movement at the end of the long room. Bolan leaped down the last few stairs to the second-floor landing, panning left and right with the suppressor-extended barrel of the eleven-inch deathbringer.

He advanced into the lobby.

Flame blazed from beside a pillar in front of a ten-foot window in the far wall. One of the 9 mm parabellum rounds thunked into the alcove divider inches from his head. Another bullet nicked his webbing belt, shearing away a metal D-ring above the AutoMag holster. The hand grenade attached to the ring fell to the floor.

Azzid fired at the gunner's muzzle-flash. Glass erupted in a shower of silver rain as the Kalashnikov's killstream smashed across one of the mirrored pillars.

A shadowy figure flitted past the deep window embrasure. It was almost dark outside now, and it was hard to see clearly in the gloom of the vaulted room. But there was more movement, quickly stilled, on the opposite side of the window.

Azzid fired again. More glass shattered and fell. The soldier was firing down the stairwell, trying to repulse an attack from below.

As the colonel's AK spit fire for the third time, lightning flashed vividly across the angry sky, followed almost at once by a prolonged roll of thunder overhead. The livid blue brilliance, reflected a thousand times, in all the colors of the spectrum, from a thousand glass shards scattered over the mosaic floor, gave Bolan an idea.

He picked up the grenade, primed it and rolled it along the floor toward the window.

The enemy's exact position was of no importance. The spherical missile, an M-50 plastic shell charged with fifty grams of explosive, hit the wall and burst with earsplitting concussion. The blast, spreading steel beads traveling at eighteen thousand feet per second, scythed through the dusk to shatter the rest of the pillared glass.

A storm of razor-sharp fragments cut the two killers to ribbons. Once more the lightning flashed—and this time the myriad points of reflected radiance showed red.

Bolan ran back to the stairway. Outside the tower, rain hissed down into the lake.

Ogano's men had taken the second guardhouse and invaded the palace courtyard. They were under fire from the long, shuttered windows on three sides of the great graveled rectangle. But there was cover behind and beneath half a dozen cars and military trucks parked there. The crew with the cannon had rushed them over the bridge: from beneath Ononu's personal, customized, ivory-colored Rolls-Royce, the twin guns slammed 40 mm shells at the huge iron-studded doors barring the main entrance to the summer palace.

One of the doors was burning. Smoke rolled up the double staircase at the far end of the entrance hall and invaded the mezzanine. It penetrated to the floor above and billowed around the tough members of the emperor's personal guard, whose guns were pinning down Bolan and his companions on the stairway inside the octagonal tower.

There were seven or eight of these Oriwady paratroopers, each of them steel-muscled and over six feet tall. They were deployed behind two Egyptian stone coffins at the entrance to the great reception hall, on the far side of a balustrade circling the central stairway, and in the shelter of seventeenth-century furniture pulled out from the walls.

Bolan, Azzid and the soldier were safe as long as they remained around the final bend in the spiral staircase. But while the paratroopers were in position they dared not advance. Bolan was unwilling to use a second grenade. He could hear women's voices from the room beyond the coffins, together with a loud bellow that he took to be Ononu issuing orders to his troops. It was possible that the tyrant had placed the hostages at the entrance to his command post, a living stockade to protect his imperial majesty. If that was the case, and the doors to the great hall were open, a bomb explosion could render the positive half of Bolan's personal crusade null and void.

He touched Azzid on the arm. "Random shots," he whispered. "Just poke the muzzle around the corner and fire, okay?"

The colonel nodded. Passing the message on to the enlisted man, he risked a single rapid burst with his head and shoulders exposed. There was a thunderous volley of automatic fire in response. Stone chips flew, ricochets screeched off pillars, the acrid odor of cordite overpowered the smoke from below.

After that, both men contented themselves with single shots fired blind, as the Executioner had suggested.

The warrior, crouched below the level of the balustrade, was speeding back up the stairs. When he had made almost a complete circuit of the tower, he stopped and peered down into the hallway.

The black paratroopers were crouched behind their ornate shelters, every sense angled toward the curve of stairs and the two gun muzzles sporadically erupting with potential death. Two of them, hidden by a sideboard, were surreptitiously sliding the piece to one side so they could get a clear field of fire on the stairway.

Bolan climbed to the top of the balustrade and jumped. An avenging angel, with fire spurting from his arm, he leaped down, spraying silent annihilation left and right.

The defenders were taken completely by surprise. four of them fell at once before the Executioner's onslaught. Two more, springing upright and whirling to frame the big guy in their fields of fire, were mowed down from behind as Azzid and the soldier, on cue, jumped down from the stairway and pumped out a staccato hail of lead.

A crescendo of shouts, stamping feet, wood splintering and a succession of different caliber shots announced that the men of the besieging force had burst their way into the palace.

Fanned by a wind whistling through the shattered doors, the fire below burned more brightly; the smoke roiling up to the other floors billowed more densely.

The remaining paratroopers, bewildered by the presence of enemies on all sides, lost their cool.

One emptied the whole magazine of his Uzi at Azzid's soldier. Hurled back against the stairs, the man died instantly, his body torn almost in two by the 9 mm fusillade.

A heartbeat later, the gunner also dropped, victim of a single deafening shot from Bolan's AutoMag.

Another bodyguard decided to call it quits, flung down his SMG and raised his hands. Foolishly, he then thought better of it and raced for the main stairway—where he was instantly cut down by Ogano's invaders, sweeping up to liaise with their colonel.

Thirty seconds more fighting and the battle was over. Ononu's personal guard lay among the wrecked furniture, slumped on bloodstained and bullet-riddled upholstery, sightless eyes staring upward. Apart from the two casualties sustained by Bolan's small party, Ogano had lost an officer and three more men rushing the palace, plus another wounded who sat nursing a shattered knee at the top of the stairs.

Led by Bolan and Azzid, the remainder of the force burst into the great reception hall.

A confused impression of women screaming, black servants huddled among some cheap wooden chairs in front of what seemed to be a stage, a man in white uniform with gold epaulets pointing a revolver at a small group of white girls. Behind him, bullish in a pale suit with his dark face a mask of rage, Ononu stood unarmed by the marble table.

"A step farther and one of the girls dies!" General Shagari shouted.

Azzid and the invaders stumbled to a halt. Ogano, uncertain, moved slightly ahead, then he, too, paused.

"Move again and two of the bitches go!" Shagari yelled.

Behind the colonel, half-hidden by his lean figure, Bolan had slid the silenced Beretta from its shoulder rig. Now he laid the barrel on Azzid's own shoulder, sucked in his breath, held it and shot the revolver from the general's hand.

Shagari jumped back with a cry of rage and pain, shaking blood from his ravaged fingers. Coolly, Bolan placed a second shot through the left side of the man's chest, transforming the multicolored medal ribbons into a uniform scarlet.

The general jerked backward and collapsed with arms and legs outflung across the marble table, a grotesque parody of the atrocities committed there previously.

Azzid and his men rushed forward.

Ononu whisked through a door in back of the huge hall. "The radio room!" Azzid cried. "He mustn't get to the transmitter!"

"I'll take him," Bolan rasped. "You mop up down here."

The Ingram's magazine was exhausted. He flung it beside the body on the table and sprinted for the doorway. Beyond it was a long passage leading to service stairs. From overhead, Bolan could hear heavy feet pounding. He unleathered both handguns and took the stairs three at a time.

A corridor ornamented by statues in niches...doors swinging...twittering cries of fright as servants disappeared...a fleeting view of rooms rich with silk and velvet hangings, piled with cushions in Oriental splendor.

And the squat back of the tyrant vanishing around a pillar at the far end.

Bolan accelerated. The pillar was one of four around a stairwell. Below, a checkerboard marble hallway; three floors above, a glassed-in cupola loud with the pelting rain.

Ononu was halfway up the stairs to the next floor.

Beyond the cupola, lightning flared, bathing the well with its sickly brilliance. Shadows flickered and danced around the curving walls. The lights dimmed. More lightning flashed, and the shadows danced again.

Including the shadows of three men, suddenly revealed, posted at the bend before the next landing.

Bolan dropped, sighted the Beretta, fired. A shape jerked up, toppled over the railing above and fell, screaming, down the well to the checkerboard floor.

One more pawn out of the game, the Executioner thought with a momentary pang of compassion. The lights brightened. He squeezed out two more rounds, wasted a second man. How many more moves before he could checkmate the king?

Gunshots flashed and reverberated as he scrambled to his feet, feeling the wind of the slugs stir his hair. The shooter was half-hidden behind an ottoman on the other side of the landing.

Only half-hidden.

The Beretta clicked. No more shells. At once Big Thunder roared, splashing the wall with blood. Behind the pillars, running footsteps receded; the others were calling it a day.

Bolan kicked the Uzi away from the nerveless hands behind the stuffed seat and continued the chase.

Ononu was barreling up a staircase that circled a turret at the southeast corner of the palace. At the top, beneath the roof, Bolan knew, was the dictator's private broadcasting studio. The warrior poured on all the speed he could muster.

Panting, he burst into the circular room.

He saw dials, tape spools, rheostat levers. He saw pilot lights winking blue and red. He saw the tyrant's huge black hand wrapped around a transportable microphone.

Bolan had one shot left in the AutoMag. He turned away from Ononu. The all-important task was to ensure that no word from the soon-to-be deposed emperor was transmitted.

He fired at the outlet where the mike was plugged in. The plastic backplate shivered; brass terminals, screws, lengths of copper wire and bright scraps of insulation leaped from the wall. A minor lightning flash and the pilot lamps faded and died. Before the echoes of the shot had died away, the tape spools stopped turning.

Ononu's suppressed rage was terrible. There was foam at the corners of his mouth. His arms, gorilla-long, hung motionless at his sides, the fingers twitching.

"It would be interesting to know," he said thickly, "what brings a renegade mercenary, a killer wanted even by the lackeys of capitalist decadence, into my country."

"A private mission," Bolan said. "We call it seek and destroy."

"Destroy!" Ononu's voice rose suddenly to a screech. "You talk of destruction? An impudent hired bully consorting with convicts in an attempt to overthrow a lawful regime? I think I will not kill you at first. I shall break your back and have you publicly exposed as the criminal you are."

"You're a little out of date," Bolan said. "You don't have a public anymore. It's finished. Azzid's men broadcast from Bomiko-Kassi a half hour ago, announcing that you were overthrown. You're through and the army's in power now."

With a yell of rage, Ononu charged at the warrior, like an enraged bull, hamlike fists flailing, in the hope of knocking Bolan aside with the sheer weight of his body and getting out.

Bolan stood solid as a rock. He drew back his right fist and slammed the African over the heart with all his strength.

Ononu's stride didn't even falter. The Executioner was astonished at the man's strength. He punched him again, hard, in the solar plexus. The blow, which would have felled most men and left them crying for breath, scarcely made the African blink.

Bolan rode a haymaker and hit the man, flat-handed, on the side of the neck, temporarily paralyzing a nerve. This time Ononu went down, gasping for air. But he was tough. He came up again, swinging a roundhouse left that caught Bolan on the side of the head and knocked him against one of the tape decks.

The emperor came in again, clawing for the Executioner's eyes. Bolan pushed himself off the steel chassis and brought his laced hands ferociously down on the back of Ononu's neck.

He dropped for the second time. As he struggled to rise, Bolan kicked him on the jaw. "That's for the girls you callously used,'' he said, panting, kicking him again and smashing his nose. ''And that's for the lives you took needlessly in order to get your dirty hands on them.''

Ononu spit out a broken tooth. A curtain of blood linked his nose and chin. ''Those little bitches?'' he choked. ''That white trash? Why, after the first time they loved it; they couldn't get enough—''

The words were blocked in his throat. Anger lent Mack Bolan an awesome strength. He picked up the ex-dictator bodily and hurled him through the arched window beside the transmitting console.

Frame and glass exploded outward as the squat form hurtled through. For an instant Ononu was limned in fire as lightning flashed again. Then he dropped with a wild cry down into the darkness and the rain.

It seemed to Bolan a long time later that he heard the splash as Ononu plunged into the deep water at the foot of the tower.

Chapter Fourteen

Mack Bolan never knew exactly what it was that made him decide to stay with . . . with what? It wasn't a mission: nobody was briefing him. It was no longer a crusade: there was no visible enemy to overcome. There didn't even seem to be a specific problem to solve.

His original aims, moreover, had been achieved: Rinaldi's evil organization was broken, Suzanne Bozuffi and the others would be returned to their fathers, Ononu's dictatorship was finished and his small country would now be ruled by more reasonable men.

But something still nagged at him. The dossier, which should have been tagged Mission Completed and filed away, obstinately stayed open. Was it simply because everything that had happened so far seemed a little too neat, too pat? Did the Executioner's subconscious mind, ever alert to the nuances of wrongdoing, evaluate the material and find the organization just a little too smart for such banal considerations as kidnapping, blackmail and mineral rights?

Partly—there could be no doubt about this—his decision was influenced by the newspaperman, Jason Mettner. But there was, too, the evidence of the extra hostage.

Bolan returned from the tower studio to join Azzid and the others in the reception hall.

Suzanne Bozuffi, long red hair tumbled about her shoulders, still shuddering after her interrupted ordeal, was naked under a blanket held over her by a tall, willowy blonde. Bolan knew from the photos that this was Joy Helder, daughter of the plastics king. In a corner with two scared-looking black female servants was a voluptuous brunette he took to be Rachel Meyerbeer.

The youngest girl was tapping an impatient foot and looking out the window at the continuous flashes of lightning illuminating the torrential rain.

Seventeen-year-old Palomar Varzi.

To Bolan's surprise there was a fifth young woman in the room—white joggers with padded ankles, fawn corduroy jeans and an orange shirt that did nothing to hide the swell of splendid breasts. She, too, was dark-haired, with a wide, sensuous mouth and brown eyes beneath straight black brows. She looked a little, maybe five years, older than the others.

Ruth Elias, she said in answer to Bolan's question. She had been taken at night from a hotel room in Milan.

"Does your father have anything to do with the mining corporation in this country?" he asked.

She frowned, shook her head. "My father died ten years ago," she said. "He was an academic, a professor of French history."

"My mistake," Bolan said. "So why did Ononu snatch you?"

Ruth Elias shrugged. "Maybe it was just because I was white, because I was there, because he wanted to show how... well, how big he was."

"Maybe," Bolan said. He turned to the other four girls.

Azzid, Ogano and the other officers, outraged by their story, had already made soothing noises. Bolan feeling a little embarrassed, added his voice.

One curious thing emerged from their tactful questioning: the youngest hostage, Palomar Varzi, had been neither raped nor tortured.

"Why do you figure you were passed over?" Bolan inquired. "It sure wasn't kindness on Ononu's part, or consideration for your age. Were you the last in line or something?"

The seventeen-year-old shrugged. "I don't know. I was in the same room as the others. We had the same food, the same attention. Look, when are we going to get out of here?"

"It can't have been that, anyway," Ruth Elias put in before Bolan could answer. "He... he abused the rest of us several times. In no particular order. He seemed to have a special hate for Suzy and me. We... well, I think we got the worst of it. More often than the others, too."

"I guess you were just lucky," Bolan said to the Varzi girl. "We'll get you out of here as soon as we can, probably early tomorrow morning, once we arrange transport to the airport."

Colonel Azzid then drew Bolan aside to report total success of the takeover. The Yanga tribesmen whom Ogano had not been able to recruit in time had neutralized the second AH-1G chopper and talked the army units at Oulad into supporting the coup. The radio announcement had been well received. Police had rounded up the few Oriwady extremists who might have caused trouble. There was dancing in the streets of Kondani and Halakaz. All that remained, once the palace had been cleaned up and the wounded attended to, was to contact the girls' fathers, the press and diplomatic circles in the capitals where Montenegria was represented.

All that remained for the Montenegrians.

For the Executioner it was only the start of a long road.

Departure point was a stray remark, a word of sympathy for Ruth Elias, with whom Bolan found himself by chance alone in the reception hall the following morning, in the center of all that frenzied activity. Having no anxious father waiting, she had tactfully drawn back while arrangements to repatriate the four other girls were rushed through.

"I guess you'll want to go *some*place," Bolan said. "I don't think this country will hold too much attraction for you, even with new rulers."

"I'll go back to Milan," she said.

"You work there?"

"I work all over. Milan this week, maybe Caracas next."

"What do you do?"

"The current term is market research," she said.

"Who buys what, and why?"

She smiled. "In my line, it's more who does what, and why?"

"I get it. Career girl! Still, even for a sophisticated woman of the world, even if you hadn't led a sheltered life like the others, what happened here . . ." Bolan hesitated. Then he said awkwardly, "I mean it must have been . . . well, pretty tough."

"It was bad." She folded her arms and hugged herself across the orange-shirted bosom. "It was real bad, and that's for sure. But it was just personal, for each one of us a private hell. What that son of a bitch was doing over in the Ogodishu and Gabotomi was hell for a whole people."

"The Ogodishu?"

"It's not a country, it's a region. Thirty thousand square miles of nothing, east and a bit south of here. I'm not even sure where the boundaries run, but it's located like somewhere between Chad, Cameroon and the Central African Republic."

"And what's happening there?"

"Nothing. That's just the point."

Bolan's eyebrows rose.

"It's a famine area," Ruth Elias explained. "Mile after mile of cracked earth, no grass, no living tree, only the skeletons of animals that have died of thirst. And the people, dying of hunger and thirst as well."

The Executioner nodded. "I don't mean to be callous, but that kind of thing is happening in many parts of the world. What's so—"

"You don't understand," the brunette interrupted. "This drought has been deliberately engineered; the famine is man-made, for a specific purpose."

Bolan stared at her. "Man-made?"

"Two rivers ran through the area. They didn't amount to much but they carried enough water for irrigation ditches to be run off here and there, for the tribal population to grow a few patches of corn, maybe raise a few animals. It was a wretched existence, but it was life."

"So what happened?"

"Three years ago, when the forecasts promised extra low rainfall for some while, the rivers were diverted. One was dammed and the outfall directed away from the region; the other was simply channeled into a different course, through a gulch that had been blasted in a bluff originally containing the flow. Result: the vegetation died."

"But why?"

"Slave labor. People dying of hunger will work twenty hours a day for peanuts."

"Why didn't the people move where the water had gone?"

"Tradition. They're not nomads. Warlike tribes who'd keep them out. Plus a deliberate policy by the crooks who stole the rivers, shooting them down if they transgressed. A kind of controlled genocide."

"You're right. I still don't understand," Bolan said. "Who are these people? Why do they need slave labor?"

"I only know what I've been told. It seems there's a particular valley on the fringe of this region that can be watered from the dam...and the climatic conditions in this valley, with the unlimited water relieving the natural dryness, make it ideal for ultraintensive cultivation of a certain crop.

"What crop?"

"Opium poppies."

Bolan whistled. "And the slave labor...?"

"Grown this way, the bumper crop requires a lot of attention. And the cheaper the labor, the higher the profit."

"Okay. But why would they bother? In the middle of Africa?"

"Two reasons. Stuff originating in the Golden Triangle—Laos, Cambodia, Burma, up in that corner—it's becoming more and more difficult to shift it without problems. The routes are too well-known, security in most countries is tightening all the time, so it costs more and more to keep clear of the narcotics squads. Nobody had found this particular route yet."

"Which is?"

Ruth Elias shrugged. "I guess they pass the refined product out through Angola or one of these Communist states—the comrades would be only too pleased if the whole of the West was to get hooked and stoned out of its mind. They'd help all they could. After that it'd be shipped to one of the old Portuguese Atlantic islands—Madeira or even Tenerife—and flown from there to Europe."

"You mentioned refined product. You mean the extraction is done right there in that valley?"

"That's the second reason," the girl told him. "You see, the normal alkaloid yield from opium—basically morphine and its derivatives—is between eight and twelve percent by weight. Well, with their system, the poppy seeds swell bigger with a more severe desiccation and the yield climbs to fifteen, maybe sixteen percent."

"But refining the morphine base into heroin is a delicate and dangerous process. You need highly qualified chemists to get away with it."

"Highly qualified chemists they've got. And the most up-to-date laboratories and equipment. All out in the open. Who's going to start police raids in the Ogodishu?"

"The entire crop's turned into heroin?"

"I would think. Because they have an extra advantage there, too. Weight for weight, heroin's normally three times less active than morphine. Theirs is half as active—two times less, if you like. So they're coining more money per square yard of cultivation down the line."

Bolan nodded. "Cheaper labor, higher yields, safer routes. Something smells to high heaven here. What did Ononu have to do with it?"

"He was interested financially...both ways. He put up some of the original capital; the bastard organized the famine, it was his idea. And now that it's all systems go... well, the kind of money he'd have gotten from renegotiated mining rights here would be chicken feed compared with the profit from the Ogodishu connection."

"That's some crazy market research you're into," Bolan said. "How come you know about all of this?"

"I'm a good listener. It's part of my job. I heard Ononu and that General Shagari talking a couple of times."

Bolan stared at the woman thoughtfully. The drug industry and the evil it entrained, the young lives it ruined, the crime its enormous profits bred, these had always been high on his list of targets, even when the Mafia was not involved.

"How far away is this valley from here?"

"I don't know exactly. It must be more than a thousand miles."

Bolan pursed his lips. "If Ononu had a stake in it, then it must be part of this operation here in a way. I mean part of the cleaning-up routine. I think I'll take a look at the place."

"Good idea!" an unexpected voice drawled. "Let me drive you there."

Bolan and the girl swung around. A tall, thin man with a cigarette drooping from one corner of his mouth was leaning indolently against a marble pillar on one side of the hall's entrance doors.

It was the newspaperman, Jason Mettner.

"What the hell are you doing here?" Bolan demanded.

Mettner grinned. "Working. I'm following up a story."

"How long have you been here?"

"Long enough."

"How did you get here?"

"Funny you should ask that. Soon as I heard about the jailbreak, I figured it might have something to do with this dump, so I rented a jalopy and headed this way. In the middle of the night, along one of those forest trails, I happened on an abandoned Land Rover. According to the license on the steering column it belonged to some Montemines consulting engineer. Guess whose face was on the license card?"

"You drove my Land Rover here?"

"Out of the kindness of my news hawk's heart," Mettner said. "I thought you might need it, and now I see you do. So how about making me your co-driver on the road to the east?"

Bolan frowned. He liked to work alone. On the other hand, a co-driver would halve the driving time. He had been impressed by the tactful way Mettner had handled the Rinaldi affair, contriving a sensational scoop without once mentioning Bolan or his part in it. Perhaps it wouldn't be so bad, having a professional along who would print a firsthand exposé of this latest drug scourge.

Apart from which, he liked the guy!

"Okay, Mettner," he said. "You got yourself a job."

Chapter Fifteen

At the desk in his hotel room, Jason Mettner began to reread his story before sending it to Allard Fielding. He planted his feet on the desktop, and slid back his chair as his eyes scanned the first page.

Believe me, Al, Mettner read, the trip we just made was unbelievable. You've heard the word desolation? Forget it and invent a new one. Overpopulation? The number of frontiers we passed outnumbered the people we saw by around seventy to one. The ones who were still alive, that is.

We had mountains, forests, desert and jungle, canyons and plains. But twelve hundred miles in a straight line? It felt more like twelve thousand by the time we arrived. Whoever heard of a straight line in *Africa*, for crying out loud.

I said when we arrived. But arrived where? It was like someone pulled the chain to let the sand and the shale out of the Sahara and this was where most of it had touched down.

"You'll be getting a color piece on this journey by separate mail. But I want you to read this as background to the drug story, *Taking the H out of the Sahara*. It's strictly For-Your-Eyes-Only material, but it should explain how a nameless one-man army flying no flags could do what it did.

Bolan won't be mentioned by name. That was the deal.

We spent several lifetimes bumping across a stretch of country that God must have had left on his hands when He was through with Nevada and Arizona. You know: sagebrush, thorn trees, a line of hills that was never closer than eighty miles.

Without really paying attention, we'd been climbing some, and suddenly the land fell away: we were on the crest of a ridge...and below us there was this colossal saucer-shaped depression, the Ogodishu.

As far as the eye could see in every direction there was this dust bowl that looked like every cracked-earth, PBS-television documentary on drought that you ever switched off.

Nothing moved. No place. Dry sticks instead of trees, brown straw where once there might have been crops, bones and skulls by the dried-up water holes, dead villages where the people looked like black skin draped over the skeletons of thorn bushes.

In that region, even the buzzards were thirsty. We had a crate of beer with us. Every time we stopped the Land Rover, I expected to get knocked down in the rush.

Iron rations, cans of beer, a dull drive across interminable wastelands—naturally two guys in a red-hot oven with wheels, stinking of gas fumes and sweat, get to talking. Bolan didn't talk much but I felt I got to know the guy a little on this trip. Because of what I found out, I'm writing this, like I say, to fill you in. Because for my money the guy himself is at least as interesting as the story.

You see, Al, this is no flat-eyed, coldhearted killing machine. Ruthless the man is, yeah. But not callous. He's a deadly fighter but he does have a conscience. Plus, despite his kill score, a load of compassion.

The way he sees it, Uncle Sam trained him to be a soldier; it's the only skill he has, so he stays with it. But since Nam the enemy has changed, that's all. The battalions he fights now are no longer Indochinese guerrillas but what he calls the mercenaries of evil, the legions of animal man.

The key to this warrior's character is Justice—and you should leave that J in caps. "My targets are soldiers, too," he told me one time while I was at the wheel and it was his turn to breathe in the dust cloud from the passenger seat. "They chose to serve in the ranks of organized crime or the international terrorist conspiracy, people whose lust for power blinds them to how much innocent blood they spill. I don't aim to pass judgment on this scum. In my book they are already condemned by their own actions. All I do is hand out the sentence they deserve."

You see what I mean, Al? In Jason Mettner's book, on the other hand, this guy was only doing what governments, law enforcement agencies and the armies of the world were too scared, too corrupt or too hemmed in by bureaucracy to do themselves: the dirty work they themselves trained him to carry out.

He lays his life on the line each hour of every day in a personal battle to preserve what he believes in—the values these others are so quick to promote and so slow to defend.

I'm telling you this because it goes some way to explain the guy's actions when we reached the far side of the new desert.

Finally there was a far side. Lack of vegetation had allowed the wind to do its worst. We passed through erosion of all kinds. Baked mud, powdered earth, dunes, places where the land had already been stripped to naked rock. But at last we thumped over another low ridge and there was this incredible sight.

Some way off, Bolan had told me, there was a dam, and away to the south a river had been diverted through another ridge. Even so the vision was one hundred percent unexpected.

A winding valley maybe one mile across and several miles long, brimming with vibrant color!

Amid this desolation of gray was a shimmering sea of candy pink, washing rose-tinted waves against the walls of the valley in the evening wind:

Opium poppy—a gold mine above the ground, given continuous care and the right specialized fertilizers. The bulbous, flat-capped seeds, when properly dried, are worth a fortune.

The higher yield, Bolan told me, was due to the particular conditions, climatic and otherwise, of the chosen site.

They sure were particular. Apart from the sight of a candy-colored ocean of flowers in the middle of a dead sea that only washed up the bones of extinct beasts, there was the question of the real water and the headquarters from which the creation of the dead sea had been cold-bloodedly planned.

The real water? Yeah, like on the Capitol lawns—thousands of sprinklers, each with its private rainbow, packed closely all along the countless rows of blooms, spiraling droplets into the hot air, and over the army of thin, drenched workers bent above the plants.

Beyond, low down along the horizon, our binoculars showed us stone-built huts, a wooden mess hall, warehouses, a drying plant, glass-roofed laboratories and something that looked very like a blockhouse behind a chain link fence.

We were approaching the place from the south west. Farther north in the manufactured desert, Bolan had been told, there would be vigilante patrols something like the notorious Selous Scouts in Rhodesia, their job to head off any of the starving tribesmen reckless enough to make a break for the country where the rivers flowed.

Right here, as our dust cloud drew nearer, we could see armed guards between the blockhouse and the gates in the chain fence. Outside the fence there was a fleet of ancient cattle trucks and, beyond, a strip with a Piper Cherokee tethered against the wind.

Bolan stopped the Land Rover when we were halfway around the perimeter track that circled the poppy fields. He toted a hidden compartment packed with arms and that was disguised as a second spare gas tank. Some of the stuff had been used up in the jailbreak and the attack on Ononu's palace, but there was plenty left. He came up with a selection, replaced the floorboards and climbed back behind the wheel.

He had unscrewed the suppressor from an Ingram, which reduced the scattergun's length, with the wire stock retracted, to no more than eleven inches. Even with a 30-round magazine clipped in, the deadly little

SMG could easily be concealed beneath the oversize cotton bush jacket that he wore. So could his holstered Beretta, the AutoMag and a selection of grenades.

As he drove, he issued my instructions, the orders that were to coincide with his own planned assault schedule. The briefing was succinct: it could be encapsulated in five words.

Stay put and do nothing.

By the time we pulled up outside the gates it was almost dusk, and for the first time in two days there was color in the western sky—a pale reflection of the evil flowers filling the valley. Water from the sprinklers lay down and died. Two of the cattle trucks, loaded with emaciated tribesmen, had already passed us on their way back to the dead villages in the wasteland where the sweatshop workers lived.

Overseers were herding the rest of the men out from among the rows of poppies and into the remaining trucks. Each man was searched before he left—in case he was trying to smuggle out a can of water, I guess. They packed fifty or sixty tribesmen into the rear of each truck.

A third group stood in line outside the open door of a storehouse, handing in crop-spraying equipment, backpack reservoirs, flexible nozzled tubes and stuff like that. The overseers were shouting at them, and several times I heard the crack of a whip.

It's not often that Bolan curses. But then he said in a barely audible voice: "By the time I leave, not one of the fucking bastards that ran this hellhole is going to be alive."

He pulled up on the hand brake savagely and we slid to a final halt. The armed guards on duty were standing in a row with their submachine guns unslung—as ugly a group of heavies as I'd seen outside of a presidential motorcade or a waterfront bar in Marseille. They looked suspicious. I guess no more than thirty or forty Land Rovers registered in Montenegria pass that way in a normal day's work.

Bolan waited for the last truck to pass through the gates and then he eased himself out from behind the wheel and walked casually toward the guards. A tall dude, clearly in shape, with eyes like chips of blue ice.

"This is private property," the meanest of the guards growled.

Bolan ignored him. "Don't close them, I'm coming in," he said politely enough to two guys dragging the gates closed.

They stopped and stared at him.

A fourth sentry hefted his SMG and snarled, "Who the fuck are you? Nobody gets in here."

"On your way," the first man said.

"I have a message from Emperor Ononu," said Bolan. He slid a hand between the edges of his jacket.

"Oh, yeah? What kind of message?"

"This kind," Bolan rasped. And then—it was the most extraordinary thing I ever saw—somehow he fired that Ingram from under his jacket. Half the magazine in one damn burst!

The cyclic rate of that baby is 1,145 rounds per minute. It sounded like ripping calico with the volume increased a million percent. Bolan swiveled left, right, left, holding the Ingram hard against his hip, stitching a figure eight across and through those hoods before even the one with his weapon at the ready could clench his finger around the trigger.

The sentries were spread all over the ground between the gates. I never saw such a lacework of scarlet sinking into Mother Earth, not even when I was on the crime beat.

The engine of the Land Rover was still running. Bolan beat out the flame licking around the scorched edges of the hole in his jacket and made it back, cool as the ice in his eyes, to take the wheel. We gunned into the compound.

There were guys running out of the blockhouse. To block us. Tough dudes in khaki shorts and safari jackets like the gatemen, each of them with some kind of shooter.

Bolan lifted a hand from the controls and lobbed a grenade.

A puff of smoke and an orange flash.

When the smoke cleared there were more guys lying dead on the ground. Bolan then jumped down from the jalopy, kicked open the door of what looked like an HQ building and blazed his way in there with that Ingram, choking out the rest of the clip.

I followed my orders. I stayed in the passenger seat. Over the knocking of my knees, I heard several more separate shots from inside, deeper toned, from more than one gun. From more than Bolan's two. Finally he came out alone.

Suddenly, from the cook house, the stores, the mess hall, there was a clatter of the inhabitants running *away* from us.

The big guy had a light in his eye. He motioned me to take the wheel, then slammed a fresh magazine into the Ingram.

"I aim to make this quick and I'll make it merciful," he told me, "but I'm sure as hell aiming to make it final. If there's any more shooting back at us," he said, "get down, the bulkhead's bulletproof."

I swallowed twice, but again I followed my orders. He followed the escapers.

I'm not going to detail the hits, Al. You'll find the count itemized in my story, anyway.

All I'll say is that by the time we left, Bolan had made good his word. There must have been twenty or thirty drug traffickers, technicians or enforcement men strewed around whose eyes were never going to open on tomorrow—many of whose guts were already open on today.

All of it due to surprise, quick decisions, *action*. And, of course, guts.

One way or another.

If the big guy had hesitated during that first eyeballing at the gates, he'd have been drilled a dozen times over before I could scream, "No, not me!" We won't even mention the time it took to make the blockhouse. As it was, he had them on the run from the start and gave yours truly a lesson on what one single guy with no fear and plenty of determination can do.

Correction. I said he made good his word. He'd promised there wouldn't be one man left alive. In the end there was one.

It could have been two if Bolan wasn't such a good shot.

Cleaning up, we saw them on the outside of the chain fence, two heavyset characters running like crazy toward a Chevy Blazer 4X4. One of them carried a canvas bag; the other wore a city hat.

Bolan dropped the guy in the hat with a single shot from the Beretta.

The one with the bag made it to the 4X4 and roared off on the far side of the Piper Cherokee in a cloud of dust.

"Are you going after him?" I asked.

Bolan shook his head. "By the time we turned this buggy around and made it back to the gates, he'd be long gone. Let him take the money or the shit or whatever he has, and tell the tale. It's more important to finish what we came here to do."

What we'd come to do was wreck the joint so thoroughly that it could never again be used as a horse factory. Bolan already had fixed ideas about the way to do this.

He went through those buildings, jerking out drawers, ravaging shelves, piling papers and files on floors. There were drums of kerosene in the stores, there was a gasoline dump and there were acid carboys in the labs. Bolan was going to torch the place.

To make quite sure, he placed several small packages of C-4, which he produced from his private arsenal in the Land Rover, in certain strategic places.

"What about the truck drivers when they fly back to the nest?" I asked. "And these patrols you say are out there discouraging the tribesmen from leaving their reserve?"

"If they show before we're through, they get zapped," he said with a shrug he must have learned while he was in Italy. "If not . . . well, there'll be no reason for them to stick around here."

The way things turned out, it was not.

I didn't get to see the inside of the labs. Bolan had found other duties for me by then. But I know he happened on one of the top men holed up in an office there, that Bolan leaned on him until he came across with certain intel, that the guy tried to soft-talk Bolan but he wasn't having any.

"He tried to buy me off by saying he was unarmed," Bolan told me afterward.

I'd heard a single shot from the AutoMag before Bolan finally came out. I figured it was his business; it was better to stay quiet as ordered.

Before I could have gotten out a question, in any case, the laboratory went up into the air like a volcano. It was quite dark by then, but the flames lent us enough light to set off the other Independence Day celebrations we'd arranged.

It didn't take long.

You heard about hell on earth? Well, by the time we'd got it all going, this was the blueprint.

The sky-high blaze was reflected in the dark surface of the water flowing out across the dry earth from the fractured pipes.

Bolan used the light to hang a final Indian sign on the traffickers' operation.

There were crop-spraying tanks fitted each side of the Cherokee's modified fuselage. Bolan knocked out the stoppers and allowed the contents to gurgle away.

He'd saved a couple of containers of sulfuric acid from the labs. The steaming liquid went into one of the empty tanks. He filled the other from a drum of herbicide he found up by the filtration plant. Then he climbed into the Cherokee's cockpit and fired up the plane's engine.

He leaned out from the cabin before he closed the door. "The wind's blowing away from the compound," he yelled down at me, "but you better find a length of cloth, dip it in the water that's going to waste over there and tie it over your mouth and nose. You don't want a lungful of the stuff I'll be laying down here."

You know me, Al, I did what I was told.

By this time Bolan had taken off, circled the valley a couple of times and made an approach run, low down over the flaming outpost. The Cherokee zoomed over the fence at around twenty feet and flew out across the sea of poppies.

Once clear of the compound, Bolan pulled whatever you pull to feed the stuff in the tanks to the spray nozzles. For the first few hundred yards, I could see a pale mist, pulsating in the light of the fires, roll out on either side of the airplane and settle slowly on the close-packed blooms. After that there was just the diminishing drone of the engine until the aircraft made the far end of the valley, climbed, banked and came in for a return run. He made three double runs, six passes in all, over those opium poppies until the two tanks were dry.

With that noxious mixture on the plants, like he said, nobody was going to refine any heroin from *that* crop again!

He taxied back to the end of the strip, switched off and walked across to the Land Rover. We'd refueled before we sent up the gasoline dump. "Okay," he told me, "that's it. We'll be on our way. We can camp for the night someplace near this famous dam."

"On our way where?" I asked.

"Out."

"Do you need the Rover that bad? Why don't we take the plane? It'd be much quicker."

"Uh-uh," he said. "It's already night, and that crate has no navigation lights. I have no flight plan, no aerial charts, no means of knowing which way the airfields that interest me lie. Apart from which the fuel tanks are close to dry."

"That isn't the real reason, is it?"

He looked at me, the flickering light making his hawk face more enigmatic than usual. "Maybe not," he said. "This isn't the end of the road. The scum running this place were only the hired help. They had—still have—very powerful connections. Okay, we killed their operation here. But there will be others. Meanwhile, the connections are going to be mad. The patrols, when they come back, are going to radio out a report. If we took this plane, it would be marked for destruction all over Africa. If we didn't run into a mountain or get shot down by frontier guards, there'd be pursuit planes, missiles maybe, homing on us before we'd made fifty miles."

"Connections *that* powerful?" I queried.

He nodded. "I'm not joking. This is big time stuff. The only living person who knows we travel in a Land Rover, on the other hand, is the guy in that Chevy. And he isn't going to stop running until morning. By which time we'll have made other arrangements."

"You learned something from the guy in the lab, didn't you?" I accused him. "Something you're keeping from me."

"Maybe, maybe not."

"You're not going to let me in on it? I thought we were on a share-and-share deal?"

"We were until now," Bolan said. "I kept my end of the bargain. You got an exclusive, on an illegal drug ring smashed. Be happy with that and don't push your luck."

I sighed. "Okay, where do we go from here?"

"I'll tell you exactly," he said. "We're heading south to Berberati and Libenge, and then we cross over into Zaire and drive southeast to Lisala. After that we follow the Zaire River to Kisangani—which I still prefer to call Stanleyville. There's an international airport there, and we're both going to need it."

"Whatever you say," I said. "And from the airport?"

"You take a plane to wherever you want. I have my own route mapped out."

"I get it," I said. "End of story."

"That's right," he said, climbing behind the wheel and starting the engine. "And until we get to Stanleyville, we travel by night...."

And that, Jason Mettner read on the last page of his letter to Allard Fielding, really was the end of that particular story. I'm writing this in the Palm Lounge of the Kisangani Hilton. Or is it the Stanleyville Holiday Inn? You never know these days. Tomorrow I take a UTA Boeing to Paris, France.

I'll telex you from the Paris bureau.

Jason Mettner folded the pages and slipped them into an envelope. Then he drummed his fingers on the desk, wondering where Mack Bolan was at that moment.

Chapter Sixteen

Four thousand feet above sea level, four floors up from the street, Mack Bolan clung to a ledge outside the open window of a police office on John Vorster Square in Johannesburg.

It was dark. Inside the office two men sat on opposite sides of a desk illuminated by a green-shaded lamp pulled low down over the papers littering the surface.

"This fellow Bolan," the older man said, "must be located with the least possible delay. And eliminated. That is imperative."

"No sweat," the other drawled. "Give me the backup I need. And the tools. After that you can leave it to me and go back to your golf at the country club."

"You can have all the backup you need. All the weapons. All the police looking the other way. But it's unofficial. You have to remember that. I'm talking to you as a private individual; you're being paid by a private organization. Step out of line or fuck up and we never heard of you. Is that clear?"

"Sure, sure," the second man said.

He was a large man, bullnecked and muscular, with crew-cut red hair and mean eyes. His name was Eddie Hanson, and he was a mercenary—a Swedish-American deserter whose skills had been for hire ever since he was chased out of Vietnam for running a chain of GI whorehouses and drug dens in and around Saigon.

Hanson had fought in Mozambique, in Biafra, in Lebanon, in Chad, Katanga, Central America and Angola—anyplace that was long on money and short on ideals. He had all Bolan's skills and none of his humanity. For Eddie Hanson, those at the receiving end of the hollowpoint, the missile, the grenade, were of no more interest than the cardboard targets at a shooting gallery.

And now his target was to be the Executioner himself!

Bolan had, in fact, run across the guy once or twice in his combat career, usually on the opposite side of the firing line. He knew the man by reputation, and he didn't like what he knew.

Merging with the gloom in his blacksuit, Bolan was stretched out at one side of the window, toes on the ledge, fingers gripping a concrete lip that ran above the window frame. He could easily have shifted one hand, drawn the Beretta from its shoulder rig and wasted both men in the office. But he wanted to learn a hell of a lot more about the guy who was hiring the mercenary.

The two of them couldn't have been more different physically. Hanson, in jeans, sneakers and a turtleneck sweater, was lounging against the back of his chair. The man behind the desk was small, spry, with white hair, a clipped mustache and penetrating blue eyes. He wore an immaculate uniform; in the harsh light from the lowered lamp his belt and buttons shone, the gold teeth that showed when he spoke looked as though they had just been polished. Even behind a desk in a swivel chair he gave the impression of being at attention.

Julius Vanderlee was a colonel in the South African National Intelligence Service—the security organization that used to be known by the acronym BOSS.

The administrative headquarters of the service were in a tall building beyond the gardens on the far side of the square. It was there, on the tenth floor, that the secret police customarily punched, slapped and kicked their prisoners, making them undress and attacking their genitals, forcing them to do strenuous physical exercise, threatening them with death, and using hooding, electric shocks and prolonged sleep deprivation to stimulate the confessions desired.

Colonel Vanderlee did not look the kind of officer who would sully his manicured hands with anything as crude as that. It was hard, Bolan thought, to imagine him attacking anyone's genitals. Less difficult to swallow was the idea of his signing an order authorizing someone else to do it.

Still, here he was, coolly organizing Bolan's own extinction. Strictly unofficially, of course.

The Executioner had choked Vanderlee's name from the laboratory boss before he killed him. But the guy had not known in what exact way the security chief was concerned with the opium farm or Ononu's Montenegria blackmail routines—only that there *was* a connection. And that all orders affecting the farm were funneled through the colonel from some person or persons higher up.

What was evident already was that the whole operation had high-level protection. Partly, according to the lab boss, from certain wildcat sectors of the old BOSS field agency owing allegiance to Vanderlee, partly from quasi-military bodies in neighboring countries, working like Vanderlee himself without the knowledge of their governments.

As Bolan had said some time before, it smelled.

Right now his main interest was to discover who gave the colonel his orders. And why it was so important that he, Bolan, should be liquidated.

He could understand it if they wanted to "punish" him for the Ogodishu operation. Sure—as a warning to others. But from what he had heard so far it seemed now that the most important reason was to block him from further investigation.

Of what?

Vanderlee was tapping a buff folder. "This man Bolan is a danger," he said. "It is important that you understand the position. You'll know that farmers, ranchers and managers of estates in the outback and away on the veldt are at the mercy of terrorists—the marauding bands that filter across the border from Botswana, Mozambique, Southwest Africa, Zimbabwe, you name it. They come in all shapes and sizes: Zulus, Swazis, Bantu from our own reserves, even Masai, sometimes, from the north. Or Xhosa. But they all have certain things in common. One, they kill, loot, rape and destroy; two, their activity threatens to put the whites who make their home there out of business."

Hanson yawned. "And so?"

"So quite often the whites form vigilante patrols, or they employ specialized posses to flush out the marauders and crucify them, to provide the protection the law is not always able to give them. It's a big country, for Chrissake. Your own position should be viewed in the light of that example."

"Meaning?"

"I mean that you are answerable to...well, to a group of private individuals who are, let us say, comparable in a figurative sense to those farmers. Except that in our case it's big business rather than agriculture. Gold, diamonds, heavy industry... You don't need to know the details, but people dealing in that kind of merchandise can't afford to have years of exploitation threatened by the terrorist activity of one crazy son of a bitch who thinks he's Superman."

"Okay," Hanson said. "Leave aside the history, Colonel. You want this guy Bolan taken out, so I'll take him out. And leave no clues pointing your way. That's what you want, right?"

"Don't underestimate him," Vanderlee warned. "He's smart, and tough. You'll need the whole group if you're going to make it."

"We'll make it, all right. You say he already hit town?"

"Three days ago. We tailed him from Gabotomi, near the dam, through Libenge to Lisala. He had some kind of newspaper creep with him, the bastard who wrote up the raid in the Chicago *Globe* last week. They changed cars at Lisala and we lost them until they made Kisangani. After that, the scandalmonger flew north and Bolan took a flight that brought him here. We don't know where he's holed up. Wherever it is, he's got to be flushed out and disposed of."

"I'll find him."

"You better. I'm driving out to Baarmbeek at the weekend. I'd like to have the file closed by then. They'll want to let Florida know that everything's taken care of this end."

On the ledge outside the window, Bolan frowned. Baarmbeek, he knew, was a small town between Pretoria and Warmbad, in the Transvaal province.

But *Florida*?

Florida, U.S.A.?

Whatever it was that he had rowed himself into, there were international ramifications, for sure. But who were "they"? And what were they doing in a small town far to the northwest? What the hell had this Euro-African conspiracy to do with Florida?

Before he made any attempt to check out any of those questions, Bolan determined to do his damnedest to penetrate Vanderlee's office sometime and take a look at his files. Even if he was acting in a private capacity, surely there should be some clue someplace. And the Executioner needed every lead he could get, however slight.

In any case, he thought sourly, it was time he initiated some indoor action; he seemed to have spent half his life, lately, clinging to roofs and walls.

He shivered. It was cold this high above the street and the wind was freshening.

He glanced sideways along the ledge, toward the corner of the building on the far side of which was the stack pipe he had climbed. Behind the rows of lights marking the steel and glass skyscrapers of the city center, a cloud bank was blotting out the stars.

The Executioner tensed.

Something was blotting out the city lights, too—first one row, and then another as the first reappeared.

There couldn't be clouds between him and those buildings!

He strained his eyes through the darkness.

Spread-eagled against the wall, toes on the ledge, hands gripping the cornice above, another dark figure had materialized around the corner from the pipe.

Inch by inch, the head still turned toward the corner, the figure was sidling toward the lit window.

And nearer to the Executioner.

He reached gloved fingers down toward the holstered Beretta.

Like Bolan himself, the second intruder was clothed entirely in black—skintight one-piece suit, black gloves, black sneakers, black woolen cap.

No more than three feet separated them when the head turned slowly to face the window.

An indrawn gasp of surprise when the newcomer found an eavesdropper already in place was echoed by Bolan himself.

In the diffuse light escaping from the office, he saw that he was face-to-face with Ruth Elias, the dark-haired woman from Milan he had rescued from Anya Ononu's summer palace.

Chapter Seventeen

"There is one other thing, Hanson," Colonel Vanderlee said. He cleared his throat. "It's better we should get it out of the way now."

The mercenary had already moved away from his chair, on the way out. He retraced his steps, frowning. "Namely?"

"The man Bolan, as you know, is on the hit list of several security agencies, among them the KGB. He is also wanted in a number of European countries and in many parts of the United States."

"So?"

"But not at present in South Africa. If, on the other hand, we could persuade one of those bodies to ask formally for his extradition..." Vanderlee left the sentence unfinished.

"What are you getting at?"

"Such a request could not involve the security forces here, but it would provide an excuse for the civil police, country-wide, to be put on the alert, with a warrant issued for his arrest."

"So why not do that?"

"The necessary procedures have been... set in motion." The security boss straightened a pile of papers on the desk, patting the edges with his fingertips. "But even if he was caught and detained, there would have to be a trial before the authorities decided whether or not there was a prima facie case for extradition. And Bolan would be permitted to advance a defense, to show reason why he should not be sent back to wherever it was. In some countries, what are known as political crimes—" the colonel pronounced the words with distaste "—are not considered sufficient reason for extradition."

"What would be the point, then? Are you trying to say—"

"I am saying that although such a move could effectively neutralize Bolan so far as activities in this country are concerned, it would take time. And time is what we lack."

"You're telling me," Hanson said, "that I could get police help to locate Bolan—given sufficient reason? Is that it?"

"I am pleased to see that we think along the same lines," Vanderlee replied.

"But that the extradition reason, though it might work in the long run, doesn't move fast enough for you?"

"Exactly."

"So what other reasons did you have in mind?"

"Assuming you cannot eliminate the man at once—"

"I figure we can."

"We have to plan for all eventualities. Assuming you cannot," Vanderlee said carefully, "it would place much more pressure on the police, give them a far more urgent reason to find him, if Bolan had committed—or was supposed to have committed—some crime in this country. Murder, for instance."

On the ledge outside the office window, the subject of the conspiracy shook his head. He had heard it all before. It was precisely because of such a frame that he was now an outlaw.

It had started with the death of a Russian test pilot during one of the Executioner's clandestine missions inside the Soviet Union. The pilot's father had sworn revenge. And the father happened to be Major General Greb Strakhov, ruthless head of the KGB's Department Thirteen terror squad.

Stage one of the revenge was the KGB-inspired assault that almost took out Stony Man Farm, Bolan's Virginia headquarters when he was working secretly for Uncle Sam, and provoked the death of his great love, April Rose.

Stage two was subtler. While the Executioner was on a mission in southeastern Europe, a double was KGB-trained to assassinate, in full view of the public, a popular labor leader. The Bolan look-alike then vanished, leaving the real man to take the blame.

Whether or not the revenge was sweet, nobody knew, for Greb Strakhov was now dead, too.

But Mack Bolan was still an outlaw.

He glanced across at the figure of Ruth Elias, flattened against the wall on the far side of the open window, and shrugged. Raised eyebrows on his part and a hesitant smile of recognition on hers were the extent so far of their communication. It wasn't the best place in the world for small talk.

For the moment, as far as Bolan was concerned, the mystery of just who this woman was—and what the hell she was doing here—must wait. Inside the office the conversation was nearing its end.

"Let me get this straight," Eddie Hanson was saying. "You want me to stage a killing, to pin a murder rap on Bolan, right?"

There was no audible reply. Bolan assumed Vanderlee had nodded.

"Okay," the mercenary continued, "so, as you say, that would bring in the local law to help find the bastard. But there'd still have to be a trial before he was topped. It'd probably take even longer to come to court than an extradition case, wouldn't it?"

The Colonel sighed in frustration. "The purpose of such a frame—the only purpose—would be to enlist all the aid possible, to hasten the search for this renegade, to help with a job that might take you too long on your own. But once Bolan was cornered—well, I should be relying on you to make damned sure he was *not* brought to trial. That, in reality, is what you are being paid for, Hanson."

"I'm with you," the hired killer said. "Okay. Right. I see."

"As a model," Colonel Vanderlee offered, "I could advance the case of Lee Harvey Oswald. You'd be playing Jack Ruby. Do I make myself clear?"

"Sure. Knock him off once the cops have fingered him. Leave it with me, okay?"

"Very well. I will contact you in the meantime if there are any developments in the extradition situation, but a murder charge would be much better."

There was the sound of papers shuffling and the closing of a drawer. "And now we must leave," the security chief said. "In five minutes the door of this office is electronically locked and nobody, not even myself, can open it until ten o'clock tomorrow morning."

Bolan held his breath as footsteps approached the window.

Ruth Elias froze.

But Vanderlee did not poke out his head to look at the sky or the city. He shut the window and they heard the sound of bolts being slid home into the frame. Seconds later the light was killed and there was the muffled slam of a heavy door.

"What the hell are *you* doing here?" Bolan whispered furiously.

"Market research," Ruth Elias replied.

Bolan choked back a retort.

"I'm going in," she added in a low voice. "If you're not going to force the window, I will."

"Great," he said, "and have every siren in town wailing when you break the alarm connection?"

"Do you have a better idea?" she snapped.

Bolan nodded. Very carefully, he moved in front of the window. Lowering one hand, he removed from a narrow pocket a short stalk with a dull industrial diamond embedded in one end.

There was a thin screeching noise as the diamond traced out the shape of a circle on the windowpane.

Bolan hit the center of the circle a single sharp blow with the heel of his hand.

The glass broke away cleanly and fell to the carpeted floor inside the office.

The opening was large enough for a big man to enter. He eased his body through the gap and then helped the woman in after him.

"I have a flashlight," she murmured.

"Save your battery," Bolan said. He pulled down a canvas blind over the window, stole across the floor to where a thread of light showed beneath the door and found a wall switch. The green-shaded lamp above the desk momentarily dazzled them.

"The passageway outside is lighted, so there will be no telltale beam under the door," he said. "In any case, nobody can get in here. And with a building this size, I guess nobody out in the night's going to notice which particular window out of several hundred shows a light. Even if any escapes around that blind."

It was a small office, with a desk, three phones and two chairs. A black-leather and chrome armchair. Shelves of reference books, a bank of gray steel filing cabinets, a wall safe.

"Okay," Bolan said softly. "I want to know who you work for and what brings you here tonight."

"I told you before," Ruth Elias said, "I like to know why people do things."

Bolan sighed in frustration. "I think you'll tell me in your own sweet time. There's too much work to be done now."

He shot her an appraising look. The one-piece garment she wore, so like his own blacksuit, clung to her body and emphasized the rounded swell of her breasts, the subtle curves of hip and waist, the provocative sweep of flesh dropping away from the belly to the top of the thighs. She pulled off the woolen cap and shook her dark hair free.

"What are you looking for?" he asked.

"His files."

"Me, too." Bolan crossed over to the row of metal cabinets. Each was secured with a combination lock that controlled all the drawers.

He swore.

"Don't worry," she said. "The window was yours, this one is for me."

From a knee pocket in the close-fitting suit she produced a metal box not much larger than a cigarette pack. Clamped magnetically over the first lock, it emitted a faint beeping sound.

Ruth knelt, her ear close to the box, and fingered two tiny wheels set into the casing. On the face of the box a needle flickered across a dial.

As the tumblers, moved by electromagnets within the box, approached or receded from the preset combination, the beep quickened, slowed, accelerated again and finally changed tone. The lock clicked open and she pulled out the top drawer.

Bolan was impressed.

"How do you want to do this?" she asked.

"Let's each take a whole drawer."

Colonel Vanderlee's filing system was predictable, as neat and precise and orderly as the man himself. Still, it did not help Bolan, because he didn't know what he was looking for.

What he *did* know was that the colonel wanted him out of the way. Vanderlee's words came back to him.

If Bolan himself was out of the way, Baarmbeek would want to let Florida know that things in South Africa had been taken care of.

Following his vigil on the ledge, that was all Bolan had in the way of a lead.

But now that he was in the office, which files should he search?

Baarmbeek and Florida, both presumably no more than place names, were the only possible entries. Files under the broad headings of Transactions and Relations seemed the obvious ones for a preliminary search. But neither name appeared under those headings.

The files under Communications could conceivably relate, but here again Bolan drew a blank.

Vanderlee had made it clear, talking to Eddie Hanson, that he was acting "unofficially," that he was, in fact, looking for a reason to *make* his interest in Bolan official—which was why he was so eager to frame a case against him.

But it wasn't official yet. So it was possible there would be *no* entries in the official files in connection with Florida or Baarmbeek. Or, if there were, that they would be in connection with some subject having nothing to do with Ononu and the opium farm.

Bolan tried all the subheads under Organization.

Zero.

From time to time he stole a covert glance at the girl. She was skimming through the Professions section of the Suspicion drawer.

Judging by her expression, she was having no better luck than he was.

He was about to make another attempt to find out who she was working for and why she was there, but he thought better of it and continued his own search. Questions could wait. Right now the important thing was to find answers.

He went to the desk and pulled open a double drawer at one side of the kneehole. Here there were folders on the everyday running of the office, furlough rosters for the security personnel working under Vanderlee, interdepartmental memos, Ministry of Interior circulars and suchlike.

No file detailing the relation between a town in the province of Transvaal, the opium trade and an American state bordering the Gulf of Mexico.

It was in the shallow drawer above the kneehole, among paper clips, rubber stamps, ink pads and elastic bands, that he found the first clue.

He spotted a small address book with imitation leather covers, bordered by a neat row of ballpoint pens.

Bolan ran his thumb down the stepped index on the outside of the pages until he came to the letter F.

Nothing under Florida.

No Baarmbeek on the B pages.

But there wouldn't be, he realized. Any entry would be under the name of a person or an organization He went through the book page by page.

He struck pay dirt when he reached the second R page.

Reinbecker.

The full entry read: Piet van der Hoek Reinbecker, Greystones, Valley Road, Baarmbeek. And there were two telephone numbers.

On Florida Bolan once more scored zero.

He went back to the filing drawers and searched for any entry under the name Reinbecker.

It took him almost an hour to find it—in the least likely place.

The name—together with a spidery signature—was at the foot of several report sheets in the section of files headed Subversion (Cases Closed).

Piet van der Hoek Reinbecker was governor of the Baarmbeek jail.

It could, of course, be no more than a coincidence. The guy might have nothing whatever to do with Vanderlee's unofficial connections—or with the state of Florida. But it had to be followed up; it was the only lead Bolan had.

Ruth Elias appeared to have none at all.

She was kneeling on the floor now, surrounded by open files from the Suspicion cabinet. Bolan had flipped through them earlier—surveillance reports on students, journalists, union organizers, petty crooks; hour-by-hour notes on stakeouts; transcriptions of tapped phone calls. Some of them were cross-referenced to Cases Pending, in the Subversion drawers.

Bolan looked over her shoulder. The sheets she had removed all dealt with suspected drug dealers, pushers, importers. The material was thin; such people only interested the National Intelligence Service archivists insofar as they might be security risks.

"I can't find the damned connection!" she said angrily.

"If I knew what you were looking for..." Bolan said.

"Distribution. The spiderweb. It was a long shot anyway, coming here. But I hoped I might find proof of a link between the Ogodishu farm and..." She shrugged. "Wherever."

Bolan frowned. "You're working for the narcotics squad?"

Ruth Elias shook her head. "I am not American."

"Then who..."

She ignored the question. Rising to her feet, she picked up the metal box. "I guess it was too much to hope that he'd keep records here," she said. "I'll have to try his home. Unless of course..." She moved toward the wall safe. "I don't think the magnets are strong enough for this, but..."

She clamped the box to the steel door next the combination dial and reached for the handle.

"Don't—" Bolan began urgently.

The warning was too late. Outside in the passageway, alarm bells jangled a deafening alert.

Ruth sprang to her feet with an exclamation and snatched away the box.

"That's what I was afraid of," Bolan said. "The alarm's actuated the moment that lock's tampered with. We have to get out. Fast."

"But nobody can get in here. Vanderlee said the door was electronically—"

"Under normal conditions," Bolan rapped. "I'd guess the safe alarm automatically disconnects the other circuit to let the security people in. No point in the alarm otherwise."

She looked helplessly around the littered floor, at the opened files, the empty cabinets. "But won't they know? How can we—"

"We can't. Out the window, back the way we came. Move!" He shoved her toward the opening. "I'll cover you until you make the corner by the stack pipe."

Already there were shouts from the floor below, footsteps in the passage outside punctuating the trilling alarm.

Ruth squeezed through the hole in the glass and balanced herself on the ledge outside. Bolan followed her through as she moved away.

Clinging to the edge of the window frame with one hand, he unleathered his silenced Beretta with the other.

The door of the office burst open. Two men in uniform leaped in with Browning automatics fisted and ready to fire.

The Beretta sneezed out a 3-round burst before they had taken in the scene.

One of the security men was slammed back against the wall with a scarlet stream pumping through the breast pocket of his safari jacket. He slid to the floor.

The second guy had dived for the desk. Crouched in the kneehole, he blasted off three shots, then ducked out of the Executioner's field of fire.

Wood splinters flew from the window frame. Glass shattered and fell.

Still holding the frame, Bolan had ducked to avoid the deathstream. Now he rose upright to drill a single shot into the desk and then glanced swiftly to his left.

At the far end of the ledge, Ruth Elias was maneuvering herself around the corner. The slender bulk of her body vanished, and he could see, beyond the condominium towers that had been financed with Witwatersrand gold, the mine dumps east of the city gilded by a late-rising moon.

Bolan jerked up a second time to trigger another round at the desk.

The security man had moved. His return shot blazed out from behind the leather-and-chrome armchair. The slug streaked dangerously close to Bolan's ear and gouged a channel in the wood near his hand.

Down once more, he glanced again at the corner of the building, wondering how far away it was.

Crouched as he was, could he move far enough from the frame to stand upright and grab the coping without presenting the gunman inside with a target he couldn't miss?

Upright and moving away, with only one hand to grip that coping, could he steady himself enough to zap the guy with the Browning if he realized the Executioner had changed position and leaned out the window to fire?

The guy with the Browning was smarter than that.

He knew Bolan was bent double on a narrow sandstone ledge just below the windowsill.

He knew that even if he was one hundred percent in shape, this guy supporting himself with one hand on the frame was in a damned precarious position.

He fired two shots in rapid succession at the upper, undamaged windowpane.

The pane exploded outward, showering razor-sharp fragments of glass around the big guy on the ledge.

Automatically, involuntarily, he jerked up an arm to protect his head from the lethal shards. His weight shifted; his center of gravity moved outward; a section of sandstone, cracking under the changed pressure, broke off and dropped into the void.

Bolan fell.

Chapter Eighteen

For Mack Bolan the urban jungles of the West had always been, would always be, as perilous as the wooded hell of Indochina where he had first learned his deadly skills. All his adult life he had lived with and accepted the notion that there had to be an end...that sometime, someplace, the final blackness would descend on him.

The roar of a grenade, the hammer blow of an assassin's bullet, the searing scorch of flame or the stupefying concussion of a booby-trapped automobile—all these were ever-present risks, the question marks on the daily calendar of his personal crusade.

At times he had even wondered in a detached way whether, in that last instant, in that thousandth of a second before the brain was pulverized, the pumping of the heart stilled, he would be aware of the blossom of fire blooming at the tunnel mouth of an SMG, the disintegration of a windshield and the up-blast of a hood as he twisted the ignition key.

What had not occurred to him was the possibility that he might die falling backward from a fourth-floor window.

Easy as falling off a log.

The childish phrase recurred with idiot insistency as he hurtled past the facade of the security police annex in John Vorster Square, Johannesburg.

Easier, in fact.

Because, dammit, he was getting used to it. Yeah, there had already been enough falls, too many falls, in this mission. He had jumped through a window of the police chief's office in Udine; he had plunged off a cliff at the wheel of an automobile; he had leaped out of Rinaldi's house in Laigueglia, into the sea from the ramparts of the prison in Montenegria, out of a chopper and down from the spiral stairway at Ononu's summer palace on Lake Gadrany.

Now he was doing it again. But not, this time, because he wanted to.

This time was different, too, because it would be the last time.

In none of the other cases had it even occurred to him that he might not survive; here there was a certainty of death.

Feeling the rush of cool air past his face, Bolan was aware of three separate reactions, a trio of distinct emotions.

Regret, satisfaction, annoyance.

Regret that now he would never know who Ruth Elias was working for or why Colonel Vanderlee had to contact Baarmbeek.

Satisfaction that he had cheated the security guard, whose receding figure he saw leaning out of the lighted window above, of his chosen target—even though it was something of an extreme way to achieve that end!

Annoyance—with himself—because of all the deaths he had envisaged, being split open like a slaughtered beast on the pavement far below was the least dignified, and the one farthest down the list he had figured.

But it didn't happen like that.

Bolan had reached his ledge via a stack pipe spanning the facade on the other side of the building. He had made the pipe under cover of trees growing in the gardens of John Vorster Square. He had made no recon of the wall in back.

He did not know that there were also some trees, of varying height, in front of the building.

He had never looked down from the ledge. That was one of the rules: you never looked down.

So he didn't know that one of the taller trees stood immediately below the window of Colonel Vanderlee's office.

Automatically, following the experienced jumper's routine, he balled himself for a bad landing, even though it would be the last.

He hit the younger and more slender branches at the top, which helped to slow his fall. At once he realized what was happening and he spread his arms and legs wide, hoping that some of the larger branches would slow his fall. They would, probably break his arms and legs, too. But at least he wouldn't splatter onto the pavement below.

Green boughs whipped at his face as he slammed into the foliage, and all he could think of was that he had to protect his eyes.

Bolan shut his eyes tight, then he heard a crack and felt a fire in his side. And he knew that he had shattered one or more of his ribs. His flexed knee caught on a branch and he hit the back of his head, jarring his teeth, but he had stopped falling. He shook his head to clear it, then groped awkwardly until his fingers closed around a limb. He unhooked his leg and swung his body upright, grimacing in agony from the blow to his diaphragm. Slowly, he eased himself down the remaining branches and dropped the few feet to the ground.

For a moment he stood there, dazed, leaning against the trunk of the tree. He could not believe what had just happened, but as he took a step forward, the fierce throbbing in his side was a painful reminder of his ordeal. But battered as he was, he knew he had to get out of there.

Around the corner of the police building, someone was shouting orders; there was a stamp of feet as the guard turned out.

The alarm bell still jangled and blue lights flashed on the far side of the square.

With every inch of his body aching now, Bolan ran.

He dodged around some benches, cannoned into a big guy with a heavy mustache who sent him sprawling. He picked himself up with difficulty, clutching his side and biting his lower lip. Suddenly he found himself on the sidewalk of a street crowded with late-night traffic.

Horns blared, brakes squealed, cabdrivers swore as he hobbled into the rush of vehicles. He made the far side of the street without further mishap—what was a mere stream of cars, trucks and buses to a guy who had just survived a fall from a fourth-floor window?—and only then had time to pause and thank the universe for his lucky escape.

The flashing blue lights and the confusion were all across on the other side of the wide busy street. Already a crowd had gathered on Bolan's side, wondering what the hell was going on. He hoped the woman had gotten away before the commotion started.

For himself, he relied on the notorious inability of witnesses to agree on descriptions, directions, anything. The great thing was not to attract attention. There were plenty of jaywalkers at this time of night.

He limped slowly to the end of the street, flagged down a cab and returned to his hotel.

But even though he had escaped, the situation in general had changed radically... for the worse.

There would be no need now for Eddie Hanson to cook up a murder and pin it on the Executioner.

He had killed a member of the security forces in the execution of his duty and had attempted to mow down another. Since he was engaged in a criminal act—the burglary of a government office—at the material time, any justifiable homicide claim or self-defense plea was out the window.

Police forces all over the republic would be marshaled for a full-scale murder hunt.

Colonel Vanderlee would be pleased. The entire weight of the justice machine would now be organized to track down the man he wanted out of the way—while Hanson lurked in the wings, waiting his chance to shoot once Bolan was located.

And he needed medical attention. But there was no time for that. Holding one edge of a bed sheet between his teeth, he tore the cloth into a long strip, then wrapped it around his torso. Satisfied with the makeshift bandage, he went into the bathroom and washed his face. The water turned pink in the basin, and he looked in the mirror. He had sustained only minor scratches.

There was a single bright spot, he thought as he left the bathroom; neither the colonel, Hanson nor the police would know of Bolan's interest in Baarmbeek.

Because they had been interrupted by the alarm, the warrior and Ruth Elias had been obliged to leave drawers opened, files scattered over the floor, a mess of papers on the desk. But there was nothing to show which way their search had been directed; the minutest examination of the dossiers removed from the filing cabinets would give no indication of their interests—if only because they themselves had not known what they were looking for.

And the address book that might have tipped off Vanderlee that Bolan was looking for a link, for names, for places—the book, thankfully, had been replaced beside the ballpoints in the desk drawer.

So the quicker he could get out of town and make it to Baarmbeek the better; he would be in no more danger there than anyplace else.

He packed his gear and checked out of the hotel. It would be too dangerous to stay there, because by now there would be an all-points alert out for him, complete with description and probably a computerized photo sent via satellite from Interpol—and the hotels would be the first places the police looked.

Bolan walked the dark streets and passed the rest of the night with the poor, at a bus station on the outskirts of the city.

Early in the morning he was on the fringe of the Soweto slum township where black workers were segregated.

Although they wouldn't know for sure that he planned to leave Johannesburg, he reckoned that the police would be heavily into identity checks at all railroad stations, airports and bus terminals.

He dared not rent a car because the clerks at each agency would have received orders to report details of all clients to police headquarters.

He went into a wrecker's yard and used car lot and spent the equivalent of fifty dollars on a beat-up Plymouth sedan with dented fenders and the chrome strip on one side missing.

Throwing his gear into the trunk, he filled up the gas tank and drove the decrepit heap northward out of the city.

Chapter Nineteen

It was thirty miles from Johannesburg to Pretoria. The early-morning traffic was heavy but it was mostly in the other direction—trucks bringing produce from the outback farms to the city, busloads of black workers for the mines. Even when the road ahead was clear, Bolan took it slow and easy, obeying the speed limit, carefully signaling each maneuver of the ancient sedan. He could ill afford, he knew, to attract the attention of the highway patrol.

Besides, the poor suspension of the Plymouth made the car seem like a tank, causing Bolan a twinge of pain in his side each time the wheels hit a pothole.

After the frantic commercial bustle of the gold and diamond city, the state capital was an oasis of calm, a city where it seemed permanently to be Sunday.

If there were shantytowns like those surrounding the slums of Soweto, or sterile and regimented hut compounds similar to the artificial townships housing the African workers of the Rand, Bolan did not see them.

Although more than eighty percent of the Transvaal population are of Bantu, Xhosa or Matabele origin, because Pretoria is mainly a government and diplomatic center, the number of black faces on the street is astonishingly small.

Warmbad lay more than fifty miles to the north, on the principal highway linking Johannesburg and Pretoria with Salisbury and the old Rhodesian frontier. The route ran between two of the Bantustan tribal reserves, and the road to Baarmbeek branched off below the more easterly of these and skirted the lake at Penskop before climbing to the high ground on which the town was built.

Away on his left Bolan occasionally saw the conical thatched roofs of a Ndebele village on the fringe of the reservation, the circular huts decorated with black, brown and blue architectural designs on the white mud walls.

Soon the acreages of cotton, soya and corn that stretched between the low hills gave way to lush European farms planted with tobacco, pineapples, avocado pears, wheat and orchards of citrus fruit. Baarmbeek lay between this rich area and the treeless grasslands of the high veld.

It was a small town of balconied brick buildings with half a dozen high-rise structures in concrete grouped around the railroad station.

There was a Dutch Reformed church behind the gardens in the central square, a tall white edifice with a bell tower and a slate roof crowning the severe curves of the facade. The only hint of industrialization was an assembly plant for combine harvesters, crop-spraying machines and mechanical cultivators imported in crates from Europe and Japan.

Bolan wondered what possible connection there could be between this sleepy, bourgeois backwater, a man-made famine fifteen hundred miles to the north and an opium crop financed by a small-time West African dictator.

Surely they weren't growing the stuff around here, too!

He put the thought from his mind: the agricultural machinery assembled in Baarmbeek was destined for the cultivation of less toxic crops than opium poppy.

Whatever the connection was, he would force it out of the jail governor and then get the hell out of there.

Unless, of course, he had jumped too quickly to conclusions, unless the whole deal was no more than a coincidence and Reinbecker's name was in Vanderlee's address book simply because he was a social acquaintance.

Bolan put that thought from his mind, too. There *had* to be a connection.

Low cloud building up over the Drakensberg Mountains far away to the east had moved nearer while the Plymouth was wheezing up the long grade leading to the town. As Bolan braked in the station yard to ask the way to Valley Road, it began to rain.

By the time he found the snobbish residential quarter where Reinbecker lived, the shower had become a downpour.

On the way he passed the only other visible connection with Montenegria—a long line of hopper cars loaded with ore being hauled out of a freight yard by a shunting locomotive. Like the northern part of Ononu's crooked kingdom, the land around Baarmbeek was rich in cassiterite, the chief source of tin.

The tin mines were discreetly hidden from view by a fold in the hills. But the wealth that they brought was clearly visible all along Valley Road.

Big properties, mostly in the Dutch Colonial style, most of them standing well back in several acres of well-manicured garden, were shaded by subtropical trees and equipped with stables and pools beyond the flowered verandas. Several of them were guarded by uniformed security men, standing with slung shotguns at the white-painted gates, chained German shepherds lying at their feet.

Greystones was something else.

It was a massive stone-structure that resembled a nineteenth-century European school or seminary, complete with clock tower, gothic window embrasures and sham battlements.

It was built around a square courtyard, entered through an arch beneath the tower. Between the house and the road, seventy yards of velvet-smooth, tree-shaded lawns had recently been mowed.

The property, which included a small wood at the rear of the main building, was surrounded by white-painted fencing. The gates, of tall wrought iron supported on imposing pillars, were overlooked from the inside by two khaki-clad local policemen armed with assault rifles.

Bolan didn't know how much a rural prison governor earned in South Africa, but it sure seemed quite a place for a civil servant, unless he had considerable private means. It was raining hard now—and the Plymouth's wipers were defective, naturally—but he glimpsed a white Cadillac Fleetwood and an Alfa-Romeo sportster parked in the courtyard as he cruised past.

He went on driving. The Plymouth would have been noted by all the security men he passed. It was anonymous, all right—but in a classy area like this it was too damned anonymous; the very fact that it was old and scratched, that its owner wasn't making a point, would render it conspicuous. It wasn't the sort of car you could park at the curbside and then pretend you were reading the racing results while you staked out a place. Not in Valley Road.

Bolan decided to circle the block. Maybe there was a service road in back from which he could work out some way of getting inside the Greystones perimeter. In any case, if he wished to avoid attracting unwelcome attention, he had better not drive past the main entrance to these mansions again.

But that was precisely what he had to do. Half a mile farther on, the road ended in a cul-de-sac fringed by tamarisk trees and oleanders in bloom.

There was just one gateway on the cul-de-sac, wrought iron again, with stone pillars topped by sculptured lions. On the far side the driveway twisted out of sight between high banks of rhododendrons. The house was not visible, but there was a small lodge inside the gates.

A tough-looking guy came out of a side door with the collar of his leather windbreaker turned up against the rain. He held a double-barreled shotgun in the crook of his arm and he was accompanied by a Doberman pinscher on a leash.

He walked across to the Plymouth as Bolan maneuvered the car in a three-point turn to head back the way he had come.

"You looking for something?" he inquired. The voice was not friendly.

Bolan wound down the driver's window. "Guess I must have missed my road," he said easily.

The gateman glanced scornfully at the Plymouth. "Damn right, you did. This is private property. We don't want any rubberneckers or insurance salesmen."

"I'm not selling anything." Bolan pretended to be down and out on his luck. "I got a call to pass by the assembly plant, where they make the tractors and stuff. Can you tell me which way to turn when I get to the end of this street?"

"Get your ass out of here and ask someone else," the man replied. His tone was suspicious. "Get out fast, and don't stop on the way."

"Look, you don't have to take that attitude with me," Bolan began, affecting an injured tone.

"Beat it."

"I don't have to take—"

The guy leveled the twin snouts of the shotgun threateningly at Bolan.

"On your way," he gritted, then swung on his heel as Bolan flipped the selector into Drive and laid rubber, in simulated anger, on the wet macadam. Between the rain spots on the outside mirror he saw the guard unhook a phone from the wall of the gate house.

Back in town Bolan found a cigar store where he could buy a large-scale map of Baarmbeek and the surrounding country.

According to the map there was a road that skirted the rear of Greystones and the other mansions. It was described in the legend as "unmetaled." Bolan guessed this meant it was a dirt road. If the scale was exact it ran within a quarter of a mile of the Reinbecker place, meandered past a couple of farms and then degenerated into what was marked as a hill track that eventually looped down to the lake.

The difficulty now was the Plymouth. It was possible that the guards he had seen patrolled the whole property, and if the same guys happened to be in back when he passed along the lane...

The car had to go, for sure.

Beyond the freight yard, on a slope of land that led down past workers' huts toward the mines, Bolan found another used-car lot.

It was surrounded by ten-foot corrugated iron fencing, which suited him fine—any transactions in there would be invisible from outside. Fifty yards from the gates, a wooden shack stood between a mound of wrecked auto bodies collected for scrap and the double line of parked vehicles that were for sale. Some of the used-car bargains were scarcely distinguishable from the wrecks on the mound. Bolan reckoned that the clientele must be drawn largely from the black workers employed in the mines.

A balding Asian wearing blue coveralls stood in the open doorway of the hut. He was about forty years old, unshaven, with dark-brown cash-register eyes.

Bolan braked outside the shack, rolled down the window and explained that he wished to trade in the Plymouth for something better. "The wipers are gone," he said.

The Asian stared at him. Dark clouds scurried low across the sky. The rain fell heavily, blown almost horizontal now by the freshening wind, bouncing knee-high off the cracked asphalt of the yard and drumming a loud tattoo on the shack's tin roof.

The Asian made no reply. He walked around the Plymouth, frowning critically. He rapped with his knuckles on the hood and side panels. He kicked a tire. "I do not see much chance here for a trade-in," he said. And then, evaluating the driver and clearly rating him a better economic risk than the car, he added, "It will depend, sir, naturally, on what you want to buy."

"Something tough," Bolan said. "For a long, rough trip. But something reliable." He pushed open the door and got out into the rain. The Asian's coveralls were already sodden, but what the hell—there was a possible sale in view.

They splashed through the rain to the double line of bargains. Bolan's glance ranged glumly over rusted Fiats, Citroëns drooping on worn-out hydraulic suspensions, nineteen-sixties American convertibles with bodywork like crumpled paper.

The salesman fielded the glance. "For you, sir," he said quickly, "frankly there is not one of these carriages I could recommend. This is shit, sir, for the poor. For you there is only one car on this lot, and she is behind my office." He gestured toward the hut. "My personal transport, but I sell her to you."

"Too kind," Bolan said. "What is it?"

"She is a Volvo station wagon. A little old maybe, and a little rough on the outside—but she goes real good. The engine, sir, is new. The brakes are fine. And she is very tough. You have my word. Also there is a thirty-gallon, supplementary gas tank beneath the floor in back."

"Show me," Bolan said.

The Volvo certainly did have a beat-up air. Beside it, the Plymouth looked almost in showroom condition.

The wagon's fenders were scratched and dented, the massive front bumper bar was crumpled and the one at the rear had disappeared altogether. The paintwork had been reduced by years of high veld sunshine to a lusterless, neutral color that was neither white nor cream nor gray.

But the salesman was right about one thing. The engine note was crisp and the acceleration brisk. Even driving up and down the muddy yard Bolan could see that the car would perform well. The brakes, too, were good, although the tread remaining on the tires was minimal.

What really made him decide was the extra gas tank: getting out of the country in a hurry, along the route he planned to take, that could be important.

"Okay," he said, climbing from the driving seat, "how much do you want?"

"For you, sir, five hundred American dollars."

"I'll givc you two-fifty."

An Oriental shrug, the rain dripping from the Asian nose, the lobes of the ears. "At that price, sir, I think maybe you should look again at the bargains by the gates. A 1976 Skoda perhaps?"

"Okay. Three hundred. Plus the Plymouth."

"Sir, I am not in the philanthropy business. I buy and sell motor carriages. Because it is raining and cold, four-fifty."

"Three twenty-five," Bolan said.

"Four hundred."

"Three hundred and fifty American dollars, cash, plus the Plymouth. As she is worth at least fifty, that meets your price."

The Asian sighed. "At this figure," he said sorrowfully, "I am practically paying you to take this beautiful machine away. You drive a hard bargain, sir. But because you are a gentleman, reluctantly, as one up-market man to another, I accept. But if I continue with such reckless generosity, sir, I am out of business."

"Try to survive," Bolan said. "Stay hard."

By the time he had transferred his belongings to the Volvo and driven to the gates, the Plymouth had joined the ranks of used-car bargains. A card behind the windshield announced that it was a steal at $130.

Bolan headed for the farm track behind Valley Road. The rain fell faster still. The Volvo's wipers worked fine.

The farms, in fact, belonged to horticulturists raising cut flowers, garden plants and ornamental shrubs under glass.

On an impulse he drove to the farm nearest Greystones, inspected the display in the long rows of greenhouses and bought a few potted flowering plants. Loading the spacious rear of the Volvo with these, he arranged a close-packed row against the double doors so that they effectively blocked any view of the interior.

This at least gave him a valid reason to be in the area of the properties on Valley Road.

Reinbecker's house was hidden on the far side of the wood. Bolan had strolled a little way up the track toward a rear entrance while the greenhouse employees carted out his purchases. He could see men among the trees, and he thought—though he could not be sure—that there were dogs with them.

There was a point of conscience here. Much though he disapproved of South Africa's racial laws, Bolan had no quarrel with individual police officers. In John Vorster Square it had been his life or theirs. But here it was different. Sure, he had to break the cordon and get to Reinbecker, get him alone, at all costs. But against the police? Normally he regarded the guardians of the law as allies. He couldn't treat Greystones as if it was a Mafia stronghold, shooting down cops and blasting his way in as he would have done if the place had been staffed by members of the Mob.

He would have to find a more subtle way of getting in and out of Reinbecker's house without spilling blood.

Except perhaps the blood of Reinbecker himself. But that would depend on the answers to Bolan's questions.

Back at the intersection where Valley Road branched off the highway linking the mines with the city center, Bolan parked on a shoulder of the road and kept watch. Apart from an occasional limo with a chauffeur at the wheel, the only traffic making it in and out of the ritzy estate was a fairly constant flow of panel trucks making deliveries.

The property owners of the neighborhood obviously preferred their supplies to be brought to the door rather than to demean themselves by entering a store.

Here, Bolan felt, was his answer.

The Reinbecker house was not a prison, even if its owner governed one. Once past the gate man and a perimeter guard, a delivery truck in Valley Road wasn't going to be subjected to a search, nor would private security men look inside a vehicle whose driver they knew.

Bolan drove the loaded Volvo back to the farm lane and left it beneath a line of trees around a bend, just out of sight of the Reinbecker property. With luck, anyone passing would think it was connected with the greenhouses.

He walked back to the intersection. The rain had stopped but the clouds racing across the sky were still low and menacing. The potholes pitting the surface of the lane brimmed with yellow water.

The Executioner allowed several vehicles to turn into Valley Road before he made his decision. He chose a panel van driven by a black youth with a cigarette hanging from one corner of his mouth. The sides of the truck carried blue lettering that announced:

Baarmbeek Laundromat: Fast Daily Service. Whiter than White.

Bolan stopped the vehicle by simply stepping into the road in front of it. The young driver hit the brake pedal, sending the van sideways across the slick pavement as the disks squealed their protest. He would have cursed, except that it paid to be careful what you said to a white man in the Transvaal.

Bolan stepped up to the window of the cab. He had decided that the only approach that would work quickly and surely was to offer money—a sum so exaggerated that it would probably be more than the driver earned in a week.

"I want you to do something for me," he said without preamble. "It's worth fifty American dollars in cash." He produced the bills and held them out. The driver's face, sullen and resigned until he realized from Bolan's accent that he was not South African, showed signs of animation.

But there was still suspicion there. Why would a foreigner be offering him such a sum?

"What do I have to do? Poison President Botha?" he asked sourly.

"You're going down Valley Road," Bolan said. "Are you delivering at Greystones?"

"Collecting—if it's anything to you."

"I want to get in there," Bolan said. "Without the guys on the gate seeing me. Here's twenty—" he handed over two ten-spots "—and you get the other three bills once I'm in the courtyard."

The driver took the bills, hesitated. What was the catch?

"I just want to see Reinbecker alone, without the sentries knowing," Bolan explained.

The young black stuffed the bills in his pocket.

"Listen, man," he said, "the number of friends of mine that son of a bitch has under lock and key in his jail, you could smash every picture in the place, take all his money and feed his wife to the wolves, and I'd be on the sidelines, applauding."

"I have something to settle with the guy," Bolan said, profiting from the youth's hostility. "Something personal."

"Don't let me stop you," the driver said. "Jump in the back among the silk sheets."

Bolan hid between the plastic sacks of neatly pressed shirts and skirts and bed linen. In fact the panel truck was waved through without being stopped at all.

Inside the Greystones courtyard the driver backed up to a service door at one side of the arch. Peering forward over his shoulder, Bolan saw that the main entrance to the big house, flanked by stone beagles on either side of an imposing flight of steps, was on the far side of the flagged enclosure.

The yard was embellished with ornamental troughs bright with geraniums and other blossoms. In the center, behind the Caddy and the Italian sporster, bronze dolphins in a fountain tried to outdo the rain, which had started to fall once more.

"You wanna get *inside* the dump?" the driver asked out of the corner of his mouth.

"That's the idea," Bolan said.

"Wait until I bring out the first hamper then. The housekeeper here's suspicious. She follows me to make sure I don't steal anything, then again when I fetch the second hamper. You can slide in after us. Take the first door on the left, the one covered in green stuff. That lets you into a passage that goes past the library, the billiard room and whatever."

"Thanks," Bolan said. He handed over the remaining three bills and ducked behind the plastic sacks.

"My pleasure," the driver said. "You've got time: the old man won't return before six, six-thirty."

He climbed out of the cab, opened the rear doors and rang a bell at the side of the service entrance.

Pretty soon the door opened and a thin, starchy white woman in a gray coverall beckoned him in with a jerk of the head.

Two minutes later the two of them emerged from the house, the driver with a large wicker basket full of linen in his hands.

He shoved it over the tailgate and toward the plastic sacks to make room for a second load, favored the hidden Executioner with a broad wink and turned away to go back into the house with the woman.

Bolan thrust aside the sacks, glanced quickly around as he crouched momentarily between the van's open doors. The courtyard was deserted. Gothic windows all around stared emptily at the rain drumming on the two cars. He jumped to the ground, ran across the wet flagstones and slipped into the house.

Bolan smelled floor polish and wood ash with a hint of some rich stew in the background. He could hear voices around a corner. The green door was immediately on his left as the youth had said.

The warrior pushed it open and edged through.

He was in a long corridor, with windows on his left following the line of the courtyard. Two doorways broke the paneling on his right; the far end of the passageway was closed off by double doors of frosted glass.

The green door hissed shut on an autostop as Bolan trod carefully along a creaking parquet floor.

Beyond the frosted glass, the corridor turned at right angles, tracing the line of the courtyard toward the main entrance. He could hear the distant drone of a vacuum cleaner but there were no voices in this part of the house.

He passed a lounge, a television room and two more closed doors and then found himself in an entrance lobby from which a wide, shallow stairway with carved posts curved to the upper floors. Behind it he could see a gun room with windows that looked out on the trees behind the house.

Bolan moved stealthily up the stairs. The gun room odors of wet raincoat, and rubber boots were overpowered by more cloying scents as he passed a huge urn of tropical flowers in the upper hallway.

Bedrooms, bathrooms, a housekeeper's cubbyhole stacked with linen. Finally the open door of what was clearly the owner's study or den. The vacuum cleaner drone was much nearer now, just around a corner in the corridor.

Bolan entered the study.

Brass-studded leather armchairs, legal reference books on glass-fronted shelves, college crests, crossed oars and golfing photos on the walls. Beyond the heavy oak desk, a window looked over the courtyard at the entrance arch.

On the far side of the yard, Bolan could see a man in a yellow slicker leading two German shepherds on a leash. It was still raining.

The hum of the vacuum cleaner was approaching the door. Bolan pushed it almost closed and looked hastily around him. Heavy velvet draperies framed a window recessed to hold a window seat. He slipped behind one, checked that his toes were not exposed and held his breath.

Looking down on either side of his feet, he saw that the waxed floorboards showed no sign of dust. Perhaps the servant had already cleaned the study.

The phone on the desk rang.

Bolan tensed. The shrill bell pealed once, twice...and then was stilled in the middle of the third ring.

Outside, the vacuuming continued, passed the half-open door, receded down the corridor. Evidently the upstairs maid had orders not to answer; the call had been taken on an extension somewhere below.

Cautiously Bolan padded out and picked up the receiver.

He assumed one of the voices was that of the starchy housekeeper; the clipped delivery of the other made it unmistakable as Colonel Julius Vanderlee's.

"As soon as he comes back, sir," the woman was saying.

"Very well," the policeman's voice barked. "His name is Hanson. Have you got that? He will arrive at seven with four other men. Be sure to tell Reinbecker that: four men."

"Yes, sir."

"He can supplement or take over completely the guarding of the house while this criminal is still at large," Vanderlee said. "That is for your employer to decide. Tell him, anyway, that this gentleman has my complete confidence."

"I won't forget, Colonel," the woman said.

When the subdued click indicated that the phone below had been hung up, Bolan gently replaced the receiver. There was a slight but satisfied smile on his face.

That did it.

No need to worry whether Reinbecker was in on the opium deal or just one of Vanderlee's golfing buddies.

If Eddie Hanson was being sent to watch over the guy—and, by inference, to guard him against Bolan—he was in it, all right.

Up to the neck.

That solved one of the Executioner's problems... but it posed another.

Hanson and his team of mercenaries were due to arrive at seven o'clock. According to the driver of the panel truck, Reinbecker should check in from the prison between six and six-thirty.

Bolan reasoned then, that Hanson at least, if not the four others, would come into the house to talk over and check out guard routines once the owner was back.

Bolan would therefore have to act fast; he would have maybe as little as thirty minutes to locate Reinbecker while he was still alone, make him talk... and get the hell out.

The Executioner looked around the room. There was an in-tray beneath a standard lamp on the desk, with three folders stacked in it. Beside the phone was a copy of that day's *Rand Daily Mail*, a scratch pad whose top page was covered with jotted notes in a spidery hand and a leather-bound diary in front of an onyx pen set.

Yeah, the study had a used air about it—as if business went on there every day. Bolan opened the diary; entries had been made up to ten days ahead. The folders contained daily reports on prison routine, copies of correspondence, circulars and telex messages from the Ministry of the Interior in Pretoria.

In each case the latest material in the file was dated the previous day.

Bolan reckoned that Reinbecker checked in to the study to tidy up his paperwork when he returned to the house each evening. Bolan decided to play that hunch and wait there for the guy.

If he was lucky, the prison governor would come to the study as soon as he arrived home, or at any rate before dinner.

If he was luckier, nobody else would come into the room before.

He went back behind the curtain. It was five-fifteen. There was a dull ache in his side.

Bolan was armed only with the silenced Beretta 93-R in its shoulder rig. He unleathered the gun, checked it over, unloaded and reloaded the magazine clip.

He put the weapon back in its holster.

Five thirty-three.

He couldn't hear the vacuum cleaner anymore. But there were other sounds of life: women's voices from the wing of the house he had not yet penetrated, distant music from a radio or television, an occasional muffled roar from some kind of heating or air conditioning plant. And of course the drumming of rain on the roof and against the window.

At five forty-five a young woman in a black raincoat with a scarf tied over her head ran down the steps of the main entrance, got into the Alfa-Romeo and drove away. Twelve minutes later a youth in an oilskin jacket rode a motorbike into the courtyard and delivered a package to the housekeeper at the service door. Bolan rechecked the Beretta.

Piet van der Hoek Reinbecker arrived home punctually at six. A black Citroën CX swished into the courtyard, braked by the entrance and disgorged a chauffeur in the uniform of a prison warden. The man ran around to open the rear door, helped out the governor, saluted and drove away as Reinbecker ran up the steps. The geranium blooms in the stone troughs were drooping under the pelting rain.

There were muffled voices below, one subservient, the other bullying. Reinbecker handing his wet garments to a manservant?

Soon afterward Bolan heard footsteps in the corridor outside. A door opened and closed. It was followed by the sound of water running, toilet flushing.

Reinbecker pushed open the study door and walked into the room.

Through a crack between two lengths of curtain Bolan saw a burly man with wide shoulders and a thick neck. His pale, flat eyes, set in a brick-red face, stared angrily at the newspaper as he opened it and scanned the headlines.

He peered shortsightedly at the newsprint and then, with a muttered exclamation, switched on the desk lamp. Beneath the low dark rain clouds it was almost dusk outside. Reinbecker turned to the window and tugged one of the cords that opened and closed the drapes.

He pulled the wrong one.

The draperies slid farther back. Reinbecker's jaw dropped as he stared incredulously at the tall, menacing figure of the Executioner. There was a cold glint in Bolan's blue eyes. The muzzle of the silenced autoloader was pointed straight at the South African's heart.

"Okay," Bolan said quietly, "tell me what Florida has to do with the Ogodishu opium—and why it's so important to them to know that everything's taken care of here."

Chapter Twenty

Reinbecker's face flushed an even deeper red. "What the hell are you doing here? Who are you? What the devil are you talking about?" he stormed.

"I need answers, fast," Bolan said softly.

"We'll soon see about that." The South African moved toward a white button recessed into the desktop. "No goddamn burglar's going to break into—"

"Don't!" Bolan's voice was suddenly a whiplash as Reinbecker's hand reached for the bell.

The pale eyes widened...took in the steely blue ones, the hawklike features, the determined chin of the tall, dark stranger standing so menacingly by the window. "Bolan!" he breathed. "You're the son of a bitch who murdered one of Vanderlee's men and ransacked the security police office. Well, don't kid yourself you can get away with that kind of thing here."

"Try me," Bolan said. He gestured with the gun. "Your last chance, I want an answer."

"Well, you won't bloody get one." Reinbecker swung around the swivel chair by the desk and dropped into it. "You won't use that thing. There's half a dozen state police in the grounds. One shot and—"

He froze. The brick-red features paled. Bolan had squeezed the trigger of the 93-R. The suppressed report made no more noise than a discreet chug. The slug smashed a hook on the wall. A golfing photo hanging from it dropped into one of the leather armchairs.

Reinbecker managed to regain his composure. "So kill me," he said. "What will it get you? A dead governor and another murder charge. You can't get away from here. You're going to hang, anyway."

"I'll get away all right," Bolan said. "Hanson's not due here with his four hired killers for another twenty-five minutes. I can deal with half a dozen cops."

For a moment Reinbecker was silent. "You're well informed," he said. His glance rested on the phone. "Of course. Eavesdropping once more. You listened in on Vanderlee."

Bolan ignored the accusation. "Vanderlee is the link between Ononu, the opium farm...and you," he said. "Whether or not there is a permanent connection between your team and the Rinaldi gang, I'm not sure. But it seems in any case that the whole deal's part of something much bigger. Something or someone you have to answer to. In Florida. I want the details. And I want to know who and where in Florida."

"Get lost," Reinbecker said.

Bolan sighed. "This is becoming boring," he said. "I never met so many guys who hate to talk. But the others all talked, finally. I think you will, too."

"Think again."

With lightning speed the Beretta came up. Bolan steadied his wrist with his left hand, and fired another single shot. The slug cored the palm of Reinbecker's left hand before it was lost in the padded leather of his chair.

Blood spurted over the files on the desk, onto the knee of his pants, across the floor.

The South African stared in disbelief at the ruined palm. He had gone very pale. "You dirty swine!" he muttered between his teeth.

"Now the other hand," Bolan snapped.

Involuntarily, Reinbecker snatched his right away from the desk and hid it behind his back.

"That won't save it," Bolan warned. "If I have to, I'll drill through your slimy body to get at the hand."

"All right, goddamn you; all *right*!" Reinbecker choked, losing some of his confidence now.

"I'm listening," Bolan said.

"It...it has to do with something bigger." The South African was trembling now. "It's all designed to...to rake in money."

"Money! So what else is new? You're stalling," Bolan snarled.

"I'm not stalling, I swear it. What I mean, the money from the drug end, the snatches, it's not profit for its own sake. It's for investing in...well, like you say, in something bigger."

"I'm waiting."

"I don't know. I'm told it's to be used to finance a big-time operation—but that's *all* I've been told. I don't know what operation."

Bolan grabbed a fistful of Reinbecker's hair and jerked the head back hard. The Executioner jammed the snout of the 93-R under the man's chin. The effort of the sudden move caused Bolan some discomfort.

"It's the truth." The voice was a strangled croak. "Ononu takes...took...a cut. Vanderlee takes a cut. I take a bigger cut. But the bulk of the money goes to Florida. I don't know how they use it."

"Guess. And guess right."

"Something to do with...with the terrorist circuit." Reinbecker was perspiring freely now, afraid to meet the diamond-hard gaze of the Executioner. "But I don't know who or where. All I have to do is keep the operation at this end trouble-free and moving."

"You said terrorists. Rinaldi?"

Reinbecker was about to shake his head, stopped just in time, quaking with horror at the thought. "Rinaldi was small time stuff," he groaned. "The hired help for that one series of snatches. Period."

"Okay. So who's the Florida contact?"

"They'll kill me if I tell you."

"At least that gives you another lease on life. Because I'll kill you now, if you don't tell me."

Reinbecker gasped out a name and address. Bolan withdrew the autoloader and scribbled the information on the top sheet of the notepad lying beside the phone. "You better get that hand looked at," he said. "It's bleeding." Reinbecker was crying. He held the shattered hand at his crotch, trying to stifle the pain as the scarlet flood flowed over his lap and down one leg of his pants.

Light from the courtyard splashed over the drawn draperies. An engine suddenly gunned, was cut.

Footsteps. Voices.

Bolan parted the draperies a crack and peered out.

A Range Rover beside the Cadillac. The driver and four other men piled out. Three carried SMGs, the other handguns. One of the state troopers ran through the arch and exchanged greetings with the driver.

Eddie Hanson and his mercs were ahead of time.

There was a sly grin forming on Reinbecker's agonized face. It didn't last.

Bolan moved fast. "Too bad about the hand. It'll have to wait now," he said. He snatched the South African by the lapels and pulled him half out of the chair. His right fist, traveling a short distance, carried all his weight. It crashed to the side of Reinbecker's jaw and knocked him cold.

Bolan lowered him back into the chair. Blood still pumped from the hole in his hand. Bolan ripped the paper from the notepad, stuffed it into his pocket, switched off the light and got out of there.

Holding his side, he raced along the upper hallway, took the stairs three at a time and sprinted for the gun room in back of the lobby.

As he pushed open the door and ran past the governor's gun room, the front door of the house opened and men crowded into the lobby.

A voice shouted, "Hey! That's Bolan! What the hell's he doin' here? After him, quick!"

The Beretta was in Bolan's hand. Jerking open the door that led to the backyard, he swung around and choked out a 3-round burst. One of the men silhouetted against the light from the lobby cursed and clutched his arm. The others scattered on either side of the open doorway.

Bolan ran into the night and the rain.

A gravel path led toward the woods sixty or seventy yards away. Weaving from side to side, he saw the dark punctuated by vivid flashes as revolver shots cracked out behind him. Slugs kicked up gravel by his feet. Hanson shouted orders. Bolan heard the engine of the Range Rover start on the far side of the house.

If only he could make the trees before the guys with the SMGs were near enough to score. His ribs were starting to throb again.

He couldn't. Two chatterguns roared when he was only halfway there. A stream of lead fanned the air on both sides of him. Before the gunners could correct their aim he turned right, pelted through a shrubbery, passed a summerhouse.

More shots—a whole fusillade this time. Bullets splatted through the leaves, chipping the woodwork of the little pavilion. A ricochet screamed off into the night. Then Bolan saw a wall surrounding a vegetable garden. He jumped for the coping, hauled himself up and dropped on the far side.

Grimacing and panting among dimly seen ranks of bean poles and raspberry canes, he staggered through rows of wet leaves, his feet clinging to the soggy earth. Before he reached the far side of the garden, Hanson's mercs were swarming over the wall, firing as they came.

Bolan found a door in the wall. He pulled it open and ran through. In front of him was a narrow belt of trees. He was at the outer fringe of the woods—and beyond it there was a stretch of rough ground and then the wall fencing off the property from the farm lane.

On the far side of the trees he reached a log pile before the SMGs were near enough to be dangerous. But the log pile was still ten or twelve yards from the boundary wall. He flung himself down behind it and looked desperately around.

He was cornered there. If he ran for it again and tried to climb the wall, he would be a sitting duck for Hanson's gunners when he pulled himself over the top. If he stayed where he was, he might be able to hold them off for a while, but his ammunition was limited and ultimately they would creep near enough to get him. It was only a question of time.

He peered over the top of the logs, straining his eyes through the blackness. There must be police allied with the mercs now; he made out seven or eight denser blurs in the dark, fanned out through the trees, moving inexorably closer. He fired two more rounds.

Hanson's voice again, something about grenades. Rays of light splashed between the tree trunks on his right. The Range Rover had been driven past the coach house, was taking the track that led to the rear entrance, was about to enfilade him.

Bolan emptied the Beretta's magazine and reloaded. His last clip. He fired again.... Somewhere out in the dark a man screamed.

The routine continued, mercs and police advancing, shooting as they came. Bolan showed himself above the log pile long enough to fire; the gunmen dropped and then blasted off again to make him duck while they approached still closer.

All the while the glare of the Range Rover's headlight through the trees grew nearer.

Then suddenly, astonishingly, gunfire blazed out in two places from the top of the wall behind the Executioner.

Gunfire that was aimed at the advancing enemy.

The clamor of the autofire was deafening. The lights of the approaching Range Rover died. Glass tinkled to the ground. In front of Bolan the darkness moved as men dived for cover. A grenade was thrown but fell short, momentarily etching the trees against the night sky with its livid exploding flash.

"This way, quick!" a voice called. "Run!"

Bolan sprinted for the wall, leaped, and pulled himself up and over, biting his lower lip to mask the agony in his side.

His Volvo had been driven across the grass and parked immediately below the wall. She was standing on the roof, a smoking mini-Uzi in each hand.

"Now get behind that wheel and drive like hell!" Ruth Elias said.

Chapter Twenty-one

Bolan knew that without headlights they'd think twice about pursuing him and the girl in the dark, even though the rear entrance to Greystones was less than two hundred yards from Bolan's Volvo. He raced to the end of the lane before Hanson's commandos could climb the wall and identify the car, turning left to take the highway leading north to Warmbad.

"They can't follow but they'll radio ahead," Ruth Elias said. "The good news is that they won't know about this particular vehicle—and they won't know your companion is female."

"And the bad news?"

She held up a small, powerful shortwave and FM radio receiver. "I'm tuned in to the police transmissions. They're looking for you all over the country. Murder while engaged in a criminal act. Dangerous. Shoot on sight. The whole works."

He smiled crookedly. "I think I heard the song before."

"Which way are you heading? Where do you want to go?"

"Out," Bolan said. "I already got what I came for."

"Any special route?"

"When I changed cars, I intended to go north, and then east after Pietersburg—bypass the Venda reserve and cross the Limpopo into Zimbabwe, then take a plane from Harare. Either that or go due east through the tail of the Drakensberg and then the Murchison range, making Mozambique on minor roads through New Agatha, Leydsdorp and Phalaborwa. Depending on the pressure."

"And now?"

"With this kind of heat—" he nodded toward the radio "—Mozambique and a boat from Laurenço Marques are out. So is Zimbabwe. I guess the only thing to do now is go west, and cross into Botswana."

"You're a long way from any airport there," the girl said.

"I'll worry about that when I get there."

"You better cut through the Blouberg," she said. "That's wild country but it's the quickest way to the border. The only thing is, we have to pass by Warmbad, Nylstroom and Pietersburg before we make the turnoff. It'd be wise to let me take the wheel first."

"How come?"

She pulled up the telescopic antenna on the radio and pressed a switch. "Listen," she said.

Through a fish fry of static, Bolan heard the voice of a police controller: "All stations west of Area Seven and north of Nine. This man is armed and he's dangerous. Repeat dangerous. He is more than six feet tall, dark, with blue eyes. Thought to be driving a pale blue 1968 Plymouth sedan with a companion as yet unidentified. Murder, armed robbery and malicious wounding of a state official are the charges so far—"

Ruth killed the transmission.

Bolan nodded. "Okay. If they're on the lookout for a blue Plymouth with two guys—"

"They may not be so anxious to flag down a Volvo if it's driven by a woman on her own."

"On her own?"

"It was smart of you to load all that garden stuff," she said. "As long as they don't stop and search, you can hide among that and leave me alone at the wheel."

"Good thinking," Bolan agreed. "We'll stop soon and change over."

The rain was falling more heavily now, gusting like blown smoke across the tunnel of light carved out by the headlights as squalls of wind shook the thorn trees beside the road.

They crossed a barren area of bush veld, passed through a region of scattered farms and stopped southeast of Warmbad, where the pale waste dumps from tin mines bulked dimly against somber hills to the left. Bolan steered the Volvo off the road, where it was partially sheltered by a huge tree, and cut the lights.

"Plymouth or whatever," he said, "they'll be expecting us to go like a bat out of hell. So the longer we wait, the less chance there is that they'll be suspicious of a woman alone in a Volvo full of plants."

"Whatever you say."

"I say thanks for getting me out of there," Bolan returned. "Now I think it's time to lay a few cards on the table."

For a moment Ruth was silent. Over the splatter of rain on the pavement, they could hear the ticking of hot metal as the engine cooled, the momentary hiss of steam each time a drop fell through the broad leaves of the tree onto the hood. Finally she said, "Okay."

"Just fill me in," Bolan said. "Who are you? Who do you work for? What's your angle on this whole deal?"

"You know my name." She paused again, and then said, "I work for Mossad."

"Mossad! What does the Israeli intelligence service have to do with Vanderlee and Reinbecker and their stinking drug racket? Why didn't you tell me before?"

"One of the things about an intelligence service," she reminded him gently, "is that it's supposed to be secret. But I guess I can't hold out on you any longer."

"And the Mossad angle?"

"As you say, drugs."

"Drugs?"

"Specifically, this opium farm and its refinery. Most of the hard stuff coming from there finds its way into Israel. Shipped in through Haifa, smuggled past the airport customs at Tel Aviv, or sent direct—overland across Africa and through the Sinai desert."

He nodded. "And your briefing?"

"Originally, to trace the source. Now we want to find out whether the operation is just a normal underworld racket, with our country up front as a largely unexploited market. Or whether there's a more sinister, possibly political, motive—a deliberate attempt to destabilize Israeli society by subverting the young, possibly financed by hostile Arab or Soviet elements."

"How come you were snatched by Ononu and... well, and maltreated like the other kids there?"

"I wasn't snatched in the sense of kidnapped. That Milan number I sold you was a phony. I was following the trail and I got too close. I guess I was careless. His security men jumped me when I was checking out his palace. The beatings and the rape were..." She shrugged. "Revenge, I suppose. He was going to have me killed if you hadn't shown."

"What were you looking for in Vanderlee's office?"

"Evidence. Some indication of who was behind the drug operation. Some kind of lead to the motivation. Anything. Because it was already clear that Ononu was not the Mr. Big—whatever he himself thought."

Bolan nodded again. "Like you, I drew a blank. But I think the operation *is* part of something bigger. I found that out from Reinbecker. It has something to do with terrorist activity, but I don't think it's particularly directed against your country."

"You're not certain?"

"It was only a hint. He didn't know for sure himself. I have to find out more," Bolan said evasively. Cards on the table were fine, but he liked to keep one or two up his sleeve.

"Where do you aim to look?"

"You were on the ledge outside the window, too. You heard what I heard. Florida." He did not say that he already had a name and address.

"Okay," Ruth said. "Your turn. Who do *you* work for? And why?"

"First of all," Bolan replied, "I was helping out a buddy. He's hospitalized, and one of Onunu's hostages was his daughter. Also, I don't go for the kind of trash we're dealing with here, and I figure they should be stopped. Permanently. But that's personal. I don't work for anyone!''

''So what are you going to do now?''

''Try to complete the puzzle. Find out who's behind Reinbecker and company, find out what they're financing with the dough from the drug operation, and why. Then stamp the whole dirty deal into the ground if I can.''

Bolan stopped speaking as headlight beams appeared over the brow of a hill behind them, swept past to illuminate the driving rain, vanished around a curve in the road. He said, ''You haven't told me yet how come you were outside Greystones just when I needed you?''

''I followed you,'' she said simply.

He stared at her blankly through the darkness. ''Followed me? From where? From Montenegria?''

''No, no,'' she said laughing. ''From Jo'burg. I knew about Vanderlee, I'd been out to the opium farm and turned over their files before Ononu's men jumped me. It was a coincidence we happened to make that ledge at the same time. The rest was...well, quite logical.

''I heard the shooting as I came down that stack pipe. I saw you saved by that tree and...I couldn't believe it. Anyway, I followed you back to your hotel. I saw you buy the Plymouth and tailed you to Baarmbeek—that was the big surprise, I did *not* know about Reinbecker. Then I saw you change the Plymouth for this Volvo. After that there was no problem.''

''I never knew I was being tailed!'' Bolan was shocked with himself. ''What were you driving?''

"A taxi when you were on foot in the city. A panel truck to Pretoria, and then a pickup. In Baarmbeek it was a motorbike."

"A bike!" Suddenly he remembered. "The boy in oilskins delivering some package while I was waiting for Reinbecker—that was you?"

"That was me."

"But how did you make it with so many different—"

Ruth tapped the radio. "I'm not the only Mossad agent in South Africa," she said. "Now I guess it's time you hid in the shrubbery and we got moving."

"Right," Bolan said.

Two rows of the potted plants were ranged on slatted wooden supports in back of the station wagon. The supports stood nine inches off the floor. Beneath these, with a tarp covering his body and the taller shrubs crowded around, the Executioner was invisible to anyone glancing through the Volvo's windows.

Ruth started the vehicle and drove on.

There was a police roadblock outside Warmbad and another in Nylstroom. In each case the Volvo was flagged down by two armed cops swinging flashlights...and in each case it was waved on without being stopped when they saw a woman alone at the wheel.

It was at a village called Moorddrift that the trouble started.

Another roadblock. A flashing white-on-blue Police sign below the revolving amber light on the roof of a patrol car. Two cops with Heckler & Koch MP-5 submachine guns waving flashlights.

This time the Volvo was required to halt. There were several cars in front of it, lined up along the lamplit street. It was still five minutes short of eight o'clock.

One of the cops approached the driver's window, the other began a slow circuit of the battered station wagon.

Ruth rolled down the glass. "What seems to be the trouble, officer?"

"Routine check, miss. Your license and papers, please."

She unzipped her purse and handed them over. The second cop flashed his light over leaves and fronds behind her. Highway patrolmen were also checking out the cars lined up ahead. Three local police stood by the open door of the patrol car listening to the garbled voice of the dispatcher broadcasting messages over the radio.

Facedown beneath his tarp, Bolan heard it all.

"What have you got in back there, miss?" the first cop asked.

"Oh, only some plants for a new house in Pietersburg," Ruth replied.

Then another policeman spoke. "You want me to take a look in there?" he asked the first cop. "Yeah, maybe you better. Where are you taking them, miss?"

"I told you. Pietersburg. My brother-in-law's place," Ruth said, beginning to get a bit edgy now.

Bolan felt a cold draft of air as the rear doors were jerked open. His head was toward those doors, his right hand, gripping the Beretta, near the edge of the tarp. Light seeped in beneath the heavy proofed material. "Like she says," the second cop reported, "garden plants." He began to close the doors.

"How come you're delivering way out here, when you're driving on Pretoria plates?" the officer near the driver's window asked.

And then they all heard it, suddenly clear of static, the radio voice: "Attention all cars! Attention all cars! Correction on the Bolan murder case intel. The two fugitives are not, repeat not, driving a blue Plymouth sedan. This vehicle was traded in at Baarmbeek earlier today. The criminals are now believed to be using a pale-colored 1977 Volvo station wagon. Any officer sighting this vehicle is ordered—"

The rest of the sentence was lost in a blur of sound and movement.

Ruth gunned the engine. The Volvo rocketed forward. The cops by the patrol wagon yelled. The guy holding Ruth's papers fell back as the spinning wheels sprayed roadside gravel against his legs. The man closing the rear doors swore as one of them, reacting to the sudden forward movement, swung wide and knocked his gun arm aside.

Among the plants, Bolan threw off the tarp and rose to his knees. It would be no good trying to bluff now. If the police knew about the Volvo they must have visited the used-car dump and questioned the Asian who sold it. They would know the license number, Bolan's description, the fact that there was an auxiliary fuel tank, the whole works.

He fired the Beretta, shattering the rear window glass. He had no wish to kill members of the police force, but he had to make them keep their heads down to stop them wasting him. He loosed off another trio burst—through the swinging doors, above the stumbling cop's head.

The Volvo snaked into the center of the road and shot away.

Behind them, cops ran into the road and fired automatics and SMGs. Their movements were hampered by the line of civilian cars halted ahead of the Volvo, and by the risk of hitting bystanders on the sidewalks.

By the time the policemen had reacted and leaped out to give themselves a clear field of fire, the station wagon was two hundred yards away, accelerating fast. More glass erupted from the rear windows and the steel body echoed to the impact of 9 mm slugs, but otherwise the vehicle was undamaged.

The Volvo howled past an intersection at the exit from the village as the patrol car was maneuvered past the stalled vehicles and launched in pursuit.

Bolan climbed over the seats and dropped down beside the woman. "They won't know we have the radio, so we can keep ahead of them until sunrise," he said. "But after that the choppers will be out and the going will be tough. You must take the first left turn, cut the lights and head for that border.

"We have to take the second turnoff, not the first. I know this country and that road will take us up toward the Blouberg. It's hilly and it's slow—but although there are farms and native villages, we hit no towns between there and the frontier."

Bolan turned to look over his shoulder. The lights of the patrol car were no more than a misty glare above a line of treetops masking a bend in the road behind.

Chapter Twenty-two

The rain stopped shortly before dawn. For more than nine hours it had been sucked in through the broken rear windows of the Volvo, soaking their arms and shoulders. Nine hours of low-gear driving through barren foothills blotched with patches of thin scrub, along a ridge of rock and sand where nothing but thorn bushes broke the monotony of scorched terrain on which the storm seemed to have made little or no impression. Nine hours that had finally brought them to this bleak upland plateau beyond which, Mack Bolan hoped, the dirt road would finally tilt down and lead them toward the distant border.

He braked the car to a halt, shaded his eyes with one hand against the dazzle of the rising sun and scanned a slope that slanted up to a bluff a thousand feet above them. Ruth Elias was asleep, her dark head lolling against the padded back of the passenger seat.

Below and behind them, the dead land dropped away in parallel crests of ocher and rust, an arid landscape rising from the high veld in which Bolan figured their pursuers must still be searching for them.

The woman had backtracked on their route constantly during the night, following narrow trails in the dark until finally she had eluded the pursuing headlights. But when Bolan relieved her sometime after midnight on the edge of the huge expanse of veld, they had no idea where they were. They had passed through no towns or villages; in the night these vast tracts of country could have been on an alien planet.

As daylight approached, Bolan had been forced to keep climbing or go back and risk running into the enemy again. He had been steering roughly west in the hope of finding some landmark that would indicate how far they were from the Botswana frontier. Now he figured it was time to make a more serious attempt at orientation.

He stepped out of the Volvo and stretched. The sky had been swept clear of clouds. His clothes were already steaming damply in the heat of the sun.

He took a western Transvaal map from the car and opened it. It was not very detailed, but as far as he could see from the scale, the high ground they were crossing should be someplace between Thabazimbi and Vaalwater, fifteen or twenty miles northeast of the Heystekrand Bantustan.

If he had guessed right—he peered at the map again, squinting against the fierce glare of the sun—they should be near the headwaters of a river called the Matlabas, which was a tributary of the Upper Limpopo. And once they located that, all they had to do was follow the valley until they arrived at the confluence, for in that region the Limpopo formed the frontier.

And the distance from their present position to that frontier, if Bolan had calculated correctly, was between forty-five and fifty-five miles.

"The longer we stick with the car," he said when Ruth awoke, "the nearer we can get to the border.

And the less chance we have of being zapped by Hanson or the South African police. On the other hand, if they get anyplace near at all, a Volvo station wagon's much more easily identifiable than two guys on foot."

"I say we stay with it," Ruth said.

Bolan nodded. "We're on our way."

A mile farther on, the dirt road twisted through a pass, a narrow cleft in the bluff. On the far side, the land dropped away and the trail was lost in a wilderness of boulders. Beyond this, scrub covered the floor of a huge depression for miles in all directions.

"And this river valley we're looking for?" Ruth inquired.

Bolan took a hand from the wheel and gestured diagonally to the right, where the ridges of a distant mountain chain stood out crisply against the sky. "On the far side of that crest," he said. "The bush veld below stretches a long way north and south, but it's no more than fifteen miles across. We should make those foothills inside an hour."

He sent the car rolling down the slope. The air was clear and sparkling now; the sun cast iron-hard shadows behind the rocks. Even with the unbroken windows wound down, the air inside the station wagon became insufferably hot.

Steering between the boulders, bumping alarmingly over patches of shale and bedrock, Bolan reached the trackless veld below. "Not a square foot of shade in the whole damn valley," he complained. None of the stunted vegetation was tall enough to throw a shadow that reached even halfway up the wheels.

But there was a darker shadow above the veld—a shadow that moved, undulating swiftly over the scrub, gliding across rock and sand and areas of cracked, dried mud. The rotors were spinning too fast to register more than a blur, but the skeletal, mosquitolike body left a recognizable enough image as it sped over the parched terrain.

The Volvo was grinding through a dried-up riverbed, so Bolan and Ruth failed to hear the whining clatter of the machine as it passed directly overhead at a height of less than five hundred feet. It was only when they saw that shadow—and then, as it turned to make another pass, a flash of light when the Plexiglas-bubble caught the sun—that the fugitives realized they had been spotted.

"A helicopter," Ruth groaned. "That's all we need."

"Not entirely unexpected," Bolan said grimly. The chopper had sunk lower on its second run. "It's a Lynx," he added. "French machine. They use them for surveying forest fires, searching for people swept out to sea—and tracking down fugitives."

The helicopter passed overhead for the third time, and then swung away to hover level with them, fifty feet above the veld. They could see the helmet and phones of the pilot as he turned his head to stare at them. Beyond him, a second man had half risen to his feet to look over the pilot's shoulder. He was speaking into a microphone.

"They're not armed?" Ruth asked.

Bolan shook his head. "Strictly recon. But whoever they're calling up will be armed. My guess is that it'll be Hanson. If the cops catch up with us, they'll try and take us alive. Vanderlee and Reinbecker would much rather know we're dead. That's why they hired mercs in the first place."

"Can't we shoot down the helicopter and stop them reporting our position?"

"Not with an Ingram and two mini-Uzis." Bolan smiled. "And that's the heaviest firepower we have left."

Bolan continued heading west between the clumps of scrub. After a while the helicopter wheeled away and flew off to the south.

"NIS crew," Bolan said. "We'll have to ditch the car."

"How long have we got?"

"Depends how far away Hanson's killers are. And what transport they use. Whatever they have, it'll be better suited to the terrain than this."

"Surely they could call up a flight of Mirages and blow us off the face of the earth with rockets," Ruth said, "in about four minutes flat?"

"That's right, but they won't." The Executioner was definite. "They'll want visual evidence of some kind of fight—bodies, weapons, a burned-out car. That way they can say it was some underworld feud. A few smoking holes in the ground, especially if they could only have been made by government planes, won't be easily explained."

"The foothills are still four or five miles away," Ruth said later. "Some of those valleys look like they have real trees in them. If we got there before they caught up with us, couldn't we stash the car and drive again at night?"

Bolan was looking into the rearview mirror. "Not if you see what I see," he said.

She turned and stared out the shattered rear window. A column of yellow dust hung above the veld. And it was moving on a course that would intercept their own some miles ahead.

"A dust storm?" Ruth asked.

"Uh-uh. We raise a cloud ourselves—but because we're in the center we don't notice it. It'll be visible for miles, to others. What we're seeing is raised by something on wheels that's traveling a hell of a lot faster than we are. Too bad the rain stopped before it reached here."

"What is it?" she asked. "Another Range Rover? One of those jumbo-size superjeeps?"

"I don't think so," Bolan said. "Not on this terrain, not going that fast."

He floored the pedal. Bouncing and slithering, the Volvo hightailed it between the thornbushes toward the rising ground, trailing its dust cloud behind it like a banner.

They made the lower slopes before the pursuers intercepted their route. Bolan was able to identify their tail after they had climbed a short distance from the veld but still not found a recognizable track.

Hot wind had blown the dust clouds off to one side, and he could see in the mirror that the vehicle was in fact a half-track—a Humber FV-1612, capable of speeds up to forty mph over rough ground.

"Basically it's an armored personnel carrier," he told his companion. "They were originally designed as radio command cars, but the models supplied to the

South Africans have been modified to act as APCs for riot-control work and guerrilla fighting."

He didn't tell her that the modifications included the installation of a 40 mm cannon in the half-track's turret.

EDDIE HANSON CROUCHED beside the APC's driver, his small eyes squinting against the sun glare as he stared at the Volvo zigzagging up the hillside among the trees ahead of them. The land was less barren on this side of the depression. A variety of vegetation dotted the slopes and here and there a clump of dry grasses stirred in the breeze.

"Hell, man, push this goddamn thing!" Hanson growled. "We were overtaking them fast on the flat, and now they're keeping their bloody distance. With caterpillar tracks on the rear wheels, you should be able to catch that Swedish tin can. What's the matter with you?"

The driver was Irish, a renegade who had been chased out of the Provisional IRA for pocketing funds destined for the purchase of arms. "Sure it's the grade," he said. "She's steep enough for the weight of our armor to slow us down, but not so steep that they have to shift to a lower gear. When they hit rougher ground, then we shall gain on them."

"I hope you're right," Hanson snarled. "I want them destroyed before they're over the crest. There's a stretch of high veld that goes almost all the way to the frontier on the far side of the ridge. We could lose them over there."

"You want me to stop so the guys in back can fire?" the Irishman asked. Apart from himself, Hanson and two survivors of the Greystones engagement, half a dozen other mercs recruited by Hanson were crammed into the rear of the truck. Three were seasoned Vietnam vets, deserters from the U.S. Army, one was an Ethiopian, the remaining couple were Cuban.

"For cryin' out loud," Hanson sneered. "They're half a mile ahead of us, on an upward slope. At that range, on a hill, with those goddamn trees in between, even the cannon could miss—and if we didn't zap them with the first shot or two, we'd be too far behind to catch them again. We could lose them altogether."

"It's your money," the driver said sullenly. He banged the lever into second to negotiate a graveled depression and then shifted up once more as they hit harder ground.

At the top of the slope the land dipped, then rose to a low escarpment that crowned the ridge. Along the foot of this weathered cliff, a dirt road ran north and south. The Volvo bumped across the last few yards of rough terrain, swung right and sped away along the track in another cloud of dust.

The helicopter made its second pass as the Humber half-track slewed onto the trail and rocketed in pursuit. The sun was lower now, and the machine's shadow flitted over the exposed rock beside the station wagon.

"Why the fuck don't they send a bloody gunship and blow them off the road?" the driver said.

"Because they are only spotters," Hanson said. "They pinpoint the target, we make the hit. There's nothing illegal about an NIS spotter reporting fugitives, but they don't want to be officially connected with..." He chuckled. "Well, call it execution without trial."

"They say Bolan's got a skirt with him," the driver said.

"That's right. In which case the execution could be...delayed a little...while we have ourselves some fun." Hanson laughed again.

Soon the rock strata forming the escarpment dipped downward, and the dirt road, playing switchback for a few hundred yards, plunged over the crest and looped down to where the landscape was gathered into wooded folds. Then it dropped to another expanse of veld beyond which, blue in the distance, rose the last mountain chain before the border.

"Now!" Hanson grated as the Volvo ahead of them took the downward grade. "Close the gap man. We only need to get within three or four hundred yards."

But the Humber—"borrowed" with Vanderlee's connivance from the motor pool of an army training unit—was unfamiliar to the driver. Although the weight of its armor should have been an advantage in a downhill situation, he found the tracked pairs of rear wheels acting as a brake. Before he had adapted his driving technique to the conditions, the old Volvo, battered and clogged with dust as it was, had actually gained several hundred yards.

The trail arrowed across the plain. This was the high veld, a great swell of grassland, golden in the light of the setting sun, that rippled with waves like an inland sea as crosscurrents of wind stirred the surface.

Apart from isolated black herdsmen with flocks of sheep or goats, pursuer and pursued passed nothing but a herd of zebra, startled into a mass gallop by the unfamiliar machines. Farther off, vultures circled above the carcass of some savanna creature.

Like another kind of vulture, the helicopter hovered above them until the Volvo reached the range of hills fifteen miles away on the far side of the veld. It was there that Hanson got his chance...and the chopper, apparently satisfied that his men could complete their mission, tactfully withdrew so that the crew could witness nothing that contravened international law.

The crunch came when the trail was passing an abandoned farm that lay in a pocket of the hills—a small upland valley covered in coarse grass with clumps of dwarf trees clustered on either side of a watercourse strewed with pale stones.

The pursuers saw Bolan's station wagon hesitate and almost halt at the nearer edge of the valley. It seemed to bounce once or twice on its springs as if the occupants were jumping up and down in their seats...rolled slowly down the slope...stopped finally at the foot of the grade climbing the far side.

Hanson was triumphant. "Got them!" he exclaimed. "They must be out of gas!"

The Irishman braked the half-track on the rim of the depression. Five hundred yards away, the doors of the Volvo opened. Two people piled out, each wearing dark clothes, one much taller than the other. Sunlight glinted on the steel of weapons as they ran for the farm buildings. The tall one was carrying some kind of suitcase.

Hanson focused his binoculars on a long, low building attached to a hollow square of stables and barns. The farm looked as though it had been uninhabited for some time. The roofs of the outbuildings had fallen in, the ten-bar gate at the entrance to the stockade leaned drunkenly on one hinge, the vanes of the windmill no longer turned. Scorch marks blackened the walls above some of the unglazed windows as if at some time the main building had been torched. Perhaps the farmer and his family had been victims of a guerrilla raid by antiapartheid rebels from across the border.

Hanson jumped to the ground, ready for a whirlwind assault on the farm. "They'll have nothing but SMGs and handguns, maybe even a grenade or two," he said. "We're way out of their range here; we can blast them any time we want."

From past experience, however, he knew it would be crazy to underestimate the Executioner or underrate his powers of recovery. The mercenary lifted the binoculars again and studied the terrain.

Behind the farm buildings what had once been neat rectangles of cultivation had run wild. The dusty track that twisted between neglected fields of maize was overgrown with weeds. Bolan and the woman had remained inside the stockade. The merc leader could make out gun barrels still glinting in the rays of the sinking sun at two of the windows.

"Making a stand," he said. "Great. We'll soften them up from here and then go in and finish it."

A quarter of a mile away, to one side of and a little behind the abandoned farm, the swell of land was broken by a bare rock outcrop that rose through the grass like a boil blemishing a smooth area of skin. It was the perfect place for an enfilade.

Hanson sent a two-man mortar crew—the Cubans—and two of the Vietnam vets, armed with M-16s, to position themselves in clefts amid the rock. "Set fire to the place if you can," he told the Cubans. "And you two guys—" he turned to the vets "—mow down anyone who tries to escape the back way."

As the four men set off along the lip of the valley, he positioned the remaining members of his ten-man team.

The third vet was stationed with his M-16 behind a clump of bushes at one side of the track. The two Greystones survivors were dispatched with their shorter-range SMGs toward the farm, with orders to make use of whatever cover they could find as they traversed the valley. Hanson and the driver were to stay with the Humber.

The Ethiopian was odd man out. A tall, thin guy with a shaved skull and skin the color of a ripe fig, he was a specialist. He had perfected the skill of firing an XM-174 automatic grenade launcher from the hip. And when the self-powered launcher's 12-round magazine was loaded with rocket-assisted projectiles, he was an accurate one-man artillery barrage at anything up to one thousand yards.

He stood now with the cumbersome twenty-five-pound weapon held loosely in his hands, a little to one side of the armored truck. At that distance there was no need for him to take cover. "Choose whichever part of the building you like, Abu," Hanson told him, "but wait until the car is destroyed. I want to do that myself."

He took a final look around. There was no sign of movement from the deserted farm. He clambered back into the half-track and squeezed his burly frame into the turret behind the 40 mm cannon. He adjusted the sights, checked the automatic loader and squinted out through the slit in the armor.

The stranded Volvo, its doors gaping open, lay at the bottom of the depression like a wounded bird.

Beneath the sandy crew cut, Hanson's face creased into an anticipatory smile. Moving the barrel fractionally, he thumbed the cannon's firing button.

The Humber rocked on its springs as the coughing detonations of the cannon shells spit flame from the front of the turret. The weapon fired alternate high-explosive and incendiary rounds at a rate of 320 per minute. The interior of the vehicle vibrated with the clamor of the first burst.

The charger belt leaped and jerked as the shells fed through the breech. Powder fumes swirled in the flat shaft of sunlight slanting through the slit in the armored windshield.

Small, bright explosions and mushrooms of dust blossomed from the hard ground fifty yards short of the Volvo. "Make it five-fifty," Hanson shouted to the Ethiopian. On the second burst he got the range right. Shells ripped into the rear of the Volvo, tearing open the roof, setting fire to the tires and showering leaves and stalks from the plants inside across the trail.

The third burst hurled the wrecked car over onto its side, and the incendiaries, each burning for one-seventieth of a second at a temperature of two thousand degrees centigrade, ignited the engine and the oil pan.

Black smoke streaked with red boiled up into the evening sky.

An instant later fumes from the two gas tanks exploded with a dull roar and the remains of the Volvo flared into an incandescent torch.

Hanson erupted from the turret of the Humber and waved his arms. The Ethiopian, then the mortar crew and the men with the M-16s opened fire.

The thudding concussions of the mortar on the rock outcrop and the crackle of automatic bursts were drowned in the belching roar of the XM-174. Flame seared the atmosphere as the RAP rounds streaked for the farmhouse, towing fiery tails.

Mortar shells pulverized the stonework in back as the Ethiopian's rocket grenades exploded against door and window frames, dropped through the sagging roof and ignited the wooden rafters. Flames and smoke streamed up through the jagged holes in the building and then, teased out by the breeze, leaned away to mingle with the oily smoke cloud rising from the blazing Volvo.

"Okay, back into the truck!" Hanson yelled. "Now we're going in to get them."

The men on the rock increased their rate of fire.

The Ethiopian and the third vet joined Hanson and the Irish driver aboard the half-track, which careered down toward the stockade, spitting cannon shells from its turret and a stream of 7.62 mm lead from a coaxially mounted machine gun.

Nearer the farm, the two guys with the SMGs emerged from their cover and advanced, shooting as they came.

The cannon pumped a stream of shells into the farmhouse, blasting still larger holes in the walls, setting fire to the interior. It was only when the Humber dipped below the stockade and approached the broken gate that Hanson realized there was no answering fire.

He pushed himself up from the turret and shouted orders, yelling at the more distant men through a bullhorn. Once through the gateway he leaped from the half-track, a Walther PPK in his hand, and led the rest of the mercs into the attack.

The assault was a model of its kind—a small, limited force softening up a target and then rushing it from two sides, with a flanker behind, to cut off any attempt to escape.

Hanson and his men lobbed hand grenades and then rushed into the shell-torn house. But when they got there, they found nobody to attack.

Bolan and the woman had disappeared.

Chapter Twenty-three

Strategically, Mack Bolan's thinking was good. If their position was to be pinpointed by NIS helicopters, clearly it would be impossible to shake off their pursuers. It was equally clear that with the armaments they had the two of them could not hope to outmaneuver Hanson and his mercs in a straight combat. The answer, therefore, must be to delay the enemy while they themselves escaped.

The best way to do this, Bolan figured, was to fool the opposition into thinking they had been cornered. And for this—although there was still plenty of gas in the tanks—it was necessary to sacrifice the Volvo.

Tactically the ploy worked well. It was the ancient principle of surprise and the unexpected; the warrior and his companion had in fact fled without the slightest attempt to make a stand.

Pausing only to position a couple of metal rods in the window in the hope they would be mistaken for gun barrels, they had run straight through the farmhouse and dodged behind a stone barn in back. Hidden by the stockade, they ran to a wall behind that, and then crept along on all fours until they were opposite the nearest patch of high grass.

Still hidden from the mercenaries by the bulk of the buildings, they dashed across thirty yards of wasteland and vanished among the fifteen-foot stalks and desiccated leaves of the neglected plantation.

By the time the Cubans set up their mortar on the rock from where they could survey the whole area of the farm, Bolan and Ruth were a quarter of a mile away, following the farm track as it snaked toward the crest of the range.

For a wild moment, when he first decided to make the pretense of running out of fuel, Bolan had toyed with the idea of drawing Hanson and his men into the farm while he outflanked them by some maneuver and stole the half-track. But the odds against them were too great: they were outnumbered, they were outgunned—and Hanson was too experienced a fighter to leave his transport unguarded.

The moment he heard the cannon open fire, Bolan knew he had been right.

Seven hours later they reached the east bank of the river that formed the frontier. It wasn't the easiest seven hours of the Executioner's life.

Once night had fallen, there were perilous descents through the dark, along rocky trails strewed with loose stones where a false step could mean a sprained ankle, a broken leg or even a shot from South African police, who Bolan was certain, would be lying in wait for them someplace ahead. The trail constantly petered out in a wilderness of scrub. But to use the dirt road that had taken them to the farm would invite another confrontation with Hanson.

As they dropped below the tree line, unexpected branches whipped their faces. Their legs were scratched by thornbushes they could not see. A late-rising remnant of moon cast shadows that resembled clumps of bushes, and the bushes themselves became confused with shadow.

But once they saw the surface of the river glimmering through the leaves below them, such natural hazards took second place to man-made dangers.

Apart from catnaps snatched in the passenger seat of the Volvo, neither of them had slept for two nights. And although there were glucose tablets and vitaminized chocolate bars among the weaponry in the bag Bolan still carried, it was more than thirty-six hours since they had had a proper meal.

But Bolan knew that before dawn he had to find a stretch of the river where they could safely cross into Botswana.

He knew it wasn't going to be easy. It meant deliberately searching for a frontier post, a bridge, a ford, anyplace an enemy could by lying in wait.

Although the aim of the operation was to avoid such places, it was only near them that crossing the swift-flowing river would be possible.

The chances of swimming over were zero. Swollen by rains in the interior, the waters swirled between high, heavily wooded banks, sometimes thirty, sometimes as much as fifty yards across.

It was more than an hour before Bolan, moving cautiously between the trees in the dark, saw light reflected on the water around a bend in the river several hundred yards ahead.

The bank was steep and wet. It was hard to move without tripping over gnarled roots or snapping the branches of unseen undergrowth, difficult to advance without making any noise. But finally, beneath an arcade of thick trunks he was able to see around the corner.

He saw a steel-and-wire suspension bridge with twin pylons on either side of the river. Floodlights cast a harsh glare over the roadway, and on the huts clustered on the South African side. Two antiriot trucks were parked near the striped barrier pole and what looked like a whole company of special police were mingling with the border guards.

This bridge would be the nearest to the deserted farm. And the chopper had flown away before the attack. Bolan guessed the NIS crew had reported to the murder hunt authorities as well as spotting for the Vanderlee-Hanson team. The mercs wouldn't be far away, either; it was the obvious area to search once they found their quarry had bolted.

Half a mile downstream was another bridge—a ropewalk for pedestrians only, slung high above the river, which narrowed there and flowed faster than ever. There was a frontier post, too: a small tin-roofed hut staffed by two guards.

Police were in evidence, as well, but the place must have been considered unlikely for an attempted crossing, because only a single jeep and four men had been sent.

At a bend in the river two hundred yards farther on, Bolan found the place he was looking for. But to gain the far bank, he would have to return to the hut and steal something.

The jeep was parked without a guard, but it was no use to the warrior. No trail followed the course of the river; all they could have done with the jeep was move back into the interior. A few yards from the vehicle, however, was a small compound behind barbed wire, and inside this lay the means of the fugitives' escape.

A stack of lumber, including some large logs.

From the edge of the clearing surrounding the small post Bolan surveyed his target area. The gate to the compound was between the hut and the riverbank; to reach it he would have to cross the bar of light streaming from the open door of the hut—and risk being seen by the six men talking inside.

The wire was strung with tin cans that would jangle at the slightest touch.

But it was less dangerous than the bar of light—and there were wire cutters in his bag.

Bolan posted the woman on the far side of the clearing with her two mini-Uzis. "Don't fire unless they trap me," he told her. "And if there's any trouble, move up the slope—don't follow the riverbank—and work your way down later to meet me at the place we chose."

In the darkness behind the hut he had no trouble worming his way to the wire, except for some painful twinges in his side. He turned and lay flat on his back, looking upward to locate the cans.

The stars continued to glitter in the blackness above him.

He moved a few feet to one side, trying to locate the cans. For an instant he was certain that one star disappeared, and then reappeared. He twisted his head this way and that, but the star stayed bright.

There was a sudden puff of wind, a thin metallic clanking. One of the cans was almost directly above his head.

Bolan brushed the sweat from his eyes with the back of his free hand. He groped carefully upward. His fingers touched a cold strand of wire; one of the barbs pricked his thumb. The tin can clanked again, louder this time.

He froze... then reached warily up once more. The snap of the cutters biting through metal sounded like an explosion in his ears. The wire coiled back, setting several cans jangling.

He could feel the moisture running between his shoulder blades and trickling down his sides. The next strand was slacker: there was no reaction from the cans when he cut it. Nor was there from the one after that.

He rose to his knees and tackled one of the higher strands. The wire sprang away from the blades like a striking snake, setting up a rattle on either side.

Bolan dropped to the ground and hid his face in his hands. The shadow of a soldier appeared in the spill of light spreading outward from the door of the hut, peering into the night. Another light squall stirred a can farther along the wire. "It's just the wind, Sergeant." The man's head turned. "There's a bit of a breeze blowing up."

Bolan went on cutting the wire. When there were no strands left he rose to his feet and tiptoed into the compound.

He selected three large logs from the woodpile and lashed them together with a long coil of rope he had seen in one corner the first time they passed.

He hefted the logs onto his back and pulled one end of the rope down over his shoulder. He took a step toward the gap in the wire...and then something caught in his pant leg and he plunged to the ground.

There was a trip wire he had missed on his way in.

Tin cans jangled, clattered and bounced all around the compound. The noise was deafening.

Voices inside the hut shouted. Tongues of flame spit into the night as the police specials fired a volley blind. By the steps leading to the bridge a searchlight glowed and then sizzled into dazzling brilliance. The beam, trained on the ropewalk, swung slowly around to sweep the clearing. The light in the hut was extinguished.

At once Ruth Elias opened fire with both SMGs.

Over the shattering double clamor of the hellfire miniatures, glass splintered and fell. The searchlight faded and died. The South Africans returned fire from outside the hut; they were too smart to be caught in a confined space.

For a moment there was silence from the far side of the glade. Then two more bursts from the Uzis—from among the trees, higher up the hillside.

Following orders, Ruth was laying down the idea of a strategic retreat. Bolan knew the police would have been ordered not to leave the bridge unguarded. Since there were so few of them he reckoned they would call for reinforcements rather than attempt to follow attackers into the forest.

He was right. After a few more sporadic volleys—returned by single shots from the woman, even higher up the hill—Bolan heard the tinkle of a hand-cranked field telephone from inside the darkened hut. And then an excited voice—the sergeant's.

He picked up the load of wood and stole quietly in among the trees himself.

A little later, alarmingly, he heard another exchange of shots—farther away from the river this time. Immediately before, he had been aware of the sound of a truck engine grinding along the forest trail that he guessed led to the rope bridge and the hut. He judged that the reinforcements called up by the sergeant in charge of the frontier detail had caught sight of Ruth.

They had—a fleeting figure momentarily seen among the tree trunks, picked up by the headlight beams when she had inadvertently strayed too near the track.

She once more shot out the lights and escaped before they could deploy into the woods and surround her. But it was another half hour before she joined Bolan at the place he had chosen for their crossing.

She was exhausted, scratched and bleeding, her hair mussed and her clothes torn. She was also distressed.

"I couldn't find the place," she gasped. "I kept hearing the river but I couldn't locate the bank. I'm so sorry, but—"

"That's okay. We've got time."

"You don't understand." She was almost in tears. "The...the bag...I don't have it. I lost it. I fell down a bank and it was torn out of my hands . . . I dared not go back to l-l-look for it. They were too near. I don't know what to say. . . ."

The bag had contained the remainder of their rations, the Ingram, grenades, spare ammunition, lightweight clothes and some burglary tools that Bolan sometimes used. It was a serious loss.

"No sweat," he said lightly. "It could happen to anyone. The important thing is that you're here; you still have the Uzis and your radio, and I still have Big Thunder and my Beretta. But we should cross over quickly."

"Bolan," she cried, "I think you're great! Some of the guys I work with, they'd have thrown me into the river. But you..." She stifled a sob.

"Come on," he said awkwardly. "Let's go."

They were by a double curve in the river, where the stream swirled west, then east, between steep slippery banks. The current was fast and deep, far too turbulent for a human being to stay afloat, an undulating surge of water with only an occasional eddy of foam at the surface to hint at the jagged rocks beneath.

The quarter moon was brighter now, streaking the far bank with caverns of darkness, casting grotesque shadows behind the boulders at the river's edge.

The Executioner's plan—ironically, one developed by South African scouts during the Boer War almost a hundred years before—was to drop into the water clinging to a log with the rope attached to it. He would then allow himself to be swept downstream, relying on the centrifugal force of the current to swing him outward against the far bank at the limit of the westward bend. He would then scramble ashore, pull up the rope and fix it so that Ruth could follow hand over hand.

But first he had to check that the treacherous stream would do what he expected. This was what the other two logs were for. He tossed them in one after the other. Each time, as he had calculated, the river dashed the wood against the opposite bank at exactly the same place, a smooth arc of sandstone where the force of the water had swept away the topsoil and gouged out the bedrock below overhanging branches.

Behind them in the forest, Bolan and Ruth could hear the shouts of security men beating the undergrowth in search of them. From time to time faint gleams of light appeared between the closely packed trunks.

Bolan hated like hell to be the quarry, forced to duck and run; it was his nature to play the hunter, fearless and enterprising. He was still fearless, yeah, but the enterprise would have to wait until he got out of the country.

He knotted one end of the rope high up around the trunk of a tree, held in place by a projecting branch, and then lashed the other around the log. "I think it's long enough," he said. "There's a lot of rope here—probably a replacement for that bridge rail—and the river's not more than twenty-five yards wide here."

"And if it's not long enough?" Ruth asked.

Bolan grinned at her in the gloom. "Then I'll be back!"

He picked up the last log and jumped with it into the raging stream.

The swirling of the river was suddenly very loud in Ruth's ears. All at once she felt very much alone. She saw Bolan for an instant, a darker blur against the turbulent surface of the water, and then he had submerged, to reappear amid the foam farther downstream. But after that she lost him in the patches of light and shadow heaving where the river swung into the curves.

She strained her eyes, striving to pierce the dark, staring at the white froth by the shoulder of rock that diverted the river from its course. It seemed a long time before she felt the rope rise from the water and pull tight. Shortly afterward it was tugged sharply three times.

That was the signal. Bolan was safely across. He had worked his way back upstream until he was opposite Ruth and had secured the other end of the rope.

All she had to do now was swing herself over to join him.

Ruth slung the radio around her neck. She shortened the webbing straps on each of the miniature SMGs so that they rose as high up on her shoulders as possible. The rope stretched away into the dark at the level of her eyes.

She gripped it with both hands, lowered herself gingerly down the bank and then stepped off over the racing stream.

The rope stretched over the river eight or ten feet above the surface. But as she began slowly working her way across, her weight dragged it down so that her feet, her calves and finally her knees were in the water.

Panting with exertion, her brow furrowed with effort and her lower lip clenched between her teeth, she inched along at the full stretch of her arms as the current swirling around her thighs tried to snatch her away and sweep her downstream.

Slowly the woman's dangling form writhed to combat the remorseless pull of the current. Sinews now crying out with fatigue, Ruth fought on hand over hand. The last few yards were the worst, for the flow was at its strongest there, hurling itself against the bank as it swept toward the curve.

She was within feet of dry land when she lost her grip with one hand. For an instant she hung perilously, her slender body carried away at an angle of forty-five degrees, and then with a despairing cry she let go and plunged into the torrent.

The Executioner moved with lightning speed. He leaped into the furious stream and grabbed one of her arms just as she went under. Then, as they were about to be swept away by the force of the water he reached up and grabbed a branch that overhung the scooped-out rock bank.

For timeless seconds he hung there, muscles straining with effort. Slowly, against the relentless downstream pressure, he drew the woman toward him until she could reach out and lace her arms around his neck. Then he lifted his arm and wrapped his free hand around the branch.

He went on fighting the river, edging shoreward along the branch until at last he could haul the two of them out of the water and onto the bank.

"Welcome to Botswana," he gasped as they collapsed exhausted on the damp ground.

Much later, striking diagonally through the woods, Bolan and Ruth hit the trail leading inland from the rope bridge. It was little more than a forest path, curling slowly uphill through the densely packed trees. But just before dawn the trunks thinned out and they emerged on the fringe of a vast savanna, sloping gently up to a distant range of hills.

There had been some cloud obscuring the stars during the latter part of the night, but the breeze had freshened and blown it away. Now the bar of orange silhouetting the treetops of the forest they had left widened to reveal a clear sky. Westward, a segment of moon rode palely in the dark. It was going to be another hot day.

Bolan decided to call a halt. "Once the sun's up," he said, "we find a sheltered place, we dry our clothes, we try to dry out the weapons. After that we must find a village, get food—and if possible transport. We're free, we're safe, but there's work to do. Any chance of raising your . . . friends . . . on that radio?"

Ruth shook her head. "Apart from water damage, the range wouldn't be enough to raise anyone. And there aren't too many Mossad agents in Botswana!"

He nodded. "Okay. We're on our own. There's still money stashed in my waterproof belt. This trail probably hits the highway from that suspension bridge not too far away. Once we make that, it shouldn't be too hard to find a village, then a town, finally an airport."

They found the highway—a dirt road wide enough for only one vehicle—a mile away. Pressing on after they had dried their clothes and their weapons, they came to an intersection. But they could turn neither right nor left. And to continue along that road would be crazy.

Fortunately the warrior was a few paces in the lead.

Glancing to one side as he drew level with the opening—the road ran below banks traversing a sugar plantation—he froze and motioned Ruth to halt.

Two hundred yards away, where the side road turned back toward the river, a truck was parked beneath a giant acacia.

A military truck, a Humber FV-1612 half-track with a 40 mm cannon installed in the turret and the South

African army identification letters and unit insignia painted out.

Beside it a handful of men in combat fatigues lounged in the shade. Their leader was a beefy dude with small, close-set eyes and crew-cut sandy hair.

After the hazards of the past two days, Bolan and Ruth had at last overcome all the obstacles and made it across the border into a country where, for political reasons, the South African security forces could no longer pursue them . . . only to find that they were still facing the threat of Hanson and his hired killers!

Chapter Twenty-four

Ruth Elias awoke beneath a flowering bush on a barren hillside many miles inside Botswana. At the foot of the hill, an immense plain stretched in every direction as far as the eye could see. The plain was totally flat. No rise or fall in the landscape varied its even surface; no river curled through it; no mountains showed above the haze veiling the horizon.

Sand and shingle covered the plain, which in that vast area could support no more than a sparse covering of thorn trees and scrub. Two or three miles away, primitive fences looped around conical thatched huts where a native village broke the monotony of the plain.

Goats were tethered outside the largest of the huts. Nearby, a group of men in combat fatigues stood around a Humber half-track.

Mack Bolan was already awake. "It's probably a Basuto village," he said. "They are simple people, not unlike the Masai farther north—warrior races still courageous but now basically farmers and herdsmen. Callous bastards like those—" he nodded toward the men around the Humber "—don't find it too hard to coax or force information from them. Or even trick them into helping."

"You're telling me we dare not go to that village and ask for help—even after Hanson leaves?" Ruth asked.

"Sure am. Those guys will stop at nothing. And as long as we stay alive they don't get paid. It's easy enough to terrorize tribesmen when you're prepared to shoot and kill, destroy livestock and crops if they refuse to cooperate." He shook his head. "Even if we did contact them, how are they supposed to know we're any different?"

"So we're still outlaws? We can't check in anyplace?"

"Not until we hit some reasonably sized town. I've been in this situation before," Bolan said dryly.

"Did you have any town in mind? Sydney? Stockholm?"

His eyebrows rose at her tone.

"I'm sorry," she said at once. "It's not like me to be bitchy and sarcastic. But I'm beat, and I'm starving. I guess it's all a little too much."

"Forget it," Bolan said. "I reckon we're about equal distance from Francistown and Gaborone. There's an airstrip at Francistown, but Gaborone, being the capital, has an international airfield. I figure on heading that way."

"How many miles is equal?" she asked.

"One hundred each way, give or take. But we could also take a train. We're on the fringe of the Kalahari Desert here, and there's kind of a trans-Kalahari line. We have a choice of railroad stations on the Francistown-Gaborone sector. If we make it that far out into the desert."

They had walked throughout the whole of the previous day and most of the night.

Eluding Hanson's team that first time by taking to the sugarcane plantation and bypassing the intersection, they had discovered when they regained the road that it led them farther toward the desert with no sign of any trail breaking the uniformity of dense woods on either side.

The sun had been blazing down from a cloudless sky for three hours when the helicopter reappeared. It bore no markings and was painted a dun color, but it was the same NIS Lynx, invariably approaching from the east and returning, once the recon was completed, in the same direction.

Bolan and Ruth took cover the moment they heard the rotors throb, but there was no way of knowing whether or not they had been seen before that. What was certain was that they heard the flailing of caterpillar tracks and saw the armored Humber lumbering along the trail perilously close soon after each run the chopper made. On more than one occasion it was only Bolan's quick reaction that enabled them to run for the bush or stop short before they rounded a bend on the far side of which the mercs were waiting.

Between noon and dusk they passed several signposts indicating villages or game reserve stations ten, fifteen, and once only two miles away. But the Executioner was adamant that the risk of a detour was too great with Hanson's killers in the vicinity.

Sweet potatoes stolen from a farmer's field and—best of all—three overripe pineapples overlooked during the harvest provided the only food they had. It was the juice of the latter, more than the starchier bulk of the potatoes, that helped most to still the pains clawing at their empty bellies.

They went on walking after dark, but they could advance only with extreme caution; it was unlikely that Hanson would allow his mercs to relax when there was money at stake.

Halfway through the afternoon, Bolan had begun to suspect that the enemy's plan—at least for the moment—was less to annihilate them than to force their flight in a particular direction. They were subtly being herded toward the desert. A move in any other direction would be blocked at once, whereas a run to the east could continue unchecked for some time.

Perhaps the murder of two people wanted by the South African police would be potentially less embarrassing for Reinbecker and Vanderlee if it took place in the desert, as far away as possible from the frontier.

As far as the Executioner was concerned, east was okay—as a direction. The railroad lay east. But it was at least twenty miles out in the desert. And a crossing of that barren plain under aerial surveillance, with the certainty that an armored vehicle could be called up by radio at any moment, was strictly no go.

For this reason, Bolan had decided late the previous day to abandon any thought of keeping to well-traveled trails. They would take to the forest and then the bush, steer by the sun and to hell with how much time they lost.

If they could lose their pursuers that way, then start out across the plain under cover of darkness, then they had a chance....

By the time dusk thickened into night, he thought he *had* lost the hunters. But he and Ruth were still nowhere near the desert. It was just before daybreak when they emerged from the bush and saw the dark void of the plain stretching out before them.

Bolan decided they should rest for the whole of that day. Then, maybe, if there had been no further sign of the mercenaries or their helicopter, they could attempt a night crossing in the direction of the railroad.

It was therefore with a sick feeling of dismay that he saw the Humber parked in the desert village below.

Since the hillside bushes hid them from watchers both on the plain and in the air, he determined to take the much-needed sleep nevertheless. After that he would be playing it by ear.

He awoke late in the afternoon to find their shelter surrounded by a group of silent figures.

There were twenty or thirty of them, men, women, a few children, all a coppery bronze in color, with tribal marks striping their faces and primitive clothing made from hides or strips of sacking. Some of the men carried bamboo spears, but their attitude was not hostile, merely curious.

Bolan rolled over and sat up, rubbing the sleep from his eyes. Ruth was lying on her back, eyes wide with fear, trying not to move. "Relax," he said. "The natives are friendly. These are no Basutos or Masai. We've been discovered by a band of Bushmen."

"Bushmen?"

"Desert people. Nomads called San or Bushmen."

Hearing their voices, the women—some of them carrying babies strapped to them with a kind of sarong, leaving their arms and breasts free—moved nervously back a few paces. "Once their ancestors inhabited the whole of central and southern Africa," Bolan told the woman. "But when the Bantu came this way they were driven even farther south, where the white colonists damned near exterminated them. There are only a few thousand left now, mostly here in the Kalahari."

"They are real nomads, moving all the time?"

"They live a Spartan existence," Bolan said. "They stick around in one area until they've used up all the roots and berries and locusts and lizards and other things they can eat. Then they move on, maybe to a place where they know water can be found, maybe following game migrations in the hope of killing an antelope or something."

"Are they on the move now?"

"I think so. They don't usually stay in the hills."

"Can you communicate with them? If they are heading east into the desert, do you think you could persuade them to take on a couple of passengers?"

Bolan's brows rose. "You mean..."

"I mean two white fugitives trying to cross that wilderness would stick out like a sore thumb to a chopper pilot. But a group of Bushmen might not attract attention. If the pilot is used to seeing nomads."

"It's worth a try anyway."

Bolan rose slowly to his feet, spread his arms to indicate that he was not aggressive and drew aside a wizened little man who seemed to be the chief. He gesticulated and drew pictures on the sand for what seemed an eternity.

Finally he returned after his long and animated conference with the headman.

"It's okay. I think they'll play ball. On one condition. They hate the game wardens, who try and chase them off the reserves; they hate the armchair hunters who go on safari in helicopters and shoot their game from the air; they hate the black pressure groups, who try to force them into a rebellion that doesn't interest them. Once I made him understand most of those guys were chasing us, too, he agreed to help."

"What's the condition?" Ruth asked.

"They will help us, provided we promise to kill them something—a gnu, a wildebeest, an antelope, whatever—with our fire-spears, our guns. That will keep the whole band in food for weeks."

"Supposing we can't find one?"

"They'll find one, all right. The problem is to get near enough with a bamboo spear, especially in flat country like this."

"The effective range of the Uzis is only 150 yards," she said dubiously.

"Big Thunder's a little more than that—and I have spare rounds in a waterproof pocket on this belt. But we'll worry about that later. Right now we have to move."

"I thought you said—"

"The farther we are out into that desert when the chopper reappears, the less chance there is of making the crew suspicious. We won't leave any tracks down there—there's only sand between the scrub, and sometimes gravel. And they must already have spotted the nomads, yesterday and maybe the day before. They don't travel very fast."

Ruth took a closer look at the nomads. All of them, especially the women, had extremely close-cropped heads. All wore armlets and anklets of elephant hair, sometimes decorated with red and yellow beads. Three teenage boys held coarse-grained spherical objects about half the size of a football.

"Ostrich eggs," Bolan explained, "With a hole in the top. They use them to carry water. Those and the stomachs of eland."

She looked out over the arid desert. "Water?"

"They're smart," he told her. "Where there is no well or water hole, they look for a certain kind of briar whose roots go down to wherever the water hides under the surface. The water moves up the plant by capillary action. And they simply break off the thorns, suck it out and then spit it into the ostrich eggs for use later."

"I think I lost my thirst," she said.

"Wait until you're out in that desert when the sun's high," Bolan said. "You'll be glad to drink anything, wherever it comes from."

The headman was surprisingly smart. He refused to move into the open until Bolan and the woman bore at least a distant resemblance to his own people. Outer clothing was removed, some of it exchanged with the Bushmen; one or two wore ragged jackets picked up nobody knew where. Shoes and weapons were bundled up in hides and carried by the women, along with their own poor possessions—tools, utensils and camp requirements they customarily moved from place to place.

Finally, there was the vital question of skin color. Giggling, the teenage boys ran to a kind of sand pit at the foot of the slope and carried back handfuls of a thick dust that was half ocher and half bauxite. Rubbed liberally into their exposed skin this lent the fugitives, from the height at which the helicopter normally flew, a tint that would not seem too different from the Bushmen.

The remaining problem was the Executioner's height. The biggest of the Bushmen was no more than five feet six inches tall, and most of them were around five feet. To hide that extra fourteen inches Bolan was to be covered with skins, leaning forward and walking with bent knees any time the helicopter appeared.

They had been walking for an hour when they saw it, flying low above the foothills. It made one pass over the plain. Ruth and Bolan looked down; most of the nomads looked up, either in anger or curiosity. Bolan felt the hairs on his neck prickle as the machine's shadow skimmed past. But the racket of the jet turbine soon diminished: the spotters seemed to think they had more chance of a strike if they kept a close watch on the higher ground.

Bolan wondered where Hanson's half-track was at that moment. The warrior hoped that it would not occur to the mercs to check out the Bushmen, just to confirm the pilot's report.

The dust raised by the rotors finally settled. The Lynx flew away, circled the foothills some way to the south, vanished, returned one hour later and hovered for several minutes fifty feet above the nomad band. The headman urged them to keep on walking, the younger men fanning out now ahead of the main group, circling around in search of anything moving, startled by the noise, that could be used as food.

Eventually the chopper flew away once more.

The Bushmen penetrated farther into the sparse bush covering the plain. The sun blazed down from an empty, leaden sky, raising shimmering heat waves over the sandy floor.

The vegetation was not quite as scarce as it had appeared from the hillside. Here and there isolated trees that resembled gnarled and distorted caricatures of European olives rose above waist-high clumps of grass scorched brown in the heat. Dead brushwood bleached bone-white lay scattered beneath ilex bushes whose papery, withered leaves rustled dryly with every puff of wind. But the arid spaces between these tracts were wide.

By midday, Bolan and Ruth found that their feet were being burned by the fissured earth they trod on. The sun's progress across the sky seemed as interminable as theirs across the plain. The dry air cracked their lips and hurt their lungs.

At some time during the afternoon, occasional squalls of hot wind clattered the dried leaves and the thorn tree spikes. One of them brought with it a miniature whirlwind, a dust column nine or ten feet high that corkscrewed along above the overheated land.

Soon afterward another column, taller and wider, moving more quickly, approached them from the east.

Only this time there was no wind.

The headman became excited, gesturing with his spear. "Damn," Bolan said, "Hanson! And I think he's going to check out the nomads!"

The headman was prepared for the suspected threat.

He issued orders rapidly in a flat, liquid monotone. Fifty yards away, a patch of yellowed elephant grass lay between two trees at the far end of a line of desiccated, thorny shrubs. The women hurried there and dumped the hide-covered bundles containing Ruth's

SMGs, the radio and the telltale clothes. The woman herself, with Bolan, was to lie up in the grass and avoid moving in any way that could stir the tall, frilled stems above them.

The Bushmen then crouched low and ran back the way they had come for two hundred yards, finally straightening up and resuming their slow pace at a tangent to their original direction.

Smart again, Bolan thought. By locating themselves some way back of the position they had actually reached, and then altering their bearing, they minimized the chance of the elephant grass being considered as a possible hiding place.

If they were questioned and denied seeing any strangers in the area, the mercs might check...but they would probably check in the immediate vicinity, perhaps behind it, not in places where the nomads had apparently yet to arrive.

Lying motionless in the long grass with his finger curled around the trigger of his Beretta, Bolan held his breath and fractionally moved two of the dry stems with his free hand.

Between them he saw the Humber pull up in a shower of sand and small pebbles. The mercs jumped down and roughly began to handle the Bushmen. Bolan saw shaken heads, shrugs. Finally Hanson seized the headman by one arm, shaking him and shouting. The little man continued to protest, feigning ignorance and innocence. Finally the mercenary boss flung out an angry finger, indicating several clumps of grass and dry thickets nearby. The killers made no attempt to search them; they simply stood back and fired, a whole clip of ammunition into each clump.

Bolan swallowed. Sweat ran down his sides and poured from behind his knees. The dry stalks had set up an uncontrollable irritation on his sunburned skin. He prepared to make the best possible use of his remaining rounds.

But since no wounded man or woman thrashed among the grasses or writhed out from beneath the bushes, Eddie Hanson seemed satisfied. He ordered his men back into the half-track, which careered away in a wide circle toward the hills. The vehicle passed so close to Bolan's hiding place that the flailing tracks scattered sand over his half-nude body.

As the nomads resumed their slow advance, Bolan called to Ruth to stay put. Hanson was no dumb muscle man. In his place, Bolan would have returned soon afterward to see if he had been tricked: he would have counted the number of nomads and then come back to make a second tally.

Again Bolan was right. When the Bushmen were a quarter of a mile away, the Humber's dust cloud rose once more in the distance. The truck drove up fast, stopping a couple of hundred yards away from the band. Bolan saw Hanson standing up in the turret, scanning them through field glasses.

Then, apparently satisfied once more that his quarry had not taken refuge with the primitives, he lowered the binoculars and settled down inside the hull. The Humber drove away: they did not see it again that day.

At sundown the headman called a halt in a depression buttressed at one side by an outcrop of bare, flaking rock. The sky flared orange to the west; eastward, the hills were still visible as a low, dark line defining the horizon.

The men of the group at once started gathering dead wood for a fire. "They make a point of it; they don't try to hide the smoke," Bolan explained. "It tells other nomad bands to keep out! This is our territory right now."

Since this was only a brief halt, the women did not begin building the hemispherical, leaf-covered frame huts that customarily sheltered the Bushmen; tonight the most important thing was food. They buried spiny cucumbers, gathered during the day from a cactuslike plant, in the hot ashes. Locusts, dried in the sun, were ground to a powder between two flat stones, and these, added to root scrapings pounded into a crude meal, were cooked in a hollowed-out gourd to form a primitive cereal cake. A small animal like a prairie rat, and lizards caught during the trek by children and grilled on a spit, completed the dinner. Together with the contents of the ostrich eggs.

It was soon after dawn that they saw the springbok.

Perhaps it was the memory of the previous night's food that prompted Ruth to notice the African antelope first, about 250 yards upwind, somehow separated from the herd, standing alone by a thorn tree beside a dried-up water hole.

She tugged at one of the hides slung around Bolan's neck and held a finger to her lips. He looked up and saw the animal at once. In turn he touched the headman on the arm and pointed.

The nomad chief uttered a sibilant whisper and the whole tribe flattened themselves to the ground.

Bolan unleathered Big Thunder, unbuckled his belt and the shoulder rig holding the Beretta, either of which could scrape on the rock and become an alarm signal, and moved out.

He wormed out of the depression and, still lying flat on his stomach, inched his way around the rock on the side hidden from the animal.

The rock was perhaps fifty yards wide. If he could creep around it and still remain downwind, the range would be reduced to two hundred yards. But even with a muzzle velocity of 1640 feet per second it would be a long shot for a 240-grain boattail to make a decisive hit.

Bolan saw the water hole slide into view as he rounded the last shoulder of rock. The springbok was still there. The bobtail was up, the ears twitching. For a moment the hunter thought that the animal had gotten wind of the danger. He hoped not, because once the beast had taken off, no handgun on earth could bring it down.

In a prone firing position, supported on his two elbows, Bolan wrapped the fingers of his left hand around his right wrist. The barrel of the 11.5 inch fleshshredder lined up with the target. The springbok pawed the ground. The head turned left, right. Another flick of the tail.

The Executioner held his breath.

He squeezed the trigger.

The report of the wildcat cartridge was deafening. The four-pound gun jerked in Bolan's hand, the massive recoil jamming his right elbow painfully against the scaly rock.

From the far side of the rock he heard a ragged cheer. The springbok was down.

But it was not dead. Despite the Executioner's expertise, the heavy .44-caliber slug had climbed fractionally in flight and only creased the animal's skull. Instinctively, the effort no longer conscious, it struggled upright on its front feet, then the rear, and staggered a few steps.

Bolan was already running. The tribesmen with their spears, too.

At forty yards out Bolan fired again, the big gun bucking in his hands. The boattail cored home and the springbok fell once more; this time it was for keeps.

The Bushmen were overjoyed. They decided to make camp there; they would remain while the carcass was skinned, disjointed, part eaten and part preserved, the hide dried in the sun, and the hoofs and horns fashioned by the women into tools, ornaments and utensils.

It was while they were dragging the animal back to the depression that Bolan noticed the hole in the ground.

It was beyond the dried-up water hole, where the land sank between two shelves of bare rock. Clearly this had been the approach to the site—when there was water.

The hole was roughly square, about twelve feet by twelve, between eight and ten feet deep. It was evidently manmade. "Covered over, it's a trap for animals when they come at dusk to drink," Bolan said. "The hunters hide themselves among the rocks and shoot them down when they're immobilized in there, maybe with a broken leg."

Equally interesting was a discovery Ruth made in a patch of elephant grass at one side of the rocks.

Half-hidden among the man-high stalks, roped down beneath a sheet of tarpaulin, was a small dump of half a dozen five-gallon jerricans full of gasoline.

"Very efficient," Bolan said acidly. "To make quite sure they get home safely after this perilous safari, the hunters have established a refueling dump for themselves!"

"Right now I'd like anything with a tank that this would fill," Ruth said.

Bolan was caressing the stubble on his jaw. "We'll get something," he said. "I'm sick of being chased. We need that damned helicopter one more time."

Ruth looked puzzled. "But I thought..." she began.

"We hated it," Bolan said. "And now we need it. This time I *want* them to find us."

"THERE'S TWO CHARACTERS out in the desert," the Lynx observer reported on his radio. "I figure they're the ones you're after."

"A man and a woman?" Vanderlee inquired.

"That's right. The guy's tall. The woman's dark and... well, just a woman. It's hard to say, they look dead beat."

"Are they armed?"

"Not that I can see. We'll go lower and... no. It looks like they got nothing but the rags they're wearing. The guy is waving a white cloth at us, like he wants to surrender or something."

"Excellent," Vanderlee said. "Is there any sign of the monkey men, the bush Indians?"

"I don't see any. I think they'd be father out to the west by now. You want me to pass on the map coordinates to the guys in that half-track?"

"You don't know anything about any half-track," Vanderlee said testily. "Report the coordinates to me. Stay in the area until... until other parties locate the fugitives. What happens after that does not concern you. Once contact is made, you fly home. Is that clear?"

"Whatever you say, Colonel," the observer replied.

Half an hour later, Eddie Hanson, compass in hand, steered his driver out into the desert. It was midday and the sun's heat turned the Humber's steel body into an oven. Hanson didn't mind the discomfort—his prize was in the bag! He had known all along that the bastard and his whore must be out there someplace. Trying to make the railroad probably.

Hanson grinned. They'd had enough, now they were offering to surrender. Well, if they thought they were going to be shown any leniency, they had another think coming!

He wouldn't shoot them down right away, though. There would be no witnesses. He didn't like Bolan, had never liked the soft-shell, holier-than-thou son of a bitch. It would be fun to watch him squirm while the boys had their fun with the skirt. He'd let Abu Fekhrouh finish her off. What that Ethiopian could do with a knife...

Soon Hanson saw the Lynx, a dark speck motionless against the aching blue of the sky some miles ahead.

Approaching the chopper, he waved his arms as soon as he could distinguish the figures in the bubble, and the pilot signaled a thumbs-up before he flew away.

The Humber roared on across the plain in a cloud of yellow dust. Bolan and the woman were standing on the cracked earth of a dried-up water hole. And, right enough, the big American was waving something white, a torn shirt or something. Behind them, bare, peeling branches of ilex and wattle and some kind of eucalyptus surrounded the one-time oasis. Hanson supposed it was as good a place as any to die.

There were also some dead trees on either side of a slight grade where the approach to the water hole sank between outcrops of flaky rock. Many of the branches had broken off and dropped across the track. The Humber's caterpillars crunched over dead wood.

Suddenly the Irish driver gave a cry of alarm. Hanson saw Bolan, the woman and the water hole shoot upward into the air. He received a violent blow on the head.

Half-stunned, he was aware of shouts and cries all around him, of the truck engine screaming and then dying. He stared dazedly around.

The driver was slumped over the wheel, knocked out when his head crashed against the windshield. In front of him was darkness and what looked like a wall of sand. The other mercs, inexplicably, were in a heap on the floor beneath the turret.

The half-track had plowed through a thin screen of branches and leaves to plunge into the game trap.

The rear half of the sixteen-foot truck was still in the open air, canted skyward at an angle of forty-five degrees, but the front wheels and the radiator were buried in soft sand at the bottom of the trap, and hood, turret and half the body were below the surface of the desert.

Hanson swore. That bastard Bolan would pay for this!

Shouting to his men, he clambered to the tail of the truck and jumped to the ground. The cannon and the coaxial machine gun were useless—they could only fire downward into the sand. But he and the mercs still had their handguns, their SMGs, their M-16s.

"Wound the motherfuckers, that's all," he yelled. "I want them both alive."

But the woman and the Executioner had vanished.

Hanson gazed furiously left and right. There was only one place they could be, the fifty-yard patch of elephant grass.

"Come on," he shouted. "Spread out and comb that damned grass. We'll have them out of there in two minutes."

With his Walther PPK in his right hand, he led the way, thrusting aside the six-foot stems and stamping them flat as he penetrated the patch.

BUT MACK BOLAN AND RUTH ELIAS had not gone into the grass; they fled around the outside and waited there. When the strung-out mercs were halfway through, Bolan set the grass afire.

It took only a single match. A sheet of flame shot upward, crackled sideways, leaned away from the wind and set neighboring clumps ablaze. Within seconds the whole fifty-yard width of the patch was a seething furnace.

As the conflagration scorched toward them, the mercs cried out in terror and turned to beat their way back to the safety of the open desert.

But there were worse horrors to come. Bolan had left five of the six jerricans of gasoline, with the screw caps removed, in strategic places among the grasses.

One by one they erupted into blazing hellbursts as the heat from the advancing wall of fire blasted the volatile vapor into flame.

Black smoke boiled up into the sky. Flaming figures screamed out from the inferno, beating at the tongues of fire licking their combat fatigues. Within the fiercely burning area ammunition from guns dropped by the fleeing mercs detonated in firecracker profusion.

One of the Vietnam vets, a Cuban and a guy carrying an SMG had been killed by the exploding jerricans. For the others it was over almost as quickly.

Bolan and Ruth were firing from among the rocks on the far side of the flaming grass. Two of the enemy—Hanson himself and one of the men with an M-16—were thrashing frenziedly on the sand, trying to extinguish the flames devouring them. That left the third vet with an M-16, the remaining Cuban and the other SMG gunner on foot and fighting. But within minutes their cover had been consumed; there was nothing left of the elephant grass but an area of blackened and smoking ruin, with three incinerated bodies crisped among the charred embers.

And now there was a silent circle of small, copper-colored men armed with bamboo spears surrounding the site of the fire.

The soldier with the SMG lost his cool. Cursing, he spun on his heel, spraying death from his hammering weapon. Two of the nomads fell. A third flung his spear with such accuracy that the tip pierced the merc's throat at the same time as a short burst from one of Ruth's mini-Uzis split open his back. He dropped face upward, the shaft of the spear still quivering above the spreading pool of scarlet that stained the sand.

Meanwhile the vet dropped to one knee and opened fire at the M-16's full 950 rpm cyclic rate. Ruth ducked behind a rock shelf to avoid the high-velocity 5.56 mm killstream. Bolan dropped, too, as the ricochets screeched into the burning sky and the flaming muzzle swung his way.

He had hated like hell to resort to fire, but they had pathetically few rounds between them—and with Hanson, he knew, they had to win or they were dead meat.

Half crouching, the merc sprang sideways to get a better line on Ruth behind her shallow shelter. He was covered by the Cuban, who was armed only with a six-shot Colt Cobra revolver. The .38 caliber, 200-grain slugs hummed Bolan's way, but as the distinctive reports cracked out, the Executioner found a fissure between two boulders through which he could sight the vet.

He triggered a single round from the AutoMag in the general direction of the Cuban and then, shifting position slightly, emptied the Beretta's magazine at the vet.

Caught off balance by the heavy parabellum rounds, the guy was hurled upward and sideways for several feet before he crashed lifeless to the ground with the dark blood pouring from half a dozen holes drilled between his hip and his shoulder.

Bolan rose menacingly from behind the rock, Big Thunder in his right hand. There were only three rounds left in the clip, but the Cuban didn't know that. Besides, his own revolver was empty.

He threw the gun onto the ground and raised his hands.

One of the two men on fire had been killed by the Bushmen. His sprawled body, transfixed by three spears, lay smoldering on the edge of the ashes. Hanson was still alive, moaning as he beat with blistered hands at his blazing garments.

Ruth's face was a mask of horror and pity. She ran forward and seized the writhing man by the shoulders, rolling him in the sand to douse the flames.

Bolan shouted a warning.

The mercenary leader's features contorted into an expression mingling anguish, fury and hatred. As the woman leaned over him trying to ease his agony, he snatched a broad-bladed commando knife from his boot and stabbed viciously upward at her stomach.

Bolan fired the AutoMag twice.

The hand holding the knife vanished in a spray of blood and bones and shredded flesh. The knife spun away, the blade glinting in the sun.

The Executioner's second shot smashed Hanson's forehead.

Bolan straightened up and looked at Ruth. "Well, I guess that wraps it up," he said grimly. "This guy—" he gestured with the gun barrel at the Cuban "—has surrendered; the driver's unconscious in the cab of the truck, and the rest . . ." He glanced around the blackened hellground between the trap and the trees. "I think you could say the rest are taken care of."

He made a mental count, his brow suddenly furrowing.

There was one missing. Where the hell was the Ethiopian?

As the thought formed in his mind, the nomad headman called out a guttural warning.

Bolan swung around. Abu Fekhrouh had run back to the Humber for his XM-174. He was standing up on the rock with the grenade launcher at his hip, the stubby barrel aimed at Bolan. From a distance of fifty yards he couldn't miss—and the grenade was in position, he was about to fire.

The nomads flung spears. They fell short. Bolan had one shot left in the AutoMag.

The mouth of the launcher tube yawned in their direction.

Bolan steadied his hand, teeth clenched, eyes squinted against the glaring desert light. This was one time in his danger-filled career when everything, other people's lives as well as his own, yeah, the whole damned future, depended on a precise coordination of hand and eye.

Bolan fired.

The last boattail took Abu Fekhrouh full in the chest. He toppled forward while he was actuating the firing mechanism of the XM-174. The rocket motor ignited. But the grenade was unable to exit from the tube; the muzzle had plowed into the sand.

There was a muffled, thudding explosion...a blinding flash of light...a terrible shower of metal fragments, shreds of cloth, bone splinters and eviscerated flesh that pockmarked the desert floor within a radius of more than thirty yards. Ruth drew back with a small gasp of revulsion as a boot with a foot still inside it landed near her.

All that remained of the Ethiopian was a red stain that slid slowly down the rock, steaming in the heat of the sun.

Half an hour later the nomads, under Mack Bolan's direction, had manhandled the Humber half-track out of the pit. Both front wheels had to be changed and the steering was erratic, but apart from buckled armor the vehicle had suffered no other damage. Bolan emptied the sixth jerrican of gasoline into the tank.

The dead had been buried, the Bushmen had taken what they wanted in the way of arms, ammunition...and the clothes and footwear of the Irish driver and the Cuban, who sat, naked and sullen, by the side of the truck.

"What are you going to do with them?" Ruth asked. "You can't kill them in cold blood."

"No," Bolan repeated. "But they don't want to stay here. I think I'll send them home."

"Home?"

"Sure. Back to South Africa. Stand," he said roughly to the two prisoners, "and start walking."

The Irishman looked at him. "What the hell d'you mean?"

"You heard me. You're going back where you came from. On foot."

"Hell, you can't do that! We have no clothes or shoes? It's inhuman, man! You wouldn't—"

"Shut up!" Bolan interrupted. "You were prepared to kill us for money. Consider yourselves damned lucky you're still alive and in a condition to walk—with or without clothes. In any case, it's no more than thirty miles before you make the trees."

The Irishman looked suspiciously at the impassive Bushmen. "Suppose these little bastards take it into their heads to follow us after you've gone?"

"We kept our bargain with them. As of now, they've no reason to feel bitter toward whites."

Bolan heaved the Irishman to his feet and ordered brusquely, "Move!"

The Cuban said nothing. He got up without being told and started toward the distant hills. The naked driver limped after him, pathetic in his nudity under the huge desert sky.

Then Bolan turned to Ruth. "We better get going. We have a train to catch."

Chapter Twenty-five

"Do you ever ask yourself why you are doing this?" Ruth Elias demanded. "I mean the fighting, the crusading, the endless battle against the evil of our society?"

"Somebody has to do it," Bolan said, "or it's no longer a society but chaos, anarchy. I don't like seeing honest people trampled upon. And I have some of the necessary skills to let the savages know that someone is prepared to oppose them, and violently, if need be."

Bolan and Ruth were sitting behind glass walls in the rooftop bar of the Hotel Mandela, Gaborone. The Humber half-track had been abandoned at Dinokwa, where a prudent display of dollar bills had secured them a place on a train to the capital. Let the South Africans explain to the Botswana authorities how one of their armored vehicles, with the identification insignia clumsily painted out, happened to be parked fifty miles inside foreign territory.

The hotel was one of the few buildings of more than two stories in the railroad station neighborhood. They had checked in there because it was close by, because they were exhausted and because stores across the street could replace the tattered rags they wore with acceptable clothes.

Approaching the bar to order refills—the Mandela didn't have table service—Mack Bolan glanced through the plate glass to find half the city had disappeared. Reducing visibility to a few hundred yards, a slow drizzle was drifting down from the darkening sky.

It was actually raining! In dusty Gaborone! At dusk! And the population wasn't ready for it.

Black shoppers rushed an ancient bus with crates of live chickens roped to the roof, jamming the interior, riding the fenders, clinging to the rear bumpers. Between the hotel and two stained concrete apartment blocks squatters took shelter in a vacant lot. An old woman covered paper sacks containing her worldly possessions with a sheet of rusted tin. A cooking pot rested on top of a fire made from discarded lumber, hissing in the rain. People huddled together in doorways: a mother with her baby, an old man whose head and hands twitched ceaselessly, listless youths with wet cigarettes dangling from their lips.

Perhaps it was some atavistic impulse, springing from the time spent with primitives in the desert, that led Bolan and Ruth in a sense to identify with those squatters, fellow outcasts and outlaws seeking warmth and shelter and human comfort in mutual protection against the elements. Human elements in Bolan's case.

Or perhaps it was no more than a simple animal attraction that suddenly became irresistible.

Whatever, the moment dinner was through, they went to bed. They had reserved two rooms; without a word being spoken, they went to one.

It seemed the most natural thing in the world, a relief after days of tension that had been almost explosive. And curiously, half naked in the desert, sleeping rough together, changing clothes in the Volvo—nowhere had he been genuinely aware of her as a woman. Ever since his first unashamedly sexual appraisal in Vanderlee's office in Johannesburg she had been no more than an ally, someone he had to protect but who would also protect him.

But the instant the trappings of civilization were around—the cool drinks, the uniformed doorman, shiny cars in the parking lot—from that moment on there was a force drawing them together that was almost tangible.

Bolan didn't try to resist it.

Tomorrow they would part, she to report back to Jerusalem, he to check out a name and address in the southeastern United States.

It was tough. But Bolan had long renounced the idea of a lasting relationship, renounced since the death of April Rose any hope of a permanent attachment.

And yet . . .

Well, tonight was tonight. And tonight was theirs.

On the wide bed in the seventh-floor hotel room, he remained staring, long after Ruth had fallen asleep, at the reflections of passing automobile headlights as they pierced the blinds and swept across the ceiling.

He shook his head, marveling still at the extraordinarily voluptuous quality of her body—so trim and contained in her blacksuit or in the neat shantung skirt and top she had bought as soon as they hit town—once she was naked in bed with him.

She was one of the most passionate and demanding—and at the same time one of the most compliant and giving—women he had ever encountered.

Somewhere in the night a clock struck the hour. Tires swished on the wet road below. Bolan did not bother to count the strokes.

How often in his hazardous life did he have time to relax this way?

To take time off from his personal crusade in order to make human contact with someone of the opposite sex? How frequently in the middle of a mission did the flux of events he controlled—or which controlled him—eddy to a halt so that for the moment there was nothing he could do, need do or even want to do? Because the affair that had begun with a train wreck in Italy had taken on its own momentum, and right now at this moment, there was nothing in the world he could do to alter it.

Not often. But this was such an occasion.

Until his plane took off tomorrow there was nothing on earth he could do to accelerate the operation. No phone call, no letter, no telex message could bring him information that would take the affair any further. Gaborone could provide no more intel on what he knew already.

He had discovered that Ononu kidnapped the daughters of men who controlled the mines in his country so that he could bargain for a bigger share in the profits. Would the extra cash have been used to finance bigger and better drug distribution? Probably. And the increased profits from that would likely have been devoted to the organization of continued terrorist activity.

Terrorist activity in aid of what? On whose behalf? To prove what?

He would find this out when he got to Florida.

He hoped.

Because although both Ononu and his opium farm were now destroyed, Bolan was certain that there were ramifications to the conspiracy, that a wider organization existed and still worked, and that so far he had only uncovered a part of the whole.

In the meantime . . . space to breathe, to make contact.

And secret agent Ruth Elias to help him do it.

The thought hardened once more into desire. He reached for her, pulling the warm smooth length of her toward him, cupping a breast in one hand.

She was awake at once, her moist lips open, feeling for his mouth, her cool, practiced fingers wrapping around him, tightening, caressing. She slid beneath him, she sat astride, she knelt on the bed.

Much later, standing mouth to mouth with him beneath the shower as the dawn filtered past the blinds, she whispered endearments against his lips.

One of his hands was in the small of her back. He arched his hips forward, feeling the curve of her belly, as he let his fingers stray downward around perfectly formed buttocks, massaging, probing.

Gasping, she pulled him out of the shower and into the bedroom.

"Do you ever ask yourself why you are doing this?" the Executioner said.

Chapter Twenty-Six

From Jacksonville, past St. Augustine and Flagler Beach, Mack Bolan's rented Thunderbird took the Highway 95 south at almost three times the legal limit. At Daytona Beach, he switched direction, heading crosscountry on Highway 4, to the outskirts of Tampa. After that it was north again on U.S.19, past Tarpon Springs, New Port Richey and Hudson, to the turn-off for Pretty Bay.

Bolan had decided not to fly direct to Tampa for several reasons. One, he needed money. He had fulfilled his promise to Bozuffi, but he was not prepared to ask for more now that the tycoon's own particular problem was settled.

There was, however, a fund specially set up from which he could draw whenever he needed. It had been organized by a White Russian refugee duchess, now dead, for whom Bolan had once smuggled a scientist out of the Soviet Union. There was a bank in Jacksonville through which he could make use of this fund.

Secondly, he had contacts in Jacksonville, though not in Tampa.

The third reason was probably the most important.

Since the heat was on in South Africa, it had clearly been impossible for him to fly from Gaborone to Cape

Town and make the connection stateside there. He had been obliged to take a Pan-African flight from Botswana to Brazzaville, a Sabena jet from Brazzaville to Dakar, in Senegal, and then a UTA jumbo to Paris. By the time the Air France AF001 night-departure Concorde deposited him at Kennedy—with fifteen minutes to spare before the connection to Jacksonville took off—several hours of air that was neither pressurized nor conditioned was the number-one priority on his list.

Driving the T-bird was great. It blew away the jet lag and cleared his mind. He was almost sorry when he saw the sign that said Welcome to Pretty Bay.

The place was new. But the land developers responsible for the glassed-in shopping mall between the unfinished condominium towers had not been able to eradicate entirely the original Gulf fishing community; their clapboard shacks, tarred and weathered, still stood on either side of the half-empty tourist marinas. There were big houses, too, on the outskirts of town, which lay between Bayport and Homosassa. Bolan's quarry lived in one of them.

Westwood Towers was surrounded by fifty acres of wooded valley with a quarter-mile frontage on the gulf. Most of the estates that ran down to the ocean were centered on pillared, colonial-style mansions. Westwood was different, it was sham Gothic. It reminded Bolan of a larger version of the Reinbecker place without the courtyard. The towers that gave it its name lay at the four corners of the huge house.

It was not visible from the road; the entire landward margin of the property was bounded by a ten-foot-high wall. But Bolan rented a small outboard from one of the Pretty Bay marinas and went fishing. Five hundred yards offshore, with a pair of powerful binoculars, he was able to make a survey.

What he saw was not encouraging.

Manicured lawns sloped down to the waterside from the terrace in front of the house. A fifty-foot fly-bridge cruiser, flanked by two powerboats glittering with chrome, lay alongside the private pier. Among the trees on either side of the valley, a nine-hole golf course had been laid out, and formal gardens surrounded the Olympic-size pool.

Bolan tightened the focus.

He could see at least three—no, four—dog handlers prowling the outskirts with leashed Dobermans. At one side of the coach-house yard a husky dude stripped to the waist was polishing a cream-colored Mercedes. Beside it was a blue Maserati.

And beside the dude—very close beside, hugging his bare, tanned skin—was a strapped shoulder rig holding a large-caliber handgun.

That was not all. Among the trees Bolan saw some posts, rising no more than eighteen inches above ground level. To the Executioner's experienced eyes that could mean only one thing: TV monitors.

If that was so, an intruder's progress could be precisely charted from somewhere within the house, night or day.

Provided he made it far enough to be charted at all.

Bolan suspected—he could not see clearly enough to be certain—that some of the posts were related to what looked like fixed-position shotguns wedged in tree forks. There would probably be trip wires, too, to set off guns or grenades.

Welcome to Pretty Bay.

For sure, anyone in the opium racket handing out orders to Reinbecker and Vanderlee was not going to be a lily-white boy; he would certainly be working on the wrong side of the law. But this was hard-pro gangland material, and Bolan had expected something more in the line of an up-market Reinbecker or perhaps a crooked senator.

What the soldier wanted here, as he had in Baarmbeek, was intel. He had assumed it might be a simple break and enter, with a search of papers and perhaps a little pressure applied to start the conversation.

Now he understood why there was no barbed wire or broken glass along the top of the wall surrounding the property.

If he was dealing with heavies, his approach had to be very different . . . and from what he had seen it was going to be difficult even getting inside the perimeter of Westwood, let alone making it to specific rooms within the house.

Bolan returned to town, turned in the boat, stashed the T-bird in an underground lot and checked in to an empty hotel.

He went out again, found a public phone booth, fed in coins and dialed a secret number.

A little inside information, he figured, would help in the case of Mr. Hugo Rostand, the proprietor of Westwood Towers.

In the receiver he heard a woman's voice speak the single word, "Listening."

Bolan repeated, twice, an identification code.

After a pause, in which he knew his voice print was being matched electronically with a master in a memory system, the voice intoned, "Accepted," and quoted him another number.

He thumbed more coins into the box and dialed again. The number—it was changed twice each day—was a sterile contact for Hal Brognola, director of the NSA's Sensitive Operations Group and sole link between the Stony Man organization and the Oval Office.

From the covert operations section of the Justice Department, Brognola was still unofficially in touch with Bolan's one-time Stony Man comrades, the men of Able Team and Phoenix Force, who were still based on the Virginia Blue Ridge stronghold.

Even less officially—clandestinely, in fact—Hal Brognola remained the sole link between Bolan the outlaw and Bolan the lone warrior. The big Fed was also the only connection between Bolan and the vast data banks storing the information gleaned over the years at Stony Man.

It was through him that Bolan had been able to acquire in Jacksonville the assortment of arms and equipment now taped beneath various parts of the Thunderbird.

And he had several times plundered the Stony Man computer memories to help the Executioner on his lonely path.

"The first question I can answer off the top of my head," the gruff, lugubrious voice affirmed when Bolan had made his requests. Bolan visualized the unlit cigar that must inevitably be wedged in Brognola's mouth. "I thought you would have known, but maybe the change was made when you were in foreign parts."

"The change?"

"Yeah, the change of name. Very discreet. Official. To go with the reformed image of the retired gentleman."

"I don't get it."

"Hugo Rostand hasn't been with us too long. Before, he was more familiarly known as Ugo Rostano."

"Rostano! But wasn't he an enforcer for one of the Detroit families?"

"That's right. He's Mob right down to the ground. Then suddenly he got too big, knew too much and... well, he figured it best to cop out."

"You said he retired?"

"Into the laundry business. He washes syndicate money through connections in Switzerland, South Africa, Italy, you name it. Any Mafia don can use his services, and it's understood all the families stay away as long as he keeps his nose clean."

"He still packs a useful-looking team around home."

"A chauffeur and seven gorillas, according to the latest intel."

"No women?"

"None that we know of," Brognola replied. "No female domestics either."

"Don't send in the fire department too quickly if flames are seen in the neighborhood," Bolan said grimly.

"Just keep it low profile, Striker," Brognola said. "I should have the rest of the stuff you want within twenty-four hours. Call me this time tomorrow, right?" He hung up.

Mack Bolan's brow was furrowed, the granite-hard features pensive as he walked back to his hotel. The wind was freshening and there were whitecaps out beyond the marinas. Beneath the glass roofs of the mall sudden currents of air shook the leaves of the potted palms and tumbled debris along the pavement.

So he was back in the frontline against the old enemy, the Mafia! He should have known they would have a finger in the pie.

The knowledge brought with it a two-way change in his thinking. First, it meant that the job was going to be much tougher, much hairier than he'd expected; second, it meant he could drop the kid-glove approach. If he was dealing with the soulless carrion of the crime syndicates, he could go in with guns blazing.

First, though, he had to figure out a way of *getting* in.

HUGO ROSTAND, A.K.A. UGO ROSTANO, sat with his bodyguard, Frank Nardi, beneath a striped umbrella beside the pool at Westwood Towers. Beyond a hibiscus hedge, the Gulf stretched past millionaires' weekend love nests to the cardboard cutouts of Pretty Bay's seafront hotels three miles to the south.

Rostand was wearing sunglasses. A brown-and-white-striped bathrobe was wrapped around his meaty body, and his pale legs and feet were bare.

"It was the damnedest thing," he said, "this Swiss creep already tells me the dollar stands at 7.938 against the French franc, and it's gonna go on climbin' for at least three days. I tell him okay, weigh in when it makes eight, but hold it until then. So what happens? The bastard central banks lower their interest rates and the fucker drops overnight to 7.16!"

Nardi was wearing a purple, violet and mauve Hawaiian shirt over his yellow swim trunks. His arms and legs were tanned the color of mahogany. "We got enough trouble with our own money without some son of a bitch screwing up on the clients'," he observed. "If that wind freshens any more, they're gonna find it hard bringing in the consignment." He reached across an ornate steel, copper and glass poolside table on wheels, and splashed whiskey from a decanter into a tumbler. He drank.

"I call this *schmuck*," Rostand said, "and I tell him, 'listen, asshole, I want my friends' money cleaned—not ripped to shreds in the machine!' "

The bodyguard was watching two hummingbirds flitting around a patch of poinsettia. "So?" he said indifferently.

"So next week you fly to Zurich, Frank, and we get us a new Swiss accountant."

"Whatever you say, boss." Nardi lifted a Smith & Wesson .357 Combat Magnum from the table, sighted it and fired. The flat crack of the report was lost in the rumble of surf from the shore. One of the hummingbirds flew away. On the shaved grass at the edge of the flower bed, a tangle of blood and bright feathers palpitated. Nardi grinned and laid the automatic back on the table.

"If there's one thing makes me mad, it's bein' crossed up on some two-bit deal that—" Rostand broke off in midsentence. A bulky, hard-faced man in a white jacket was walking across the sun-drenched lawn toward them. He was carrying a white cordless telephone. "Call for you, boss," he said. "From Number One."

Rostand reached out for the instrument. He fished a crocodile cigar case from the pocket of his bathrobe as he listened. His heavy brows drew together in a scowl; his lower lip thrust out sullenly; behind the smoked lenses his eyes grew mean. He took a cigar from the case and clamped his teeth over it.

Nardi rose to his feet and approached with a gold cigar cutter. Rostand waved him away and signaled him to listen, holding the receiver slightly away from his ear.

The bodyguard leaned his expressionless face toward his boss's angry features. A waft of Polo after-shave rose from the open neck of the bathrobe.

Nardi heard the slow, deep voice in the earpiece. "The guy already loused up an important business deal in Central Africa and put the bite on certain friends of mine in Italy and the Union. Now my boy in immigration at Kennedy tips me off that he hit town day before yesterday, and when I tell him to run a check he comes up with the information that he had an onward flight booked for Jacksonville."

"You mean he's heading this way?"

"I don't think he takes his vacations in Florida," the voice from the receiver said.

"That bastard!" Rostand exploded. "I ran across the motherfucker a coupla times...and he's still doing it to the Family. It's time the interfering son of a bitch was out of business... for keeps."

"That's what you're going to do, Ugo," the voice said softly. "Put him out of business. If he don't come your way, you go find him. They tell me he's driving a green T-bird. But whatever happens, I want to hear news that he's been eliminated within the next twenty-four hours. Do you read me?"

Rostand bit off the tip of his cigar and spit it into the pool. He replaced the cigar in his mouth, waving away Nardi, who proffered a gold lighter. "Leave it to me, sir," he said.

"That's exactly what I aim to do," the voice rasped. "Make sure I'm not disappointed, hey." There was a click and the line went dead.

Rostand handed the receiver to Nardi, who pushed in the telescoping antenna. Then the capo turned a rock-hard face toward the muscle man. "Well, howdya like that," he said.

"I told you," Nardi said. "With this onshore breeze, if them waves get any higher, Sanchez is gonna have to use a different boat if he aims to land that consignment tonight."

"I wasn't talking about the goddamn consignment, Frank. This Bolan. You better alert the local cops on the payroll and send out a coupla boys to keep watch. And if the bastard does come here...well, you know what to do."

Chapter Twenty-seven

Wind roared through the treetops as the highway patrol sedan coasted to a stop outside the tall wrought-iron gates of Westwood Towers. Then the driver jammed impatiently on the horn three times.

A guy with a shotgun slung across the back of his leather windbreaker sauntered out from the brick gate house and stared through the bars. The sedan's headlights were on full, both scanner spotlights were illuminated and the amber roof light was revolving. The gateman shielded his eyes against the dazzling glare. "What the hell..." he called.

"I have to see Mr. Rostand, fast," the driver shouted.

"You have an appointment?"

"Nah. No time. I said urgent."

The guard pulled one of the gates open far enough to let him through. "Dammit," he grumbled, "we pay you guys enough to keep off our backs. Don't you have no phones at county police—"

"I told you fast, I told you urgent—now I'm telling you it's important. For chrissake, open those gates and let me into the driveway."

A second man had emerged from the gate house. The butt of a holstered revolver swung behind the open lapel of his bush jacket as he walked, but he carried no shotgun. He jerked his head at the first man and together they opened the gates. The car rolled through and stopped again.

"We'll have to check with the house," the second guard said, trying to squint through the blaze of light into the sedan's interior. "Who is it, please?"

"Chief Harris."

The first guard went into the gate house. The second approached the car and shone a flashlight through the windshield at the uniformed trooper behind the wheel. "Wait a minute—you're not Harris! We know Harris," the guy exclaimed.

"Of course I'm not, asshole. I'm bringing a *message* from Harris. Look, if you don't believe me, here's the chief's shield. He told me to show it to you as proof that I was on the level. He has some character holed up that he thinks might interest Mr. Rostand and he wants advice, okay?"

"What kind of character?"

"Dangerous."

The first man came out of the gate house. "The boss wants to know if it can't wait."

"Like hell!"

"Then you have to speak to him on the phone."

The trooper sighed. He opened the door and clambered out of the car. He was a big man, his muscles straining at his uniform jacket and his arms too long for the sleeves. He strode to the gate house with the second guard and spoke on the phone.

"Yes, sir, it's some kind of hit man. The chief figured you might want— No, he has him cornered but he was scared it might be a contract.... Yes, on you, sir.... He'd welcome your opinion if you'd just— Yes sir. Right away." He turned to the guard. "He wants me to go up there."

The sentry took the phone, checked with Rostand, hung up the instrument and led the trooper back to his car.

Behind the wheel again, the cop nodded to the two hardmen. "No offense, guys. I know you have a job to do. But next time..." He raised a languid hand and drove away.

"Your door's not latched!" one of the guards called after him.

"I know!" Mack Bolan shouted back, elbowing the door open a little wider as he dropped the two L-5 grenades onto the driveway. They burst with a hollow plop, spewing out dense clouds of white phosphorus smoke that blistered the skin and seared the lungs. With the strong onshore breeze, the noxious fumes would billow the few yards to the gate house and incapacitate the two hoods within seconds... and there would certainly be no question of them calling the house.

Okay, two down. Now there were Rostand, the chauffeur-bodyguard and another five to go.

The driveway looped for several hundred yards through the trees. Bolan wondered if the dogs were still with their handlers, or if they roamed free at night. It would be vital to know. They were probably loose. It would leave the house defense thin on the ground if four of those five gorillas were out on patrol.

Yeah—there was one of the Dobermans now, red eyes blazing in the headlights' reflection as it stood snarling on one of the golf course greens.

Bolan braked the police sedan to a halt on a graveled turnaround. He hoped Chief Harris and his driver, shackled hand to foot with their own cuffs in the woods half a mile away, would understand when they woke up. Bolan had parked the Thunderbird across the country road on a dangerous curve after making a phone call to police headquarters. Before trussing them up, they had revealed that they were on the mobster's payroll…and had been warned to watch out for Bolan. Bolan made his plans accordingly.

He glanced quickly around, checking out escape routes before he went in.

Archway to the coach house, left. Portico straight ahead. Shrubbery surrounding the pool at the far end of the facade, right. Dogs in the woods behind. The lawns leading to the shore were the obvious choice.

Rostand's Mercedes was in the yard but the blue Maserati was missing. Did that mean that one or more of the soldiers was away? No time to check now. Bolan ran up the portico steps.

The double doors were already open. A hard-faced houseman in a white jacket stood waiting in a wide lobby. "Second floor, left, third door on the right," he growled. "The boss is expectin' you, but he ain't pleased."

Bolan noticed the telltale bulge beneath the left shoulder of the guy's jacket. The warrior's right hand rested on the butt of the silenced Beretta, which he had substituted for Chief Harris's police pistol, holstered on his hip.

"Thanks," the Executioner said, "but I'll be surprised if he is expecting . . . *me*!"

The tip of the suppressor, projecting through the open base of the holster, tilted upward as he leaned down on the autoloader and fired.

Three slugs whispered out of the silenced killer, and all at once the white jacket was reprocessed in Technicolor. The hardman inside it, minus a lot of his chest, thumped to the floor.

Bolan ran up the curving stairway. No time to hide the body. He had to get to Rostand before someone raised an alarm. He could hear voices along the left-hand hallway. Yeah, behind the third door on the right. He tiptoed close and laid his ear against the cream, gold-lined panels.

"Great if Harris has this Bolan bastard nailed, but we have to get rid of his errand-boy officer quick if Sanchez is bringing this boat in on schedule."

"Why send the bum, anyway? I don't get it." A second voice, gravelly and harsh.

"We'll find out, Frank. Guy should show any minute. You're sure it's on the level that Sanchez switched to the outboard?"

"That's what they tell me. I would hope. After the African fuck-up, we can't afford to lose this Mexican consignment."

"Relax, Frank. Any case, Sakol's down at the pier, waiting to flag them in."

"He better be," Frank said somberly. "Seeing as he's the organization man for the whole damned circus."

Outside the door, Bolan frowned. Sakol?

"He handled the Cuban consignment fine, Frank."

"So what? It's his job. If you ask me, boss, we'd be better off on our—"

"Shove it." Rostand's voice hardened. "Who the hell you think you are, questioning the status quo?"

"Status what?" There was the sound of liquid splashing.

"Cut that out," Rostand snapped. "You drink too much. Put that goddamn glass down and get out those figures. Sakol will want to go over the hit checklist as well as the market figures."

Behind Bolan a door opened at the far end of the hallway and two hoods, talking loudly, walked out and headed for the stairs.

Crouched with his ear to the door, the Executioner had no time to hide the fact that he was listening in.

The conversation ceased abruptly. Two hands dived between two pairs of lapels. One of the hoods called out, "What the hell d'you think you're—"

Bolan swiveled up the holster and fired again from the hip—a series of 3-shot autobursts that cut down those two gorillas like corn razed by a sickle. Unfortunately, one was a shade fast on the draw: before he collapsed across the riddled body of his companion, he had time to whip a police special from his shoulder rig and fire a single shot.

The slug plowed through the wall-to-wall carpet covering the hallway, but the sound of the report was deafening.

No more subterfuge now. Bolan kicked open the door, unleathering the Beretta as he moved.

He leaped inside the room and flattened himself against the nearest wall with the long-snouted death-bringer at the full stretch of his arm, tracking left and right in search of targets.

The room was lined with books. He saw wooden filing cabinets, a wall safe with the thick door open, leather chairs and a wide desk with a green top tooled in gold. An open folder on the desk spilled out papers.

Behind the desk, Rostand was wearing a cream-colored suit, a black shirt and a pale blue silk necktie. Frank Nardi had been sitting beside him. He'd had time to rise halfway out of his chair, his right hand flipping aside his jacket as he reached for the gun in back of his waistband.

"Don't try it!" Bolan growled.

The bodyguard remained on his feet, bent forward, his hands now held loosely at his sides. "What the—" he rasped. "Who—"

"It's Bolan," Rostand snarled. He hadn't moved since the door crashed open.

"Both hands on the desk, palms downward," Bolan ordered. "You, Frank, toss your iron over here, then put your hands on top of your head. Move it."

The combat Magnum thumped to the floor.

"Do you really think you can get away—" Rostand began.

"Shut up!" Bolan rasped.

"Cool it, boss," Nardi advised. "Let the creep find out for himself."

"If you're thinking of your gun muscle," Bolan said, "three guys decided to take a vacation already. And the two soldiers at the gate will probably need a vacation; right now they're suffering a little lung trouble. That leaves the last two, right?"

He saw a covert glance pass between the two mobsters. Did this mean that the missing two were in fact out with the Maserati? Or if they weren't, they might be around the property someplace.

Bolan decided to play it by ear, but to remain watchful.

And watchful was right. Without moving the upper half of his body, Nardi surreptitiously slid a foot across the carpet to a small protuberance just below the corner of the desk. The button of an alarm bell, projecting through the floor.

Bolan fired a single shot. The 9 mm parabellum round cored the bodyguard's instep. He pitched sideways with a yelp and collapsed against a chair as a scarlet stream pumped out past the splintered bones of his foot.

"I've played this whole scene before—at Rinaldi's pad in Italy," Bolan said. "Okay, I know you operate an international drug distribution racket through Africa, Mexico, Cuba, wherever. The profits are laundered along with your regular contracts. I want to know who the drug money goes to—and who's the link man with your terrorists." A pause, and then, "Sakol?"

He saw at once that he had scored. Nardi, cursing on the floor, glanced swiftly at his boss and then shot a look of pure hatred at the Executioner. Rostand's eyes dropped involuntarily to the folder on the desk, and then quickly up again. "Sakol?" he repeated, shaking his head. "I don't..."

"Cut the bull," Bolan grated.

He paused again. The whine of a high-performance engine sounded over the rumble of surf and the wind whistling through the trees.

The Maserati returning?

Rostand and Nardi also heard the noise. Once more they exchanged glances. Nardi's pain-contorted features even relaxed momentarily into a half smile, rapidly suppressed. The whine came nearer, there was a sudden brisk crescendo as the driver shifted down, and then nothing but a low grumble of exhaust while the engine idled. The sportster had arrived at the open gates; in seconds the hoods would find the half-asphyxiated guards.

There wasn't going to be much time.

Hugo Rostand tried to cut it short altogether. Stealthily pressing his leg against a spring concealed in the kneehole of the desk, he released a shallow drawer that slid out slowly and silently twelve inches below his right arm. In the drawer, loaded and charged, was a gun.

Rostand moved very fast for a bulky, middle-aged man. His right hand, snatched from the desk top while the Maserati momentarily diverted Bolan's concentration, streaked down to the drawer and came up wrapped around the butt of a big-bore Detonics Combat Master.

Bolan had no choice. He fired two rapid rounds. Rostand fired one. The .45-caliber slug from the Combat Master barely missed the Executioner's head and smashed into the wall. While the roar of the report still numbed the ears, the 9 mm stingers from Bolan's Beretta slammed into the racketeer's chest.

Even at the silenced, subsonic muzzle velocity, the impact was enough to send Rostand and the swivel chair in which he sat crashing back against the draperies covering the window. His head flopped forward on the gory ruin of his chest. Then the limp body twisted sideways and slid to the floor.

Nardi dived for the Combat Magnum that was still on the floor at Bolan's feet. Bolan stamped on the outstretched hand and shot him through the head. A fan of gray brain tissue complicated the pattern of the Turkish carpet.

Bolan turned to the door. No more questions answered in here. That was too bad... but half a minute of eavesdropping plus a couple of guilty glances had, in fact, told him most of what he had come all this way to find out.

He shoveled together the papers on the desk, scooped up the folder containing them and shoved it under his arm. On the far side of the house he heard a squeal of brakes as the Maserati pulled up outside the portico.

He had to act fast before the two hoods—if there were two-recovered from finding the body of the guy in the white jacket.

Bolan seized Nardi's collar and dragged the dead man out into the hallway.

There were two heavies down in the lobby all right. One was still stooped over White Jacket's body. Both held police specials.

Bolan picked up the bodyguard's inert form and hurled it over the stair rail at the standing hood. It caught him just as he was raising his gun arm, and the two of them, the living and the dead, crashed to the floor in an ungainly heap.

Bolan vaulted lightly over the rail, dropped fifteen feet to the lobby and sprang up catlike, the Beretta sneezing out the last few rounds in the magazine at the second astonished mobster.

The mafioso collapsed before he had time to fire a shot.

By the time the other man heaved himself out from under Frank Nardi's body, Bolan was out of the lobby, down a service passageway and through the kitchens on his way out into the gardens.

Wind gusting up the grassy slope tore at his hair and clothes as he ran. There was a light bobbing among the waves near the pier, and nearby a green signal lamp winked. Behind him the remaining gorilla shouted.

Faintly against the buffeting of the wind Bolan heard shots, but none came near him. He sprinted, swerving left and right, toward the boats.

He saw shadowy figures moving on the pier. Was the mysterious Sakol among them?

A long, narrow launch of a type unfamiliar to him was now moored beyond the fifty-foot cruiser. At the far end of the planking, some small craft heaved up and down on the angry swell. As far as he could make out, a guy standing in the bow was trying to hold it close to the pier, but it was not tied up.

Men shouted in several languages. The green light still flashed on and off.

"Not until Señor Rostand or his partner are here," someone yelled in a Spanish accent. Bolan thought the voice came from the small boat. "That was the arrangement."

There was an angry reply from the pier but the wind snatched the words away.

"For cryin' out loud!" A Southern drawl. "Why won't they land the goddamn stuff?"

"I tell you no. We have a deal; we keep it." The accent again.

A chorus of complaints, pleading from the men on the pier.

"I warn: soon it shall be too late."

"Come off it, Sanchez!"

"Where the fuck—"

The hood behind Bolan was shooting again. Heavy-caliber revolver stuff, by the sound. He felt the wind of one of the slugs on his cheek. Out on the pier a powerful flashlight beam lanced through the dark.

The light swept over Bolan as he ran.

"*¡Policía!* I saw the uniform. We are not prepared—"

"Don't be a damned fool."

Abruptly a submachine gun chattered from somewhere above the whitecaps. Bolan threw himself flat. Behind him he heard a shrill cry. There were no more shots from the mobster.

An outboard burst to life with a clattering roar. The small boat wheeled away from the pier and headed out into the Gulf, leaving a phosphorescent wake curving among the foam-tipped waves.

Bolan could hear the men on the pier more clearly now. For a moment the wind had dropped. It was clearly an angry council of war.

"The stupid fools. There was no need to..."

"What can you expect of Mexicans?"

"To refuse to land the shipment just because..."

"Rostand's laxity is unpardonable. It is not just the consignment; we were supposed also to collect his market reports and send them to Ischia."

"What do we do now? Go on up the house?" The flashlight beam swung this way and that. The green signal lamp was extinguished.

"We leave." An authoritative voice, used to being obeyed. "There may still be gunmen out there, and we don't know who they are. Without Rostand's assurance..."

"They could still be Hugo's boys." The Southern drawl. "But there was a cop, all right. I saw him. Shouldn't we..."

"I said we leave. From the hotel we telephone. If all is well, we return later by road."

"What about the stuff? Will Sanchez return later?"

"We shall see."

The speaker stepped down into the launch, followed by his two companions. There was a deep-throated, burbling drone as the rakish craft knifed away through the rising waves.

Facedown in the grass, Mack Bolan let out his breath in a long whistle of astonishment.

The three men in the launch had been speaking in Russian!

And the leader—revealed for a brief instant in the flashlight beam as it swept past—was Sakol.

Bolan even knew him.

Piotr Anatolevitch Sakol, of the infamous KGB's First Chief Directorate. To be precise, a high official of that organization's S subdirectorate, which was responsible for the planting of illegals and the recruitment of sleepers in foreign countries.

Smiling to himself, Bolan ran onto the pier, stripped the covers from one of the powerboats and headed back to Pretty Bay.

Chapter Twenty-eight

The commuters in Washington, D.C. were working late. Capitol Hill was still jammed bumper to bumper long after dark. Bolan impatiently drummed his fingers on the steering wheel of the Thunderbird, wondering how long it would be before he got out of the traffic snarl.

He saw Jason Mettner first at Columbus Circle, the lean, pale face and the inevitable dangling cigarette unmistakable in the greenish light reflected from the dashboard of an Olds sedan. Before Bolan could signal, the line moved forward a few yards and a panel truck cut in between the two cars. By the time he had maneuvered the T-bird around it, the Olds was no longer in view.

They drifted together again going around DuPont.

Mettner's face was blue. Then Bolan watched it change from orange to red to yellow in the colored lights illuminating the fountain in the center of the circle.

This time he called out. Mettner glanced sideways through his open window. "Hi, there!" he cried across the low-slung hood of some foreign sportster. "What brings you to the land of the free?"

"Freedom," Bolan replied.

"That's good to hear. I figured you might be in the market for thermonuclear waste. Half-life only fifty years. Buy while stocks last."

Bolan grinned. "You keep it," he said. "You might need it to heat up one of your stories."

"Why don't we leave the pack and go hunt a martini on our own?" the newspaperman suggested. "There's no emission control on alcohol."

They drank at the Federal City Club. Such an august administration haunt, Bolan felt, would be the least likely place he'd be noticed by anyone who knew he was on the Wanted list in twenty-one states.

"What can I do for you, squire?" Mettner asked when they were comfortably installed in deep chairs with tall glasses. "I'm not actually in the freedom business, but if there's anything..."

"You may be," Bolan said soberly. "In this kind. Again, it's something I'd like you to find out for me."

Mettner stubbed out a half-smoked cigarette. "What's in it for me?"

"A story. It could be a very big one...if the stuff you come up with is twenty-four carat."

"Okay, shoot."

And Bolan couldn't help but smile at Mettner's choice of words.

"A comrade. Apparently outposted in this country. Piotr Anatolevitch Sakol. Member of the KGB First Chief Directorate, Subdirectorate S."

"That's the department dealing with illegals, right?" Mettner was scribbling on the back of an envelope he had taken from his pocket.

"Right. At one time he was seconded to Department V, the wet affairs, executive action team. I want to know what he's doing here now. If you have counterintelligence or FBI contacts, or any in to their computer linkups, I'm in the market for intel on his present cover in the U.S. And of course any educated guesses or newspaper gossip on the real reason."

Mettner nodded. "Can do. But it may take a little time. I'll have to make a few calls. You want to meet me tomorrow, or can you wait?"

"I'll wait," Bolan said.

The newspaperman shook a cigarette halfway out of his pack and put it between his lips. He rose to his feet. "I'll have the same again," he said, then walked out of the bar and into the lobby.

While he was away, Bolan ran over in his mind the disparate elements of the puzzle he was trying to solve. He was on the brink, he felt certain, of killing some particularly dirty underworld operation. But there were still too many unconnected pieces in the puzzle. It was more like one of those carved ivory balls the Chinese craftsmen made. If you looked through the gaps in the lacy carving you could see that there was a second ball inside, another one inside that, and so on.

Rinaldi, Ononu, Vanderlee, Reinbecker, Rostand... each evil plot had revealed an even more sinister one behind it.

Then he corrected himself. Instead of Chinese balls, make that Russian dolls.

Because now it seemed that the mastermind behind it all was not Mafia but KGB.

Bolan had foiled Soviet plans to make use of the Mob worldwide before, and if Sakol's dramatic appearance late in the game added an unexpected new dimension, it was not a dimension that refused to fit in with the rest of the conspiracy.

The various layers the Executioner had stripped away were each connected with the provision of money for the financing of terrorist activity. So it was not unreasonable to find the KGB at the center, because the destabilization of Western society was one of that evil organization's primary aims.

What was much less understandable was the big business involvement that seemed to surface with bewildering regularity. For that was the sector of society most likely to suffer if the plan succeeded.

There was Ononu's manic interest in the acquisition of the mines in Montenegria, when his profits from the drug industry must have been immeasurably higher.

There were mines, too, around Baarmbeek.

Vanderlee, Bolan recalled, had said to the mercenary, Eddie Hanson, that the Executioner must be eliminated because his activity threatened "years of exploitation" by private individuals heavily into "gold, diamonds, heavy industry."

The fathers of the kidnapped girls had all been industrialists.

Finally here was Hugo Rostand, an ex-Mafia capo and launderer of syndicate money, deeply involved in the Dow Jones index and recent trading on Wall Street, the Bourse in Paris and the London Stock Exchange. For there was little doubt that the market reports Sakol had needed were those connected with the file Bolan had snatched from the mobster's desk before he, Bolan, had fled.

He had it with him now. Sipping his drink, he opened the manila envelope and prepared to go through the contents again.

Market reports, underlined and annotated in various colors. Tables and graphs from *The Wall Street Journal*, *The Financial Times* and *Le Monde*, accompanied by digests encapsulating the movements illustrated. A sheaf of typed documents evaluating and forecasting trends. Most of the in-depth analyses concerned the market in gold and certain industrial metals. There was no material on industrial stock or shares in non-mining companies.

Behind these papers were press clippings, many of them dealing with unexpected fluctuations in the world price of silver, zinc, titanium and manganese, along with expert appraisal of the relation between these and various government decisions on space research, and on the defense budget's effect on the armaments industry.

A cutting from the London *Daily Telegraph* was headlined: London Metal Exchange Members Call for Tin Market Closure. The story forecast the total collapse of trading in this metal, in which dealings had already been suspended for two weeks. A feature from Kuala Lumpur in *Der Spiegel* reported that the number of Chinese working in gravel-pump tin mines, scouring quarry faces with powerful jets of water, had been cut by more than fifty-percent. The London *Times* headlined a story: Tin Crisis into Third Month.

The last group of papers were also press clippings, but they dated back over a couple of years and they all dealt with terrorist activity. Bolan saw stories relating to the explosion that destroyed an Air India jumbo over the Atlantic, bomb attacks that killed Christmas shoppers at Harrod's in London and two major department stores in Paris, the sabotage of a French high-speed train and the carnage resulting from bombing of railroad stations in Bologna and Marseille.

There were pieces on the Lod airport massacre, the suicide-bomber attack that cost 240 American Marine Corps lives in Beirut, several different skyjacks, and the machine-gunning of women and children at the airports of Rome and Vienna during a recent Christmas. Bolan found no reference to the Entebbe skyjack, in which the terrorists were annihilated by an Israeli commando force.

There was nothing about drugs in any of the extracts, but Bolan had little doubt that this was just a selection of atrocities, claimed by a variety of murderous fanatic organizations, which had in fact been financed with money from the chain he was following through.

As he closed the file a small, crumpled slip of paper fell out. It was the fragment torn from Reinbecker's notepad on which he had jotted down Rostand's name and address.

It had already been half covered by doodles and scrawls in the South African's spidery hand. Bolan had not bothered to examine them before, but a single word caught his eye now and he smoothed out the paper and scrutinized the phrases.

Some were readable enough: Cassiterite (tin) assoc. + alluvial copper...Sphalerite isomorphs inc. gallium, indium...semiconduct. transistors, telecom detectors.

At the foot of the page, in smaller, neater handwriting, he read: Malaysia—1000 tin mines red. 458 today: 360 g-pump, 51 open-cast, 38 dredged, only 19 underground. The last phrase had been underscored.

Bolan folded the paper and replaced it carefully in the file. An idea was beginning to take shape in his mind, though as yet it had no structure. It was as though he saw the leaves and twigs and branches of a tree appear, with no trunk connecting them with solid earth. But it was something; it filled what had previously been a blank space.

Why then did the word Ischia keep recurring in his mind?

The file he was holding. Sakol had said, "We were supposed also to collect his market reports and send them to Ischia."

Why Ischia? What did it have to do with the KGB? Was there yet another boss behind them? And why did the name of the place echo? Somewhere along the line he had heard it mentioned before. Where? What was the connection? He knew there was one, like a half-remembered name it kept floating almost to the surface of his memory...then submerging again before he could grasp it.

He was still struggling to remember when Mettner returned.

"Pay dirt," the newspaperman announced. "Your man Sakol is seconded to a Russian trade delegation—at present in this country for import-export negotiations with chambers of commerce in New York, Chicago, San Francisco, Philadelphia, Detroit, St. Louis, Kansas City, Tampa and New Orleans."

"I'll bet!" Bolan said. "And the real reasons?"

"That's the screwy part. According to the bureau and the NSA spooks, there is no evidence of recruiting or any attempt to place—or even trace—illegals. The guy seems to be genuinely on a commercial kick, following the markets and all."

"Any special interests there?"

"Funny you should ask. Yep—it seems he's very hot on metals, especially gold."

"That figures. Where does this trade delegation hang out?" Bolan asked. "When it's not selling vodka, caviar and sets of Russian dolls to the natives, I mean."

"Georgetown. One of the mansions leased to the Soviet embassy. Sakol himself is based in another Russian outpost, on O Street."

Bolan drained his glass and pushed himself upright. "The story will be red-hot," he said, "but you have to work for it."

"Meaning?"

"There's a place for a backup man in tonight's break-in," Bolan said. "A house rented to foreigners. Over on O Street."

As NEAT AS BOOKS arranged on a library shelf, the colonial houses on O Street allowed only a single break in their semicontinuous facade—a construction site.

Breaking into the Soviet outpost was not all that difficult—provided you could operate the swing crane whose long arm stretched out far enough to encompass the far side of the street and the houses on either side of the site if it was necessary.

It was necessary for the Executioner. The house assigned to Piotr Sakol as his private quarters flanked the site. It was unlikely that the place would be protected with the most ultrasophisticated of Soviet security gadgetry—it was, after all, a dormitory site, not an office or an offshoot of the embassy itself. But still there would be a certain amount of electronic alarm equipment and Bolan preferred to bypass it. The roof then seemed to him the best way in, with the crane the obvious way to get there.

The crane was motorized; when the construction gangs were working the site its arm with the pulleys and grappling hooks was operated mechanically. For Bolan this had to be a silent manual task. Fortunately the counterweight machinery and the huge roller bearings on which the arm pivoted were sensitive enough for him to make it.

But the timing was vital. Leaving the Thunderbird parked on the tree-lined, lamplit avenue beside the Potomac, he had realized that the gantry was visible from the river—silhouetted against the night sky above the rooftops. And there was an almost continuous police presence on the water.

Since Georgetown was one of the most burgled arcas in thc United States, patrol cars also cruised every street between ten and twelve times an hour. So speed was as important as silence.

The workers had left the pulley halfway along the arm, which was angled toward the rear of the site. Bolan wanted the pulley at the far end of the arm, and the crane swung around until it was directly over the roof of Sakol's house.

In the dark, it was nerve-racking negotiating the site, which was partly excavated, partly cluttered with stonecrushers, concrete mixers and stacks of lumber. But they made it without mishap and Bolan left Mettner as lookout by a heap of gravel at the base of the crane. Each of them had a long-range walkie-talkie; when the Executioner was ready, he would contact Mettner in time for him to have the car outside as he left the house.

The newspaperman had already checked that Sakol would be at an official embassy function until after midnight. That left just three male servants—probably all KGB—in the building.

For Bolan the slowest part was climbing the girdered telescopic pillar on which the crane arm was mounted, freezing each time a car passed or a boat could be heard on the river. At the top he found the lightweight arm moved silently, but the pulley creaked. Very slowly he maneuvered the wire hawsers so that the pulley slid outward and the grappling hooks descended almost to roof level. Only when he was sure the shrill squeaking had alerted nobody did he swing the arm until it was over the house.

All he had to do then was inch his way out along the slender, narrowing gantry, traversing the void until he was directly above the slates of the roof. Then he lowered himself down the wire, hung for an instant from the hooks, and dropped lightly beside the parapet.

There were two skylights among the slate ridges, one dark and one lit. Bolan moved warily across to the second. It was a clear, cool night; the roof was dry. Cautiously, he leaned out far enough to see down into the room below.

Clearly it had once been a servant's attic bedroom. A wide-shouldered man with long arms and a shaved head was sitting at a table covered with pages torn from newspapers, running a pencil down the columns of type—they looked to Bolan like market reports—marking some and making notations in a ledger.

Apart from the table and chair, the room contained only a bed, a chest of drawers and a shelf bearing a small radio transmitter—short-range local stuff only, Bolan judged from the antenna attached to a nearby chimney stack.

The Russian wore gray pants and a white vest. His jacket hung with his shoulder rig on a hook behind the door.

Bolan crept across a flat part of the roof to the dark skylight. It was bolted on the inside. With the same technique he had used outside Vanderlee's office in Johannesburg, he removed one pane, reached in to release the bolt, lifted the hatch and dropped into the unlit room below.

At once each of his arms was seized in a viselike grip and he felt the muzzle of a gun jammed into the back of his neck.

Evidently the Soviet alarm system was less rudimentary than he had thought.

Bolan was hustled out of the room, down a flight of dimly lit stairs and into a book-lined area that looked like a study. A standard lamp by the curtained window threw a discreet light over a desk once again littered with newspaper cuttings. For the first time Bolan got a good look at his captors.

Both medium height, muscular, hard-eyed, with close-cropped hair and flat Slavic faces. One was dark and one sandy, but you didn't need the buttoned jackets and wide, cuffed pants to know where they came from. Peter Lorre and Moshe Dayan without the eye patch—Central Europe and Central Casting.

"Okay," Bolan said with a theatrical sigh. "You caught me before I had a chance to take anything. Just call the cops and let's get it over with, huh?"

"Do you take us for fools?" the man who looked like Dayan grated. "Do you really expect us to believe that you do not know where you are? To swallow the story that you are a common thief?" His voice was deep and almost accentless. Maybe a couple of steps up the KGB ladder from the chauffeur-bodyguard rank.

"I can't think of any other reason for coming in through the roof," the Executioner said.

"With a silenced 93-R, a transceiver and—let me see—yes! A customized stainless-steel AutoMag?" Peter Lorre, who had a higher, more sibilant voice, took the items from Bolan's hip and shoulder rig as he enumerated them. "This is spy equipment if ever I saw any. Who sent you? The dogs of national security, so-called? The FBI? The CIA?"

"You ought to know the CIA doesn't operate within the United States," Bolan said. "As for the others, are *you* crazy enough to imagine this place hasn't already been screened, swept, bugged and gone over at least a dozen times?"

"So we drop this pathetic burglar pretense?" sneered Moshe Dayan, still covering Bolan with a steady hand. The gun, he saw, was a Tokarev automatic. "In any case, there is no reason to: the house belongs to the commercial consulate; it is not as though—" The Russian stopped in midsentence.

"You mean it's not the embassy," Bolan finished for him, "where the wet-affairs boys work over suspects in the cellars and the dirtier subversion plots are hatched? Where it's really worthwhile listening in?"

"Impertinence and insults will do you no good," Peter Lorre said. "What are you doing here? Who sent you?"

"Find out."

"Oh, we will. It depends upon you how quickly—and how painlessly. But we will in the end."

"For you it may *be* the end," the man with gun said. "In any case, protests will be made at the highest level. This is Soviet territory. Such an unwarranted intrusion is inadmissible at all levels."

"Even the lowest, bottom-of-the-dunghill level like yours?" Bolan asked.

Peter Lorre drew back a meaty fist and hit him as hard as he could in the pit of the stomach. Bolan folded as the breath whooshed from his lungs. The other man kicked him in the crotch, pistol-whipping the side of his head savagely as he went down.

Bolan lay on the floor fighting off waves of nausea. Through a red mist of pain he heard Peter Lorre say, "What shall we do with him?"

"Call Sakol and wait for orders."

One of the goons went out into the hallway and shouted up the stairs, "Igor! We have caught a spy. Call Comrade Sakol."

"He is with the bankers. Orders are that he is on no account to be disturbed," the voice of the giant in the attic replied.

"Then we will follow the usual routine—inject him and then call the embassy to come and collect. You had better come down and lend a hand."

Heavy footsteps. Creaking stairs. Bolan opened an eye and saw the man in the vest lumber into the room. He was carrying a metal first-aid box.

Bolan was hauled roughly to his feet and held upright by the giant as Peter Lorre opened the box, took out a heavy-duty nondisposable hypodermic and sucked fluid into the barrel from a dark brown vial.

Breath was still creaking back into the warrior's lungs. His loins were on fire and he could feel warm blood trickling down his cheek. But he was not quite as punch-drunk as he made out.

The grip on his biceps tightened as Peter Lorre ripped open the sleeve of the blacksuit and pinched up a fold of flesh near the elbow. He brought the syringe closer with his other hand.

Bolan stamped down suddenly, with all his force, on the giant's instep. The Russian cried out in pain, snatching his foot from the floor involuntarily and slackening his grasp on the Executioner's arms.

It was all Bolan needed. He jabbed an elbow viciously backward into the guy's solar plexus, reaching forward at the same time to seize the hand holding the hypodermic. He bent the man's arm upward with manic force, slamming the heel of his own hand against the syringe so that the needle plunged into the goon's temple beside the eye and the plunger went home.

He flung the Russian sideways just as Dayan fired the Tokarev, the body cannoning into the gunman and deflecting his aim. The slug drilled a hole between the giant's eyes. He fell with a crash that shook the house.

The remaining Russian was regaining his balance, the Tokarev swinging back in Bolan's direction, when the big guy's foot flashed out, straight-legged, and kicked it from his hand.

The heavy automatic spun away. Before it thumped to the floor the Russian's curse was killed in his throat by the edge of Bolan's hand, hard as a seasoned plank, slamming into his windpipe.

The cartilage was crushed, the blood vessels ruptured, muscles and nerves paralyzed by the blow. Dayan sank to his knees, choking on his own blood. Bolan picked up the Tokarev and made it easy for him.

After the flat, ringing report, the house seemed very silent. Bolan recovered his hardware and thumbed a switch on his transceiver.

"Ranger to Rider, are you receiving me loud and clear? Over."

He pressed the button marked Receive. Mettner's voice responded almost at once. "Rider to Ranger. Five on five. How's the weather in your part of the country? Over."

"Variable," Bolan said. "Bright intervals right now, but it could blow up a storm. I have a small survey to carry out, but I'll need transport at the door in, say, fifteen minutes. Over."

"Willco," said the newspaperman. "There's a gang of blank pages in my notebook, remember. Over and out."

"Well," Bolan said thirty minutes later, "you get your story, all right. I can wipe out the scum carrying out these deals, but I don't have the means to expose the plot as a whole. You do."

"I'm listening," Mettner said. They were parked beneath trees on MacArthur Drive, between Washington and Bethesda. Some way off to their left, the lights of a police patrol boat cast wavering reflections on the moving surface of the Potomac.

"I'll give you the story briefly, first," Bolan told him. "You can ask questions and fill in details later."

"Suits me," Mettner said. He fished a notebook from his pocket.

"I found the clincher during the fifteen minutes I was alone in that house," Bolan said. "Apart from more specific market intel, I dug out a whole sheaf of directives in Russian from Sakol's room. I have them here." He tapped his breast pocket. "You can take them with you. They prove the truth of my story."

"Okay," Mettner said. "Even radar beams couldn't bounce off a bug and listen in on us here. Go ahead."

"You're familiar with the cash-collecting stages of the scheme," Bolan said. "And you know the cash is used, ultimately, to finance terrorist activity. You know the aim of that activity is to destabilize Western society. But for what specific reason?"

"Promote anarchy, so that the Russians can step in and take over?" Mettner offered.

Bolan shook his head. "If such a project is on the cards at all," he said, "it's a very long-term one. This one is short-term. You have to remember two things: one, Russia desperately needs hard currency. For the installation of heavy industrial plants, to buy Western know-how and to purchase our grain surplus to make up the deficit in her own five-year agricultural plan. Two, Russia has an enormous gold surplus."

Mettner lit a cigarette and flicked the spent match out of the open window. "Go on," he said.

"Now, what will happen if terrorist activity—bombs and hijacks and machine gunning of innocent people—escalates so much that everyone panics and the stock market takes a plunge?"

Mettner nodded slowly. "I get it. As the shares slide, everybody will put their money into gold. So the shares slide still more."

"And the price of gold goes sky-high. Right. At which time our Soviet friends, in a brilliantly organized worldwide operation, slowly begin to unload their gold surplus on a seller's market—reaping so much hard cash you wouldn't believe. I've seen the estimates."

"But wouldn't that bring the price tumbling down? If they unloaded all that at the same time?" Mettner objected.

"Not the way they have it planned. Not in a graduated market assault in London, New York, Paris, Amsterdam, Tokyo, Hong Kong, Bonn and Zurich. Orchestrated with a new series of vicious terrorist atrocities, to keep up the demand any time the price does show signs of flagging."

"Very neat," Mettner said. "And you have written proof of all this?"

"I have the directions for the unloading operation. In Russian, from Moscow, right here. Obviously that's why Sakol has been seconded from the KGB: to tie up the loose ends and watch over Wall Street.

"I have the Rostand file that Sakol was supposed to collect. It shows clearly that they were relating downward market movements with past and present terrorist activity. The rest you have in your head. And don't forget this is not a case for a judge and jury; you only need enough proof to make the story stand up. Once the plot's blown wide open, whether or not there is enough proof to satisfy a court of law, the whole deal is dead."

"You're right," the newspaperman said. "What a story!"

"It's yours if you'll delay breaking it until I've checked out one more thing. There's a single piece of the puzzle that doesn't quite fit and I'd like to straighten it out before we go for broke."

"Sold," Mettner said. "I'm kind of surprised, though, that this guy Sakol's the front man, working openly through their trade delegation. I'm surprised they even let him in the country. I thought he was thrown out persona non grata years ago."

"For organizing illegals and blackmailing guys in sensitive positions to spy for the Soviets?"

"For organizing one particular illegal. Sakol was the contact man in the Varzi affair. He was Varzi's case officer."

"Varzi? The *Varzi* case?" Bolan frowned.

"Sure. I'm surprised you don't remember. It was soon after we went into Vietnam. It was a big scandal at the time, but I guess maybe it was eclipsed by the war news."

"I had other things on my mind," the Executioner said grimly. "Tell me about it."

"Varzi was a big wheel in the Mob. Sicilian, of course. A very smart operator who worked with families based in Vegas, the Coast and southern Texas. On his own, he was into prostitution, gambling, numbers, fixed horseraces and drugs imported through Galveston."

"I know the scenario," Bolan said.

"Yeah. Familiar story. But this one has the payoff you already guessed. Varzi was a longtime sleeper, recruited by the Reds back in the late twenties. They activated him during the Nam crisis. He used his Mob connections to instigate trouble in unions working on Defense Department contracts, to spread unrest in the

Army, and most of all to stir up antiwar feeling among students. Half the campus protest movements that sapped the war effort originated with Varzi."

"Nice guy," Bolan commented. His mind was racing.

"They don't come any nicer. They got him in the end the way they got Lucky Luciano—nailed him on an illegal entry rap, plus tax evasion and white slavery charges. He was deported...oh, I guess it must have been in the late sixties."

"Somehow I don't think he retired," Bolan said. And then, "What was Varzi's first name?"

Mettner flicked his cigarette out the window. "Something not too far from Luciano, oddly enough. Luigi? Lucio? No—Lucino. Yeah, that's it, Lucino Varzi."

Bolan released his breath in a long sigh. It all figured. Just that one piece of the puzzle to fit in now. But apart from that it was green all the way.

Lucino Varzi was the fourth director of the Montemines Corporation; he had a seat on the board but he held very little stock. He was not on the board of Negrimin International.

Lucino Varzi's seventeen-year-old daughter, Palomar, was the only one of the five girls held hostage by Anya Ononu who was neither tortured nor raped.

Why? Because the whole kidnap deal in her case was a setup, a cover to distract attention from the fact that her father was actually in cahoots with the dictator, probably masterminded the whole show.

Through Ononu, Varzi planned to get his hands on all the stock of both companies.

But—this was Bolan's missing piece of the puzzle—what exactly did this have to do with the unloading of Russia's gold surplus? Were Sakol and Varzi still connected? And why, above all, were Vanderlee's big-time industrialists concerned with a scheme that, if it succeeded, would ruin them?

He turned toward Mettner. "One more thing," he said. "Varzi's still a millionaire, he still plays the world markets. Would you know where he's based since he was thrown out of the U.S.?"

"Sure," Mettner said. "He has a place on the island of Ischia."

Chapter Twenty-nine

The waterfront at Ischia resembles a slice of downtown Naples carved out of the gulf and deposited into the Mediterranean a dozen miles offshore.

Bolan and Jason Mettner checked in to the Hotel Punta Molino at Ischia Porto—an Italianate building set among pines above the flat-roofed jumble of fishermen's houses that tumbled down between stone stairways to the balconied facades overlooking the quays.

The Varzi property was at the other end of the island. They rented a scooter with a pillion to make a preliminary recon. Beyond the villages clustered on the vine-covered slopes of Mount Epomeo, they came to Ischia Ponte, where a *castello*—a complex of fortress, cathedral, prison and baroque churches—crowned a massive highland connected to the island by a fifteenth-century bridge.

The ex-Mafia sleeper's retreat was even more isolated—a medieval fortress on an islet half-hidden behind a wall of rock that rose from the cliff top. A tunnel pierced the outcrop, and beyond this a narrow footbridge spanned a chasm separating two sheer one hundred-foot cliffs rising straight from the sea.

The bridge was the only way of reaching the fortress. There was no landing stage and no visible way down the rock faces between the ancient walls and the waves frothing among the jagged boulders below. Varzi's automobiles, and those of his visitors, were housed in a walled compound on the landward side of the tunnel.

"And there'll be guys with guns behind those walls," Bolan said. They had already seen, focusing field glasses from a vantage point a quarter of a mile away along the cliff top, that there were two armed guards at the far end of the bridge.

"Below the ramparts, too, all around the rock," Mettner said, handing the glasses back to the Executioner.

Bolan refocused. The journalist was right. A path circled the islet below the huge stone walls supporting the central redoubt, and here and there small dugouts had been quarried from the rock. Most of them housed one or two men, tanned, muscular guys in swim trunks. They could have been guests at the castle sunbathing, but in several cases the bright midday light struck reflections from the breech or barrel of a gun leaning against the dugout wall.

"Okay," Bolan said. "Direct approach across the bridge is out. Likewise any attempt to land from a boat. The cliffs can be scaled—but I wouldn't rate my chances high with those goons on the watch."

"How are you going to get in?"

"Underwater," the warrior said. "Let's go back to town before the stores close for siesta."

Past groves of lemon trees and a volcanic lake, the scooter carried them back down through the pinewoods to Ischia Porto. It was after they had bought scuba equipment that Bolan spotted Piotr Sakol.

The Russian was paying off a cab outside the Gennaro Restaurant—a slim, hard-bitten man with dark wiry hair who could have been north German or even Welsh rather than Slav.

"The vultures are gathering," Bolan said. "I reckon things are about to happen. They'll know the Russian unloading directives are in enemy hands. My guess is that they'll put the whole deal forward now, try to get it off the ground before anyone makes use of that information."

"You better work out a way of getting in there quickly, then," Mettner urged. "Because Ivan's gonna be given the big hand, if what you say is right. They'll have that red carpet rolled clear across the bridge and through the tunnel when he shows."

"Okay," Bolan said. "While he's getting the VIP treatment, I'll be going up the back stairs."

Shortly before dusk, Mettner tilted down the forty-horsepower Evinrude engine, so that the shaft and propellor were submerged, and punched the rented boat out from among the yachts and power cruisers moored along the waterfront.

On half throttle they cleared the harbor and chugged westward toward the *castello* and Varzi's place beyond. Bolan was already wearing a wetsuit, with oxygen tank strapped to his back. His two guns, spare ammunition clips, the transceiver and a couple of stun grenades were zippered into waterproof pouches clipped to his belt.

Approaching the islet several hundred yards offshore, he slipped flippers on his feet and sloshed seawater around the inside of his mask so that the glass eyepiece would not fog up. The intense, startling blue of the ocean had already faded through a leaden hue to inky black. Above the western horizon a tiny sliver of moon lay beneath the evening star in the darkening sky. It would be night in a few minutes.

Bolan coiled rope around his waist, picked up a harpoon gun and slid backward into the water on the side of the boat away from the islet. Mettner was instructed to await a call on the transceiver.

Bolan swam steadily toward Varzi's retreat, at first on the surface, then underwater, correcting his direction with the aid of a luminous compass strapped to his wrist. He was aiming for a section of cliff where slabs of rock formed a series of natural steps plunging below the waves.

According to charts he had read, the water there should be around thirty feet deep...and the rock shelves were halfway between two of the lookout posts. A preliminary recon while the light was still good had persuaded him that it would not be too difficult for an agile man to scale the weathered face in the dark. After that it would be the Montenegria prison tape played over—the rope, the grappling hook and the silent climb over the ramparts.

Then it would be playing by ear. There was no plan of the fortress in the Ischia public library or town-hall record office.

Ten feet below the surface, the water was pitch-black and surprisingly cold, pressing the rubber suit to Bolan's body with clammy insistence. Approaching the islet, he dived deeper and made the last few yards along the seafloor.

He was perhaps thirty feet out in his reckoning. The error saved his life.

Switching on the underwater lamp clamped to the front of his helmet, he groped his way past wave-smoothed boulders covered with barnacles, across clefts alive with fronds waving in the receding tide, to the lowest of the rock shelves.

A shoal of brightly colored fish, suspended in the viridian depths like the elements of a mobile, flicked their tails and darted away. Something large and scaly slithered out of sight into a crevice surrounded by sea anemones.

Suddenly Bolan saw that there was a cavern penetrating the base of the cliffs—a cavern that reached from the bed of the ocean to a point a few feet above the surface, a cavern whose low, arched entrance would have been hidden by the boulders from anyone approaching from the sea. But a cavern, nevertheless, that must give access by means of some system of tunnels and stairways carved from the rock to the fortress one hundred feet above. *Because even here, five fathoms deep, there were guards.*

He saw them first as dim shapes at the outermost range of his lamp. Then gradually, as they split up to outflank him, he realized they were frogmen like himself, but hostile—sinister figures now moving with a slow but remorseless scissoring of the legs toward his telltale light.

He killed the beam and thrust himself upward. The underwater guards followed. There were three of them, one who switched on his own lamp to identify the target, two others circling silently in the dark. The one with the lamp held a harpoon gun; the others clutched broad-bladed knives.

Bolan aborted the operation. Speed, strength, dexterity, mastery of the martial arts were all useless here, where action was in slow motion because of the pressure of the water. Three against one was a no-go situation. The only line he could take was to get out, fast. If he could.

The two with the knives were kicking hard, closing fast. Bolan somersaulted, propelled himself downward and then rolled to shoot toward the surface again. One of the attackers drifted away and down; the other sailed in with an upraised arm.

Bolan saw the filtered light gleam on the knife blade. He twisted sideways, feeling the razor-sharp point rip through the sleeve of his wet suit and score his left arm.

Then he had hold of the attacker's wrist, backflipping so that his knee came up and he was able to snap the bone of the guy's forearm across it like a dry stick. A stream of bubbles floated upward as the attacker screamed. The knife seesawed down into the dark.

Bolan turned. The second guard had switched on his headlight. The two beams were converging on him in the semiopaque water at the foot of the rock shelf. The first man was about to launch his harpoon at the Executioner.

Bolan fired first. The steel shaft arrowed through the deep to pierce the killer's chest. At once the man's limbs became as limp as the feelers of a squid. A murky cloud stained the depths, spread rapidly and roiled slowly toward the surface. The deadly harpoon hissed harmlessly past Bolan two feet away.

But the last defender was on him. The knife flashed, not menacing Bolan directly but above his head. Seawater gushed suddenly into his mouth and nose as a cascade of bubbles fountained upward. The blade had severed his oxygen tube.

Choking and spluttering, Bolan discarded the cylinder and shot to the surface.

He swam away from the islet with long, powerful strokes, actuating the bleeper attached to his waist belt so that Mettner, waiting with the sister device, could home on the signal and pick him up.

"Zero for that one," Bolan said when he had regained his breath and staunched the flow of blood from his arm. "We'll have to put Plan B into operation at once."

"You mean tonight?" The newspaperman was astonished. "Don't you think you've done enough—"

"Look," Bolan cut in. "This little comedy beneath the ocean will have tipped them off that someone wants in. My fault, I should have done a soft probe. The whole place will be on the alert now. The quicker we strike, the more likely we are to catch them on the move."

Mettner shrugged. "Okay, guy, it's your dream."

It didn't take Bolan long to ready himself. Bind up the arm. Keep the rope and the weapons, junk headlight and harpoon gun. Check the chute and strap on quick-release skis.

"Someone—anyone who's watching—is going to think somebody's out of his skull," Mettner observed. "Para-sailing in the dark, for chrissake!"

Bolan grinned. "You forget, this is a tourist center. If anyone does see, they'll take us for Brits."

He grabbed the towrope and lowered himself into the ocean for the second time that night. Mettner gunned the Evinrude, the bow rose, the double wake creamed out in a wide V and Bolan was up.

Mettner approached the islet in a shallow curve as the chute lifted the Executioner from the ripples rolling in toward the port.

Bolan manipulated the shrouds so that the onshore breeze buoyed up the rectangular canopy of the aerofoil chute, flying him higher and higher as Mettner gave the vessel full power and paid out the special towrope from the stern. At the same time the parachute was being carried sideways so that as the boat passed the rocky boss it flew over the islet itself.

From his position twenty feet above the rooftops, Bolan saw that the place was much bigger than he had imagined. In the center of the medieval buildings clustered above the ramparts was a domed chapel, and outside this a wide piazza encompassed a pool, a sunken garden and lawns planted with floodlit orange trees.

Bolan had intended to maneuver the shrouds so that he was able to lower himself from the sky, let go the towrope and float down to a narrow, grass-covered ledge beneath the ramparts.

This would have been dangerous enough. There was a risk that the towrope would snag on the cliff face and spill him 150 feet into the ocean; there was a risk that he might miss his footing or overrun such a small landing area. And, of course, despite the blacksuit, the helmet and the matt black nylon parachute canopy, there was always a chance that the dugouts would still be manned after dark and someone would see him silhouetted against the stars.

What he decided to do now was more perilous still.

Since he had enough height, he would forget about scaling the rampart; he would land on the inside of the fortress.

He would be at a wider angle from the boat, there was more chance of the cliff snaring the rope and the complexity of the surfaces available to him for a landing could easily result in a broken leg or a fatal fall. Because in practice this meant that he had to land on the roofs.

The towrope snaked away down into the dark. Bolan heard the wooden bar he had been holding clatter against the rock face before it dropped into the sea. The wake from the outboard faded and then dissolved into the night as Mettner throttled down and coasted.

Bolan spilled air from the canopy. A slope raced up to meet him. He landed heavily, pitching forward across the roof to dislodge a tile that shattered on the rock below.

Had anyone heard the wooden bar rattling down?

Had the smashing tile alerted one of Varzi's guards?

Affirmative.

Peering over the edge of the roof, Bolan heard a shout below, saw first one, then another, dark figure scrambling upward between the cliff outcrops. He sighed. He knew what the score would be if the positions were reversed; he already had evidence of the lethal intentions of Varzi's guards. He took the silenced Beretta from the pouch at his waist and sighted carefully down toward the clifftop.

It wasn't an easy shot. The sliver of moon had already sunk below the horizon; he had to wait for that brief instant when a man shape was outlined against the lacework of white foam circling the rocks below.

Now!

He squeezed the trigger. A single shot.

One of the figures jerked, appeared to leap outward, dived down and vanished into the surf heaving against the base of the cliff.

The second was even more difficult. Because of the flash-hider and subsonic rounds, Bolan's position was impossible to define. But the guard had heard the breaking tile; he had seen his companion fall. He dived for a crevice in the rock.

In the faint light from the stars it was hard to distinguish shapes. Bolan was forced to trigger three 3-round autobursts before he was convinced he had hit his target. He ventured a quick look with the flashlight he carried in the pouch. The hardman was wedged into his crevice with half his head blown away.

Bolan redistributed the contents of the pouches: the Beretta and the AutoMag holstered in their usual positions, grenades and flashlight clipped to belt, transceiver attached to his shoulder strap. He gathered the chute canopy, packed it into one of the pouches and left it beside a chimney stack. On the far side of the stack he fixed the grappling hook and then paid out the rope over the edge of the roof and down into the piazza.

He let himself down among the orange trees on the floodlit lawn. Standing still for two minutes, he took in the scene around the open space.

Two guards patrolled the arched gateway that led to the bridge and the tunnel beyond. At least another couple, Bolan surmised, at the landward end of the bridge. The piazza itself was deserted. On the sea side, a couple of lights showed in upper windows. Above the arch and to the south the facades were dark. But the building rising from the northern ramparts was ablaze with illumination.

Behind stone balconies on the second floor, light showed in the cracks between heavy draperies covering most of the windows; it streamed down a flight of steps leading to double glass doors behind which an ornate hallway was visible; it outlined three uncurtained windows on the ground floor overlooking the sunken garden; and it glowed behind a whole row of casements beneath the overhanging eaves.

Nobody inside the redoubt seemed to have been alerted that a stranger was on the rock. Perhaps they expected him to make another attempt on the cave below. If they had missed out on the parachute, the presence of the outboard could support that theory.

Bolan stole between the orange trees to a patch of shadow below the lighted facade. Through the glass doors he could see a typical Mob hardman sitting reading a newspaper in back of the hallway.

The uncurtained windows beyond the sunken garden revealed officelike interiors with gray steel desks, filing cabinets and telex terminals. There was also a small computer console with a display screen, but no operator.

From the upper floor, a hum of voices floated on the night air. Bolan crossed the sunken garden, skirted the pool and climbed a pillar to the nearest balcony.

It was the only one with darkened windows. Two small tools from a pocket in his belt enabled him to spring the lock. Warily, he pressed down the latch and opened the window.

Darkness.

A presence nevertheless. Breathing, heavy breathing and something else—vocal but muffled.

Bolan dropped to his hands and knees, the AutoMag fisted in his right. He reached up and swung the window wide.

In the diffused light reflected from the floodlit piazza he saw an iron bedstead. A figure spread-eagled on it. He stifled an exclamation and switched on the flashlight.

Ruth Elias.

Her wrists and ankles were handcuffed to the four corners of the iron frame. Wide adhesive tape strapped across her mouth held a gag in place, and her eyes were taped shut.

The Executioner's breath hissed between his teeth. The Israeli woman's skirt was pulled up around her waist and her blouse had been ripped open. Angry red blotches visible between the torn edges showed where the slopes of her breasts had been burned with cigarettes. When he had pried off the tapes as gently as he could, he saw that one of her eyes was blackened and both lips swollen and split.

He pulled a rubber sponge from her mouth. "You!" she gasped. "The last person I would— My God, am I glad to see you!"

"What happened?" Bolan whispered.

"I got too close again." Ruth spoke with difficulty, grimacing with pain as she moved her lacerated mouth. "Bluffed my way in, pretending I wanted to interview Varzi, but someone recognized me."

Bolan began opening the handcuffs with his picks. "How did you get on to Varzi?" he asked.

"Still on the same antidrug assignment. One of our operatives in the South managed to penetrate the gang operating the Mexican supply line. After that it was no sweat making the connection through Rostand to his old boss."

"You shortcut my own research by one round trip to Washington, D.C.," Bolan admitted. "On the other hand, you won't know about the Comrades."

"What about them?" she asked.

Bolan told her.

"But there are still things I don't understand," she complained, pulling the ragged edges of her garment together and massaging the circulation back into her cramped limbs.

"Me, too," he said. He helped her off the bed. "Come on, we'll see what we can find out. Did they find out anything from you?"

Ruth hung her head. "Only that I'm on an Israeli antidrug mission," she whispered. "I couldn't hold out any longer. But no other names. There was going to be another... session... tomorrow morning."

Bolan pressed her arm in sympathy. Somebody was going to pay for this. He handed her his Beretta, unsheathed Big Thunder and led the way out of the room.

They were in a long dimly lit corridor. The voices came from behind a door near the stairway at the far end. In between, light streamed from a small empty room.

The door was ajar. Bolan pushed it open and they stole inside. The place looked like the anteroom to an office. He saw typewriters, ledgers, a nest of trays filled with papers and documents, another telex machine. On a table in front of the window he scanned a dozen clipboards holding printed share certificates, extracts from company registers, invoices, correspondence from brokers, details of short-cover dealings and washed sales.

"Here, right here on this table, is the missing piece of the puzzle," Bolan murmured. Ruth raised her eyebrows, but he shook his head and held up a warning finger. The voices, which had been distant, were approaching. A door opened and closed. They had moved into the next room.

He laid his ear against a communicating door.

There were two voices: one a baritone, the other deep, guttural, oddly familiar. Varzi and...who else?

A phone rang. Varzi's voice. "Well, go out there, you fool, and check.... If there was an attempt to penetrate the cavern earlier and now you can't raise Ricardo and Pasquale— No, don't come whining to me. Get out there, the whole lot of you. I want the whole rock searched, inch by inch. And alert the guys guarding the tunnel." The receiver was slammed down.

Voices now from an upper floor. Feet tramping down the stairs, perhaps six or eight men, following Mr. Big's orders. The front door slammed and the voices spread out across the piazza.

With the soldiers out, now was as good a time as any.

Bolan kicked open the communicating door, having motioned Ruth to remain in reserve, and leaped into the next room with the AutoMag held out in front of him. "Don't anyone move!" he ordered.

And gasped with astonishment.

He was as dumbfounded as the two men in the room, a luxuriously furnished study with leather-bound books behind glass, white leather armchairs and spotlit paintings on the gold-paneled walls. One man stood frozen on either side of a wide, flat-topped desk.

Varzi was sixty-five years old, a tall, bulky individual with crimped silver hair, a pink face that testified to the daily application of hot towels and small green eyes above a widely smiling mouth. He was wearing a bright blue mohair suit with a white open-necked shirt.

The second man, taller, bulkier, more muscular, was black. His right arm was in a sling and he rested his left on an aluminum crutch that supported a leg in plaster.

Anya Ononu!

"You're supposed to be dead," Bolan rasped. No prizes now for guessing who had blown Ruth's cover.

"It's not only capitalist mercenaries who can dive from a height and survive," the ex-dictator snarled.

"But it's only 'capitalist mercenaries,'" Bolan said evenly, "who seem able to expose the lies and betrayals of a mobster who's tricked you, Rinaldi, Vanderlee, Reinbecker and Rostand, and even the KGB, that you've been working for the good of the socialist revolution... while all the time you've been risking your lives to make money for him, and him alone."

"What the hell do you mean, betrayals?" Ononu blustered, his hate-filled eyes glaring at the man who had lost him his kingdom.

"The bastard's crazy, don't listen," Varzi said. "My boys will be reporting back any time. We'll see who's lying then."

"You thought you were financing terrorist activity to create a situation in which your Russian friends could unload their gold and make a killing," Bolan said. "All to help the balance of payments in the socialist paradise. But all you were doing, all of you, was improving the balance of payments into this vulture's pocket."

"You're out of your skull," Varzi said.

"You really believed the plot to take over the mines in your country was to help the Arabs train skyjackers and urban guerrillas?'' Bolan said directly to Ononu. ''And you figured that would keep you in favor with Moscow and ensure a further supply of cheap arms? Ask your racketeer friend here about some of the other mines he's taken over?''

Varzi's pink face suddenly paled. The lips stretched into a reptilian grimace, and his eyes were malevolent. ''Don't listen to him, Anya,'' he said. ''This madman's obviously trying to—''

''What *are* these mines in Montenegria?'' Bolan interrupted. ''They're tin mines. There's a crisis in the world tin market right now. In London they ceased trading already. It's not too difficult to pick up stock cheap—if you're discreet. Ask Varzi who has a controlling interest in the tin mines in Baarmbeek, Indonesia, Bolivia, Malaya.''

''Shut your fucking mouth!'' Varzi roared. ''I'll have you—'' He began a dive for the desk, but Bolan stopped him with a threatening gesture from the AutoMag.

Ononu's face was a study in bewilderment. ''But why...''

''Because buying cheap and on the sly, using holding companies and front men in different countries so as not to jack up the price, your friend has made a corner in tin,'' Bolan said. ''And carved himself a man-size slice of the copper and silver market as well. What do you think is going to happen when the Russian gold floods the market? Chaos! Every speculator's going to rush out of gold into...guess what?''

Bolan paused to lend emphasis to his next words.

"This bastard's going to bring himself the world's biggest one-time jackpot when that gold's unloaded on an artificially inflated market and upsets the West's economic balance. Because he'll have a virtual monopoly in those other metals and will be able to name his own price."

The African was gaping.

Bolan continued. "And you and the other fools have been helping him do it. He's tricked all of you. If you don't believe me, take a look in the other room. It's all there on paper. That's why the story's been complicated all along the line with talk about big business and industrialists."

"You won't get out of here alive," Varzi said.

"The truth," Bolan said relentlessly, "is that Varzi's not a double but a *triple* agent—and the third party is Lucino Varzi. The big joke is that he's been crossing not only you and the Mob and the terrorists and the drug barons, but also his Russian masters. He's actually been using the KGB without their knowledge—to prepare the ground for his own coup!"

Before Varzi, flushing darkly now with fury, could answer, the door to the corridor swung open.

Bolan whirled. Piotr Sakol stood there with a tall hardman on either side of him. All three of them held guns. The Russian's sallow face was set in a grim expression. "I think it would be advisable to drop that pistol, Mr. Bolan," he said.

Three guns—Stetchkin automatics of the kind once issued to Soviet army officers—against one. He allowed the AutoMag to drop to the floor.

Sakol turned to Varzi. "I think I heard enough," he said. Curiously, he spoke English with a French accent. "Betrayal and abuse of confidence are not qualities that find favor with the Central Committee." He raised his left hand, snapped fingers.

Expressionless, the heavies on either side opened fire. Each of them emptied an entire magazine.

Varzi crashed backward against the wall under the impact of the heavy slugs, remained pinned there for an instant as the hollowpoints continued to drum into his body, then slumped to the floor with blood pouring from a dozen holes piercing the white shirtfront and the mohair jacket.

Ononu's crutch spun away. He twisted sideways and fell across the desk as the first shot penetrated his heart, the rest of the magazine pulverizing his head and shoulder so that the dark blood spurted across the tooled green leather desk top and dripped heavily to the Persian prayer rug below.

Smoke drifted lazily beneath the ceiling light as the roar of the multiple explosions died away. Small streams of white plaster trickled to the floor from the holes gouged in the wall above Varzi's body.

"What about this one?" the killer on Sakol's right asked, nodding at the Executioner. Bolan recognized the Southern drawl of the man he had heard talking at Rostand's Florida pier.

Before Sakol could reply, Ruth Elias's voice spoke from the passageway. "Now that it's only one gun against one, Comrade, and I have the drop on you, I figure it's a good idea if you toss your automatic on the floor."

The KGB goons stiffened. Sakol smiled thinly and dropped his gun. Bolan picked up the AutoMag.

There were shouts and footsteps from the piazza below. Alerted by the shooting, Varzi's soldiers were calling off the search and returning to the rescue.

Then Sakol spoke directly to Bolan for the first time. "We have no quarrel with you, Mr. Bolan," he said. "At least not tonight. Indeed, if only temporarily, we are grateful to you for exposing this thief." He pointed the toe of a carefully polished shoe at the bodies on the floor. "But since we all hope to get out of here and—" a faint smile "—the natives appear hostile, I suggest that for this one time we pool our resources."

The Executioner hesitated only an instant. Then he nodded. "Just this once," he agreed. "Seeing that it's the commercial consulate and not the KGB!" He picked up the Stetchkin and handed it back to the Russian. Sakol reached into the pockets of his suit and tossed spare clips to each of the gunmen.

"Look out!" Ruth cried suddenly from the passageway. She threw herself flat as a blast of gunfire erupted from the head of the stairs. Bolan shouldered the Russians aside and dragged her into the room.

He switched off the light and pulled back the draperies. "Shoot your way to the stairs when I draw the fire from below," he told Sakol. "And these could help smooth your path." He unclipped the two stun grenades and handed them over. Then, opening the window, he went out onto the balcony and vaulted the fifteen feet to the flagstones of the sunken garden below.

Varzi's men were crowded around the entrance steps and up the stairs leading out of the lobby. Bolan dropped behind a row of flowers and let Big Thunder loose.

The stainless-steel hand cannon roared and two men fell. A third spiraled around and collapsed across the steps as Ruth Elias fired the silenced Beretta from the darkened balcony.

The mafiosi crowded indoors, shooting blind as they retreated...to meet a heavy burst of gunfire from the head of the stairs as the three Russians advanced from the study.

Bolan heard the flat, cracking explosion of a stun grenade, a brief volley of automatic fire and then another detonation. He sprang to his feet and raced out of the sunken garden, across the floodlit lawn and between the orange trees to the archway that led to the bridge. The guards were running across from the compound on the far side of the tunnel.

The Executioner stood there like an avenging angel in black, pumping death across the void.

Lead whistled around him as the hoods fired on the run.

Big Thunder delivered its lethal message. One guy threw up his arms and pitched over the rail to plummet into the ocean one hundred feet below. The other two dropped on the footway.

A final eruption of gunfire from inside the fortress had ceased. Three figures emerged from the floodlight and walked toward the arch.

Sakol, the man with the Southern accent...and Ruth.

"I lost a man," the Russian said matter-of-factly. "But the traitors lost everything. That is their destiny."

He led the way across the bridge to the tunnel. The wind had freshened again and whitecaps grumbled against the rocks below. In the compound a black Mercedes 350 sedan was parked. Sakol opened the rear door. "I am obliged for your assistance," he said formally. "Perhaps I can offer you a ride back into town?"

"Thanks—" Bolan touched the transceiver strapped to his shoulder "—but if I can find a way down these cliffs, I have a water taxi on call!"

LATE THAT NIGHT the Executioner stood on the balcony of his hotel room, looking out across the lamplit quayside at the masts and rigging of the moored boats rocking on the swell. Velvet-dark, the sky above was diamonded with stars.

For once, for a short while, he had fought on the same side as the enemy. Was the move justified? Did he have the right?

On the whole, he figured yes. The vacationers and merchants and fishermen whose lives centered around this port—and their counterparts all over the Western world—could continue a little longer in peace and stability.

But next time?

In his war there always was a next time...and it was likely that next time he and Piotr Anatolevitch Sakol would be fighting face-to-face rather than side by side.

"Somebody's getting kind of cold with that window open," Ruth's voice said behind him.

He turned, smiling, came in and shut the window.

"Some body!" he repeated admiringly.

She was lying naked on the bed, hands clasped behind her head. The one low-power lamp in the room sculptured the softly rounded mounds of her breasts, emphasized the subtle scoop of her waist and left a tantalizing shadow that ran from her crossed ankles to the tuft of dark hair between her thighs. She didn't look cold at all.

"That's one hell of a sexy lady there," Bolan observed.

She moved slightly, aware of his gaze and welcoming it, provoking it. She uncrossed her ankles, shifting her legs slightly apart. "If a guy was to promise not to kiss my mouth and not lean too heavily on my burns," she said, "I guess I wouldn't be able to resist his advances."

"WHAT NOW?" BOLAN ASKED RUTH the following morning as the three of them sat over breakfast on a hotel terrace flooded with sunlight.

Ruth poured more coffee. "For me," she said, "a ferry to Naples, the train to Rome, then Fumicino airport and the El-Al flight to Tel Aviv."

"Watch out for gunmen," Mettner said seriously.

"That's why I have to go back," Ruth said. "We have to clean up the drug channels and the Libyan-based terrorist networks already financed by Varzi's dupes. I unearthed some names and locations before they jumped me. Do you think the Soviets will still unload their gold now the plan's blown?"

Bolan sipped orange juice. "It'll certainly come on the market," he said. "But once Mettner's exclusive has been splashed, along with the evidence, I guess the world's stock markets won't be panicked; they should be stable enough to remain unshaken." He set down his glass. "Until the next time."

Ruth rose to her feet. "I hate to leave," she said, "but there's this ferry. So...I'll just echo your own words. Until the next time!" She held out her hand.

"This story," Jason Mettner said when she had left, "could have won me a Pulitzer prize. The Mafia, Red illegals, a Soviet plot, Israeli antiterrorist operations, a beautiful spy, a drug ring busted—it's got everything! What more could a newsman want!"

He poured himself another cup of coffee.

"I'll tell you," he said. "Just one more thing. Speaking professionally and for the record, one word, a single quote, from the guy whose courage and tenacity made it all possible. Come on, Bolan."

The Executioner smiled. "No comment," he said.